Night

BERNARD MINIER

Translated by Alison Anderson

MULHOLLAND
BOOKS
HODDER

First published as *Nuit* in France in 2017 by XO Éditions

First published in Great Britain in 2019 by Mulholland Books
An Hachette UK company

This paperback edition published in 2019

I

A CIP catalogue record for this title is available from the British Library

Paperback ISBN 978 1 473 67816 3
eBook ISBN 978 1 473 67817 0

Typeset in Plantin Light by
Palimpsest Book Production Ltd, Falkirk, Stirlingshire

Printed and bound in Great Britain by Clays Ltd, Elcograf S.p.A.

Hodder & Stoughton policy is to use papers that are natural,
renewable and recyclable products and made from wood
grown in sustainable forests. The logging and manufacturing
processes are expected to conform to the environmental
regulations of the country of origin.

Hodder & Stoughton Ltd
Carmelite House
50 Victoria Embankment
London EC4Y 0DZ

www.hodder.co.uk

For Laura Muñoz,
This novel that is also hers

For Jo (1953–2016)

Prelude

She checks her watch. It will be midnight soon.

A night train. Night trains are like rifts in space-time, parallel worlds: the sudden suspension of life, the silence, the immobility. Drowsy bodies; somnolence, dreams, snoring ... And then the regular clatter of wheels on rails, the speed carrying bodies forward – every life, with its past and future – towards an elsewhere that is still hidden in the gloom.

Because who knows what might happen between point A and point B?

A tree across the line, a passenger with evil intentions, a sleepy driver ... She thinks about it, not really worrying, more for something to do. She has been alone in the carriage since Geilo and – as far as she can tell – no one has boarded since. This train stops everywhere. Asker. Drammen. Hønefoss. Gol. Ål. Sometimes it stops at stations where the platform has vanished beneath the snow, stations reduced to one or two symbolic outbuildings, like in Ustaoset, where only one person got off. She can see lights in the distance, utterly insignificant in the vast Norwegian night. A few isolated houses.

There is no one in the carriage: it's Wednesday. During the winter, from Thursday to Monday the train is almost full, mainly with young people and Asian tourists, because it stops at the ski resorts. In the summer, the 484-kilometre Oslo–Bergen line has the reputation of being one of the most spectacular in the world, with 182 tunnels, viaducts, lakes and fjords. But in the middle of the Nordic autumn, on a freezing night like this, in the middle of the week, there is not a soul. The silence that reigns from one end of the central aisle to the other is oppressive. As if an alarm had emptied out the train without her knowing.

She yawns. In spite of the blanket and the eye mask at her disposal, she cannot get to sleep. From the moment she leaves her house she is always on the lookout. It's because of her job. And this empty train is hardly conducive to relaxation.

She listens carefully. She can hear no voices, not even the sound of someone stirring, a door closing or luggage being moved.

Her gaze lingers over the empty seats and the dark windows. She sighs and closes her eyes.

The red train burst out of the dark tunnel, like a tongue lapping at the icy landscape. Slate blue of night, opaque black of the tunnel, bluish whiteness of the snow and the slightly darker grey of the ice. And then suddenly this bright red – like a spurt of blood flowing all the way to the end of the platform.

Finse station. Altitude 1,222 metres. The highest point on the line.

The station buildings were caught in a carapace of snow and ice, their roofs covered with white eiderdowns. One couple and a woman were waiting on the platform beneath the yellow lamps.

Kirsten drew away from the window and everything outside fell back into the darkness, eclipsed by the lighting inside the carriage. She heard the door sigh and glimpsed movement at the end of the carriage. A woman in her forties, like her. Kirsten went back to her reading. She had managed to sleep for only an hour, even though she had left Oslo over four hours ago. She would rather have flown, or booked a sleeper, but her boss had handed her a ticket for the night train. Just a seat, in view of the budgetary cuts. The notes she had taken over the phone were now displayed on the screen of her tablet: a body found in a church in Bergen. Mariakirken: Saint Mary's church. A woman killed on the altar, among all the items of worship. Amen.

'Excuse me.'

She looked up. The woman who had boarded the train was standing next to her, smiling, with her luggage in her hand.

'Do you mind if I sit across from you? I won't be a bother, it's just that . . . Well, an empty train at night. I don't know, I'd feel safer.'

Yes, she did mind. She gave a half-hearted smile.

'No, no, I don't mind. Are you going to Bergen?'

'Uh . . . yes, yes, Bergen. You too?'

She went back to her notes. The guy from Bergen hadn't exactly been talkative on the phone. Kasper Strand. She wondered if he was as off-hand with his own investigations. According to what he'd told her, night had been falling when a homeless man walking past the Mariakirken heard shouting inside the church. Instead of going to investigate, he had thought it wiser to turn tail, and he practically collided with a passing patrol. The two cops wanted to know where he was going and why the hurry, so he told them. Kasper Strand reported that the two officers on patrol had been openly sceptical (she thought she could tell, from his intonation and certain allusions, that the police were well acquainted with the homeless man), but it was cold and damp that night, and they were bored stiff; even the icy nave of a church would be better than the wind and rain 'from the open ocean'. (That was how Kasper Strand put it – *a poet in the police force*, she mused.)

She hesitated to play the little film Strand had sent her, the video taken in the church, because of the woman now sitting opposite her. Kirsten sighed. She had hoped the woman would doze off. Kirsten shot her a furtive gaze. The woman was staring at her, a little smile on her lips; Kirsten couldn't tell whether it was friendly or mocking. Then her gaze focused on the screen of the tablet and she frowned, clearly trying to make out what was written there.

'Are you in the police?'

Kirsten repressed a burst of anger. She studied the little icon in the corner of her screen: a lion and a crown, with the word *POLITIET* underneath. Then looked up at the woman, her expression neither hostile nor friendly. At police headquarters in Oslo, Kirsten Nigaard was not known for her warmth.

'Yes.'

'Which branch, if it's not indiscreet?'

Here we go, she thought.

'Kripos.'*

'Oh, I see; well, no, no, I don't see. It's a strange sort of job, isn't it?'

'You could say that.'

'And you're going to Bergen for . . . for . . .'

Kirsten was determined not to make it easy for her.

---

* Norway's National Criminal Investigation Service, in charge of combatting organised crime and other 'serious' crimes.

'For . . . well, you know, a . . . crime – that's it, isn't it?'

'Yes.' Her tone was curt.

Perhaps the woman realised she had gone too far. 'Forgive me, it's really not my business.' She motioned towards her suitcase. 'I have a thermos full of coffee. Would you like some?'

Kirsten hesitated.

'All right,' she replied eventually.

'It's going to be a long night,' said the woman. 'My name is Helga.'

'Kirsten.'

'So, you live alone and you're not seeing anyone at the moment, right?'

Kirsten gave her a cautious look. She had said too much. Without realising it, she had allowed Helga to worm things out of her. This woman was even nosier than a journalist. As an investigator, Kirsten knew that even in the most ordinary interpersonal relations, when you were listening to someone, it always had something to do with a search for truth. It occurred to her that this Helga woman would have excelled at interviewing witnesses. Initially this made her smile. She knew Kripos officers with less talent for interrogation. But now she had stopped smiling. Now, Helga's nosiness was starting to get on her nerves.

'Helga, I think I'm going to try to get some sleep. I have a long day ahead of me tomorrow. Or rather, today,' she said, checking her watch. 'There are only two hours left to Bergen.'

Helga gave her a funny look and nodded.

'Of course. If that's what you want.'

Her abrupt tone was disconcerting. There was something about this woman, Kirsten thought, something she hadn't noticed at the start but which now seemed perfectly obvious: she liked to get her own way; she didn't like others to stand up to her. She clearly had a low tolerance for frustration, a tendency to get carried away, Kirsten concluded. She remembered her classes at police college and the attitudes one was supposed to adopt in response to this or that personality type.

She closed her eyes, hoping this would put an end to the discussion.

'I'm sorry,' said Helga suddenly.

She opened them.

4

'I'm sorry I disturbed you,' Helga repeated. 'I'll go and sit somewhere else.' She sniffed and gave a condescending little smile, her pupils dilated.

'You must not make friends easily.'

'I beg your pardon?'

'With your nasty character. The way you give people the brush-off, your arrogance. It's no wonder you're on your own.'

Kirsten stiffened. She was about to reply when Helga got up abruptly and reached up to the overhead rack for her bag.

'I'm sorry I disturbed you,' she barked again as she moved away.

Perfect, thought Kirsten. *Find another victim.*

She had nodded off. In her dream, an insinuating, venomous voice was whispering in her ear, *'Bütch, ssstupid bütch.'* She woke up with a start. And gave another start when she saw that Helga was right next to her. In the adjacent seat. Her face angled over Kirsten's, peering at her, like a researcher studying an amoeba under a microscope.

'What the hell are you doing here?'

Did Helga really say that? Bitch? *Did she actually say it, or was it just in her dream?*

'I just wanted to tell you to go fuck yourself.'

Kirsten felt a surge of dark anger, as black as a storm cloud.

'What did you say?'

At 7.01 the train pulled into Bergen station. *Ten minutes late, which is nothing for the NSB*, thought Kasper Strand, stamping his feet on the platform. It was pitch black and on days like today when the weather was overcast it would stay pitch black until nine o'clock in the morning. He saw her alight from the train and step onto the platform. She looked up and immediately spotted him, with only a handful of people there at this early hour.

Cop, he read in her gaze, when it settled on him. And he knew what she was seeing: a somewhat oafish, poorly shaven policeman with thinning hair and a paunch, owing to the can of Hansa pressing against his old-fashioned leather jacket.

He walked up to her. Trying not to look at her legs. He was somewhat surprised by her outfit. Beneath her winter coat with its fur-lined hood, already fairly short to begin with, she was wearing a strict skirt suit, flesh-coloured tights, and heeled boots. Was this the fashion in the Oslo police this year? He could picture her leaving one of the conference rooms at the Radisson Plaza near the central station, or a DNB Bank building. She was undeniably pretty, in any case. He reckoned she must be in her forties.

'Kirsten Nigaard?'

'Yes.'

She gave him her gloved hand and he hesitated to squeeze it, it was so soft.

'Kasper Strand, Bergen police,' he said. 'Welcome.'

'Thank you.'

'I hope the trip was not too long?'

'It was.'

'Did you get some sleep?'

'Not really.'

'Follow me.' And he held out a red fist towards the handle of her bag but she motioned with her chin that it was all right, she would rather carry it herself. 'We've got coffee at the police station. And there's bread and cold meat and fruit juice, and some *brunost*. After that we'll get to work.'

'I'd like to see the crime scene first. It's not far from here, if I'm not mistaken?'

He raised an eyebrow and rubbed his six-day beard.

'What, now? Right away?'

'If you don't mind.'

Kasper tried to hide his annoyance, but he wasn't very good at that game. He saw her smile. A smile without warmth, not aimed at him, but that no doubt was to confirm some thought she'd had about him from the start. *Well fuck that.*

Scaffolding and a huge tarpaulin hid the big luminous clock dedicated to the glory of the *Bergens Tidende*. The most important newspaper in the west of Norway would no doubt run the murder in the church as its lead story this morning. In the main hall they turned to the right, walked past the Deli de Luca and entered the damp, windy corridor leading to the taxi rank. Not a single taxi in sight, as usual, despite the half-dozen or so customers who were waiting, getting splattered by horizontal rain. He had parked his Saab 9-3 on the other side of the street, on the cobblestones. There was something undeniably provincial about these modest

6

gardens and buildings. Or at least what Oslo people would mean by 'provincial', anyway.

He was hungry. He had spent all night beavering away with the rest of the Hordaland investigation team.

When she flopped down in the seat next to him, her dark coat opened and her skirt rode up, revealing her lovely knees. Her blonde hair tangled in rebellious curls on her collar, but elsewhere it was straight, divided by a sharp parting on the left-hand side.

There was nothing natural about her blondness: he could make out dark roots and eyebrows, which were tweezed thinner. Her eyes were so blue as to be disturbing; her straight nose was on the long side, and her lips were thin but finely drawn. And there was a beauty spot on the tip of her chin, slightly to the left.

Everything about her face said determination.

A woman in control, calm and obsessive.

He had known her for only ten minutes but he was surprised to find himself thinking that he wouldn't like to have her as a partner. He wasn't sure he could put up with her personality for long, or with constantly having to avoid looking at her legs.

KIRSTEN

I

Mariakirken

The nave was dimly lit. Kirsten was surprised that they let the candles go on burning near the crime scene, which was cordoned off by a length of orange and white tape that barred access to the sanctuary and the choir.

The smell of hot wax tickled her nostrils. She took a metal box from her coat; inside were three little pre-rolled cigarettes. She placed one between her lips.

'You're not allowed to smoke in here,' said Kasper Strand.

She shot him a smile, not saying a thing, and lit the thin, uneven tube with a cheap lighter. Her gaze swept over the nave and came to rest on the altar. The corpse was gone. As was the white linen that must have covered the altar; she pictured the cloth, stained with brown streaks and large spots that had become thick and stiff on drying.

Kirsten had not attended mass since childhood, but she recalled that when the priest came in to celebrate mass he would bend down and kiss the altar. Once the service was over, before leaving the church, he would kiss it again.

She closed her eyes, massaged her eyelids, cursed the woman on the train, took a puff of her cigarette, and opened her eyes again. The spurt of blood had not reached the big crucifix up there, but it had splattered the Virgin and Child, and the tabernacle a bit lower down. She could see constellations of little reddish-brown spots on the gilt and on Mary's indifferent face. Close to 3 metres: the distance the geyser had travelled.

The Vikings burning their dead at night on tomb-ships; Loki, god of fire and deviousness; Jesus next to Odin and Thor; Christians evangelising the pagan people of the north by force, cutting off their hands and feet, gouging and mutilating; Viking princes converted to Christianity through pure political interest. The end of a civilisation. Kirsten thought of this in the silence of the church.

Outside, the city was still sleeping in the rain. As was the harbour, where an enormous bulk carrier spiked with antennae and cranes, and painted grey like a battleship, was moored in front of the wooden houses of Bryggen. Was it time to invoke the spirit of place? The past of this church went much further back than that of the churches in Oslo – to the early twelfth century, in fact. There might be no national theatre here, no royal palace, no Nobel Peace Prize or Vigelands Park. But here the savagery of the ancient past had always been present. For every sign of civilisation there is a corresponding sign of barbarity; every light struggles against obscurity, every door that opens on a home full of light hides a door opening onto darkness.

She had been ten years old when she and her sister spent their winter holiday with their grandparents in a small town not far from Trondheim called Hell. She adored her grandfather; he had the funniest face, and he loved to tell them all sorts of silly stories and sit them together on his lap. One night he asked them to take some food out to Heimdall, the German shepherd that slept in the barn. When she emerged from the well-heated farmhouse into the December night it was so cold it felt as if the blood in her veins would freeze. Her boots crunched on the snow, her shadow led the way through the moonlight like a huge butterfly as she headed towards the barn. It was completely dark when she entered the barn, and her heart was in her boots. It was sadistic of her grandfather to send her out there when it was so dark. Heimdall greeted her with a bark, pulling on his chain. He was grateful for her caresses, and licked her face affectionately while she hugged his warm, throbbing body, burying her face in his musky coat and telling herself it was cruel to make him sleep outside on such a night. Then she heard the whimpering. So faint that if Heimdall had not been silent for a moment she would not have noticed it. The sound came from outside, and she began to be truly frightened, her little girl's fertile imagination picturing some strange creature adopting a plaintive voice to lure her outside. And yet she went. And to her left, glowing faintly in the corner between the barn and the lean-to, were the bars of a cage. Kirsten went closer, her heart pounding, as the high-pitched whimper grew louder. She had a terrible sense of foreboding. After half a dozen steps through the snow, her fingers touched the bars, and she looked between them. There was something, there at the back, against the cement wall. She squinted. A young dog, hardly bigger than a puppy. A little mongrel with a long nose, low-lying ears, and short tawny fur. His head was practically glued to the cement wall because his collar was attached to a ring, and he trembled violently. Even now she could still see the gentle, affectionate, imploring look that the little dog sent her. A look that said, 'Help me, please.' It was the saddest thing she had ever seen. She felt her heart shatter into a thousand pieces. The little dog didn't have the strength to bark, and his eyes opened and closed with fatigue. She grabbed hold of the icy bars, wanting to break open the cage and run away with him in her arms. Overcome with despair, she staggered back to the farm to plead with her grandfather. But he was adamant. For the first time he would not give in to her whims. It was a stray, a mongrel that had stolen some meat: it had to be punished. She knew it would be dead by dawn if she did nothing. She had cried, pleaded, shouted with rage in front of her stunned, frightened sister, who began to cry too. Her grandmother had tried to calm her down, but Grandfather looked at her sternly, and in that moment she saw herself locked up in the dog's place, the collar tight around her neck, fastened to the metal ring on the wall.

'Put me in the cage!' she screamed. 'Put me in there with him!'

'You're completely mad, my poor child,' said Grandfather, his voice hard and pitiless.

She recalled that episode when she read in the newspapers that the Norwegian state had created a police force that would be charged with combatting cruelty towards animals: the first on the planet.

Shortly before Grandfather died in hospital she waited until her sister and the rest of the family who were at his bedside were out of earshot, then she leaned over to murmur in his ear. She saw his loving gaze as she leaned closer.

'Old bastard,' she murmured. 'I hope you go straight to hell.'

She had used the word in English to refer to his village, but she was sure he got her point.

Now she gazed at the pulpit, the altarpiece, the large crucifix up on the wall, and the frescoes, and she remembered that even Agnes Gonxha Bojaxhiu – better known as Mother Teresa – had spent the greater part of her life in the dark night of faith, that in her letters she had spoken of a 'tunnel', of 'terrible darkness in [her], as if everything were dead'. How many believers lived like this, in utter darkness, making their way through a spiritual desert which they kept secret?

'Are you all right?' asked Strand.

'Yes.'

She touched the screen on her tablet. The images of the little film from the Bergen police reappeared.

Ecce homo.

1. The woman lying on her back on the altar, her back arched as if she has just received an electric shock or is about to have an orgasm;
2. Her head dangling off the side of the altar into the void, her mouth wide open, her tongue out; she seems to be waiting for the host, with her head upside down;
3. A blurry close-up: her face is red and swollen, and almost all the bones – nasal, zygomatic, ethmoid, upper maxilla, mandible – have been broken. There is also a deep rectilinear crushing of the middle of the frontal bone, which makes it look as if a furrow has been dug there, the crushing no doubt caused by an extremely violent blow with a long blunt object, probably a metal bar;
4. Finally, her clothes have been partially torn, with the exception of the missing right shoe, revealing a white woollen sock with a dirty heel.

She took in every detail. *A scene with the imprint of profound truth*, she thought. The truth of humankind. Two hundred thousand years of barbarity and the hope of a hypothetical afterlife where humankind, supposedly, would be better.

According to the initial findings, the woman had been beaten to death, initially with an iron bar, which had been used to crush her ribcage and skull, and then with the monstrance. The technicians had drawn this last conclusion from the presence of the object itself on the altar, bloodied and overturned, and the very particular pattern of the wounds: the monstrance was surrounded by bands which made it look like a sun; these bands had left deep gashes on the victim's face and hands. Her throat must have been cut just afterwards, and it had caused blood to splatter in the direction of the tabernacle, before her heart stopped beating. Kirsten focused. At every crime scene, there is one detail that matters more than the others.

The shoe. A North Face walking boot, black with white motifs and a fluorescent yellow sole; it had been found upside down at the foot of the rostrum, a good 2 metres from the altar. Why?

'Did she have any papers on her?'

'Yes. Her name was Inger Paulsen. No criminal record.'

'Age?'

'Thirty-eight.'

'Married, any children?'

'Single.'

She looked at Kasper. He wasn't wearing a wedding ring but maybe he took it off for work. He had the air of a married man. She moved a bit closer to him, shifting from personal space to intimate – less than 50 centimetres – and she sensed him stiffen.

'Have you found out what she did for a living?'

'She was a worker on a North Sea oil platform. Oh, and blood tests showed elevated alcohol intake.'

Kirsten knew all the statistics by heart. She knew that the homicide figures in Norway were considerably lower than in Sweden, one and a half times lower than in France, almost half that of Great Britain, and seven times lower than in the United States. She knew that even in Norway, the country that according to the United Nations had the highest index of human development, violence was proportional to the level of education, that only 34 per cent of murderers were not unemployed, that 89 per cent were men, and 46 per cent were under the influence of alcohol when the crime was committed. Hence there was a by no means insignificant probability that the murderer was a man, and a fifty-fifty chance that like his victim he had been under the influence of alcohol. There was an equally significant chance that he had been known to his victim: spouse, friend, lover, co-worker . . . But the mistake all the novice cops made was to let themselves be blinded by statistics.

'What do you think?' she asked, blowing her smoke in his face.

'What do *you* think?'

She smiled. And thought.

'There was a struggle,' she said. 'A secret meeting and a struggle that turned ugly. Look at her torn clothes: the shirt collar almost pulled off from underneath her jumper, and the shoe, all that way from the altar. They fought, and he got the upper hand. Then, in his fury, he killed her. All this theatrical setting is just for show.'

She removed a fleck of tobacco from her lips.

'What the hell were they doing in the church?' she added. 'Shouldn't it have been locked?'

'Clearly one of them got hold of a spare key,' he said. 'Because the church is closed most of the time. And there's something else.'

He motioned to her to follow him. She brushed off the ash that had fallen on her coat, buttoned it up against the chill, then followed him. They went out the way they had come in, through a side door. Kasper pointed to footprints in the thin layer of snow – the first of the season, it was early this year – which the rain was already effacing. She had noticed them when she came up the path marked off between the tombstones by the forensics team. Two sets of footprints in one direction, and one in the other.

'The murderer followed his victim into the church,' he said, as if he were reading her thoughts.

Had they arrived together, or one after the other? Were they thieves fighting over their loot? Two people who had arranged to meet there? A druggie and her dealer? A priest? Lovers who were turned on by fucking in church?

'Was this Paulsen woman a practising Christian?'

'No idea.'

'Which platform did she work on?'

He told her. She stubbed her cigarette out against the wall of the church, leaving a black streak on the stone, then she kept it in the palm of her hand and glanced at the lit windows of the building across the way. It was still dark. The typical wooden houses of the Bryggen district, which dated from the eighteenth century, shone with rain. The storm sketched sparks in the glow of the streetlamps, and her hair was damp.

'I imagine you questioned the neighbours?'

'Nothing gained from the house-to-house,' said Kasper. 'Apart from the homeless man, no one saw or heard anything.'

He locked the church door and they headed back to his car through the little gate.

'And the bishop?'

'They dragged him out of bed. They're interviewing him right now.'

She thought again of the metal bar the murderer had had on him. Then something else occurred to her.

'And what if it was the other way around?' she said.

Kasper glanced at her as he turned the key in the ignition.

'The other way round from what?'

'What if it was the murderer who arrived first and the victim followed him?'

'Into a trap?' asked Kasper, frowning.

She looked at him but said nothing.

Hordaland Police Headquarters. On the seventh floor police chief Birgit Strøm was examining Kirsten with her deep-set little eyes. She had the broad, flat face of a grouper fish, her mouth reduced to a slit whose corners stubbornly refused to curve either up or down.

'A fight?' she said, with her raspy voice. (*Too many cigarettes*, thought Kirsten.) 'Then in that case, if it wasn't premeditated, why would the murderer go into a church with an iron bar?'

'It was premeditated, quite clearly,' Kirsten replied. 'But Paulsen fought back. She has cuts on her palms from the monstrance. As if she had been trying to defend herself. They fought, and at some point Paulsen lost one of her shoes.'

Kirsten noted a fleeting gleam in the grouper's eyes. The police chief's gaze settled briefly on Kasper then returned to Kirsten.

'Fine. In that case, how do you explain that we found this in one of the victim's pockets?'

She leaned back and reached for a transparent bag on the desk where she had placed her voluminous behind. Which had the effect of accentuating her no less voluptuous bosom. Kasper and the other officers of the Hordaland police investigation team followed her movements as if she were Serena Williams preparing to serve for the match.

Kirsten took the evidence bag.

She already knew what was inside. It was because of this that they had called *her*. They had made her come in to the police station not through the main entrance on Allehelgens gate, but through the little bulletproof door at the rear, on Halfdan Kjerulfs gate – as if they were afraid someone might see her.

A scrap of paper. Handwritten. Block capitals. Kasper had

informed her over the telephone the day before, when she was still at Kripos headquarters, less than an hour after they discovered the body, so this was no surprise, she already knew.

It was her name on the scrap of paper.

KIRSTEN NIGAARD

2

83 Souls

The helicopter hurtled through the gusts. In the half-light Kirsten could just make out the necks of the two pilots, and their headphones and helmets.

The pilot was going to need all his skill tonight because there was quite a storm out there. That was what she was thinking, sitting at the rear, cramped in her survival suit, while the single windscreen wiper did its best to fight off the torrential rain. In the glow of the dashboard instruments, thick drops rolled skyward from the air pressure. Kirsten knew that the most recent accident involving a helicopter headed to one of the offshore platforms had been in 2013. A Super Puma L2. Eighteen people on board. *Four dead.* Before that, a Puma AS332 had crashed off the Scottish coast in 2009. *Sixteen dead.* And two other accidents, without casualties, in 2012.

These last few days the weather conditions had stranded over 2,000 offshore workers between Stavanger, Bergen and Florø. This evening the helicopters had at last been able to take off and get everyone home again. But the conditions remained borderline.

She glanced over at Kasper. Sitting on her right, his gaze was glassy, his mouth open. Kirsten focused her attention ahead of her again. And at last she saw it. Emerging from the darkness, perched 20 metres above the invisible surface of the ocean, it seemed to be floating in the night like a spaceship.

Latitude: 56° 4' 41.16" N

Longitude: 4° 13' 55.8012" E

Two hundred and fifty kilometres from the coast. Hardly more isolated than if it had been lost in space . . .

Below them was total obscurity and Kirsten tried in vain to make out the tall steel pylons that plunged straight into the raging waves.

She knew they touched bottom, 146 metres below the surface, in other words the height of a forty-eight-storey building. The difference being that instead of solid walls, there were only four frail metal legs surrounded by a roaring, tumultuous ocean to bear all the weight of that floating city . . .

The closer the helicopter came, the more the Statoil platform began to look like a chaotic, precarious pile. Not one square inch of space was clear between the decks, footbridges, stairways, cranes, containers, miles of cables, pipes, fences and derricks, and on top of it all, six floors of living space stacked up like prefab modules on a construction site. There were brilliantly lit sections then others that were invisible, swallowed by the dark.

A sudden gust, stronger than before, caused the helicopter to swerve off its path.

What a bloody night, she thought.

There were thirty nationalities down there: Poles, Scots, Norwegians, Russians, Croats, Latvians, French . . . ninety-seven men and twenty-three women, split into night teams and day teams. One week working nights, one week days, in twelve-hour shifts, the same for a whole month. After four weeks, bingo! You were entitled to twenty-eight days off. Some of them went surfing in Australia, others went skiing in the Alps, others went back to their families; the divorced men – the most numerous – partied hard, blew a good part of their wages or went off looking for a new, scarcely pubescent, companion in Thailand. That was the upside of the job: you earned a good living, you had a lot of time off and travel was cheap with the airline miles you racked up. But then stress, mental health problems and conflicts were probably frequent on the rigs, she figured. There was bound to be a certain number of hotheads in a place like that, borderline cases, Type As. She wondered if Kasper had already put her in this category: *Pain in the arse, for sure.* With his chubby, teddy-bear demeanour he must be a Type B: tolerant, unambitious, rarely aggressive . . . Calm, too calm. Except tonight: when they left solid ground he had finally abandoned his good-natured manner and now, in spite of his build, he looked like a little boy.

Only thirty more metres or so to go. The landing pad consisted of a poorly lit hexagon with a big H in the middle, covered by a net stretched across the ground, all of it suspended above the void at the edge of the platform. A metal stairway led to the superstructure.

Kirsten glimpsed the flame of a torch burning at the top of a derrick. The hexagon was getting closer. The H225 pivoted on itself and the landing pad disappeared from their field of vision for a moment. Then, after one last swerve, the skids touched the helipad, and in spite of the noise she heard Kasper gasp. No doubt about it, she thought, the pilot was a champion.

What was waiting for them outside was no less violent: a stinging cold rain, and wind that was so strong she wondered if it mightn't just blow her overboard. She stepped forward and felt the net beneath her feet. The whole area was plunged in darkness, apart from the neon lights at ground level. A man wearing huge earmuffs came out of nowhere and grabbed her by the arm.

'Don't face into the wind!' he shouted, spinning her around like a top. 'Don't face into the wind!'

Okay, but where were the gusts coming from? It felt like the raging wind was blowing from every direction at once. He shoved her towards the steel stairway that led downwards. Between the steps you could see the void; Kirsten was overcome with dizziness when she saw the raging, roiling waves below, churning up the ocean and smashing against the platform piles before continuing on their way through the murk of the North Sea.

'Fuck!' said Kasper behind her and, turning around, she saw him clinging to the guardrail.

She wanted to keep going down but couldn't. Impossible. The wind was like a wall, the rain and hail lashing at her cheeks. She felt as if she was in a wind tunnel for aerodynamic tests.

'*Shit, shit, shit!*' she bellowed, humiliated but incapable of moving forward.

Two hands pushed her from behind and at last she made it, one step at a time.

The platform captain – a tall, bearded guy in his forties – was waiting for them at the bottom of the steps, together with another fellow who held out orange jackets with reflective tapes for them to wear.

'Are you all right?' asked the bearded man from beneath his helmet.

'Captain, I'm Kirsten Nigaard from the Kripos, and this is Kasper Strand, investigator with the Hordaland crime unit,' she said, holding out her hand.

'Jesper Nilsen. I'm not the captain, I'm the supervisor. Put these on: it's obligatory around here.'

His tone was authoritarian, his face inscrutable. Kirsten reached for the heavy jacket, which was not at all comfortable and far too big: her hands disappeared up the sleeves.

'Where is the captain?'

'He's busy!' Nilsen shouted to make himself heard above the racket, motioning to them to follow. 'It's a constant scramble around here, it never stops. Given how much it costs to keep a rig going even for just one day, there's no time to waste.'

She made her way, gripping the fence, buffeted from one side to the other and blinded by rain. They turned right, then left, then right again, went down a few steps, along a footbridge with metal grate flooring, then turned behind a big container which sheltered them for a moment. Helmeted men wearing protective goggles came and went. She looked up. Everything here was vertical, vertiginous, hostile. A labyrinth of neon and steel, haunted by North Sea storms. Everywhere there were signs, prohibitions: NO SMOKING, DO NOT REMOVE YOUR HELMET, DO NOT CROSS, NO WHISTLING (perhaps because, in spite of the noise, any unusual sounds could mean danger and, therefore, important information). There was vibrating, throbbing, roaring from all sides, with the clanking of pipes knocking together, the clamour of machines, and the breaking of waves further down. Right, left, right . . . Finally, a door. They were out of the wet in a sort of vestibule with benches and lockers. The supervisor opened a locker and removed his helmet, gloves and safety shoes.

'Here, safety is everybody's business,' he said. 'We don't have a lot of accidents but when we do they're serious. There is constant danger lurking around a platform. There's a welding operation under way on the drill floor, an urgent repair job. We call that "hot work". It's a delicate phase we can't delay. I don't want you in the way while we're doing it. That's why you're going to do exactly what we tell you,' he added, his tone final.

'No problem,' she replied. 'Provided you ensure we have access to everything.'

'I don't think that will be possible,' he replied.

'Uh . . . Jesper, right? This is a criminal investigation and the victim was one of your—'

'You didn't hear what I just said,' he interrupted. 'My priority is safety. Not your investigation. Is that clear enough for you, now?'

Kirsten wiped her forehead and happened to catch the scowl on

Kasper's face. Like her, he had seen right through the supervisor and his captain: they were like two tomcats who had pissed all over the place to mark their territory. They must have finalised their strategy with the company bigwigs: they were sole masters on board, and consequently the Norwegian police could operate only within the perimeter and under the conditions that they had set. She was about to intervene when Kasper said, placidly, 'Your captain, does he ever get any sleep?'

The bearded guy with the subversive air gave him a condescending look.

'Of course he does.'

'Then when he's asleep, does someone fill in for him?'

'What are you driving at?'

'I asked you a question.'

His tone made both the supervisor and Kirsten jump. Not so Type B after all, our Kasper Strand.

'So you did.'

Kasper moved closer to the man, who was a good half a head taller than him; so close that the man was forced to step back.

'What am I driving at? What am I driving at? Do you have a place where you hold meetings?'

The bearded man nodded warily.

'Good. Then here's what you're going to do—'

'I get the feeling you don't understand, either one of you. You're going to have to—'

'Shut up.'

Kirsten smiled. Nilsen turned crimson.

'Now do I have your attention?' said Kasper.

Nilsen nodded, jaws clenched, glowering.

'Fine. You are going to take us to that meeting room. Then I want your captain and everyone responsible for personnel management on the platform to meet us there. Everyone whose work at this moment is not *absolutely vital*, do you understand? Hot work or no hot work, I don't give a fuck. This rig is a Norwegian rig, there is only one authority in charge here, and that's the Norwegian Ministry of Justice and the Norwegian National Police. Have I made myself clear?'

Captain Tord Christensen had a tic he was possibly not aware of: he pinched his nostrils every time something annoyed him. And the presence of two cops on board annoyed him supremely. The gathering

23

consisted of himself, Nilsen, the rig's doctor, several team leaders who were not essential to the operation under way, a brown-haired woman who, if Kirsten had understood correctly, was in charge of maintenance, and a blonde woman who was introduced to her as the supervisor for job security.

'A little over twenty-four hours ago, Inger Paulsen, a worker on this platform, was beaten to death in a church in Bergen,' Kirsten began. 'We have official authorisation from the public prosecutor's office to conduct an investigation on this rig. And this order means that all personnel must put themselves at our disposal to facilitate the investigation.'

'Hmm. Provided these investigations do not put the personnel working on the rig in any danger,' objected the blonde woman curtly. 'Otherwise, I will personally oppose it.'

Clearly everyone was playing the game of who could piss the farthest, thought Kirsten.

'We have no intention of endangering anyone,' Kasper replied diplomatically. 'All those who cannot leave their post will be interrogated later.'

'Did Inger Paulsen have a private cabin?' Kirsten asked.

'No,' replied Christensen. 'Production technicians share their cabins, two in each: one on the day shift, the other on the night shift.'

'Do you have a list of all the workers who went ashore yesterday?'

'Yes, I can get that for you.'

'Have they all come back?'

The captain turned to the supervisor.

'Uh, no,' he answered. 'Given the weather conditions, there is still one flight that's not back, with seven people still ashore. They should be here soon.'

'Do you have any patients with problematic psychiatric histories?' Kirsten asked the rig's doctor.

'That is subject to medical confidentiality,' replied the little man, staring at her from behind his round glasses.

'Which is suspended in the case of a criminal investigation,' she replied briskly.

'If I thought that were the case, I would have immediately asked for the patient to be removed from his or her functions.'

'Then do you have any patients who have, let's say, shown signs of less serious psychological problems?'

'I could have.'

'Does that mean yes or no?'

'Yes.'

'I will need a list.'

'I don't know if I can—'

'I take full responsibility. If you refuse, I will have to arrest you.'

She was bluffing, of course, but she saw the little doctor shudder.

'How many men are on board tonight?'

The captain gestured towards what she had initially taken to be a clock with a rotary display. The number '83' stood out in big white letters against a black background. Then she saw what was written underneath, in English: '*souls on platform*'.

'This is indispensable, for reasons of security,' explained the captain. 'We have to be aware at all times of the exact number of people on board.'

'How many women?' asked Kasper.

'Twenty-three.'

'And how many cabins?'

'There are fifty double cabins. And then individual cabins for the captain, the supervisors, the team leaders, and the engineers.'

Kirsten thought for a moment.

'How do you keep track of where everyone is at all times?'

Now the blonde woman spoke up. 'The control room. All the work to be done on board is subject to prior authorisation. That way the people in the control room know where everyone is and what they're doing.'

'I see. And the people who are not working just now, what are they doing?'

Christensen gave a little smile.

'Given the hour, I would assume they're asleep.'

'Right. Wake them up, get them out of their cabins and gather them somewhere. We're going to search Inger Paulsen's cabin, then all the others.'

'You must be joking!'

'Do I look like I am?'

Inger Paulsen's cabin was less than nine metres square. The other occupant was one Pernilla Madsen. She was presently in the control room, so the cabin was empty. There were two bunk beds with blue sheets, and white drawers underneath, identified by the letters A and B; each one had a curtain and a tiny television fixed up in a corner, under the ceiling for one, under the upper bunk for the other. There was a little porthole in the centre of the cabin, a few shelves, a desk with two laptop computers, and two wardrobes behind the door.

'It may seem spartan,' said the blonde woman, who had guided them there, 'but they only spend five months a year on board, and a lot of that, outside of work hours, is in the canteen or the cafeteria. They've also got a wide-screen satellite television, three billiard rooms, a movie room, a gym, a library, a sauna, and even a music room.'

Kirsten took off the safety jacket and put it on the back of the chair. After the biting cold outside, the heat in the cabin was stifling.

'The toughest thing is Christmas and New Year's,' added the woman, 'when they're away from their families.'

Her voice was monotonous, toneless. Full of a dull hostility.

Kirsten went through the shelves and drawers. Female underwear, T-shirts, jeans, some paperwork, a dog-eared paperback crime novel, video games . . . nothing. There was nothing here. The woman was still speaking behind her, but Kirsten wasn't listening any more. One of the bunks had been neatly made, and the other was a mess. It was hot. Very hot. She could feel the sweat trickling under the back of her bra. She was getting a headache.

Kasper finished going through the wardrobes. He motioned to her that he'd found nothing. They went back out into the long corridor.

'Show us the cabins of the men who went ashore the night of the murder,' she said.

The blonde turned on her heels and led them down the corridor, its thick blue wall-to-wall carpet muffling their steps, and pointed to several doors. Kasper went into one cabin and she another. The woman didn't move. Kirsten saw she was watching her from the corridor through the open door. Watching *her*, not Kasper. She felt obliged to search the cabin. Less than five minutes later, she had to face the facts: there was nothing to report here either.

She went to the next door.

The cabin was exactly like the others. She opened one of the drawers under the bunk and saw them right away, among the other clothes: female underwear. Soiled. She turned around.

'Is this a woman's cabin?'

26

The blonde shook her head.

Kirsten went on searching.

Men's clothing. Brand names: Hugo Boss, Calvin Klein, Ralph Lauren, Paul Smith. She opened another drawer and frowned. Again, women's underwear. There was blood on one pair. What on earth was this? She could feel her pulse accelerate.

She turned towards the door. The hard blonde was watching her. Maybe she had sensed something. Maybe Kirsten's own body language had sent her a signal that something was happening.

Kirsten bent down and searched through the underwear. All the same size, more or less.

She turned around. The woman had moved. Now she was standing with her shoulder against the doorframe. Right by her, staring. She looked up at the woman.

'Whose cabin is this?'

'I don't know.'

'But you have a way to find out?'

'Of course.'

'Well then, let's go. Show us.'

On hearing Kirsten's voice, Kasper joined them. She showed him the open drawer, the blood-stained pants. He nodded. He understood.

'There's something not right,' she said to him. 'It's too obvious. It's like a treasure hunt.'

'If that's the case,' said Kasper, 'then it's you they planned it for.'

She looked at him. *Not so stupid.*

'Follow me,' said the woman.

'Their names are Laszlo Szabo and Philippe Neveu.'

They were in a windowless little office, full of papers.

Neveu, a French name . . .

'Which one went ashore last night?'

'Neveu.'

'Where is he now?'

The woman looked at the big wall planner with little coloured cards slipped into slots.

'Right now he is at one of the welding posts on the drill floor.'

'Is he French?'

The blonde woman searched in the drawer of a metal filing cabinet, took out a file and handed it to them. There was a photograph of a

27

man with a thin face and close-cropped brown hair. She figured he must be about forty-five.

'That's what he says he is, yes,' said the woman. 'What exactly is going on?'

Kirsten looked at the bag containing the bloodied pants, then up at Kasper. When their eyes met she felt a rush of adrenaline. On his face was the same expression she must have: that of two dogs on the trail of their quarry.

'What should we do?' she asked him quietly.

'Can't exactly ask for backup, here,' he replied.

She turned to the woman.

'Do you have any weapons on board? Who is in charge of security? You must have something lined up in case of pirates, or a terrorist attack.'

Kirsten knew that offshore companies were extremely discreet on the matter; no one wanted to admit to the vulnerability of what were highly strategic targets for well-prepared terrorists. Kirsten had twice participated in the annual Gemini exercise, which involved the police, special forces, the coast guard, and several oil and gas companies. She had also attended seminars. All the experts were unanimous: Norway was not as well prepared as her neighbours to deal with a terrorist attack. Until recently her country had been naïve, living with an assumption that terrorism didn't concern them and would always spare them. But their naïvety had been shattered on 22 July 2011, with Anders Breivik and the massacre at Utøya. Nevertheless, even today, while oil rigs in Scotland were protected by police and armed guards, Norway still had not recognised the full extent of the danger. What would happen if well-trained men armed with assault rifles landed a helicopter on a rig and took it hostage? If they loaded it with explosives? And the workers who came back from the mainland: were they searched? What would stop one of them from bringing a weapon on board?

She saw the woman press a button and lean into a microphone.

'Mikkel, can you come right away, please?'

Three minutes later a hefty guy who walked like a cowboy came into the little office.

'Mikkel,' said the woman, 'this lady and gentleman are from the police. They want to know if you are carrying a weapon.'

Mikkel looked at them with a frown and rippled his muscular shoulders.

'I am, why?'

Kirsten asked him what sort of weapon he had. His reply made her grimace.

'Is anyone else on board armed?' she asked.

'The captain has a gun in his cabin. That's all.'

Shit, she thought. She looked at the storm lashing against the black porthole, then turned again to Kasper. He nodded. His expression showed what he thought about the situation.

'We're on our own,' she concluded.

'And unlike us, he's on his own territory,' added Kasper.

'Can I ask what's going on?' said the brawny guy.

Kirsten opened the case at her waist without removing her gun.

'Take your weapon with you. But don't use it unless I tell you to.'

She saw the big guy go pale.

'What are you talking about?'

'We are going to apprehend someone.'

She turned back to the woman, whose eyes were wide with shock.

'Take us there.'

This time, the woman hurried to comply, grabbing her waterproof from a peg. She had dropped all signs of hostility; clearly, she was frightened. They left her little office and went down a narrow corridor to a metal stairway as steep as all the others.

As they stepped out into the night, the roar of the wild ocean once again filled Kirsten's ears.

The blonde woman took them through the rain-swept labyrinth. The downpour gleamed in the lamps against the opaque background of night. Kirsten turned up her collar. She could feel the icy rain against her neck, running down her back. Their steps vibrated on the footbridges, but the sound was drowned out by the din from the platform.

Huge pipes rose like organs above them, suspended in rows from the superstructure, each one taller than a house. The storm made them dance, sing and bang together like the tubes of a wind chime. They found themselves on a deck covered in greasy, oily slime and cluttered with machines and conduits. Kirsten could make out a vague form kneeling at the rear, lit intermittently. The adrenaline was spreading through her veins. Putting her hand discreetly on her lower back she made sure her gun was easily accessible. The welder's opaque visor lit up every time the powerful white light burst from his arc;

sparks and smoke rose all around. His helmet made her think of a medieval knight. Focused on his task, he didn't hear them arrive.

'Neveu!' shouted the blonde woman.

Helmet and visor looked up, the sun went dark. For a brief moment, Kirsten thought she saw a smile through the visor.

'Out of the way,' she said calmly, pushing the woman to one side. 'Philippe Neveu? Norwegian police!' she shouted, in English.

The man stayed there, saying nothing, motionless, his welding torch in his gloved hand. Kirsten could not see his eyes or his face. Still on his knees, he placed the nozzle of his tool on the metal floor and slowly removed his thick gloves. Then he raised his pale hands towards his helmet. Kirsten followed his every gesture. She had her right hand behind her, near her lower back. At last his face appeared beneath the helmet. The man in the photograph.

There was a strange gleam in his eyes and all of Kirsten's senses were instantly on the alert.

'Slowly,' she said.

She felt for the cable ties in her right pocket and couldn't find them. *Damn!* She put her hand in her left pocket. They were there. She glanced at Kasper. He was as tense as she was, and didn't take his eyes off the man; Kirsten saw his jaw muscles working under his cheeks.

Six metres.

She was going to have to cross that distance if she wanted to put the handcuffs on him. She looked around. Kasper had taken out his gun. The security agent had his hand on his holster, as if he were a cowboy in some Western. The blonde woman's eyes were wide open and frightened.

'Keep quiet!' shouted Kirsten, taking out the handcuffs. 'Understand?'

The man didn't move. He still had that gleam in his eyes: the look of a hunted animal.

Shit, she didn't like this. She brushed away a lock of wet hair that had fallen across her face.

'Put your hands behind your head!' she ordered.

He obeyed. Still with the same careful slowness. As if he were afraid he would trigger a police blunder. And yet he never stopped looking at her. At *her*, and no one else.

He really was very tall. She was going to have to be extremely cautious as she went closer.

'Now turn around very slowly and get back on your knees. Keep your hands on your head, is that clear?'

He didn't answer, but he did as she asked, slowly pivoting his body. A moment later he was gone. Out of their field of vision. As if he had performed a magic trick, he had vanished behind a huge cylindrical tank and an electric panel on the right.

'Shit!'

Kirsten pulled out her gun, shoved a cartridge into the barrel and went after him. She went around the tank, the metal grating of the flooring vibrating as she ran. She saw him turn left then run down some steps a dozen metres further along. She rushed after him. At the bottom of the steps, a narrow footbridge spanned the furious waves to reach another part of the platform, not nearly as well lit.

'Kirsten, come back!' bellowed Kasper behind her. 'Come back! He can't get far!'

Too annoyed to think, she hurried down the steps and began in turn to cross the long footbridge, hurrying towards the part of the platform that was plunged in darkness.

'Kirsten! Come back! For Christ's sake!'

Through the floor grating she could see the giant waves beneath her, seething with foam. *What the fuck are you playing at?* She ran as fast as she could, her gun in her hand, towards the other side of the platform; it seemed unusually dark and deserted.

A labyrinth, that's what it was. A maze of steel beams, stairways and barriers. Yes, she knew that she shouldn't have gone there, but this guy with his stupid smile was wearing a boiler suit that must weigh a ton, after all, and he wasn't armed, whereas she was. That is what she would tell them, should they ask why she had taken such a risk. That is what she would claim to have been thinking at that moment.

Just as she set foot on the other side (it made her think of the corner towers of a castle connected by a parapet walk), a huge wave struck one of the piles below and the icy spray stung her face. She looked for him – in vain. He could have been any of the shadows around her. All he had to do was stay still.

'Neveu!' she screamed. 'Don't be stupid! You can't go anywhere!'

She heard only the wind in reply. She turned her head just in time to see him step out of the darkness and rush further back.

'Hey! Hey! Come back, dammit!'

She ran towards him, but he had disappeared again, and she was alone. Alone with him. Neither Kasper nor the security guard had followed her. She continued to move forward. A mass of shadows and glinting lights around her; the veils of the night, floating back and forth. She moved with her legs slightly bent, her gun held out with both hands.

It was so dark she could hardly see. Fuck, this was madness! What was the point? She knew very well she was doing it to show off. Or was it just for the thrill?

Her foot met something soft and she looked down at the dark mass of a tarpaulin piled on the floor. She stepped over it cautiously, constantly looking around her. She had just put her foot firmly on the other side when she felt fingers closing around her ankle. Before she knew it, her leg was yanked backwards and she fell.

In boxing jargon that was called being floored.

Her back and elbow hit the metal floor, and her gun went flying with a clang. The tarpaulin was pushed back and a figure leapt to his feet with surprising agility, and then he pounced on her. She saw a grimacing face. She was preparing to kick him when the night sky exploded. Dozens of lamps were lit all at the same time, and Kasper's voice cried out:

'Get back! Get back! Hands on your head! Neveu! Don't be foolish!'

Kirsten turned her head towards Kasper, then focused her attention on the Frenchman again.

The man was looking at her anxiously. He raised his hands, never taking his eyes off her.

3

Telephoto Lens

Kirsten and Kasper had been sitting across from the Frenchman for over three hours. She had chosen the most neutral location possible, a windowless room with no décor, so that nothing would distract their interlocutor's attention and he would remain focused on her and her questions.

She had resorted to flattery, emphasising the unique nature of the *mise en scène* in the church, and questioning him on his profession as a welder. Then she made a complete U-turn and began to make fun of his ineptitude, jeering at the ease with which he'd allowed himself to be caught, and the clues he'd left behind.

All the while the man did not stop proclaiming his innocence.

'The underwear belongs to my girlfriend,' he groaned. 'It reminds me of her and it, well, you know . . .'

She looked at him. His imploring, wet, snot-filled face made her want to slap him.

'And the blood?' said Kasper.

'She had her period, dammit! With all your technology you ought to have a way of checking that!'

She pictured him sniffing the underwear in his bunk at night, and shuddered.

'Okay. So why did you run away?'

'I told you.'

'Tell me again.'

'I've told you ten times already!'

She shrugged.

'Well, this will make eleven.'

He remained silent for so long that she felt like shaking him.

'I bring back a bit of hash on the sly and slip it to my friends on board.'

'Are you a dealer?'

'No, I give it to them.'

'Stop taking me for a fool.'

'Yeah, okay. I sell a little bit: I do them favours. Life on board isn't always easy. But I'm not a murderer, shit! I've never hurt anyone!'

He began sobbing again; his eyes were red. They left the room.

'Could we be wrong?' she said.

'Are you kidding?'

'No.'

She went down the corridor and climbed the steps towards the control room. She was beginning to know her way around the labyrinth. Christensen watched her come in.

'Well?'

'We have to search the cabins of the workers who aren't back yet.'

'What for?'

Kirsten didn't answer.

'Fine,' he said reluctantly, sensing that this woman would be unyielding no matter the circumstances, and that he would be wasting his time trying to talk sense to her. 'I'll show you.'

In the fourth one, she found it.

Among the clothes: a brown A4 envelope. She opened it; inside were paper copies of photographs. The first was the portrait of a blond child, four or five years old. She turned the photograph over. The name 'Gustav' was written on the back. Behind him you could see a lake, a village and snowy mountains. She looked at the other pictures.

They had been taken with a telephoto lens.

A man. Always the same one. In his forties, brown hair.

Kirsten leafed through them. There must have been twenty or so. The target parking his car; the target getting out, locking it. Walking down the street, in the middle of a crowd. Sitting at the window of a café. Kirsten saw a plaque with the name of the street.

The photos had been taken in France.

In one of the last ones, the man was entering a tall building. A tricolour flag – the French flag – floated above the door, and underneath, the words 'HÔTEL DE POLICE'. She didn't speak French, but to understand the last word she didn't need to.

Police: *politiet*.

In the close-ups the man had a pleasant face, but he seemed tired, preoccupied. Kirsten could see shadows under his eyes, and his mouth had a bitter set to it. Sometimes his face was clear, sometimes his entire form was blurry – or else there was a car, or foliage, or passers-by between him and the lens. The target was obviously completely unaware of the shadow that was following him everywhere, echoing each one of his footsteps.

Again she turned over the picture of the child.

GUSTAV.

The handwriting was the same as on the paper that had been found in Inger Paulsen's pocket at the church.

The paper with her name on it.

MARTIN

4

Thunderstruck

It was raining in Toulouse, too, but there was no snow. In early October, the temperature was around fifteen degrees.

'*The House at the End of the Street*,' said Lieutenant Vincent Espérandieu.

'Huh?'

'Nothing. It's the title of a horror film.'

Inside the car, Commandant Martin Servaz did not immediately look at the tall building near the railway embankment. It had a lugubrious air – two floors, slick roof and a tall tree projecting a sinister shadow on the facade. Night had fallen, and the curtains of rain sweeping across the strip of lawn leading to the house made them feel as if they had reached the end of the world.

What a strange place to live, Servaz thought: stuck between the railway line and the river, 100 metres from the last houses in this dingy neighbourhood; the only other buildings nearby were warehouses covered in graffiti. It was the river, in fact, that had brought them out here. Three women had been out jogging along the Garonne; the first two were assaulted and raped, the third was stabbed many times over. She had just succumbed to her injuries, at the intensive care unit at the University Hospital in Toulouse. The three attacks had taken place less than two kilometres from the house. And the man who lived there was in the police database of sexual offenders – had committed multiple offences, in fact. He had been released from prison 147 days earlier, after serving two-thirds of his sentence, upon the decision of the sentence enforcement judge.

'Are you sure this is it?'

'Florian Jensen, 29, chemin du Paradis,' confirmed Espérandieu, his tablet open on his lap.

His forehead pressed against the rain-streaked window, Servaz turned to look at the vacant lot on the left – a dark plot of fallow land overrun by tall grasses and acacia. He had heard that a major company had plans to build eighty-five apartments, a children's nursery and a residence for senior citizens. Except that this was a former industrial site, and the levels of lead and arsenic in the ground were twice the norm. According to certain local environmental protection associations, the pollution had reached even the groundwater. Which did not stop locals from using their well water to water their vegetable gardens.

'He's there,' said Vincent.

'How do you know?'

Espérandieu showed him his tablet.

'The arsehole has logged on to Tinder.'

Servaz shot him a puzzled look.

'It's an app,' said his assistant with a smile. If Espérandieu was a tech geek, his boss was the opposite, having apparently zero interest in the wonders of modern computing .'The man's a rapist. So I figured there was a chance he might have downloaded Tinder. It's a dating app – it locates all the women in a given radius who also have the app on their phone. Practical, no, for scum like him?'

'A dating app?' echoed Servas, as if he were being told about a planet at the far-flung end of the universe.

'Yes.'

'And?'

'And I created a fake profile. I just got a match. Here, look.'

Servaz leaned over the screen and saw a picture of a young man. He recognised the suspect. Next to him was a picture of a pretty blonde no older than twenty.

'Except now we have to get a move on. We've been *spotted*. Or rather, Joanna has.'

'Joanna?'

'My fake profile. Blonde, one metre seventy, eighteen years old, liberated. Fuck, I've already had over two hundred matches! In less than three days. This thing must be revolutionising dating.'

Servaz didn't dare ask him what he was talking about. Vincent was barely ten years younger than him, but they could not have been more dissimilar. Whereas at the age of forty-six Servaz felt nothing but stupor and bewilderment when confronted with modern life – this unnatural marriage of technology, voyeurism, advertising and mass commerce – his assistant scoured forums and social networks and spent much more time on his computer than in front of his TV. As for Servaz, he knew he was a man of the past, and that the past was no longer relevant. He was like the character played by Burt Lancaster in *Conversation Piece* – an old professor who leads a reclusive life in his art-filled Roman palazzo until the day he has the misfortune of renting out the top floor to a modern family who are noisy and vulgar. Then he is confronted, unwillingly, with the sudden appearance of a world he doesn't understand, but which ends up fascinating him. Similarly, Servaz had to admit he was at a loss to understand this herd of people with their childish gadgets and infantile busyness.

'He keeps sending one message after another,' said Vincent. 'He's completely hooked.'

His assistant pulled the cover over his tablet and was about to shove it into the glove compartment when suddenly he paused.

'Your gun is in there,' he said.

'I know.'

'You're not taking it?'

'What for? This guy always uses knives. And whenever we've arrested him, he's never put up any resistance. Besides, you have your gun.'

On that note, Servaz got out. Espérandieu shrugged. He checked to make sure his gun was in its case, removed the safety catch and climbed out in turn.

'You're as stubborn as a mule, you know that?' he said, walking into the downpour.

'*Cedant arma togae*. Let arms yield to the toga.'

'They should teach Latin at police school,' said Espérandieu ironically.

'The wisdom of the ancients,' Servaz amended. 'I know some people who could learn something from it.'

They crossed the muddy lawn towards a little patch of garden surrounded at the front of the house by a fence. The entire south wall, where the only window was, was almost completely covered by a gigantic tag. There were two windows on each floor at the front of the house on the garden side, but the shutters were closed.

The gate creaked with rust when Servaz opened it. He knew at once it must have been audible inside the house, in spite of the storm. He glanced at Vincent, who nodded.

They walked up the short drive past neglected plants overrun by weeds.

Suddenly Servaz froze. There was a dark shape over on the right. Near the house. A huge dog had come out of its kennel and was looking at them. Silently. Without moving.

'A pit bull,' said Espérandieu, his voice tense and quiet as he moved closer to Servaz. 'There shouldn't be any first-category dogs around any more, not since '99.'

'True,' replied Servaz. 'But there are still a hundred and fifty-odd in Toulouse – plus a thousand second-category dogs, apparently. People are obviously reluctant to give up their "protection".'

Servaz checked the chain: it was long enough for the dog to reach them. Vincent had taken out his gun. Martin wondered if that would be enough to check the dog's momentum, if it suddenly felt like tearing a couple of throats to bits.

'We'd have had a better chance to stop it with two guns,' his assistant remarked wisely.

But the dog didn't blink. It was as silent as a shadow; a shadow with two shining little eyes. Servaz went up the single rain-splattered step, keeping an eye on the dog, and pressed the metal door buzzer. Through the frosted glass he could hear the shrill sound spreading through the house. It was dark on the other side, like the inside of an oven.

Then he heard footsteps, and the door opened.

'What the fuck d'you want?'

The man was shorter than him and very slender, almost thin. Younger, too – in his thirties. His head was completely shaved. Servaz took note of certain signs: hollow cheeks, deep-set eyes and pupils the size of pinheads, even though there was almost no light where they were standing.

'Good evening,' he said politely, taking out his badge. 'Crime unit. May we come in?'

He saw the shaved head hesitate.

'We would just like to ask you a few questions about the three women who were attacked by the river,' he hastened to add. 'You must have read about it in the newspapers.'

'I don't read the papers.'

'Well, on the Internet.'

'Don't do that either.'

'Ah. We've been visiting all the houses in the radius of a kilometre,' he lied. 'A house-to-house, routine check.'

The man's pinhead eyes went from Servaz to Vincent and back again. Servaz mused that he must be thinking about the blonde woman he thought he had matched with on Tinder – a real miracle, surely, with a face like his? – and he was in a hurry for only one reason: to get them out of there so he could go back to his electronic pick-up job. What would he have done with her if she'd been real and had actually taken the bait? Servaz had read the man's file . . .

'Is there a problem, monsieur?'

Servaz deliberately adopted a worried tone, raising his eyebrows as if he were puzzled.

'Huh? No, no, no problem. Come in. But be quick, all right? I have to give my mum her medication.'

Jensen stepped back and Servaz crossed the threshold. The hallway was as dark and narrow as the gallery of a mine, with a dimly lit area at the rear and a strip of grey light coming from a door 2 metres along on the left. It made him think of a network of caves fleetingly illuminated by speleologists' lamps, smelling of cat piss, pizza, sweat and stale tobacco. And there was another smell, which he could identify for having sniffed it many times over in flats in the centre of town where they found the corpses of old ladies forgotten by God and man: the cloying smell of medication and old age. He took another step. On either side were walls of cardboard boxes piled up almost to shoulder level, collapsing under the weight of whatever they contained: old lampshades, piles of dusty magazines, wicker baskets full of useless things. Elsewhere, heavy, graceless furniture left scarcely any room to get past. It was more of a warehouse than a residence . . .

He reached the door and glanced over to his left. Initially he saw only the dark shapes of the clutter of furniture with, in the middle, the little star of a bedside lamp on the night table. Then the picture became clearer and he could make out the creature in her bed. *The ailing mother* – it must be. He hadn't been prepared for this – who would have been? – and inadvertently he gulped. The old woman was propped against an unbelievable number of pillows, which in turn were propped against a carved oak bedstead. Her threadbare nightgown gaped open to reveal a marked, bony chest. Her face, with

43

its prominent cheekbones and deep-set cavernous eyes, and the sparse tufts of grey hair on her temples, clearly indicated the outline of the skull it would soon become; the whole scene was almost like a vanitas. Servaz noticed dozens of boxes of medication on the mat on the night table, and a tube connecting the old woman's gnarled arm to a drip. There was a great deal more death in this bedroom than there was life. But the most shocking thing was her eyes – in spite of the fatigue, listlessness and illness, they shone with malice. When he thought again of the name of the cul-de-sac – chemin du Paradis – he wondered if he hadn't taken the path to hell instead.

The mummy had a yellowed cigarette butt pressed between her cracked lips and was smoking like a chimney. Startled by this vision, Servaz moved on to the living room, which was dimly lit by the flickering glow of a television and several computer screens. He could make out an entire network of rooms, a wooden stairway and a host of nooks and crannies. Something rubbed against his legs and he could see shapes going back and forth in the half-light, jumping from one piece of furniture to another. There were dozens of them, of varying sizes and colours. It was swarming with cats. Saucers were set here and there throughout the darkness, filled with drying and decaying food. Servaz was careful where he put his feet.

The air was even heavier and harder to breathe than in the corridor; he thought he could make out a vague mustiness underneath the smell of decomposing cat food – he pinched his nostrils.

'Can't we put the lights on?' he said. 'It's as dark as a furnace in here.'

Their host reached out. The dim halo of an anglepoise lamp lit up the part of the desk that was cluttered with screens, leaving all the rest in shadow. Servaz did at least manage to glimpse a sofa and a sideboard in the gloom.

'You going to ask me those questions or not?'

Jensen had a faint lisp; Servaz suspected that underneath the confrontational attitude the man was pathologically shy.

'Do you ever go for walks along the river?' asked Espérandieu from behind Jensen, obliging him to turn around.

'Nah.'

'Never?'

'I told you, no,' said Jensen, watching Servaz out of the corner of his eye.

44

'You haven't heard any rumours about what happened?'

'Are you taking the piss or what? Don't you see where we live, me and my mum? Who'd go bringing us rumours, in your opinion? The postman? No one ever comes here.'

'Except the people who go running along the river,' Servaz pointed out.

'Yeah. Some of them park their cars down there, on that bloody wasteland, that's true.'

'Men? Women?'

'Well, both. Some of the women even have dogs with them, and that makes Fantôme bark.'

'And you see them go by your windows.'

'Yeah, so what?'

There was something, there, under the sideboard. Servaz had noticed it as soon as he walked into the room. It wasn't moving, or only just. He took a step closer.

'Hey! Where are you going? If this is a search, you—'

'Three women were assaulted on the path less than two kilometres from here,' interrupted Vincent. Jensen turned to look at him again. 'They all gave the same description.'

Servaz sensed that the young man was getting tense. He moved closer to the sideboard.

'They described a man wearing a hoodie, height roughly one metre seventy, weight sixty kilos or so.'

In fact, the three women had given three facial composites that varied considerably, as they often did. The only point they had in common was that the attacker was short and thin, but very strong.

'What were you doing on the evenings of 20 September, 5 September and 5 October between five and six p.m.?'

Jensen frowned, acting as if he were thinking very hard, digging intensely in his brain, and Servaz recalled the performance of the Japanese extras in *Seven Samurai*.

'On the eleventh I was with my mates Angel and Roland. We were playing cards at Angel's place. On the twenty-third, same thing. On 8 November Angel and me went to the cinema.'

'What film did you see?'

'Something with zombies and scouts in the title.'

'Zombies and scouts?' said Vincent. '*Scout's Guide to the Zombie Apocalypse*,' he confirmed. 'I've seen that too.'

Servaz looked at his assistant, eyebrows raised.

'That's odd,' he said quietly, forcing Jensen to turn his head once more. 'I generally have a good memory. But just now, like that, spontaneously, I'm not sure I recall what I was doing on 20 September in the evening, or on 30 September, do you follow me? I remember the fifth, because that's the day a co-worker retired. That was a special day, so to speak . . . but going to the cinema or playing cards with mates, is that special?'

'All you got to do is ask them, and you'll see,' said Jensen sullenly.

'Oh, I'm sure they'll say yes,' said Servaz. 'Do you have their surnames?'

Just as he expected, Jensen hurried to provide them.

'Listen,' he added. 'I know why I remember so well.'

'Oh? Really?'

'Because when I saw in the newspaper that the girl had been raped, I immediately wrote down what I'd been doing that day.'

'I thought you didn't read the paper.'

'Yeah, well, I lied.'

'And why did you do that?'

Jensen shrugged. His bald scalp shone in the darkness. He rubbed his hand full of rings over it, from forehead to neck, where he had a tattoo.

'Because I didn't feel like talking to you, that's why. I just wanted you to clear out.'

'Maybe you were busy?'

'Maybe I was.'

'So every time, you write down what you were doing, is that it?'

'That's it. And you know very well that we all do that.'

'"We"? Who do you mean, "we"?'

'Blokes like me, blokes who've done time for that stuff. We all know that the first thing little coppers like you are going to ask us is where we were at the time. If a bloke who's already been convicted can't remember what the fuck he was doing when a girl was raped nearby, well then, there's a good chance that he's the one, the nonce, you get me?'

'And your two mates, Angel and Thingummy – have they ever been convicted?'

They saw Jensen bristle.

'Yeah. So what?'

Servaz glanced under the sideboard. The shadow had moved. Two fearful eyes were watching him.

'How old were you the first time?' asked Espérandieu out of the blue.

Thunder caused the windowpanes to rattle, and lightning briefly lit up the living room.

'The first time?'

'The first time you sexually assaulted a woman.'

Servaz caught Jensen's gaze. His expression had changed. It was literally glowing.

'Fourteen,' he said, his voice suddenly very cold and clear.

Servaz leaned forward a little more. The little white cat under the sideboard raised its head and looked up at him from the shadow, torn between fear and a desire to come and rub against his legs.

'I read your file. She was a classmate. You raped her behind the gym.'

'She provoked me.'

'You insulted her. Then you slapped her, hit her—'

'She was a bitch; she was already sleeping with everyone. One more prick, what difference was it to her?'

'Several times . . . On the head. Very violently. *Cranial trauma* . . . And then, after that, you raped her in the gym with a pump – a pump for blowing up balls . . . She'll never be able to have children, do you know that?'

'It was a long time ago.'

'And what did you feel at the time, do you remember?'

Silence.

'You can't understand,' suggested Jensen, his voice unpleasant and suddenly full of boastfulness.

Servaz stiffened. That voice. Arrogance and selfishness of the purest kind. He put his hand out towards the underside of the sideboard. The little white cat slowly came out and went fearfully up to Servaz. He felt a tiny, coarse tongue at his fingertips. Other cats immediately joined him, but Servaz waved them away to concentrate on the little white ball.

'Would you explain?' said Espérandieu, and beneath his assistant's patient tone Servaz could hear an echo of rage and disgust.

'What for? You're talking about things you know nothing about; you have no idea what people like us feel . . . the *intensity* of our

47

emotions, the *power* of our experiences. The fantasies that people like you have – people who stick to order and morality, who live in fear of the law and what other people might think – will always be light years away from true freedom and true power.'

Jensen was hissing now.

'I've been to prison, I've done my time, you have nothing more on me. Nowadays I respect the law.'

'Oh yeah? And how do you do that? Keep your impulses in check, I mean? Not go through with it? Do you masturbate? Do you go to prostitutes? Do you take medication?'

'But I haven't forgotten any of it,' continued Jensen, disregarding the interruption. 'I'm not sorry about any of it, I don't disown any of it, I don't feel any guilt. I'm not going to apologise for being the way God made me.'

'Is that how you felt when you tried to rape those three women on the banks of the Garonne?' asked Espérandieu patiently. 'I say tried, because you didn't even come. If you stabbed that girl with so much rage, it's because you couldn't even get hard – isn't that it?'

Servaz knew what his assistant was trying to do: to rankle Jensen, make him react, drive him to justify himself and boast. *It won't work.*

'I raped four women and I paid for it,' Jensen answered coldly. 'I sent three of them to hospital.' He said it like a football player bragging about scoring goals. 'Mind you, I'm not in the habit of doing things by halves.' He gave a little squeal of a laugh, which made the hair on Servaz's neck stand on end. 'So you see it can't possibly be me.'

The scum was telling the truth. Right from the start, Servaz had been convinced it wasn't him. Not this time, anyway. He looked at the white cat.

It was missing an ear. In its place was a pink scar.

A little white cat missing an ear: where had he already seen that?

'Leave my cat alone,' said Jensen.

'*Leave my cat alone . . .*'

Suddenly it came to him. The woman who'd been murdered in her country house near Montauban, in June. He'd read the report. She lived alone, she had been raped then strangled, after breakfast: the pathologist had found coffee, the remains of wholewheat bread, marmalade, and kiwi in her stomach. The weather had been hot. The windows were wide open to let in the cool morning air. All the attacker had to do was step over the windowsill. Seven o'clock in the morning and neighbours less than thirty metres away. But no one had seen or heard a thing, and the gendarmes had no leads. No clues. The only thing they noticed was that the woman's cat had vanished.

A white cat with one ear.

'That's not your cat,' said Servaz quietly, pulling himself up straight.

It felt as if the air was getting thicker. Servaz made a face. All his muscles were hardening from the toxins of tension. Jensen stopped moving. He was silent. Another flash of lightning lit up the living room; only the pinheads of the man's eyes were moving in his chalky face as he looked from one policeman to the other.

'Back up,' he said suddenly.

The hand covered in rings was holding a gun. *My mistake*, thought Servaz, quickly glancing at Vincent.

'Back up.'

They obeyed.

'Don't do anything stupid,' said Espérandieu.

Jensen rushed forward. Quick as a mouse he wove through the furniture, opened a door at the rear, and vanished, while wind and rain came blowing into the room. Servaz stood there stunned for a moment – then went running after him.

'Where are you going?' screamed Vincent behind him. 'Martin! Where are you going? You don't even have a gun!'

The French window was banging in the wind. It opened onto the railway embankment, which was blocked off by a chain-link fence. Instead of climbing it, Jensen had run along the side and was now dashing across the rain-swept patch of grass. Servaz emerged in turn at the rear. In the flash of lightning, he looked up at the electric railway lines at the top of the embankment, searching for Jensen, then he turned and saw him dashing towards the little tunnel through which he and Espérandieu had come, and which passed underneath other railway lines that went to join the main line.

There was a gate to the right of the tunnel, above where the lines met. A cement ramp climbed up to a sort of concrete blockhouse, which might be a signal box. Neither the gate – where a large collection of signs warned of the danger of electrocution – nor the fence had dissuaded the taggers: every square inch of concrete was covered with big coloured letters. Drops of water glittered against the black backdrop of night, lit intermittently by lightning, while the thunder boomed: the storm was circling over Toulouse. Streams of water poured down the grassy embankment.

Servaz began running through the torrents of water. Jensen was already climbing over the gate. Then he saw him run towards the top of the cement ramp, around the signal box at the top, and on towards the railway lines. Several steel pylons stood just there supporting a complex network of grids, primary and secondary electric lines, transformers and catenaries. It looked like a sub-station and Servaz immediately thought, *high voltage*. He thought, *storm, thunder, lightning, rain, conductivity* – and the thousands of volts, amperes, or whatever the hell circulated through those lines like a death-trap. *Bloody fucking hell, where are you going?* he thought. Jensen did not seem aware of the trap. What concerned him was the goods train rolling slowly ahead of him and blocking his way.

Now Servaz reached the gate. His socks were squelching in his sodden shoes; his shirt collar was drenched, his hair sticking to his forehead.

He felt duty-bound to climb over the gate and drop down to the other side. His jacket must have got caught somewhere, because he heard a tearing sound when he landed on the cement.

Up there, Jensen was hesitating.

Servaz saw him lean forward to look under the carriages, then between the two. He reached out towards the moving train, grabbed the rungs of a carriage, and climbed up towards the roof.

Don't do that!

Not here, it's crazy!

'Jensen!' he called.

The man turned, saw him, and began climbing even faster. The rails were slick with rain. Servaz reached the top of the ballast and in turn seized the metal rungs on the side of the carriage.

'Martin! What the hell are you doing?'

5

In a Region Close to Death

Espérandieu's voice, below him. Servaz puts his foot on a rung, pulls himself up with his hand closed around a slippery bar, puts down the other foot. He can hear the buzzing of electricity in the lines above his head, like the sound of a thousand wasps.

He has come out level with the roof. Jensen is still there. He hesitates, his form standing out in the gleam of lightning, only a few metres away from the catenaries and the lines. For a moment there is a sizzling of overvoltage from one end of the lines to the other: *fff-chhhhhhh*. Servaz can feel every hair on his body standing on end. He wipes his streaming face. Climbs onto the roof and finds his footing. The rain is pounding onto the carriage. Jensen turns his head, left then right, as if paralysed by uncertainty; he has his back to Servaz, his legs spread.

'Jensen,' says Servaz. 'We'll both fry if we stay here.'

No reaction.

'Jensen!'

The din is so loud that it's a waste of time.

'JENSEN!'

And then . . .

. . . and then it comes in a sort of fog of sensations mingling and contradicting one another; a brutal acceleration of time; a sudden, unexpected and inexplicable swerve: just as Jensen pivots towards him, gun in hand (and a flame bursts from the black mouth of the barrel), an electric arc of such luminous white that it dazzles him flashes from the catenary and sweeps towards Jensen, striking him, oddly, not at the top of his head but on the left side of his face, then finds a path through his body, connecting through his legs and feet with the flooded roof of the carriage, transforming the fugitive into

51

a toaster and instantly projecting him several metres further along. Servaz feels the residual electric charge as it follows the roof of the wet carriage right under the soles of his shoes, and his hair stands on end – but an event that will have far greater significance for his future occurs in the same instant: in the tenth of a second that follows, the projectile that left the gun enters into contact with his rain-soaked mohair wool jacket, goes through it at the speed of 350 metres a second – in other words ten times faster than the speed of sound – then passes through the fabric of his polo-neck jumper (42 per cent polyamide, 30 per cent wool and 28 per cent alpaca), the epidermis, dermis and hypodermis of his wet skin, a few centimetres from his left nipple, through the external oblique muscle and the intercostal muscles, narrowly missing the thoracic artery and the breastbone, and then pierces the front edge of his left lung, with its spongy, elastic texture, then the pericardium, and finally penetrates his heart right next to the left ventricle – his heart pumping and expelling blood at a speed accelerated by fear – before coming out the other side.

The shock projects him backwards.

And the last thing Martin Servaz notices is the static electricity under his feet, the drops of cold rain on his cheeks, the smell of ozone in the air and the screams of his assistant from the bottom of the embankment, just as a fatal metal wasp pierces his heart.

'We've got a TMGSW,' says the woman's voice next to him. 'I repeat: transmediastinal gunshot wound. Strong indication of a penetrating wound to the heart. Bullet entry in the precordial region; dorsal exit. CRT: over three seconds. Tachycardia over 120 bpm. No response to pain and no reaction of pupils to light. Cyanosis of the lips, extremities cold. Very unstable situation. Prepare for surgery as quickly as possible.'

The voice reaches him through several layers of gauze. It is calm, but he can sense the urgency; it is not talking to him but to someone else, but he can only hear this voice.

'We have a second casualty,' adds the voice. 'Third-degree burns from electrocution, a high-voltage wire. Stabilised. We need a spot in the burn unit. Hurry up. We've got a mess, here.'

'Where's the other cop?' bellows a second voice, a bit further away. 'I want to know what calibre the weapon was and the type of ammunition.'

As the lightning draws bright intermittent streaks across the sky, he can sense through his eyelashes the glow of other, more colourful, rhythmic pulsations, on his right. He hears sounds, too: voices, further away, many of them; the echo of sirens; a train rattling and squealing over the points . . .

It was really stupid to run after that guy without your gun.

All at once he feels completely bewildered. It's his father. His father is looking at him, standing next to where he is lying on the gurney. *What the hell are you doing here?* he thinks. You committed suicide when I was twenty; I'm the one who found you. You committed suicide like Socrates, like Seneca. In your study where you always went to correct your students' homework. With Mahler on full blast. I had just got home from uni that day. So, tell me how, for Christ's sake, you can possibly be here?

It was stupid, really stupid.

Papa? Papa? Shit, where did he go? There is a great deal of agitation around him. The mask on his face bothers him – it feels like a big paw – but he's pretty sure this is how life is reaching his lungs. He hears another familiar voice, a terribly anxious voice. *Is he alive? Is he alive? Will he make it?* Vincent, it's Vincent. Why is Vincent panicking? He feels fine. It's true: he feels astonishingly well. Everything is fine, is what he'd like to tell him. But he can neither speak nor move.

'Number one priority, maintain the blood volume: fill it up!' shouts a new voice right next to him.

That voice, too, is close to panic. He would like to say to them everything is fine, I assure you. I even think I've never felt this good in my entire life. All at once he gets the feeling he's not facing the right way, that he's floating above his own body. He's resting on air, suspended in the void. He can see them, busy all around him, methodical, precise, disciplined. He has another self lying there below. He sees himself the way he sees the others. *Good Lord, you don't look very well! You look like a corpse!* He can feel no pain. Nothing but an inner peace of a sort he has never known. He watches them rushing around. He likes all these people. Every one of them.

That too, he would like to tell them. How much he loves them. How much they matter to him – all of them, even the people he doesn't know. Why has he never managed to tell the people he loves that he loves them? Now it's too late. Too late. He wishes Margot were here. And Alexandra. And Charlène, too. And Marianne . . . It is as if someone has poked him with a cattle prod. *Marianne . . . where is she? What has become of her? Is she alive or dead? Is he going to leave without getting an answer?*

'Right, here we go!' says the voice. 'On the count of three: one . . . two . . .'

Sometimes – like now – he disconnects completely. There can be no doubt: he's on his way towards death. *I feel fine. I feel splendid. I'm ready, lads, don't you worry.* The ambulance doors open wide.

Hospital.

OR3!
  Haemostasis!
  We've got to maintain haemostasis!

Clicking. Voices. The parade of neon lights past his eyelashes. Corridors. He can hear the gurney's little wheels squeaking on the floor. Doors banging. The smell of ethanol. His eyes are half closed, he's not supposed to be able to see: 'Coma stage two,' said someone at some point. He's not supposed to be able to hear, either. Maybe he's dreaming? But who can dream up words like 'haemostasis'. He'll have to get to the bottom of this, when the time comes.

He's so conditioned by his job, he thinks with a smile – an inner smile, of course.

He is constantly alternating between erratic lucidity and total fog. All of a sudden he sees several people bending over him, with their caps and their blue scrubs. Gazes. All focused on him.

'I want a full list of lesions. Where are the red blood cell concentrates, the platelets, the plasma?'

They pick him up and put him down again, cautiously. He vanishes into the fog once more.

'Prepare all instruments for a left anterolateral thoracotomy.'

He emerges one last time. A little light passes before his pupils, from one eye to the other.

'His pupils aren't reacting. No reaction to pain, either.'

'Is the anaesthesia ready?'

Once again, the mask over his face is like a grizzly's paw. He can hear one voice, louder than the others:

'Let's go!'

Suddenly he sees a long tunnel leading endlessly upwards. Like in that bloody painting by Hieronymus Bosch – what was it called again? He is climbing up the tunnel. What is this thing? He is . . . *flying*. There is light at the end. Shit, where am I going? The closer he gets, the brighter the light. Brighter than any light he has ever seen.

Where am I?

He is lying on the operating table, and yet he is walking through a remarkable landscape full of light. How is this possible? The landscape is breathtaking ('breathtaking': *haven't lost your sense of humour, mate!* he muses, thinking about the oxygen mask). He sees blue mountains in the distance, a sky that is absolutely pure, hills, *and light*. A great deal of light. A brilliant, sparkling, magnificent, tangible light. He knows where he is: in a region close to death, perhaps even already on the other side, but he is not afraid.

Everything is beautiful, luminous, fantastic. *Welcoming.*

He is standing on a ridge overlooking the hills, with shimmering streams winding their way through the terrain, embracing its contours. Below him, a river is slowly approaching. He follows a path down to the river and the further he goes, the more unusual the river seems. It is an unimaginable marvel, this river! And suddenly, as he draws closer, he begins to understand: the river is made of human beings walking side by side, and what he sees is the river of humanity: past, present and future.

Hundreds of thousands, millions, billions of human beings . . .

He walks the last hundred metres and when he joins the huge crowd he feels submerged, surrounded by a palpable love. Immersed in the middle of this enormous river of people, he begins sobbing with joy. He realises that never – not for one minute in his entire life – has he been this happy. Never has he felt so at peace with himself, and with others. Never has the perfume of life been so sweet.

(*Life?* says a dissonant voice inside him. *Can't you see that this light, this love, is death?*)

He wonders where this dissonance has come from, these sudden, harsh chords – as powerful as the ones that resonate at the end of the adagio in Mahler's 10th Symphony.

Through his eyelashes he sees someone at his bedside, at the edge of his field of vision. He does not know her name, this beautiful young woman with the tragic face. She must be twenty-two or twenty-three years old. Then the fog lifts and his lucidity returns. Margot. His daughter. When did she get here? She is supposed to be in Quebec.

Margot is weeping. He can *feel* his daughter's thoughts, can feel how unhappy she is – and suddenly he is ashamed.

He realises he is no longer in the operating theatre but in a hospital room.

Recovery, he thinks. The recovery room.

Then the door opens and a man in a white coat comes in with a nurse. For a moment he is filled with panic when the man turns to Margot. He is going to tell her that her father is dead.

No, no, I'm not dead! Don't listen to him!

'He's in a coma,' says the man.

He can hear Margot asking questions. She is standing outside of his field of vision and he cannot move. He cannot hear everything they are saying. *Hey, you lot, I'm here!* he would like to shout. *It's me you're talking about!* But he cannot make a single sound – and, in any case, he's got this thing stuck in his mouth.

'Can you hear me?'

He cannot remember very well where he went nor for how long. He has the vague sensation that there was light, and a human river, but he's not sure about that either. In any case, he is back in the hospital room. He recognises the ceiling, with its brown spot that vaguely resembles the African continent.

'Can you hear me?'

Yes, yes, I can hear you.

'Can you hear me, Dad?'

Yes, yes, I can hear you!

'Dad. Can. You. Hear. Me?'

He would like to take her hand, give her a sign, any sign – flicker an eyelash, wiggle a finger, make a sound – so that she will understand, but he is a prisoner of this sarcophagus that is his lifeless body.

You are so beautiful, my little girl, he thinks as she leans towards him.

He is beginning to feel at home. There are other rooms, other patients in recovery: sometimes he hears them calling the nurses or pressing their call buttons, triggering a strident ringing.

During his moments of lucidity, however, he has become aware of one important thing: he is in the middle of a spider's web of tubes, bandages, electric wires, electrodes and pumps; and the sound of the machine on his right – which he will soon begin to call the 'spider machine' – is like a sign of some modern sorcery, an evil spell that is holding him captive, its greatest perversion the silicone tube entering his mouth. He has no autonomy, no movement, no defence; he is at the mercy of the machine, as inert as a corpse.

But perhaps he is . . . dead?

Because in the evening, when there is no one left in his room, the dead take the place of the living.

Silence reigns at night, in the ward and in his room, and suddenly they are there. His father, for example, saying, *Do you remember your uncle Ferenc?*

Ferenc was his mother's brother. He was a poet. Papa said that if Maman and Uncle Ferenc were so fond of the French language, it was because they were born in Hungary.

You are going to die, said his father gently. *You are going to join us. It's not so bad, you'll see. You'll be fine here with us.*

He looks at them. Because at night, in his visions, he can turn his head. They are everywhere in the room. He knows them all. Like Aunt Cezarina, a beautiful brown-haired woman with a magnificent bosom, whom he was in love with when he was fifteen.

Come, says Aunt Cezarina in turn.

And Matthias, his cousin, who died from leukaemia at the age of twelve. Madame Garson, his French teacher when he was thirteen, who read his essays to the rest of the class. And Eric Lombard, the billionaire who was killed in an avalanche – the man who loved horses; and Mila, the astronaut, who slit her wrists in the bathtub – no doubt someone was there next to her that night, but Servaz gave up trying to prove it. And Mahler himself, the great Mahler, the genius with tired features, wearing his pince-nez and a strange hat, speaking of the curse of the number 9: *Beethoven, Bruckner, Schubert . . . they all died after their ninth symphony . . . so I went directly from the eighth to the tenth . . . I wanted to trick God – such arrogance! – but it was not enough.*

Every time they appear, he is enveloped in the same love. And yes, he is beginning to find it suspicious. He knows what they want from him: *to go with them*. But he's not ready. His time has not come. He tries to explain, but they don't want to know. To be sure, the grass is greener where they have come from; the sky is bluer, the light is a thousand times more intense, and yet, he cannot possibly stay there, now that he has seen Margot next to his bed.

One day Samira shows up, dressed as usual in one of her weird get-ups.

When she leans over him, he briefly glimpses a huge skull on her sweatshirt, and a face in the shadow of a hood. Then she removes the hood and it takes him half a second to identify the unbelievably ugly face – although the ugliness is fairly difficult to pinpoint, in fact, because it's the overall effect of individually minor details: a too-short nose and protuberant eyes; a too-big mouth, a certain dissymmetry in her features . . . Samira Cheung: the finest member of his investigation team, along with Vincent.

'Fuck, boss, if you could see your face.'

He wishes he could smile. And he does, internally. This is pure Samira . . . she insists on calling him 'boss', even though he has frequently pointed out that he finds the title ridiculous. She walks around his bed and out of sight, to open the blinds, and he notes in passing that she still has the nicest arse of anyone in the brigade.

That is the Samira paradox: a perfect body and one of the ugliest faces he has ever seen. Is this sexist? Could be. Samira herself does not refrain from passing judgement on the anatomical particularities of the men she encounters.

'. . . *How are the nurses? . . . The fantasy of the nurse, naked under her uniform, do you like that . . . boss? . . . I'll be back tomorrow . . . boss . . . I promise . . .*'

The days go by. And the nights. How many, he hasn't a clue.

Because time does not exist here. His only point of reference is the nurses. They are the ones who give rhythm to time, conducting a relay by his bedside.

He is perfectly aware of their unlimited power over his person, and although on the whole they are competent, devoted, meticulous, *swamped*, they never fail to make him aware of this, through their gestures, the tone of their voices, and their words, all of which signify the same thing: 'You are gravely ill, and you depend entirely and exclusively on us.'

Another morning, another visit. Two blurry faces by the bed. One of them is Margot, the other . . . Alexandra, her mother. His ex-wife has gone to the trouble to come. Her eyes are red. Is she upset? He remembers their disagreements after the divorce; then their complicity returned, to a degree, no doubt thanks to common memories of happy days, the time when Margot was growing up. .

'. . . say that you can't hear anything,' says Vincent from his chair.

They are alone in the room, the door open onto the corridor, as always.

And . . . oh, Lord! That music! That theme – the most beautiful ever written! Oh, the tumult, the bleeding, the words of love! Mahler . . . his beloved Mahler . . . Why didn't anyone think of it before now? He thinks that tears must be welling in his eyes, flowing down his cheeks. But then he sees the face of his assistant – who is clearly watching out for the least little sign – and he can read nothing in his eyes but disappointment, when Vincent removes the headphones and sits back down.

He would like to cry out: *More! More! I've been in tears!*

But only his brain cries out.

Another night. His father is there again, in the room. Sitting on the chair. Reading a book, out loud. As he did when Servaz was a child. He recognises the passage:

SQUIRE TRELAWNEY, Dr Livesey and the rest of these gentlemen having asked me to write down the whole particulars about Treasure Island, from the beginning to the end, keeping nothing back but the bearings of the island, and that only because there is still treasure not yet lifted, I take up my pen in the year of grace 17__ and go back to the time when my father kept the Admiral Benbow inn and the brown old seaman with the sabre cut first took up his lodging under our roof.

What do you think, son? This is quite a change from what you usually read, isn't it?

His father must be referring to his numerous volumes of science fiction. Or perhaps his current reading material. And suddenly he remembers another book he read – a terrifying one; he must have been twelve or thirteen years old:

To the vanished Herbert West and to me the disgust and horror were supreme. I shudder tonight as I think of it; shudder even more than I did that morning when West muttered through his bandages, 'Dammit, it wasn't quite fresh enough!'

Why has this memory suddenly surfaced? No doubt because tonight more than other nights he shivers on feeling its presence in the dark nooks and crannies: what he felt in that dismal house by the railway, on the chemin du Paradis; what has been clinging to his footsteps ever since, and has followed him all the way here, like a curse in a film that spreads from one victim to another.

Dammit, it must be saying, *he isn't quite ready . . .*

6

Awakening

He opened his eyes.

Blinked.

This time, it wasn't an imaginary movement. His eyelids really did move. The nurse on duty had her back to him. He could see how her shoulders and hips made her uniform taut while she examined the treatment forms.

'I'm going to give you a blood test,' she said, without turning around or expecting any answer from him.

'Mmmh.'

This time, she turned around. Looked closely at him. He blinked. She frowned. He blinked again.

'Oh, goodness,' she said. 'Can you hear me?'

'Mmmhhh.'

'Oh, goodness.'

She rushed out and a few seconds later came back with a young intern. An unfamiliar face. Glasses with a steel frame. A bit of stubble on his chin. He moved closer, leaned down. Servaz could smell coffee and tobacco on the intern's breath.

'Can you hear me?'

He nodded his head and felt a pain in his spine.

'Mmmh.'

'I'm Dr Cavalli,' said the intern, taking his left hand. 'If you understand what I'm saying, squeeze my hand.'

Servaz squeezed. Limply. But he could see the doctor smile. The doctor and the nurse exchanged a look.

'Go and inform Dr Cauchois,' the young intern said to the nurse. 'Tell him to come right away.'

Then he turned back to Servaz and held a pen up in front of his eyes, moving it slowly from left to right and right to left.

'Can you follow this pen with your eyes, please? Don't move. Just your eyes.'

Servaz did as he was asked.

'Great. We're going to remove this tube and get you some water. Above all, don't move. I'll be back. If you understood what I said, squeeze my hand twice.'

Servaz squeezed.

He woke again. Opened his eyes and saw Margot's face right in front of him. His daughter's eyes were moist but he could tell that this time, these were tears of joy.

'Oh, Dad,' she said. 'Are you awake? Can you hear me?'

'Of course.'

He took his daughter's hand. It was warm and dry in his own, which was cold and damp.

'Oh, Dad, I'm so happy!'

'Me too, I . . .' He cleared his throat; it felt as if he had sandpaper for vocal chords. 'I . . . am . . . glad you are here . . .'

He managed to say these words almost in one go. He pointed towards the glass of water on the night table. Margot picked it up and held it to his dry lips. He looked at his daughter.

'Ha . . . have you been here long?'

'In this room or in Toulouse? A few days, Dad.'

'And your work, in Quebec?' he asked.

Margot had landed several jobs there, over the last few years, and had eventually settled down in a Canadian publishing house. She worked in foreign acquisitions. Servaz had been out there twice to see her and, each time, the flight had been an ordeal.

'I've taken unpaid leave. Don't worry, everything has been arranged. Dad,' she added, 'it's great that you're . . . *awake*.'

'I love you,' he said. 'You're the one who's great.'

Why had he said such a thing? She looked at him, surprised. And blushed.

'Me too. Do you remember what I told you the time you ended up in hospital after the avalanche?'

'No.'

'Don't ever do anything like that again.'

It came back to him. Winter 2008–9. The chase through the mountains on a snowmobile, and the avalanche. Margot at his bedside when he woke up. He smiled at her, as if in apology.

'Fuck, boss. You gave us a real fright!'

He was having his breakfast, which consisted of dreadful coffee, toast and strawberry jam – with a side order of medication – and reading the newspaper, when Samira swept in, followed by Vincent. He looked up from his article, where he had read that Toulouse was taking in 19,000 new inhabitants every year, and at that rate in ten years it would be larger than Lyon; that the city was home to 95,789 students and 12,000 researchers; that it offered flights to 43 European cities, and to Paris more than 30 times a day, but – the sting in the tail – the article then stated that between 2005 and 2011, for strictly budgetary reasons, the number of police officers in Toulouse, and indeed the national police as a whole, had declined year on year, and that this dramatic decrease had not been fully offset since. Further budget cuts meant that in 2014 they had even scrapped technical training for certain officers in the criminal division. However, the terrorist attacks in Paris on 13 November 2015 had radically changed the situation. The forces of law and order had suddenly become a priority again, and night-time searches were now authorised (Servaz had always wondered why the hell it wasn't possible to arrest a dangerous individual before six o'clock in the morning – it was as if, during a war, there was a truce every night which only one of the two sides respected), and this made procedures much simpler. The debate over the restriction of civil liberties and the wisdom of extending these measures had come quickly to the forefront again, however – which was healthy in a democracy, he supposed.

He folded the newspaper noisily. Samira was pacing round the bed like a lion in a cage; she was wearing a black motorcycle jacket covered in zips and buckles. Vincent was wearing a grey woollen cardigan over a Breton shirt and jeans. As usual, they looked like anything but cops. Vincent took out his phone and held it up towards Servaz.

'No pho-to,' articulated Servaz.

'Not even as a souvenir?'

'Mmmh.'

'When are you getting out, boss?' Samira asked.

'Stop calling me boss, it's ridiculous.'

'All right.'

'Don't know. Depends on the tests.'

'And afterwards, are they going to prescribe rest?'

'Same answer.'

'We need you on the team, boss.'

He sighed. Then his face lit up.

'Samira?'

'Yes?'

'You'll manage very well without me.'

He opened his newspaper and immersed himself in it again.

'Yeah . . . maybe . . . but that doesn't mean . . .' She swung around. 'I'm going to get a Coke.'

He heard her six-inch heels move away down the corridor.

'She has a problem with hospitals,' Vincent explained. 'How do you feel?'

'All right.'

'All right, all right, or really all right?'

'Raring to go.'

'Regarding work, you mean?'

'What else?'

Espérandieu sighed. With his brooding expression and his hair falling over his forehead, he looked like a student.

'Shit, Martin, only a few days ago you were still in a coma. You haven't even got out of bed yet, dammit! And you've just had your heart operated on.'

A finger tapped gently on the door, and Servaz turned his head. He instantly felt his stomach lurch.

Charlène, his assistant's too-beautiful wife, was standing on the threshold. Charlène, her ginger hair like the flames of an autumn fire mingling with the thick tawny and white fur of her oversized collar; her milky white skin and huge green eyes promising paradise to all.

When she bent over him, he felt that primitive desire he always experienced in her presence.

He knew that she knew. She knew everything about the violent desire she inspired in him, in all men. She ran her fingernail over his cheek, almost pressing it into his skin, and smiled.

'I'm glad, Martin.'

That's all. *I'm glad.* Nothing else. And he knew she was being absolutely sincere.

In the days that followed, all the members of the investigation team, the majority of the crime unit, officers from Narcotics, the Banditry Repression Brigade and the rest of the directorate for criminal affairs, and even crime scene investigators, paraded through his room. Once the plague victim, he was now the miraculous survivor. He'd been shot, and he had made it. Every cop in Toulouse hoped that if the day came, it would be the same for them; their passage through his room was a sort of pilgrimage, a quasi-religious act of devotion. They wanted to see him, touch him and learn from him, this man who had come back from the dead. They wanted to be contaminated by his *baraka*.

The head of the Toulouse crime unit himself, Stehlin, took the trouble to visit one day at the end of the afternoon.

'Dammit, Martin, you got a bullet to the heart. And you survived. That's a miracle, is it not?'

'Over sixty per cent of those who receive a wound to the heart die on the spot,' answered Servaz calmly. 'But eighty per cent of those who make it alive to the hospital survive. It's true that mortality in the case of a gunshot wound is four times higher than in the case of a stabbing . . . Cardiac wounds from a trauma penetrating the thorax concern, in order of frequency, the right ventricle, the left ventricle and the auricles . . . Light ammunition is more unstable, and after the first trajectory of penetration has a tendency to swerve; bullets without a full metal jacket have an augmented cavitation tunnel, the bullet enlarging its diameter on impact. Buckshot has a different effect depending on the distance, with cut-and-dried lesions at less than three metres and shrapnel at more than ten.'

Stehlin stared at him, flabbergasted, then smiled. As always, when he was on an investigation, Martin had thoroughly studied his subject – or else he had grilled the doctors.

'That guy, Jensen, is he dead?' Servaz asked.

'No,' replied the Divisional Commissioner, placing his grey jacket on the back of a chair. 'They sent him for treatment in the severe burns unit. I think he's having rehabilitation sessions now at a special-ised centre.'

'Are you serious? You mean the man went free, then?'

'The guy's got a lawyer, he's suing us.'

'What?'

Stehlin was pacing back and forth in the little room, the way he always did in his big office – except that here he didn't have enough space, and he bumped into the wall.

'He says you threatened him with a weapon and forced him to climb onto the train, that you knew very well that he risked being electrocuted, and you did everything you could to ensure he would be.'

'He was electrified,' amended Servaz. 'He survived.'

He held one hand to his chest. He felt as if the stitches were pulling on the wound. They had sliced into his breastbone with cutters or a saw, and it would take weeks for the bone to fuse back together completely, weeks during which he could put no pressure on his arms or lift the slightest weight.

'It doesn't matter. According to his lawyer, there was "criminal intent", and "an initiation of offence constituted by acts tending directly to the perpetration of the offence".'

'What offence?'

'Attempted murder.'

'Huh?'

'According to his lawyer, you tried to kill him by electrocution. It was raining, you must have seen the warnings on the gate, and you ran after him in spite of that and obliged him to climb onto the train, while threatening him with your gun . . .' Stehlin waved his hands. 'I know, you didn't even have your gun on you. But he claims you did. He's just trying to intimidate us; we cannot allow ourselves to add oil to the fire at the moment.'

'The man is a murderer.'

'Martin, he was not charged for the rapes and the murder of the jogger . . .'

Through the window, Servaz saw the clouds grimacing above the flat hospital roofs.

'He's a murderer,' he stated.

'Martin, the culprit was arrested, he confessed. We found overwhelming proof at his house. Jensen is innocent.'

'Not as innocent as all that.' He leaned over to take the bitter-tasting corticosteroid that had dissolved in the glass. 'He killed someone else.'

'What?'

'The woman who was murdered in Montauban: it was him.'

He saw Stehlin frown. Over the years his boss had learned to respect his opinion.

'What makes you say that?'

'What did you do with Jensen's mother and all those cats?'

'His mother is in hospital, the cats were given to the SPCA.'

'Call them right away. See if they still have a young white cat that's missing an ear. Then find out what Jensen was doing at the time of the assault. And whether his phone activated a cell tower identifier in the sector during that same period.'

Servaz described the visit to Jensen's place, with the cat hiding under the sideboard and Jensen running away when Servaz told him – in all likelihood too quietly for Vincent to have heard – that it wasn't his cat.

'A young white cat,' said Stehlin, his tone openly sceptical.

'That's it.'

'Hell, Martin, are you sure of what you saw? I mean . . . blimey, a cat! You don't want me to go arresting a bloke because you saw a cat in his house?'

'And why not?'

'Because no judge will buy it, dammit!'

Stehlin said 'dammit' where others would have said 'for fuck's sake'.

'Well, we could remand him in custody, couldn't we?'

'What proof do you have? Apart from a cat?'

7

Séfar

'No one refutes testimonies of near-death experiences any more,' said Dr Xavier. 'On the other hand, the reality of a life after life is still just as open to debate. Those who, like you, have had a brush with death are, by definition, not dead. Since you are here.'

The psychiatrist gave him a warm smile, which widened his mouth in his salt and pepper beard, as if to say, 'And we are all very glad of it.' Servaz reflected that the events of the winter 2008–9 had changed Xavier – not just psychologically but also physically. When Servaz had met him, Xavier had been head of the Wargnier Institute. He was a precious, pedantic little man who dyed his hair and wore ostentatious red glasses.

'All near-death experiences can be explained by a dysfunction of the brain, a neurological correlate.'

Correlate. Servaz savoured the word. A touch of pedantry could do no harm when it came to establishing one's authority: it has always been thus, ever since Molière's doctors. In this respect Xavier had not changed. But it was nevertheless a changed man that Servaz saw before him. Wrinkles had appeared on his brow and at the corners of his eyes, which were no longer as bright, but rather like two bits of old metal. Xavier still had his passion for scholarly words, but he used them more circumspectly now, and he and Servaz had forged ties that were fairly close to true friendship. After the fire at the Wargnier Institute, Xavier had opened a surgery in Saint-Martin-de-Comminges, in the Pyrenees, only a few miles from the ruins of the establishment he had once run. Servaz went to see him two or three times a year. The two men went for long walks in the mountains, mindful not to stir up the past. Nevertheless, the past did hover over all their conversations, the way the shadow of the mountain hovered over the town after four o'clock in the afternoon.

'You were in a coma. This "out of body experience" you mention: there are researchers in neuroscience at the University of Lausanne who have succeeded in triggering it in people who are in good health, by stimulating different regions of the brain before an operation. Similarly, the famous *tunnel* would seem, in fact, to be due to a lack of irrigation to the brain, which causes hyperactivity on the level of the visual cortex. A hyperactivity that is said to produce this intense frontal light and, consequently, a loss of peripheral vision, whence the impression of tunnel vision.'

'And the feeling of plenitude, of unconditional love?' asked Servaz, sure the shrink was going to pull another explanation out of his hat.

Where has your rationality gone, dammit? he wondered. *Good grief, you're agnostic, and you've never believed in little green men or telepathy.*

'A secretion of hormones,' answered Xavier. 'An influx of endorphins. In the 1990s, German researchers who were studying the phenomenon of blackouts realised that after they lost consciousness, a number of patients claimed to have felt extraordinarily good, had witnessed scenes from their past and had even seen themselves above their own bodies.'

'And all the dead people I saw? That crowd?'

'On the one hand, don't forget there will have been side effects from the drugs you were given, not only during anaesthesia, but also in recovery. And then, think about your dreams. When you dream, you can experience incredible things: you can fly, or fall off a cliff without dying, you can be transported from one place to another, you can see people who have died or people who, in real life, don't know one another.'

'It wasn't a dream.'

The shrink ignored his interruption.

'Have you never had the impression, in any of your dreams, that you were brighter, more intelligent?' He gave a little wave of his hand. 'Have you never had the feeling, sometimes, that you knew more in your dreams, and understood things that you would not normally have understood; that you were stronger, cleverer, more talented, more powerful? And when you wake up, and the memory of your dream is still very vivid, you are astonished by the force of it, and how it seemed so . . . so real.'

69

Of course, thought Servaz. Hasn't everyone? When he was a student and he wanted to try his hand at writing, he would dream that he was composing the most beautiful pages ever written with disconcerting ease, and when he woke up, he had the disturbing impression that those words, those magnificent phrases had truly existed in his mind, for the space of a few seconds, and he was furious that he could no longer find them.

'So,' he asked, 'how do you explain that all the people who have experienced something like this, even the most rational types, the most hardened atheists, come out of it changed for good?'

The psychologist crossed his slender hands above his knees.

'Were they really such atheists? As far as I know, there have not been any truly serious scientific studies regarding the philosophical and religious presuppositions of those people *before* their near-death experience. But I will admit that the change observed in nearly all of them is irrefutable. With the exception of the usual quota of compulsive liars and eccentrics – the same lot who call police switchboards to falsely confess to crimes, I suppose; or who, perhaps, see it as an opportunity to give a few *paid* lectures, forgive my poor wit, we do have very some serious testimonies from eminent personalities whose sincerity cannot be doubted, regarding these . . . "radical changes of personality and values systems" following a coma or a near-death experience . . .'

I'm the one who should be talking like this, thought Servaz. *I'm the one who would have talked like this, before. What's happening to me?*

'This is why we have to listen to these testimonies,' continued the psychologist, his tone appeasing, almost purring, and he put Servaz in mind of a Cheshire cat curled up in an armchair. 'They mustn't be dismissed with a simple shrug of the shoulders. I can guess what you must be going through, Martin. It doesn't matter whether there are explanations; what does matter, is what it changed inside you.'

A pale autumnal beam came in through the window and caressed a bouquet in a Chinese vase. Servaz looked at it, fascinated. He suddenly felt like weeping at the sight of so much beauty.

'You *came back* and everything has changed. It's a difficult time. Have you talked about it with your family and friends?'

'Not yet.'

'Is there someone you can talk about it with?'

'My daughter.'

70

'Try. If need be, send her to me.'

'I'm not the first or the last person to have been through this. There is nothing exceptional about it.'

'But it concerns *you*. And that means a lot to you, since you've come here.'

Servaz did not react.

'You went through a great upheaval. A traumatic experience, which will produce profound changes in your personality. You feel as if you have acquired knowledge you did not go looking for, knowledge that will not be without consequences. But I can help you confront it. I know what you will have to go through: I've already had patients like you. You will feel more alive, more lucid, more attentive to others; you will resume your old routines, but they will seem devoid of meaning. Everything material will lose its importance. No doubt you will feel the need to tell people that you love them, but they won't understand what is happening to you or what you're doing. That's often how it is . . . You'll have periods of euphoria and a desire to live, but you'll also be very fragile and subject to depression.'

The little man tightened the knot of his Ermenegildo Zegna tie, slipped on his jacket, and got to his feet as he was buttoning it. There was nothing fragile, euphoric or depressive about him.

'Whatever the case may be, here you are among us, in fine form. I suppose the doctors have prescribed rest . . .'

'I'd like to go back to work.'

'What, now? Right away? I thought your . . . priorities had changed.'

'I believe everyone has a mission here on earth, and mine is to *catch evildoers*,' said Servaz with a smile.

He saw the shrink frown.

'A *mission*? Are you serious?'

Servaz flashed him his smile number 3, the one that meant, 'Got you there'.

'That's what people expect me to say, isn't it? If I were convinced I'd come back from the dead . . . Don't worry, Doctor, I still don't believe in UFOs.'

The shrink gave a faint smile, but his gaze suddenly sharpened, as if he'd remembered something important.

'Do you know the Tassili n'Ajjer, in the Algerian Sahara?' he asked.

'On the Séfar plateau,' answered Servaz in the affirmative.

'Yes. The Séfar. I had a chance to visit that extraordinary, unique site over thirty years ago. I was twenty-two at the time. I was able to admire the fifteen thousand rock paintings, that great and wonderful book of the desert that tells of the wars and civilisations that existed at the turn of the Neolithic era to the millennia to come – including that three-metre-high work some people have baptised the *Great Martian Man*, or even the *Great God of Séfar*. To this day I'm still not sure what I saw. And this is a scientist talking.'

Five o'clock in the evening, and darkness had already begun to fall by the time he emerged from Xavier's office into the streets of Saint-Martin. These streets no longer terrified him the way they had for years, in his memory. In those days, all he had to do was think about them for his heart to start racing.

Now for him the place had once again regained its somewhat old-fashioned charm as a spa town and holiday resort, with the ski slopes perched in the nearby mountains, and the memory of past grandeur still visible in the hotels, tree-lined walks and gardens. Xavier's words had not totally convinced him, but they had brought him back down to more earthly realities.

He headed towards his car. The doctors had only recently given him permission to drive again, and only for short distances: he put the four-hour journey in this category. Once he was on the road, which left the narrow valley of Saint-Martin for a much wider one 20 kilometres further along and then wound through mountains that gradually diminished in height until they reached the plain between Montréjeau and Toulouse, he was filled with a childlike wonder. These hills vanishing into the blue night, their kindly presence, the tiny delicate lights of these 'end of the world' villages which the road skirted around without going through, the horses he glimpsed in the misty gloom, not yet brought in for the night, even the simple rest area shining with the bright windows of a fast-food place . . .

An hour and a half later he headed into Toulouse via the port of l'Embouchure, along the Brienne canal and its pink brick facades, then he parked his Volvo in the Victor-Hugo car park above the market of the same name. As he typed the code to enter his building, it suddenly seemed to him that the real world resembled a dream. And that the world he had left behind in that hospital room was reality.

Reanimation = reality? he wondered.

He was perfectly aware that what he had seen in his coma could

72

be attributed to the chemical substances he had absorbed, and the dysfunctioning of his freewheeling brain. So why did he feel such loss? Why this nostalgia for the state of bliss he had found himself in? He had read a few works on the subject since he'd regained consciousness. As Xavier had emphasised, there was no questioning the sincerity of these testimonies. And yet Servaz was not prepared to accept that what he had seen was anything other than a phantasmagoria. He was far too rational for that. And besides, dammit – a river of happy people? It was absurd.

He went up the stairs and into his flat. Margot was wearing a brown woollen cardigan over light trousers. Her gaze had the superior sweetness of the healthy for the ill, and he felt like pointing out to her that he was perfectly healthy too, but he refrained.

The table was set; he noticed candles. There was a smell of spices from the kitchen. Servaz immediately recognised the music on the stereo. Mahler . . . her thoughtfulness moved him to tears. He tried to hide them but Margot didn't miss a thing.

'What's wrong, Dad?'

'Nothing. It smells good.'

'Tandoori chicken. I warn you, I'm not a gourmet chef.'

Once again, he had to hold back his emotion: his urge to tell her how much she had always meant to him, that he was sorry for all the times when, in one way or another, he had screwed up their relationship. *Easy does it*, he thought.

'Margot, I would like to apologise for—'

'Hush. You don't need to, Dad. I know.'

'No, you don't know.'

'I don't know what?'

'What I saw there.'

'What do you mean? Where?'

'There . . . when I was in a coma . . .'

'What are you talking about, Dad?'

'I saw things there . . . while I was in a coma.'

'I don't need to know,' she said.

'Don't you want to hear?'

'No.'

'Why not? Aren't you interested?'

'No . . . yes . . . it's not that, but I don't want to know, Dad. It makes me uneasy, all that sort of stuff.'

Suddenly he wished he could be alone. His daughter had told him she had taken unpaid leave and that she would stay as long as he needed. What did this mean? How long? Two weeks? A month? More? The first time he went into his study after he got back from hospital, he had been annoyed to see that she had tidied up without asking his permission. She'd done the same in the kitchen, the living room, the bathroom – and he'd felt equally annoyed. But not for long. That was the way it had been since he got out of hospital: there were times he felt like hugging people, taking them in his arms, talking to them endlessly – and a second later, he had only one desire: to seek refuge in silence and solitude, isolate himself. Once again, he felt a twinge in his heart when he thought of that landscape full of light, and all those people – and their unconditional love.

He looked at the tablets in his palm. Fat capsules and tiny pills. Since he'd been taking them he'd had nausea, diarrhoea and cold sweats. Or were these the after-effects of the coma? He knew he should mention it to the doctors, but he was fed up with the lot of them, and with hospitals. For two months he'd been seeing cardiologists, dieticians, psychologists, physiotherapists, and nurses, twice a week. He had successfully completed a physical rehabilitation programme, attended respiratory physiotherapy sessions, and his second stress test had shown a marked improvement.

He opened his hand and the pills rolled into the sink. He ran the cold water over them and watched them disappear down the plughole. He didn't need them. He had survived a coma, had nearly gone to the other side. He wanted to be in full possession of his faculties to start work again. His chest felt perfectly fine now, and if it weren't for the ugly scar he saw when he got undressed he might almost believe it had happened to someone else.

He wasn't sleepy. In a few hours he would be back at police headquarters and he knew his return would arouse considerable curiosity. Were they going to let him resume his position as team leader? Who had filled it in his absence? He hadn't even thought about that until now. He wondered if it was really what he wanted: to go back to his former life.

8

Night-time Visit

It was pitch black. The house looked empty and abandoned, no light behind the closed shutters. Up there on top of the railway embankment trains still passed just as slowly over the points, screeching and swaying, and with every train Servaz felt his hair stand on end.

Sitting behind the wheel, he looked at the empty lot, the warehouses covered with graffiti and the tall building on its own, everything just as it had been the last time he was here.

Nothing had changed. And yet everything had changed. As in the famous words of Heraclitus, he was no longer the man who had come here two months earlier. He wondered if his colleagues would notice these changes tomorrow.

He opened the car door and got out.

The sky was clear, and the moon lit up the lot. The puddles had dried and disappeared. Everything was silent, apart from the faraway rumble of the city and the passage of trains. He looked around. He was alone. The tall tree still cast its unsettling shadow over the facade of the house. He felt a rush of nerves as he walked up to the small garden at the front and pushed the little gate, which opened with a squeal. Where was the pit bull? The kennel was still there, but the chain slithered across the ground, inert, like a snake's shed skin. The dog had probably been put to sleep.

He went up the steps of the porch and rang the bell. He heard the shrill sound echoing through the empty rooms, but nothing moved. No answer. He put his hand on the doorknob and turned it. Locked. Where had Jensen gone? Stehlin had said something about a thermal cure at a spa. Who were they kidding? This man had committed rape and murder and now he was being pampered by gentle hands, jets of water and bubbling hot baths at a spa? Servaz looked around him.

No one in sight. From his pocket he took a dozen or so keys, wrapped in a dirty rag. So-called bump keys used by burglars to pick pin locks. A 'Mexican': that's what they called an illegal search. He'd already practised this kind of sport at the house of Léonard Fontaine, the astronaut, during another investigation. *I'm not even back at work and I'm already performing an illegal act.*

The rusty lock gave him a hard time. Inside was the same odour of cat piss, stale tobacco and old age, and he squeezed his nostrils. The bulb in the corridor had not been replaced and he had to look for another switch to get the vaguest light in this dark cave. Nothing had changed in the old woman's room; even the drip pouch and the mountain of pillows on the unmade bed were still in place. Although it was practically a skeleton, her emaciated body had left an imprint on the mattress.

He shuddered.

He walked into the living room. What was he looking for? What sort of proof did he think he might find? He began by searching the desk drawers. Nothing but papers, and some hash in aluminium foil. He looked at the computer screens set up on the big desk. Perhaps the answer was in there, but he wasn't a specialist, let alone a geek like Vincent. And he couldn't exactly call the Computer and Technological Tracking Services to retrieve the data from the hard drive. On the off chance, he switched on one of the computers. Which immediately asked him for a password. *Bloody hell . . .*

The sound of an engine outside.

A car was headed this way; he heard it stop, doors slamming. *They've parked on the lot.* The shutters were closed; there was no way he could see what was going on outside. Men's voices. He thought he recognised one of them. A cop from the crime unit. Someone had decided to reopen the investigation.

He switched off all the lights and rushed towards the back door in complete darkness. It was locked. *Shit!* He didn't have time to pick it. He could hear footsteps coming up the path. Servaz hurried down a corridor and into a room, switched on the light, opened the window and shutters. He was about to climb out, then changed his mind. They were bound to have written down his registration number.

He closed the window and went back into the living room. The bell rang. He tried to quiet his pounding heart and prepare to come out with as casual a 'Hello, lads!' as possible. The footsteps went back down the path and receded. Apparently they had no search warrant. He listened to the sound of the car pulling away, waiting a short while in complete darkness, his heart pounding, then went back out.

KIRSTEN AND MARTIN

9

It Was Still Dark Out

On Monday morning, he came out of the Canal-du-Midi Métro station, and it was still dark out. He walked across the esplanade and past the guards in bulletproof jackets who, since the events of 13 November 2015 in Paris, had been monitoring access to the building. He went through the glass doors and headed towards the lifts on his left. There was not yet the usual queue of victims and complainants at reception.

Toulouse was a city that secreted delinquents the way a gland releases hormones. If the university was its brain, the Hôtel de Ville its heart, and the avenues its arteries, the police force was the liver, the lungs, the kidneys . . . Like those organs it maintained the equilibrium of the organism by filtering impure elements, eliminating toxic substances, and temporarily stocking certain impurities. The unsalvageable waste ended up in jail or back out on the street – in other words, in the city's intestines. Naturally, like every organ, they occasionally failed to function properly.

Not convinced by his analogy, Servaz came out on the second floor and headed towards the director's corridor. Stehlin had called him the night before, asking him if he felt okay. On a Sunday. Servaz had been surprised. He felt ready to go back into the field, even if he knew that to do so he would have to hide the changes that had taken place in him, and that he mustn't speak to anyone about what he had seen when he was in a coma. Or about his strange mood swings, which flung him from euphoria to sadness and vice versa. And still less about what the cardiologist had said: 'It's out of the question. Park yourself behind a desk if you feel like it, but I forbid you, do you hear? I forbid you to do anything that will make demands on your heart.'

However, Stehlin's impatience to see him come back did surprise him somewhat.

The smell of coffee wafted down the deserted corridors; the rare civil servants who were already at their posts – or had not yet gone to bed – worked silently, as if, by tacit agreement, all outbursts, excesses or outrageous remarks were forbidden at such an early hour.

Servaz turned right, past the bulletproof door that stayed open summer and winter alike, past the leather sofas in the waiting room, and knocked at the director's double door.

'Come in.'

He went through and saw two people looking at him. The first was Divisional Commissioner Stehlin; the second was a blonde woman he had never seen before. Sitting in one of the chairs opposite Stehlin's wide desk, she had turned to look at him over her shoulder. A cold, analytical, professional look. He got the unpleasant sensation that he was being dissected. *A cop*, he concluded. She didn't smile, or make any effort to appear friendly.

Stehlin got up and so did she, pulling on her skirt. She was wearing a dark blue suit, the skirt somewhat tight around the hips, a light grey scarf over a white shirt with mother of pearl buttons, and shiny black heels. A black coat with big buttons had been tossed over the back of the adjacent chair.

'How are you feeling?' asked Stehlin. He had walked around his desk to approach Servaz, passing in front of the big filing cabinet, and he could not help but glance at Servaz's chest. 'Do you feel up to this? What did the doctors say?'

'I'm all right. What's going on?'

'This is rushing things a bit, I know. We won't be sending you back in the field right away, Martin, you must realise that. We'll give you time to get back in the swing of things. But we absolutely had to have you here this morning.'

He looked steadily at Servaz then turned to the woman in a somewhat theatrical way. He had been speaking quietly.

'Martin, I'd like to introduce Kirsten Nigaard, from the Norwegian police. Kripos, the unit in charge of combatting major crime. Kirsten Nigaard, this is Commandant Martin Servaz, from the Toulouse crime brigade.'

He had ended his introduction in English. *So was she the delicate matter?* he wondered. A little Norwegian cop in Toulouse. What was she doing here, so far from home? He noticed that she had a big beauty spot on her chin.

'Hello,' she said, with a slight accent.

He returned her greeting and shook the hand she held out. She took the opportunity to look him right in the eye, with that chilly gaze of hers, and again he felt assessed, judged, evaluated. Given what had happened to him, and the changes in him, he wondered what this woman saw.

'Sit down, Martin. I'll speak English if you don't mind,' Stehlin warned him, going back behind his desk.

The director seemed incredibly preoccupied. But perhaps it was just a manner he was adopting in the presence of this representative of the Norwegian police (what was her rank, anyway? Stehlin hadn't said) so that she wouldn't think the French police took things lightly.

'To start with, we got a request for information from Kirsten's department, through Scopol, and we responded.' Scopol was the police service for international technical cooperation, based in Nanterre: they provided a link between Europol, the European police forces, and the French agencies. 'Then we got a request for mutual judicial assistance from the Norwegian Ministry of Justice. Kirsten's boss at the Kripos called me at the same time, and we agreed on how to proceed.'

Servaz nodded: this was the usual procedure for international investigations.

'I don't know where to begin,' continued Stehlin, looking back and forth from the blonde woman to Servaz. 'It's fairly . . . *incredible*, what is going on. Officer Nigaard belongs to the Oslo police, but she was asked to intervene in Bergen.' Servaz thought Stehlin's accent in English was even more ridiculous than his own. 'Bergen is on the west coast of Norway,' his boss deemed it necessary to point out. 'It's the second largest city in the country.' He glanced at the Norwegian policewoman for approval, but she neither confirmed nor denied it. 'There was a murder there. The victim, a young woman, was a worker on an oil platform in the North Sea.'

Stehlin coughed. He glanced over at Martin, who was immediately on the alert. It suddenly occurred to him: this was why Stehlin had asked him to come – not because it was a delicate matter *but because it concerned him, Martin, personally.*

'Officer Nigaard went to Bergen because in the victim's pocket there was a, um, scrap of paper with her name on it,' continued Stehlin, glancing at Kirsten. 'One of the workers who was on land at the time never came back. In his cabin, Officer Nigaard found photographs taken with a telephoto lens,' he said, this time training his gaze on Servaz.

To him it seemed as if some demiurge hidden in a fly loft was manipulating all three of them like puppets, pulling on invisible wires – a shadow, and even before its name was uttered, Servaz knew what it was and that it was going to grow and envelop them in its darkness.

'This is you, Martin, in these photographs,' said Stehlin, shoving the pictures across the desk to him. 'They were taken over a fairly long time period, judging by the change of seasons in the trees and the light.' Stehlin paused. 'And there is also a photograph of a little four- or five-year-old boy. On the back of the photograph it says "Gustav". We suppose it must be his first name.'

GUSTAV.

The name exploded in his ears like a grenade. Could it be?

'We found these photographs among his things,' said Kirsten in English. Her voice was melodious, veiled, and hoarse all at the same time. 'And through them we were able to trace you. First we identified the words "hôtel de police" in French. Then your Ministry of the Interior told us which . . . *politistasjonen* . . . um, commissariat it was. And it was your . . . boss, here, who, um, identified you.'

Which was why they had called him on a Sunday, concluded Servaz, his heart racing.

He held his breath, his eyes glued to the photographs. The brain is a remarkable computer; he had never seen himself from this angle, even in the mirror, but it took him only a fraction of a second to recognise himself in the prints.

Taken from a distance with a telephoto lens. In the morning, at midday, in the evening . . . leaving his building, or the commissariat . . . getting in his car . . . going into a bookshop . . . strolling down the pavement . . . having lunch outside on the place du Capitole . . . and even in the Métro and a car park in the centre of town, shot from a distance, from between two cars . . .

For how long? When had it started?

The questions went rushing through his mind.

Someone had been following him like a shadow – in his footsteps, observing him, spying on him. Every hour of the day and night.

It was as if icy fingers were stroking his neck. Stehlin's office was huge, but it suddenly seemed small and stifling. Why didn't they switch on the overhead lights? It was so dark.

He looked over at the windows, where the sky was beginning to turn grey. Instinctively he put his hand to the left-hand side of his chest, and Stehlin noticed.

'Martin, are you all right?'

'Yes. Go on.'

He was having trouble breathing. The shadow following him had a name. A name he had been trying for five years to forget.

'DNA tests were carried out in the man's cabin and in the common areas of the rig,' continued Stehlin uneasily. Servaz could guess what was coming. 'It would seem that the cabin was cleaned regularly by its occupant. Not regularly enough, however. One trace of DNA did give us a result.'

Again the director cleared his throat and looked Servaz straight in the eye.

'Well, in short, Martin, it would seem that the Norwegian police have picked up the trail of . . . Julian Hirtmann.'

10

Group

Was this yet another hallucination? Was he back in recovery, hostage to the spider machine, seeing and hearing things that did not exist?

The last time he had heard from the Swiss killer was when Hirtmann had sent him a human heart, and he had thought it was Marianne's. *Five years*. And since then, nothing. Not a sign. Not the slightest embryo of a lead. The former Geneva high court prosecutor, the alleged torturer of more than forty women in at least five countries, had disappeared from their radar screens, and as far as he knew, from the radar screens of every police force.

Vanished. Into thin air.

And suddenly a Norwegian policewoman shows up and swears they've picked up his trail by chance? Is that even possible?

With growing unease he listened to Stehlin's description of the butchery at the Mariakirken. In fact, it sounded just like the Hirtmann he knew. Or the profile of the victim did, in any case. As for the way she had died and subsequently been displayed – well, with the exception of some traces left on a farm in Poland, the bodies of the Swiss killer's victims had never been found. So why so many clues now? If Servaz had understood correctly, the dead woman had worked on the same platform as Hirtmann. Maybe she had found out something about him? And he had wanted to shut her up, then figured it was time to make himself scarce. Maybe he'd been after her for a long time, seeing her every day like that, and then when the time had come for him to disappear he had seized the opportunity to act. No. Something was not right. And this business about the scrap of paper in the victim's pocket? What did that mean?

'This is not like him,' said Servaz finally.

The Norwegian policewoman gave him a sharp look.

'What do you mean?'

'I mean it's not like Hirtmann to leave so many clues behind.'

She nodded approvingly.

'I agree. Um . . . I don't know him as well as you do, of course,' she said, with a wave of her hand which was no doubt meant to clarify their relative positions, 'but I did do my homework and I studied his file. However . . .'

He waited for her to continue.

'. . . given the scene of the crime and the footprints in the snow, as well as the probable use of an iron bar, I wondered if it wasn't a trap.'

'What do you mean?'

'Let's suppose Hirtmann found out she had unmasked him, or that she wanted to blackmail him and, one way or another, they arranged to meet in the church.'

There was a moment's pause.

'He kills her and then he vanishes,' she concluded, her eyes still riveted to his.

'Something's not right,' he said. 'If he had decided to vanish, he didn't need to kill her.'

'Perhaps he wanted to punish her. Or did it for his own pleasure. Or both.'

'In that case, why would he leave all those photographs behind? And besides, what's this business with the piece of paper in the victim's pocket? It had your name on it, didn't it?'

She nodded and went on looking at him, not speaking. She put a hand on his wrist. The intimacy of the gesture surprised him. She had long fingernails, painted in a shimmery pinkish-coral. He quivered.

'I don't know what it means,' she said. 'And why me, I haven't the slightest idea. But I heard that you and Hirtmann go back a number of years.' She stared at him. 'Maybe that's just it – he wanted us to find those photographs. Maybe he wanted to send you . . .'

She groped for the words.

'. . . a friendly greeting.'

'Who is this boy?' Servaz asked, pointing to the photograph of Gustav. 'Do we have any idea?'

'Not remotely,' she answered. 'Could it be his son?'

He stared at her.

'His son?'

'Why not?'

'Hirtmann doesn't have any children.'

'Maybe he's had one since he disappeared. If this is a recent photograph, the boy is four or five years old. Julian Hirtmann hasn't been seen for six years, am I right?'

He nodded. And suddenly, his throat went dry. *Six years.* That would correspond to the time when Marianne was kidnapped . . .

'Perhaps he has had a child since then,' she continued. 'He began working on the platform two years ago. We don't know what he did before that. And platform workers have a lot of time off.'

He turned his red, tired eyes to her and Kirsten looked back at him, as if she realised what was happening to him. She left her fingers on his wrist and said, 'Tell me what is on your mind. We won't be able to work together if we hide things. Tell me everything that is going through your head.'

He stared at her for half a second. Hesitated. Then gave a nod.

'I met Hirtmann for the first time at a psychiatric hospital in the heart of the Pyrenees,' he said, in English.

'Pi-re-nee?'

She saw him wave towards the windows.

'Mountains . . . Nearby . . .'

She nodded in turn.

'A place for the criminally insane. Hirtmann was incarcerated in a special wing, with the most dangerous individuals. They had found his DNA at a crime scene a few kilometres from there. That's why I went to see him.'

Kirsten raised her eyebrow.

'Was he allowed out?'

'No. No way. The security measures were very tight.'

'So, how did you meet him?'

'It's a long story,' he replied, thinking back to the strange, apocalyptic investigation when he'd nearly lost his life; there had been a decapitated horse, and a power plant perched at an altitude of 2,000 metres, buried 70 metres in the side of the mountain.

He felt as if her fingers were burning his wrist. He moved slightly, and she withdrew them.

'When I went into his cell, he was listening to music. His favourite composer. And mine, as well. Mahler. *Gustav* Mahler.'

'Oh,' she said. 'There was music in his cabin. CDs.'

She took out her mobile and searched through the gallery of photographs, then with her index finger she opened one of the pictures and held out the screen.

'Gustav Mahler,' she confirmed.

Servaz pointed to the photograph of Gustav.

'Were you able to identify the village and the lake in this picture?'

She nodded.

'It was easy: Hallstatt, one of the most beautiful villages in Austria. A magnificent place. A UNESCO World Heritage site. The Austrian federal police, and the local police from Styria are conducting their own investigations. But we don't know if the boy lives there, or was just visiting. It's very popular with tourists.'

Servaz tried to imagine Hirtmann acting the tourist, holding a five-year-old by the hand. Stehlin checked his watch.

'Time for the meeting,' he said.

Servaz gave him an enquiring look.

'I've taken the liberty of calling your team in, Martin. Do you feel up to it?'

Servaz again nodded his head emphatically, but it wasn't true. He felt as if Kirsten's gaze was piercing right through him.

It was ten a.m. Present at the meeting were Vincent Espérandieu, Samira Cheung, and four other members of investigation team number 1, as well as Malleval, who was head of the Criminal Affairs Department; Stehlin himself; Escande, one of the five cops from the Financial Crime unit in charge of cybercrime; and Roxane Varin, who had come down from the Public Security floor to represent Child Protection.

When their attention was elsewhere, Kirsten took a good look at them all, Servaz included: sitting on her left, he seemed distracted. He had given her a brief description of his long-distance relationship with Hirtmann. How the Swiss killer had escaped from the psychiatric hospital in the Pyrenees. How he had abducted a woman Servaz knew (and, from the way he hesitated, she thought she could tell that this 'acquaintance' was not one of mere friendship). How both had disappeared leaving no other sign of life than an insulated box sent five years earlier from Poland, containing a *heart* – and how at first Servaz had believed the heart belonged to his friend Marianne, until the DNA tests proved otherwise.

It was an incredible story, but as he told it to her, the French cop had seemed strangely detached, as if all these horrible things had not happened to him and didn't concern him. There was something about his attitude that she couldn't understand.

'I would like to introduce Kirsten Nigaard, from the Oslo police,' he began. 'In Norway,' he added, just in case.

She examined each face while he summed up what he himself had just learned. She got the impression they were all staring at Servaz very attentively. It was not just his words; he himself was of interest.

Then, when he announced that they had picked up the trail of Julian Hirtmann in Norway, the attitude of the people gathered there changed noticeably. They stopped staring at him and exchanged looks with each other. The relaxed atmosphere of the opening minutes disappeared, and she noticed a morbid mood, a heavier atmosphere taking over.

'Kirsten,' he said finally, turning to her.

She was silent for a second, and you could hear the sound of the rain outside, like a heartbeat. She turned to the participants and raised her voice:

'We have contacted Eurojust,' she said. 'An international investigation is being organised, in five countries to start with: Norway, France, Poland, Switzerland and Austria.'

Eurojust was a judicial cooperation unit on a European scale, in charge of combatting cross-border crime. Magistrates from all over Europe coordinated international investigations and activated the judicial systems and police forces of their respective countries. She paused. She knew what they must be thinking: wasn't Norway one of those Scandinavian countries where the prisons looked like Nordic versions of Club Med, and where the policemen were not allowed to ask awkward questions? The cops in the room were no doubt unaware of the fact that for decades Norway had come under criticism for improperly resorting to detention cells in its police stations, and solitary confinement in its prisons. And that the Norwegian extremist Kristian Vikernes, arrested and then released in France, had praised the exemplary behaviour of the French police officers in comparison to 'that gang of hooligans otherwise known as the Norwegian police'.

Personally, Kirsten would have liked to ram that shit-faced little Nazi's metalhead guitar into one of his orifices. And in any case, she'd heard all sorts of stories about what went on in French police stations.

She pressed the button on the remote control and a TV screen at the back of the room lit up. Everyone turned to look. After a few seconds of snow, the first images appeared. Metallic cross struts, a footbridge with a steel grating floor, a raging ocean beyond: images from the platform's video surveillance cameras.

At the end of the footbridge a figure appeared and walked up to the camera. Kirsten paused the video. Servaz stared at the ghost from the past frozen on-screen. It was him, indisputably. His hair was a bit longer and danced around his face in the wind. But otherwise, he was exactly as Servaz remembered him.

'Hirtmann worked on this platform for two years. The address he gave his employer was fake, as were his CV and ID papers. The documents found in his cabin do not provide much information – with one exception, which I will get to. After requisitioning the bank where he had an account for depositing his salary, we were able to piece together some of his movements, at least; but only partially, because Hirtmann transferred quite a bit of money into other accounts in tax havens. The Norwegian police suspect him not only of this woman's murder but also of being behind the disappearance of several other women in the Oslo region. That is one of the reasons for my presence here.'

She refrained from mentioning the other reasons at this stage, looking all around the room.

'In all likelihood Hirtmann left Norwegian territory quite a while ago. He escaped from the, uh . . .' she checked her notes '. . . Wargnier Institute in December 2008. He passed through your region in June 2010. Then through Poland in 2011. In Poland, the remains of several of his victims were found in an isolated house near the Bialowieza forest. Young women only. That was five years ago now. Five years amounting to a black hole, other than these last two years when he worked on this oil rig in the North Sea. Let's be under no illusions: a man like Julian Hirtmann is capable of disappearing for a long time, and we may not find his trail again for months, or even years.' She glanced over at Servaz, but he still seemed lost in thought, staring at the screen where the apparition was frozen in the position Kirsten had left him. 'In addition, a man like this cannot spend five years without killing. It's unthinkable. The purpose of this investigation is to track his criminal career, taking full advantage of the fact that at last we have recent data concerning him to try and retrace his steps. We will proceed on the assumption that he has been on European soil all this time, but even then – given his profession, which enabled him to accumulate air miles and therefore to travel cheaply anywhere in the world – there is no guarantee of that, either. We will issue a description of him. We know the way he works from his writing, and we know the profile of his previous victims. Nearly all of them were young women who lived in regions bordering on Switzerland: the Dolomites, Bavaria, the Austrian Alps. Then a few in Poland. Previous attempts to locate him have yielded nothing. I don't need to tell you that our chances of success are extremely slim . . .'

She broke off and looked at Servaz, who translated as best he could for those who didn't speak English. Then she handed the photograph of Gustav to her neighbour on the right.

'Pass it around,' Servaz said.

'The second element of the investigation concerns this child. This photograph was found among Hirtmann's belongings. We do not know who this boy is. Or where he is. Or even if he is still alive. We know nothing about him.'

'Hirtmann never went after children,' said the ugly young woman, the one called Samira; her English was impeccable. 'He's not a paedophile. His victims have always been adult women – young and attractive, as you pointed out.'

Kirsten noticed that she was wearing a little death's-head necklace beneath her leather jacket and that she had propped her feet, clad in a pair of imitation python boots, on the edge of the table, while her chair rocked on its two rear legs.

'Exactly. We think this child might be his son. Or the son of one of his victims.'

'What else do we know about him?' asked a tall bald man as he scribbled something on his notepad – a portrait of the Norwegian policewoman, by the looks of it.

'Nothing at all, beyond his first name. We don't even know his nationality. We just know where this photograph was taken. In Hallstatt, in Austria. The Austrian federal police are involved. But as it's very popular with tourists, it could be the boy was only passing through.'

'Hirtmann playing the tourist?' said Samira, her tone sceptical.

'In the middle of a crowd of other people,' added Vincent. 'Not such a bad idea . . . where better to hide a tree than in the middle of the forest?'

'Yeah, but what is our role in all this?' asked the tall bald man. 'Aren't we beginning to waste our time, here? I don't know about you lot, but I have other things to do.'

The man had spoken in French and Kirsten didn't understand, but she could tell from his tone and the others' awkward silence that he had made a rude comment.

'Naturally at the oil platform we questioned his roommate and colleagues at length,' she said. 'It would seem he was fairly solitary and extremely discreet about his activities on land. On board, he spent his free time reading and listening to music. Classical.'

She looked over at Servaz.

'But the most important thing is the photographs of your commandant. They show that Hirtmann stayed in your town for a long time, and that, inexplicably, something always brings him back here and, um, to you, Martin,' she said, keeping her eyes on him. 'The requisition at the bank regarding his finances has confirmed our hunch: over the last two years Hirtmann came here quite often.

'It could well be that he will try to come back here again,' she said, addressing everyone in the room now. 'Since he already has on numerous occasions. I'll say it again: we know the way he operates. And the profile of his victims. We'll search the region and beyond for any similar crimes: disappearances of young women over these past few months.'

'We already have,' said Samira, 'and we came up with nothing.'

She saw several heads nodding in agreement.

'That was a few years ago,' said Servaz. 'Since then, we've been working on other things.'

Kirsten saw Vincent exchange a look with Samira. She knew what they were thinking: *too simple, too easy.*

'I know you've been doing remarkable work,' she said diplomatically, 'even if it hasn't yielded any results. I intend to stay here for a while. I have permission from Commissioner Stehlin to collaborate with Commandant Servaz. I know you have other things to do and that this is not a priority for you, but just bear this in mind: if Hirtmann is here, it might be worth keeping your eyes open and digging a little deeper, don't you think?'

If Hirtmann is here. Clever, thought Servaz. Very clever. He saw her words spreading over their consciousness like a layer of ice. She was bluffing but it had worked: he could see it in their eyes. The Swiss ghost was going to infect their thoughts the way he had already infected Servaz's, and he would not leave them alone.

That was what Kirsten wanted.

I I

Evening

On the Karlsplatz in Vienna, the neo-classical facade of the Musikverein – full name *Haus des Wiener Musikvereins*, House of the Friends of Music in Vienna – stood out against the Austrian night, where a few snowflakes were drifting. With its Doric columns, high arched windows and triangular pediment, all bathed in light, it evoked a temple, which indeed, it was: a temple of music, with some of the best acoustics in the world, a unique sound experience for music lovers. At least officially, because among themselves the Viennese specialists sometimes complained that the programming was insipid, with nothing but Mozart and Beethoven concerts *ad nauseam* – a lot of schmaltz for tourists with lazy ears.

This evening, however, beneath the gilt of the Musikverein, the Vienna Philharmonic Orchestra was performing Gustav Mahler's *Kindertotenlieder*, 'Songs on the Death of Children', conducted by Bernhard Zehetmayer. At the age of eighty-three, 'the Emperor', as he was known, had lost none of his spirit. Or his demanding passion for the right note, which sometimes caused him to ruthlessly lecture any musicians who struck him as amateurish during rehearsal. Legend had it that he once left his podium and wove his way through the members of the orchestra to a mediocre second violin who was talking to his neighbour, and slapped him so hard that the violinist fell off his chair.

'Did you hear how that slap was in tune?' he was said to have declared before returning to his podium.

It was a myth, of course. But there were plenty of others surrounding the most 'Mahlerian' conductor in Vienna since Bernstein. Given the very personal nature of these lieder, the concert was not held in the prestigious Golden Hall but in the smaller Brahms Hall. It was the Emperor who had decided this, despite the administrator's protests, because the Golden Hall could seat 1700 people, whereas the Brahms Hall held only 600. Zehetmayer was merely following the master himself, at the time the work was first performed in January 1905. Similarly, although nowadays most of the lieder were performed by female soloists, he had called, like Mahler before him, for a tenor and two baritones.

The ceiling of the Brahms Hall resounded with the last bars of the coda, elegiac and full of serenity after the uncontrolled furore of the opening bars; the horn's hazy voice joined the dying tremolo of the cellos in a final sigh. For a few seconds, silence reigned, then the hall exploded. The audience leapt to their feet to acclaim the Emperor and his orchestra. Zehetmayer lapped up the praise quite openly, because all his life the old man had been vain. He gave a deep bow, as deep as his bad back, the pain in his lumbar region, and his pride would allow, then he caught a glimpse of a face in the audience, made a discreet sign, and returned to his dressing room.

Two minutes later there was a knock on the door.

'Come in!'

The man who entered was roughly the same age – eighty-two – with bushy eyebrows, but while Zehetmayer was nearly bald, this man had a fine white mane, and he was small and stocky where the musician was tall and thin. It would never have occurred to him to label the conductor of the Vienna Philharmonic Orchestra 'the Emperor'. If there was one *imperator* in this room, it was him, Josef Wieser: he had built one of the most powerful industrial empires in Austria – of petrochemicals, cellulose and paper – thanks firstly to the generous Austrian forests, and then to an excellent marriage, which had brought him capital as well as the necessary introductions into the little Viennese circle of wheeler-dealers and decision-makers (he had remarried twice, since, and was now contemplating a fourth marriage to a financial journalist forty years his junior).

'What's going on?' said the visitor.

'There has been a development,' said the conductor, slipping a clean, starched white shirt over a vest.

'A development?'

Zehetmayer gave him a look that was sparkling and feverish, a look worthy of German expressionist cinema.

'We've picked up his trail.'

96

The billionaire stood there with his mouth open.

'*What?*' His voice trembled with emotion. 'Where?'

'In Norway. On an oil rig. One of our sources sent me the information.'

When his friend did not react, Zehetmayer continued: 'Apparently,
the bastard was working there. He killed a woman in a church in
Bergen, then vanished into thin air.'

'He managed to get away?'

'Yes.'

'Shit . . .'

'It will be easier to get at him outside than in prison,' the conductor
pointed out.

'I'm not so sure about that.'

'There is something else . . .'

'What?'

'A child.'

Wieser gave the conductor at a funny look.

'What do you mean, a child?'

'They found a photograph of a five-year-old kid in his belongings.
And guess what his name is?'

The billionaire shook his head.

'Gustav.'

Wieser stared at the musician with round eyes, clearly experiencing
an onslaught of thoughts and contradictory emotions – perplexity,
hope, incomprehension.

'Do you think it could be—'

'His son? It's possible.' The conductor's gaze vanished into the
mirror opposite him, where he contemplated his own stern, sad face,
lost in the mean little eyes beneath his old man's eyebrows that were
every bit as bushy as his friend's. 'This opens up possibilities, don't
you think?'

'What more do we know about the boy?'

'At the moment, not a great deal.' The Emperor hesitated. 'Other
than that he must care about the kid, if he hangs on to his photograph,' he added, handing Wieser the picture of Gustav.

The two men looked at each other. They had 'found' one another
– twist of fate or pure chance – at the end of another performance
of the *Kindertotenlieder*, one that had been a triumph for Bernhard
Zehetmayer. Sitting in the hall, Josef Wieser had been deeply moved

by this interpretation of the lieder, and by the time the music stopped, the billionaire was weeping, something that he had not done for a long time. For these lieder spoke directly to the ravaged heart of a father who had lost his daughter. And the interpretation the orchestra had just given was proof that its conductor had a deep, personal understanding of this premonitory work – since Mahler himself went on to lose his eldest daughter to scarlet fever not long after the lieder were first performed.

At the end of the concert, Wieser had asked to greet the prestigious Viennese conductor, and the organisers had led him to Zehetmayer's dressing room. Still very moved, he congratulated the maestro and asked him what his secret was, to have attained such truth in the interpretation.

'You have to have lost a child, that's all,' Zehetmayer replied.

Wieser was both astonished and upset.

'And did you?' he asked, his voice trembling.

The conductor looked at him coldly.

'A daughter. The sweetest, most beautiful creature. She was studying music in Salzburg.'

'How did she die?' Wieser ventured to ask.

'She was killed by a monster.'

The billionaire felt as if the floor was opening beneath him.

'A monster?'

'Julian Hirtmann. Prosecutor at the high court of Geneva. He has killed more than—'

'I know who Julian Hirtmann is,' interrupted Wieser.

'Ah. You read the papers.'

Wieser turned to face him.

'No. I myself have . . . a daughter who was . . . murdered by that monster. At least, that is what we suppose. We never found her body. But Hirtmann was in the vicinity when she disappeared. The police are almost certain . . .'

He had spoken so quietly he was not sure the other man had heard him. But the Emperor was staring at him, stunned, then he motioned to the other people in the room to leave.

'And what do you feel?' he asked when they were alone.

Wieser lowered his head and looked at the floor.

'Despair, anger, unbearable yearning, a father's heartbroken love . . .'

'And any desire for revenge? Hatred?'

Wieser looked up again and straight into the eyes of the conductor, who was much taller than he. And there he saw a deep, ferocious hatred – and a spark of madness.

'I have hated him since the day I found out what happened to my daughter,' said Zehetmayer. 'That was fifteen years ago. Since then I have awoken every morning with this hatred. Pure, intact, unchanged. I thought it would diminish over time, but the opposite is happening. Has it occurred to you that the police might never find him if we don't help them?'

So they had become friends – a strange friendship, founded not on love but on hatred, two old men communing in grief and a cult of vengeance. Two monomaniacal friends with a shared secret obsession. And just like others who spend all their savings on a passion, living only for and through that passion, they did not care about expense. In the beginning, they merely joined hunting parties together and had desultory conversations in Vienna cafés. They constructed their theories and exchanged information. Mainly in one direction: Zehetmayer had read and seen nearly everything that had been published and broadcast about Hirtmann in German, English or French: books, articles, television programmes, documentaries . . . But madness is contagious, and before long Wieser began immersing himself with ever-increasing interest in the mass of documentation the conductor had passed on to him. They went on talking. For weeks, months. Their plan began to take shape. Initially it only meant using their money and their contacts – Wieser's above all – to try to track down the Swiss killer. They had resorted to private detectives, without much success. Wieser had also contacted a few Austrian policemen he knew. To no avail. They then decided to use the Internet and social networks. They managed to raise over €10 million, which would be a reward for anyone who knew Hirtmann's whereabouts; €1 million would also be paid for any valuable information. A website had been created to enable the candidates for the generous reward to get in touch. They had received hundreds of useless messages, but they had also been contacted by professionals: detectives, hacks, and even cops from a number of countries.

'This is Hallstatt, isn't it?' said Wieser, pointing to the picture.

'Of course it's Hallstatt,' said Zehetmayer curtly, as if the billionaire had said, 'Is this the Eiffel Tower?'

'It's a bit too obvious, don't you think?'

'What do you mean?'

'Well honestly! He might as well have sent us a map of Austria and written on it, "Here I am."'

'The photograph wasn't supposed to end up in our hands, or in the police's.'

'Hirtmann left it in his cabin before he cleared off. Let's suppose it is his son.' Zehetmayer hesitated: he still couldn't accept the idea that the Swiss killer might have a son. 'Why wouldn't he take the photo with him?'

'Maybe he had others.'

The musician gave a sniff of annoyance.

'Or perhaps he wanted someone to find it. To send all the police on the planet down the wrong trail. Because in actual fact the kid is miles away from there.'

The conductor reached for a little pear-shaped vaporiser on the dresser – a bespoke eau de Cologne he'd had made by an esteemed French perfumer.

'What are we going to do?' asked Wieser, pinching his nostrils when the musician squeezed the pear and the sweet-smelling cloud spread through the room.

Zehetmayer studied him disdainfully. How had this imbecile become a billionaire when he seemed incapable of making even the slightest decision?

'We'll find the kid,' he said. 'We'll start by putting his photograph on the website. Then we'll use all our resources.'

12

Evening 2

'Martin,' said Stehlin, 'I've given it some thought. In the end, I think I'll ask someone else to take over.'

Servaz wondered if he'd misheard.

'Huh?'

'If it really is Hirtmann behind all this, you're in no fit state to—'

'I don't understand,' said the Norwegian policewoman suddenly. 'No one knows this man better than Commandant Servaz, and he's the one who's in the photographs. Why?'

'Well, um . . . Commandant Servaz is convalescing.'

'But he's recovered, hasn't he? Since he is back at work.'

'Yes, yes, of course, but—'

'I want to work with Commandant Servaz, if you don't mind,' she declared firmly. 'It seems to me that he is the most competent person to deal with this matter.'

Servaz smiled when he saw Stehlin scowl.

'Fine,' he said reluctantly.

'How many days did your superiors give you?'

'Five. After that, I go home. Unless, of course, we find something.'

Servaz wondered what he was going to do with this Norwegian policewoman. He didn't feel like playing tour guide, or spending his time jabbering in English trying to make himself understood. It was already complicated enough to be back at work and prove to everyone that he was up to it. By burdening him with this foreign officer they were putting him on the sidelines, that was the truth of it. Yet he was the one who was in the photographs. And the thought that Hirtmann himself had taken them made his blood run cold.

'Of course, if by some unlikely chance you do find something significant, I want to be informed at once,' said Stehlin.

By some unlikely chance . . . Servaz contemplated his words.

'And what if, "by some unlikely chance", the photograph of the kid was meant to lead us up the garden path?'

Kirsten and Stehlin stared at him for a moment.

'Do you mean the photograph is meant to send us in the wrong direction?' said Kirsten.

He nodded.

'So he left the photograph of the kid lying around on purpose? Of course, we did think about that,' she added, narrowing her eyes. 'It seems a bit too obvious, don't you think?'

'And what else have you come up with?' he asked.

'What?'

'Regarding the photograph.'

'There might be some other information we can get from it.'

Now they both had their eyes glued to him, Kirsten with a mixture of curiosity and bewilderment, Stehlin looking as if he was waiting for him to finish so they could move on to something else. That had been the predominant sentiment in the meeting room, too, by the time everyone got to their feet. Even Vincent and Samira had seemed only moderately interested, and after enquiring after his health had been in a hurry to get back to outstanding business.

'Why would Hirtmann try to send us in the wrong direction when he can simply hide – with the child – anywhere in the world? What would be the point?' asked Stehlin.

'I'm listening,' Kirsten said.

'I know him too well to believe he would use such crude subterfuge. However, one thing does seem obvious: between the photographs of me and your name on the scrap of paper, his purpose has been to bring us together. The question is, why?'

She put the chain on the door and walked over to the bed, laid down her suitcase and opened it.

She took out shirts, skirts, trousers. Two jumpers, a toilet bag, a make-up bag and her pyjamas: flowery flannelette bottoms and a T-shirt. She spread them on the bed. Then the lace lingerie she had bought at Steen & Strøm. Underwear from Agent Provocateur and Victoria's Secret. She knew that no one would see the little panties with their delicate satin bow at the back, but she didn't care: what she got a kick out of was hiding this provocative finery beneath the austerity of her external appearance, like a treasure reserved for whoever was bold enough to explore further. As she put things away in the wardrobe, she wondered if such an intrepid individual might make himself known to her during her stay in France.

She had noticed Vincent Espérandieu's gaze and immediately categorised him. *Bisexual.* Kirsten had a sixth sense for such things. On the shelf in the bathroom she set out her day cream, perfume, shampoo (she didn't trust hotel shampoos) and toothbrush. Looking at herself in the mirror, she nodded. What she saw was a handsome face that nevertheless betrayed an excess of control and a tendency to be obstinate. In short, a woman in her forties, serious and a bit uptight. Perfect. What she saw was what she wanted others to see . . .

Two men at the same time: that could be an interesting experience, she thought, removing her make-up. In Oslo, it was unthinkable. One way or another it would get back to her colleagues and be round the department in no time. But here, far from home . . .

She also took out the toy. She had found it at the back of the Kondomeriet on Karl Johans gate, opposite the arcades of the bazaar, amidst a crowd of couples, women her own age, and very young women giggling and nudging each other. One of the women among the couples had slowly placed her hand around an impressive sex toy as if to masturbate it. At Oslo-Gardermoen airport she had waited for the reaction of the man sitting at his screen, scanning her carry-on baggage. She caught him turning his head to look at her as she took the bag from the conveyor belt, once it had come out of the scanning tunnel.

She felt a sudden pressing desire. Hurrying into the bathroom, she thought about Servaz. Definitely not an easy man to figure out. Heterosexual, beyond a shadow of a doubt. But there was something about him that defied analysis. Something fragile, but also strong. And then there was that Samira woman – so ugly and so sexy at the same time. She, too, was difficult to figure out.

She pushed her knickers and tights down around her ankles.

She sat down and reached for her mobile.

Then dialled the number she shouldn't have known.

The boy was watching the way the moonlight shone on the freshly fallen snow. The first of the season. And he saw that an animal had left deep prints that went around the barn and off into the woods.

The mountains on the other side of the valley formed an almost impassable frontier, which the boy vaguely perceived as a rampart, the guarantee that his safety and the cosy world of his childhood would be preserved forever. The boy did not watch the news, but his grandfather did, and from time to time the boy saw images on the screen. So, despite his youth, he could imagine the wars and battles that took place beyond these peaceful, protective mountains. He was only five years old, it was all quite confusing, but like a young animal he could sense danger.

And the boy knew the danger could come from outside the valley, from strangers who lived there. Grandfather had told him: never speak to strangers, never let strangers or even the tourists at the ski resorts speak to you. And anyway, outside of school, the boy saw almost no one, apart from his doctor and his grandparents. He didn't have many friends, and the ones who did come to the house had been hand-picked by his grandfather.

The little boy went back to the farm and was immediately greeted by an enveloping warmth. He shook the snow from his shoes onto the doormat, leaving little white crusts in his wake, then removed his shoes, hat, quilted jacket and scarf, which was damp with saliva and melted snow, and hung it on a peg. He could hear the fire crackling in the fireplace, and when he went closer, waves of heat caressed his bright red face.

'What were you doing outside again at this time of night, Gustav?' said his grandfather from his armchair.

'I was looking at a wolf's pawprints,' he replied, going over to Grandfather to let him pick him up with his big hands and sit him on his lap.

Grandfather didn't smell very good: he didn't wash enough, and rarely changed his clothes, but Gustav didn't care. He liked to stroke his beard, and he liked it when Grandfather read him a story.

'There aren't any wolves around here,' said Grandfather.

'Yes there are. They're in the forest. They come out at night.'

'Did you see them?'

'No. Just their prints.'

'And you're not afraid they'll eat you?'

'They're not nasty. And they like me.'

'How do you know?'

'Because they guard the house.'

'Oh, I see. Would you like me to read to you?'

'I have a tummy-ache,' said the boy.

For a moment Grandfather didn't say anything.

'A bad tummy-ache?'

'Sort of. When is Papa coming?' he asked, suddenly.

'I don't know, son.'

'I want my papa.'

'You'll see him soon.'

'When is soon?'

'You know Papa can't do as he pleases.'

'And Maman?'

'It's the same for Maman.'

The little boy suddenly felt like crying.

'They never come.'

'That's not true. Papa will come soon. Or we'll go together to see them.'

'Both of them?' said the boy, suddenly hopeful.

It had been so long since he had seen his papa and maman together.

'Both of them, I promise.'

'Don't make promises you can't keep,' said a stern voice from the door to the kitchen.

'Leave me alone,' said the grandfather, his tone irritable.

'You're only putting ideas in his head, poor lad.'

Grandmother dried her hands on her apron, hands covered in veins as thick as roots. Gustav looked away, fascinated by the flames licking the logs in the fireplace. Didn't they look like snakes, the way they wound themselves around the logs – or maybe dragons, dancing, pulling away, then rolling around the logs again? He tried not to pay attention to what Grandmother had said. He didn't like Grandmother. She spent her time complaining and criticising Grandfather. He knew she wasn't his real grandmother. He wasn't his real grandfather, either – but he loved Gustav, whereas Grandmother hardly even pretended. The boy was not fully aware of all this – he was far too young – it was, rather, a vague feeling. The boy felt a great many things without really understanding them; it was simply an instinct he had developed, like a wolf cub's.

'You mustn't be afraid of who you are, Gustav,' his papa had told him one day, and Gustav hadn't exactly understood that either, and yet he knew what Papa was trying to tell him.

Oh, yes.

13

Dream

It was half past nine in the morning when he was woken by the sun filtering through the blinds. He had not fallen asleep until around four in the morning, and then he had dreamt about the boy, Gustav. In his dream he was standing at the top of a huge dam in the heart of the Pyrenees. An arch dam. The child had climbed over the railing and was standing at the edge of the void. Just beyond his toes was a vertiginous abyss of over one hundred metres, where the most solid thing was air.

Servaz stood about five metres away on the other side of the railing.

'Gustav,' he called.

'Don't come near me, or I'll jump.'

A few snowflakes fluttered through the icy night, and the dam, like the mountains, was white with snow and ice. Servaz was petrified. The concrete edge where the child was standing was covered with a thick layer of ice. If he let go of the handrail, he could slip and fall into the void. He would be crushed against the rocks 100 metres below.

'Gustav . . .'

'I want my papa.'

'Your papa is a monster,' he answered, in his dream.

'You're lying!'

'If you don't believe me, just read the newspaper.'

Servaz was holding a copy of *La Dépêche*, and the wind, blowing harder and harder, tried to rip it from him. The paper was wet with snow and the ink was beginning to run.

'It says so, in here.'

'I want my papa,' said the child again, 'otherwise I'll jump. Or my maman . . .'

'Your maman – what's her name?'

'Marianne.'

The mountains around them, almost phosphorescent in the moonlight, seemed to be waiting for something. A denouement. Servaz's heart was pounding fit to burst. *Marianne* . . .

Another step.

And another.

The child had his back to him and was looking into the abyss. Servaz could see his graceful neck and the fine, rebellious blond hair dancing around his ears in the raging wind.

Another step.

He held out his arm. And then the child turned around. It wasn't him. Not Gustav's innocent face. A woman's face. Big, frightened green eyes. Marianne . . .

'Martin, is that you?' she said.

How could he have confused them? He was sure he had seen Gustav. What sort of evil spell was this? She was already letting go of the handrail to turn around and reach out to him, but she slipped, and her green eyes grew bigger and bigger with terror, her mouth open on a silent cry as she fell backwards.

That was when he woke up.

He looked around the room streaked with sunlight, his heart going at a hundred miles an hour, his chest covered in sweat. What had Xavier said about dreams? 'When you wake up, and the memory of your dream is still very vivid, you are astonished by the force of it, and how it seemed so . . . *real*.'

Yes, that was it. So real. He had seen that boy. He hadn't merely dreamt about him.

He shivered with cold; the sweat on his chest was icy. With fear and sadness, too. He threw back the sheet and got up. Who was that child? Was he really Hirtmann's son? The very thought of it was terrifying in itself, but another thought had formed in his mind, even more appalling, and his dream had reflected it: *what if Marianne actually was his mother?*

He went into the kitchen. Margot had left him a note on the countertop. *Running.* In English. What was this fashion of English words tirelessly invading their everyday life? For every old word that was left out of the dictionary, ten new ones barged in. Then he returned to the persistent sense of unease the discovery of the photographs had given him. A child. What was he looking for now? An evil killer or a child? Or both? And where should he look? Nearby, or further away? With his coffee cup in his hand he walked over to the bookshelf and let his mind wander at the same time as his gaze, until it came to rest on a title. An old edition of Edgar Allan Poe's stories, translated by Charles Baudelaire. He sat back down at the kitchen table and drank his coffee.

The sound of the front door. Margot appeared, flushed from running. She smiled, went over to the sink, poured a big glass of water and drank it almost in one go.

Then she sat down opposite her father. In spite of himself he felt slightly annoyed. He liked to eat breakfast on his own, and this was the first time since Margot's arrival he'd had the opportunity to do so.

'How do you spend your days?' he asked her suddenly.

She seemed to understand immediately what he was getting at and was instantly on her guard.

'Does my presence here bother you?' she asked. 'Am I in your way?'

Margot had always been very direct – and sometimes unfair. She was of the opinion that she must always tell the truth, but there were times when there was more than one truth, and his daughter was incapable of grasping this notion. You always had to stick to your position. However, he was ashamed and denied it vehemently.

'Not at all! Why do you say that?'

She observed him, but did not smile. She could see right through him.

'I don't know. Just an impression I've been getting for a while. I'm going to have a shower.'

She got up and left the room.

14

Saint-Martin

Servaz was browsing through the 440 when Kirsten came into his office. The 440 was a newsletter fed daily by the telegrams that circulated nationally for each case. Most of the cops in the crime unit consulted it every morning. Servaz didn't know who had named it the 440, but the name derived from the musical note A and its frequency of 440 Hz – the pitch standard used for tuning the instruments of an orchestra. (Servaz knew that the practice had evolved, however, and that most orchestras now tuned to 442 Hz.) In the same manner, the 440 newsletter served to circulate information and keep the various departments in harmony.

He had found nothing special. He certainly didn't expect to find any mention of Hirtmann in there, he was simply getting back into his old routine. Now he gave a shudder. He couldn't rid himself of the uneasy sensation the dream had left him with, that one way or another, the past was about to resurface. For months, after he'd found out that the insulated box did not contain Marianne's heart, he had tried to trace her, along with Hirtmann. He had laboriously worked on his English, sent hundreds of emails to cops all over Europe, made just as many phone calls, spent many a sleepless night going through reports his colleagues sent to him, searched through piles of national and international files, and regularly checked online for even the most trivial news item that might bear the stamp of the Swiss killer. In vain. He had not turned up a single thing.

He had even got back in touch with Irène Ziegler, the gendarme who had helped him track Hirtmann in the past. She was no further ahead than he was. She had, however, exhibited no lack of ingenuity in trying to find him. She explained to Servaz how, for example, she had cross-referenced the files of missing young women all over Europe with the concert halls performing Mahler's music, but she'd met a dead end there, too. Julian Hirtmann had vanished from the face of the earth. And Marianne along with him. And so, after months of frustration, he had eventually concluded she must be dead; perhaps they both were – in an accident, a fire, who knew? He resolved to erase them from his memory. And he had more or less succeeded. Because time had done its work, as always. Two years, three, four, five . . . Marianne and Hirtmann had vanished into the mist. Shadows, the trace of a smile, a voice, a gesture – little more.

And now everything that had been so painfully erased was resurfacing. The black heart that had been waiting in the past to come and beat again in the present. And infect his every thought.

'*Bonjour,*' said Kirsten in French.

'Hey.'

'Sleep well?'

'Not really.'

'What are you doing?'

'Nothing. I'm checking a file.'

'What sort of file?'

He explained to her what the 440 was. She told him they had roughly the same sort of newsletter in Norway.

He closed the 440 and typed something on his keyboard. Read the result of his search.

Scrolled down the screen.

'There are 116 nursery schools in Toulouse,' he said, finally. 'And roughly the same number of primary schools. I counted them.'

She raised her eyebrows.

'Do you think he's already in school?' she asked, somewhat surprised.

'I have no idea.'

'And do you intend to show the photograph to every school?'

'It would take weeks. And besides, we would need a requisition.'

'A what?'

Servaz winked at her and picked up his telephone.

'Roxane, can you come? Thank you.' Turning to Kirsten he said, 'When a child is involved, and no crime has been committed, we can't search just like that without permission. It really falls under the remit of the unit for the protection of minors in each *département.*'

She wondered if it was this complicated in her country. Roxane

Varin came in two minutes later. A rather pretty little woman with round cheeks and a brown fringe, Kirsten had seen her during the meeting. She reminded her of the French actress Juliette Binoche. She was wearing a denim shirt over a pair of skinny grey jeans.

'Hey,' she said, giving Servaz a kiss on the cheek.

She shook Kirsten's hand somewhat timidly. Kirsten thought perhaps she was more at ease with children than with adults. Roxane was holding the photograph of Gustav and collapsed in the last free chair.

'I've launched a search with the bureau of academic affairs to see if he's enrolled,' she said. 'They're the ones who keep track of this sort of thing. Unfortunately there are no photographs in the pupil database. They can search using the first name, as it's an unusual one,' she added, not hiding her scepticism that anything would come up.

'What's the pupil database?' asked Servaz.

'A computer application: it's used to manage and monitor a pupil's school career for the first stage of their education – from nursery school to the end of primary school, when they're ten years old, or thereabouts.'

'For every school? Both public and private?'

'Yes.'

'And do you have access to it?'

Kirsten saw her smile. A pretty smile, which lit up her gaze.

'No. No administration outside the Éducation Nationale has access. With the exception of the local council, who enrol the children. And even then, there's some data the council doesn't see – for example if the child requires psychological support. The problem is that first and last names are visible up to the level of the regional education authority, but they disappear from the database at the level of the national authority in order to protect confidentiality.'

She turned to Kirsten and summed up in English what she had just said – with frequent hesitations and corrections and a few frowns of incomprehension on the part of the Norwegian visitor.

'The second problem is that the data is not kept beyond the child's enrolment in primary school. Once they leave, everything is erased.'

Again, she translated as best she could. Kirsten nodded.

'Naturally, I also sent a standard search request with a photograph, which will be transmitted to the schools, I hope, once the pupil database comes up negative. How long that will take is another story.'

She stood up.

'Do you really think the boy is here, Martin?'

Her tone conveyed the same scepticism as that of his colleagues during the meeting. Servaz did not answer. He merely took the photograph that Roxane handed him and placed it in full view on his desk. He seemed lost in thought. Roxane shot a look and a smile at Kirsten then went out, shrugging her shoulders. Kirsten returned her smile then looked at Servaz, who was gazing out of the window with his back to her.

'Do you feel like going for a little walk?' he asked suddenly.

She stared at Servaz's back.

'Do you know "The Purloined Letter", by Edgar Allan Poe?'

He had quoted the title in English, having found it the night before on the Internet. Now he turned around.

'Explain,' she said.

'*Nil sapientiae odiosius acumine nimio:* Nothing is more hateful to wisdom than excessive cleverness. A sentence from Seneca that is the epigraph to the story. "The Purloined Letter" tells us that very often the thing we are looking for at some distance is right there in front of our nose.'

'Do you really think that Gustav might be here?' she echoed Roxane's question.

'In the story, the police cannot find a letter in an apartment because they assume it is well hidden,' he continued, ignoring her interruption. 'Dupin, Poe's character, has understood that the best way to hide the letter is to leave it on the desk in plain sight: it has simply been folded backwards, and marked with a different seal and different handwriting.'

'Oh, you really are crazy, you know,' she said in English. 'What are you driving at?'

'Replace the desk in Poe's story with Saint-Martin-de-Comminges, where everything began. You said so yourself: Hirtmann came back through the region on several occasions. Why did he do that?'

'Because of you. Because he's obsessed with you.'

'And what if there was another reason? More compelling than just some obsession with a cop. *A son*, for example.'

Kirsten didn't reply. She was waiting for what came next.

'A son in disguise, but in plain sight, like the purloined letter on the desk in the short story. Simply give him a different surname. But he goes to school, and he is raised by someone who looks after him when Hirtmann is not there, which means most of the time.'

'And no one would notice?'

'Notice what? A boy like any other. Going to school.'

'True. But wouldn't anyone at the school wonder who this child is?'

'Maybe the people who take him to school have passed themselves off as his adoptive parents? I don't know, something like that.'

'Saint-Martin, you said?'

'Saint-Martin.'

'Why there in particular?'

Why there indeed? Just supposing Hirtmann came back to the region to see his son, why would Gustav necessarily be in Saint-Martin? Why not just anywhere in the region?

'Because Hirtmann spent several years in Saint-Martin.'

'Locked up in an asylum.'

'Yes. But he had accomplices on the outside, people like Lisa Ferney.'

'The head nurse at the Wargnier Institute, am I right? She worked there. She wasn't simply living here.'

He paused to think. Why had he always assumed that Hirtmann must have other accomplices? Accomplices that his associates didn't find at the time? He knew that his reasoning had no logic to it. Or that, at best, his logic was skewed, and he was seeing signs and coincidences where there were none – the way paranoid people did. Nevertheless, his mind kept swinging back to Saint-Martin, magnetised like the needle of a compass.

'Saint-Martin, that's where you nearly got killed, isn't it?' Kirsten asked.

She was well informed. He nodded.

'I've always thought there was someone else there who helped him,' he said. 'The way he escaped that night. On foot over the mountains – his car was wrecked in an accident – in the middle of a snowstorm. He couldn't have got very far without help.'

'And so it could be this accomplice who is raising Gustav?'

Her tone was no less sceptical than Roxane's.

'Who else?'

'You do realise that's a very thin lead to go on?'

'I know.'

They came off the motorway at Montréjeau, leaving the monotony of the plain behind them, and began to head up into the mountains.

They went through a dogleg tunnel and when they emerged at the other end they saw it below the stone parapet: Saint-Martin-de-Comminges, population 20,863. The road went back down and they entered the town.

The pavements were thronged with people: skiers who had come back down by gondola from the ski resort at the top of the mountain; guests from spas who had forsaken the hot springs for the cafés and restaurants in the centre of town; families with children and push-chairs. Servaz wondered whether Hirtmann could have walked along these streets without being noticed. His face had been on the front page of all the local and even national newspapers, and it was not a face you could easily forget. Might he have resorted to cosmetic surgery? Servaz didn't know much about it, but he had heard that they could work miracles nowadays.

As they parked in front of the town hall and got out of the car (he could hear the roar of the waterfall that left a vertical silver line against the wooded flank of the mountain), he felt a little shiver go all down his spine: it would be just like Hirtmann to come back to the scene of the crime and mingle incognito with the crowd. The thought caused him to cast his gaze over the square, the café terraces, the bandstand, and the faces. Beyond the roofs, draped in its cloak of fir trees, the mountain contemplated their arrival with the same indifference with which it had greeted the crimes of the winter of 2008–9.

'What are we doing here?' he asked, suddenly.

'What?'

'If we're both here, it's because he wants us to be. Why? Why did he bring us together?'

She gave him a questioning look before they entered the town hall.

There was a different mayor now. He was a young man, tall and corpulent, with a thick beard that hid much of his face and huge bags under his pale, rather watery eyes. It was hard to determine just what colour his beard was: somewhere between brown and ginger, with white streaks in the middle.

'Servaz: that name rings a bell,' he said, in a strident voice.

He took the cop's hand in his huge paw, which was damp and cool. Then he flashed his most charming smile at Kirsten. Servaz looked at his hands: no wedding ring. The big man observed him again.

'My assistant told me you are looking for a child,' he said, turning around and striding ahead of them into an office that was impressive in size, well lit and aired by two tall French windows with a balcony that offered a view on the highest summits of the range.

There were advantages to being mayor in Saint-Martin.

He went to sit back down at his desk. Servaz placed the photograph of Gustav on the desk before taking a seat.

'He may have been at school here,' he said.

'What makes you say that?'

'I'm afraid I can't tell you. We're in the middle of the investigation.'

The mayor shrugged and typed on his computer keyboard.

'If he is here, he should show up in the pupil database. Come and have a look.'

They got up and walked around the desk to stand behind him. From his desk drawer the mayor took a sort of plastic key with a little digital screen in the middle, and gave them a quick course on the database.

'It is protected, of course.'

On the computer screen they saw the words 'Login', 'ID number' and 'Password'.

'I have to enter my ID number. Then the password, which consists of my personal four-digit code, and the six-digit number that appears on this security key. And the login address is different for every regional authority.'

Servaz watched him click on 'Enrolment and Admissions'.

'What's his name?'

'We only have his first name.'

The mayor swivelled his seat round to look at them, puzzled. His watery gaze went from one to the other.

'Are you serious? Just the first name? Up to now I've always had first and last name. Besides, look: there is an asterisk. The last name is a required field.'

Roxane's mistake. No sooner had they begun than they had come up against a brick wall.

'His name is Gustav,' said Servaz. 'Surely you must have archives somewhere, with the classes over the last couple of years: there aren't that many schools in Saint-Martin.'

The mayor paused and thought.

'Do you have a requisition?' he asked suddenly.

Servaz took it from his pocket.

'I should be able to find out for you,' replied the mayor. 'Besides, Gustav is not a very common name nowadays.'

Servaz knew it was unlikely that Hirtmann would have enrolled the child under his real name. But then, why not? Who would make the connection between a child and a Swiss serial killer? Who could ever imagine he would put his child in school in Saint-Martin? Was there any hiding place less likely to arouse suspicion than this one?

Servaz glanced out at the square. Clouds must have appeared on the peaks, because the square was veiled in shadow and a strange greyish-green haze lay over things, as if he were looking at them through a filter. A little spot of light clung to the roof of the band-stand.

'I'll see what I can do. It might take me a few hours, all right?'

'We'll stay here.'

There was a man down on the square. Because of the hazy light, Servaz could not see him very clearly. A tall man. In a dark winter coat. His face was turned up towards the windows of the town hall. It even seemed to Servaz that the man was looking at him.

'Try Gustav Servaz,' came Kirsten's voice suddenly, behind him.

Servaz gave a start and turned around briskly. The mayor was examining her again, in surprise, then he looked over at Martin.

'Shall I try Gustave Servaz?' he translated.

'Yes. Gustav without the e.'

'And Servaz, how do you spell it?'

She told him.

'But that's your name!' said the mayor, who clearly no longer understood what was going on.

Nor did Servaz. There was a buzzing in his ears. He wanted to tell him to stop, but he nodded.

'Do what she said.'

His heart began beating more quickly. He was having trouble

breathing. He looked out of the window. Now he was sure that the man was looking at him. He was standing straight and motionless right in the middle of one of the pathways on the square, his face raised towards the windows of the town hall, and adults and children alike flowed around him like a stream around a large rock.

'Here we go,' said the mayor.

The silence lasted only a few seconds.

'Servaz, Gustave: with an e,' he announced triumphantly.

15

School

Servaz felt an icy shiver. He looked outside. In the place where a second earlier the man had been standing, there was no one, other than the usual traffic of passers-by.

Who was that child, for God's sake?

'He was enrolled at Jules Verne School until last year,' said the mayor, as if he had heard the question. 'But he's not here any more.'

'And you don't know where he is?' asked Kirsten.

'What I do know,' said the mayor in English, 'is that he has left the region. Otherwise he would show up in the database.'

He turned to Servaz. Servaz saw his eyes narrow; the man must be puzzled by his pallor and his haggard expression, and he must be wondering what was going on.

'Show us where it is, this Jules Verne School,' said Kirsten, pointing at the map pinned to the wall.

In the face of Servaz's shock and apparent paralysis, she was taking charge. He wondered how the idea had occurred to her. Clearly she was better acquainted with Hirtmann and his thought process than she let on.

'Right. I'll show you,' said the mayor.

They arrived at a long white avenue between two rows of ancient plane trees already leafless from the early winter. Their heavy, gnarled branches, crowned with snow, evoked living characters, like the Disney cartoons of Servaz's childhood, their anthropomorphic nature giving them branches for arms. The snowplough had gone by and had cleared the middle of the drive that led to the school gates. They passed a little snowman, probably made by very young children, because he stood crookedly and had an oddly shaped head. He looked like a nasty, unsightly gnome.

On the far side of the drive and the gates was an old-fashioned playground, which made Servaz think of the novel *Le Grand Meaulnes* and his own childhood in the southwest. How many children had passed through here? Was it here that lives were decided, as some people claimed? How many children had their first experience of life in society here in school, discovering the cruelty of their peers, or exerting their own? Servaz himself had almost no memories of this period.

The playground was deserted; the children were in class. As Servaz and Kirsten crossed it, evanescent plumes of cold escaped their lips, and both of them were buffeted by the wind that blew the snow from the trees. A woman appeared in the covered part of the playground, tugging her coat closer around herself for warmth. Servaz gauged her to be in her fifties; her hair was dyed blonde, and she had an open but stern face.

'The mayor told me you would be coming. You're from the police, is that right?'

'Regional crime unit, Toulouse,' Servaz replied, going up to the woman and showing her his badge. 'And this is Kirsten Nigaard, from the Norwegian police.'

The headmistress frowned, then held out her hand.

'May I have a look?'

Servaz gave her his badge.

'I don't understand,' she said, looking at it. 'That's what the mayor told me. You have the same name as Gustave. Is he your son?'

'A coincidence,' answered Servaz, but he could see she didn't believe him.

'Hmm. What do you want with the boy?'

'He has disappeared. He may be in danger.'

'Ah. Could you be a little more precise?'

'No.'

He saw her scowl.

'What would you like to know?'

'Couldn't we go inside? It's cold out here.'

One hour later, they knew a bit more about Gustave. The headmistress had given them a fairly detailed portrait. A very bright boy, occasionally subject to strange mood swings. Melancholy, too, and fairly solitary; he didn't have many friends to play with during break and, consequently, for a time he had served as the others' whipping boy. Rousseau be damned, thought Servaz; children don't need anyone to be cruel and nasty and hypocritical: they have it in them, just like the rest of humankind. Rather than society making us brutal, contact with others sometimes teaches us to be better and, with a bit of luck, we can stay that way our entire life. Or not. Servaz had learned integrity at the age of ten, or so he believed, reading *Bob Morane* and following the adventures of Jules Verne's exemplary heroes.

It was Gustave's grandparents who had been appointed to take care of him. Like the mayor, the headmistress had found this out through the pupil database.

She called up his file for them and they could see that only the fields with his name were filled in: there was no address.

'Monsieur and Madame Mahler,' read Servaz.

It was as if the blood had frozen in his veins. He exchanged glances with Kirsten and he was sure his eyes reflected the stupefaction he could see in hers. For the fields marked 'relationship to the child,' 'grandfather' and 'grandmother' had been ticked.

That was all.

'Did you ever speak to his grandparents?' he asked, his voice so hoarse it grated like a saw. He cleared his throat.

'Only to his grandfather,' she answered, frowning to see how unsettled Servaz clearly was. 'I was concerned. As I told you, Gustave had been bullied in the playground by his classmates and no matter how often I separated them it would start again the next day. But he didn't say a word, didn't cry.' She shot them a pained look. 'He was a puny child, too, sickly. He looked a good year younger than the others. He often missed school – flu, a cold, an upset stomach . . . His grandfather always had an explanation. And the boy looked sad. He never smiled. It broke your heart to see him in the playground during break. Can you imagine it, a child who never smiles? Anyway, you could tell something wasn't right. And I needed to find out what it was. So I mentioned it to the grandfather . . .'

'How did he strike you?'

'What do you mean?'

'What sort of man was he?'

She hesitated. Servaz could clearly see a precise thought surface in her gaze.

'The nice old granddad type, of course. The boy always jumped into his arms, they seemed very close and affectionate, it was obvious. But . . .' Again they saw her hesitate. 'I don't know . . . there was something else about him, the way he would look at you. He was clearly very fond of the boy, but whenever I tried to dig a bit deeper . . . how can I put it? . . . his attitude would change. I even wondered what he used to do before he retired.'

'What do you mean?'

'Well, he wasn't the kind of person you would want to cross, do you know what I mean? He must have been nearly eighty but, I don't know why, I thought that if ever any burglars broke into his house, they'd better watch out . . .'

Servaz could see how puzzled she was. He realised he was sweating profusely under his jacket and coat. Was this an after-effect of the coma?

'And did he enlighten you in any way about Gustave's situation?'

She nodded.

'Yes. He told me his son was often away, and for long stretches, because of his work. And that this upset the boy, who was always asking for him. But he also told me that the father would be coming soon, because he got plenty of leave, and that meant he could be with his son.'

'Did he tell you what Gustave's father's profession was?' Servaz was speaking hurriedly, his words spilling out.

'Yes, I was about to get to that. He worked on an oil platform. In the North Sea, I think it was.'

Servaz and Kirsten looked at each other again, and the headmistress noticed.

'What's the matter?' she said.

'This corroborates certain findings of our own.'

'And, naturally, you can't tell me what they are,' she said, annoyed.

'Exactly.'

The headmistress flushed.

'Might you have the grandparents' address somewhere else?'

'No.'

'And you never saw the grandmother?'

'No, never. Just her husband.'

Servaz nodded. 'I'm going to have to ask you to come to Toulouse, to the regional crime unit, to help construct a facial composite and answer a few other questions. Ask for Captain Roxane Varin, from Child Protection.'

'When?'

'As soon as possible. Take a day off. And the mother – did you ask Gustave's grandfather about the mother?'

'Of course.'

'And what did he say?'

The headmistress gave them a dark look.

'Nothing. That was one of those instances I mentioned, where you could tell you couldn't get anything more out of him.'

'And you didn't insist?' he asked, astonished.

Servaz's tone made her sit up straight in her chair.

'Um, no.'

He saw her cheeks go red.

'Has something happened to Gustave?' she said. 'Have they found—?'

'No, no. You would have seen it in the papers. He has disappeared, that's all. Thank you for your help.'

They stood up and shook her hand.

'Commandant,' she said, 'I have one more question.'

They were already on the threshold, and he turned around.

'What is your tie to this boy?'

He looked at her, taken aback. Gripped by a sudden, terrifying foreboding.

They went back to the car along the avenue of cartoon plane trees. Oddly, the snowman had been decapitated – or could the wind have toppled the big head, which was now lying on the ground? – and even more oddly, it made him think of the propaganda images of Islamic State which had managed, with the passive or active complicity of the media, to infect the Western imagination. In another era, not that long ago, such images would never have seen the light of day, let alone reached the general public. Was it a blessing or a curse that everyone had access to them now?

'So he lived here,' said Kirsten, once Servaz had translated everything that had been said in the headmistress's office.

Her voice was tense.

'Servaz, Mahler . . . he staged the whole thing. He knew that one day you would trace him back to this place. How can that be?'

He turned the ignition without replying. Reversed cautiously onto the wet road, with its patches of black ice. He was about to shift into first gear when he turned to her:

'How,' he said, 'did you come up with the idea of joining his first name to my last name?'

16

Return

He drove in silence along the A61 motorway, the 'Pyrénéenne', and couldn't stop thinking about Kirsten's reply. 'A hunch.' It was like slow poison – ricin, or amatoxins – spreading through all his thoughts, contaminating them. Was it a hunch that in any way resembled the one he'd had when the headmistress asked him what his tie with Gustav was?

What if . . . *what if Marianne was already pregnant before Hirtmann kidnapped her?* At the thought a wave of terror went through him – he felt nauseous. He opened his mouth as if to gulp for air. No: it mustn't, it couldn't have happened. It was out of the question. He could not go there, the shrink had said as much: he was too fragile, too vulnerable.

He let his gaze drift over some huge goods vehicles as he overtook them. One thing was certain: Hirtmann had left these clues for them. So he had stayed here, according to what the grandfather had told the headmistress: he had come regularly to see his son when he had leave – and platform workers had plenty of leave. Thus he had probably altered his face to be able to go around unnoticed in Saint-Martin. Unless he merely used some form of disguise. And Marianne. Was she even still alive? When he had found out that the heart in the insulated box was not hers, he had thought she was, but now he was beginning to have his doubts. Why would Hirtmann have kept her alive for so long? That was not the way he worked. And from a practical point of view it would be very complicated. At the same time, wouldn't Hirtmann have let him know one way or another if she was dead? He would certainly not have let pass without comment an event that was so important to his policeman 'friend'.

His fingers tensed around the steering wheel, and he felt as if his head was about to explode.

'Hey! Watch out!' said Kirsten next to him. 'Slow down!'

He looked at the speedometer. Good Lord! One hundred and eighty kilometres an hour. He lifted his foot from the pedal and the roar of the motor abated.

'Are you sure you're all right?' she asked.

He nodded, his throat tight. He glanced over at her. She was observing him, calmly, coldly. Her skirt had ridden up above her knees but her dark coat cinched her waist and was carefully buttoned all the way up. There was a sharp parting in her blonde hair with its dark roots, and her shiny nails were impeccable. He wondered what was hidden beneath that cold exterior. Was it typical of Norwegians, such a strict, spartan temperament? Or was it just Kirsten? Something buried in her childhood, in her upbringing?

She did not offer much in the way of opportunity for human warmth or contact. She had told him she had six days here. What could the Norwegian police hope to accomplish in such a short time? It was no doubt a question of budget, as it would be here. Well, it was all to the good: he didn't feel he had the stamina to put up with her Jansenist presence for much longer, even if he himself was hardly a chatterbox or a live wire. He felt as if she were constantly watching him, sizing him up, and he didn't like it. Was it just her nature, or was she adapting her behaviour to the situation? Either way, the sooner she went back to Norway, the better.

'It's really kind of sickening,' she said suddenly.

'What? What's sickening?'

'If that kid is his son . . . It's really sickening.'

He thought about her words. Yes, it was sickening – but there could be even worse to come.

17

Footprints

Night was falling by the time the skiers reached the refuge. It was almost six o'clock and the temperature was one degree above zero. The sun had already been hidden behind the mountains for several hours, and they had been following the white trail through the forest for even longer. They advanced in single file through the trees: five figures bundled up in down parkas gliding on their skis. It had been a very long day and they had stopped talking. They were too tired. They merely concentrated on breathing faster and faster, their breath forming an origami of white vapour before their lips.

They were invigorated by the sight of the refuge. Its dark shape huddled in the snowy clearing gave them a final boost.

Logs, slate, stone, fir trees all around: a postcard of Canada coming closer to them, even if they were the ones who were moving through the early darkness. Gilbert Beltran thought of *White Fang* and *The Call of the Wild*, all his childhood reading filled with adventure, wide-open spaces and freedom. When he was ten he'd thought that this was what life was about: adventure and freedom. And instead, he had found out that once you were headed in a certain direction it was almost impossible to change, and that it was all much less exciting than it had seemed at the start. He was now over fifty and he had just broken up with his twenty-six-year-old girlfriend (rather, she was the one who had left him). Now he was close to exhaustion and his muscles were aching, like his oxygen-starved lungs. He was breathing, and breathing.

Like all the participants on the trek he was following a treatment for depression and insomnia at the spa in Saint-Martin-de-Comminges, and he was not yet in peak physical form – far from it.

The voice of the woman behind him roused him from his thoughts.

'I'm knackered.'

He turned around. It was the blonde. A pretty specimen, healthy and unpretentious, in her mid-thirties. He mused that he would have liked to have heard her say that in his bed. He would try to get closer to her this evening. On the condition, of course, that there was sufficient privacy in the refuge.

Their guide, a young blond man who was about the same age as Beltran's ex-girlfriend, unlocked the door and hit a switch. A yellow puddle of light immediately spilled out of the door onto the patch of snow where they had been walking. It lit up their footprints – but also others; recent, deeper ones, from snowshoes and feet.

Fresh footprints.

Gilbert looked around him. His gaze lingered on the other man, the strange one who always wore his hood up, who had a kind of crazed look in his eyes, and burn marks around his mouth and on his left cheek. Beltran had heard at the spa that the burns were from being electrocuted by a catenary. People said he had spent weeks in a severe burns unit to start with, then in a rehabilitation centre, before ending up here. Normally he would have felt compassion for someone whose face was partially disfigured, but there was something about this particular man that made your blood run cold. Maybe it was the way his demented gaze moved slowly from one person to the next, with what struck Beltran as pure evil. Or maybe it was because he would stare at the arse and breasts of the two girls in the group, the blonde and the brunette, whenever he got the chance. Or was it the way he licked his hand-rolled cigarettes just a touch obscenely, staring you straight in the eyes as he did so?

Beltran noticed that the guy was watching him from under his hood and he shuddered. He was the first one to go in. He felt uneasy, in the middle of the forest, with night falling; he was little Gilbert again, curled up in his bed reading Jack London. *You're completely regressing, you pathetic man . . .*

Emmanuelle Vengud smiled at the young guide and took a packet of cigarettes out of her anorak. To smoke one in this pure air suddenly seemed like the appropriate thing to do. A deliciously transgressive act. The oxygen that had filled her lungs during the climb had made her tipsy, as had the altitude. Suddenly a lugubrious cry, high-pitched and grating like the scraping of a saw, tore through the falling darkness.

'What was that?'

Matthieu, their guide, looked at the forest and gave a shrug.

'No idea. I know nothing about birds.'

'It was a bird?'

'What else could it be?' He held his gloved fingers out towards the packet of cigarettes. 'May I?'

'A healthy, sporty young man like you?'

Was it a bit too obvious, the way she had already said *tu* to him? If so, too bad.

'That's not my only vice,' he answered, looking at her.

She looked back at him. Was this a veiled come-on? Or just an innocent game? If it had been her husband, she would have known immediately. In her husband's mental Scrabble, the word *innocent* did not earn you a single point – unlike *adultery*, *cheating*, *fucking*, *pussy*, *pornography* and above all *betrayal*. When your best girlfriend sleeps with your husband, who do you turn to? Your household pet? Your sister-in-law? She inhaled the smoke, drawing it as deeply into her lungs as she could.

'Does your husband not like cross-country skiing?'

She shivered – he was behind her, and he said the words very close to her ear.

'No, not really.'

'What about you, do you like it?'

She shivered again, but for a different reason. Because of the voice. It wasn't the same as before. It wasn't the guide's voice; this voice hissed, like . . . She gave a start. The burned face. The one who had a strange way of looking at you, and scars around his mouth and on his left cheek. Only then did she notice they were alone. The guide had just left her there and gone inside. It was cold and damp, but suddenly she felt a warmth that had nothing pleasant about it. A rush of adrenaline that made her feel dizzy. She avoided moving her eyes, so she wouldn't be tempted to look at his scars.

'Your husband – why didn't he come?'

She was surprised, both by the fact he now said *tu* to her, and by the implicit indiscretion of his question. It was her turn to shrug.

'He likes his creature comforts. Spending the night in a sleeping bag in the middle of a shared room with people snoring – that's not his thing. And besides, as I said, he doesn't like cross-country skiing. He prefers Alpine.' (*And being slapped*, she thought.)

'What is he doing all this time you're away?'

She stiffened. Now he was going too far. (*He's sleeping with my best girlfriend*, she thought. Maybe that would shut him up.) And besides, she had noticed the way the burned man had stared at her breasts and her arse during the climb. She turned around to look at him, and to stop him brushing against her from behind.

'Why do you want to know?'

'No particular reason . . . Did you know something terrible happened in this refuge ten years ago? Something horrible . . .'

She shuddered. He had said it in such a strange voice: deeper, more serious. As if he enjoyed it. It was getting darker and darker. She wanted to go back inside.

'What was this horrible thing you refer to?'

'A woman was raped. By two skiers. In front of her husband . . . It went on almost all night until the two guys collapsed with tiredness.'

She felt a twist of apprehension in her belly.

'That's horrible,' she said. 'Did they catch them?'

'Yes. A few days later. They both had police records as long as your arm. And you know what? Their sentences were reduced for good conduct.'

'And the woman, did she die?'

'No, she survived.'

'Do you know what happened to her?'

He shook his head in the thickening gloom.

'They say her husband committed suicide. But it's probably some stupid rumour. People around here love rumours. Thanks for the cigarette,' he said in his soft, sibilant voice. 'And for the rest.'

'What rest?'

'The two of us here, quiet, speaking freely . . . I fancy you.'

He took a step closer. She looked up at him, not liking what she saw.

It was as if the night that was moving through the tree trunks had poured brutally into his pupils, devouring the entire iris. His dark, opaque gaze was like a bottomless well of such pure, avid carnality that she recoiled.

'Hey, watch it,' she heard herself saying.

'Watch what, Emmanuelle?' She hated the way he said her name. 'You've been making eyes at me for a while now.'

'*What?*'

There was something wilder, more violent, in the burned man's voice now, and her heart started racing.

'Are you out of your mind!'

She saw anger replace the animal lust in his gaze. Then the mocking little smile returned. His lips parted, pulling at the scars around his mouth, and she waited to hear the words that would demean her, reduce her to less than nothing, but they didn't come. He merely turned on his heels and headed with a shrug to the door of the refuge.

She could feel her pulse beating all the way into her throat. The bird shrieked again deep in the woods, and a chill ran from her neck all the way down to the base of her spine, like an electrical impulse. She hurried to join the others.

Beltran watched the blonde woman removing her boots at the entrance. She had been outside with the burned guy for more than five minutes, and her cheeks were as red as the checks on the tablecloth where he had his elbows. Something had happened out there, something she didn't seem to have found amusing or even remotely pleasant.

'Everything all right?' he asked.

She replied with a nod, but her expression indicated quite the contrary.

Emmanuelle Vengud spread her sleeping bag on a mattress in silence, off to one side. There wasn't enough room on the bunks and she had difficulty putting up with smells and snoring at night. And besides, she didn't want to sleep near the man with the burned face. Six days out of seven she was a chartered accountant. She worked at home, in a quiet study. This was her first time at a spa and her first time ski-touring in a group. She had thought everyone would be tired when they got to the refuge – too tired to talk, in fact – but they wouldn't stop chatting. Especially the three men.

'You say they raped her in front of a guy?' asked the one in his fifties whose name was Beltran.

'Yup, after they tied her up, there.'

The burned man pointed to the central beam that held up the roof of the refuge. He refilled their glasses.

'To a torture post, in other words,' said the guide, looking disgusted, knocking back his drink as if it were water.

'And when did this happen?' asked Beltran.

'Ten years ago.'

The burned man gave a sadistic smile. He had not removed his hood, no doubt to hide a scalp that was bare in places, or deeper wounds, thought Beltran.

'On 10 December, to be precise.'

'Today is 10 December,' pointed out the brunette, with a catch in her voice. She had short hair and a suntanned face. Her name was Corinne.

'I'm joking,' he said, winking at her.

No one seemed to think it was funny, and silence fell over the room.

'Where did you hear that story?' asked Beltran eventually.

'Everyone knows it.'

'I didn't know it,' said Corinne, 'and I'm from around here.'

'I mean all the guides know, the mountain people. You're a dentist.'

'Well she might have been my patient. What was her name?'

'No idea.'

'Can't we talk about something else?' interrupted Emmanuelle brusquely.

Her voice expressed a mixture of annoyance and something deeper: fear. Suddenly there was a loud noise on the roof above them. Emmanuelle and the others jumped and looked up. Everyone, except the burned man.

'What was that?' she said.

'What?'

'Don't tell me you didn't hear it.'

'Hear what?'

'The loud noise on the roof.'

'It was probably a mound of snow,' said the young guide.

'A mound of snow doesn't make a sound like that.'

'Then a branch that broke under the weight of the snow,' said Corinne, shooting a scornful look at Emmanuelle.

They fell silent for a moment. The wind was blowing against the shingles outside; the flames were hissing in the stove.

'She wasn't just raped,' continued the burned man in the shadow of his hood, in his curious sibilant voice. 'They were tortured, too, she and her husband. All night long. Left for dead. It was a guide who found them the next morning. A friend of mine.'

Emmanuelle could see Corinne's eyes shining with curiosity – as well as desire for the guide.

'That's horrible,' she said, but there was something else in her voice, an undertone that said to the guide, 'It's so exciting to be talking about this here with you, knowing we're going to sleep near each other . . .'

She was in her mid-forties, her hair styled in a short, tousled, blunt cut, almost a man's cut, over her ears. She had a dark complexion and her eyes were hazel and slightly slanting. She could not stop brushing her elbow against the guide's, and Emmanuelle saw her foot beneath the big table doing the same thing. She felt her cheeks flush. Were they going to do it here, tonight, in front of everyone?

'The worst of it,' added the guide, 'was that—'

'Enough, for Christ's sake!'

She saw the other four turn and look at her. The young guide was smiling, mockingly.

'I'm sorry,' she said.

'I think everyone must be tired,' said Beltran. 'Why don't we call it a night?'

Corinne shot him a look of irritation. She and the guide had not flirted enough.

'Good idea,' said the man with the burned face, in his cold, high-pitched voice.

'I'm going to have one last smoke before I turn in,' said the guide, getting to his feet. 'Care to join me?' he asked Corinne.

She nodded with a smile and followed him. She was at least fifteen years older than him. Bitch, thought Emmanuelle.

'It was pretty scary all the same, that story,' said Corinne, once they were outside.

He smiled and took a cigarette from the packet. She held her hand out to take it, but he moved it away from her fingers to place it between his lips and pretend to suck the filter end. Now it was her turn to smile. She did not take her eyes off his fine lips, red as fruit in the middle of his blond beard. He slipped the cigarette into her mouth and brought the quivering flame of the lighter closer, never taking his eyes off her.

'Matthieu, that's your name, right?' she asked.

'Yup.'

'I don't like sleeping alone, Matthieu.'

They were very close; not as close, however, as she would have liked, because of the cigarettes. She was divorced, free to do as she pleased, and she didn't refrain from enjoying her freedom whenever the opportunity arose.

'You're hardly alone,' he answered. 'You'll have three guys around you.'

'I mean alone in my sleeping bag.'

Almost simultaneously they moved their cigarettes to one side and their faces came closer together. She could feel his breath on her face, with its faint smell of wine.

'You want to do it with the others sleeping right next to you,' he said. 'That's what turns you on.'

It wasn't a question.

'I hope at least one of them won't be asleep,' she replied.

'Why don't we do it here, right now?'

'It's too cold.'

She looked deep into his eyes. His gaze was vacant, devoid of any expression; it filled almost her entire field of vision and yet she could see something moving in the thicket behind him, in the angle between his neck and his shoulder: a moving shadow.

'What was that?'

'What?' he said as she slipped out from between him and the wall.

'I saw something.'

He turned around reluctantly and gazed out at the dark forest.

'There's nothing there.'

'I'm sure I saw something! There, in the woods.'

Her voice trembled with panic now.

'I told you, there's nothing. You saw a branch moving with the wind, that's all.'

'No, it was something else,' she insisted.

'Then it was an animal . . . Shit, what are you playing at?'

'Let's go in,' she said, tossing her cigarette butt into the snow.

'There's someone out there,' she said.

They all looked at her; behind her, the guide rolled his eyes towards the ceiling.

'I saw someone,' she said again. 'There was someone out there.'

'Shadows,' said the guide, walking in front of her to join the others.

'Shadows in the forest, trees moving in the wind. There's no one's there. Honestly, who would be out in the forest on a cold evening like this? And what for? To steal our iPhones and our skis?'

'I'm sure I saw someone,' she said, annoyed, having lost all desire to flirt with this imbecile.

'Let's go and see,' said Beltran. 'Do we have torches?'

The guide sighed, went over to his bag and took two out.

'Let's go,' he said.

The two men headed out of the door.

'I was right,' said the guide. 'There's no one.'

The beams of their torches danced among the trees, a jerky, strobe-light ballet, revealing the frightening depths of the forest. And in those depths, night was endless. Like snow, night levels everything; it absorbs, conceals . . .

'There are footprints here. They look recent.'

Reluctantly, the young guide went closer. There were indeed deep footprints at the edge of the forest. A few metres from the refuge, where the snow was thickest, where Corinne thought she had seen something. The snow sparkled in the light from their torches.

'So what? Someone came through here. These prints could even be from yesterday. With the cold, nothing moves, perhaps they're not as recent as all that.'

Beltran look at the guide and pulled a face. He didn't like it, but the young man was probably right. If that nutter hadn't told his story, they wouldn't all be imagining things.

'Right, shall we go back?' said the guide.

Beltran nodded. 'Yeah, let's go back.'

'We didn't see anything, okay? No footprints. No reason to frighten the others.'

18

Strong Sensations

Kirsten went back to the hotel room shortly before midnight. She stepped into the shower and soaped herself for a long time under the steaming spray. Martin had left her in the centre of town before heading home, because she had told him she needed to get some fresh air.

When she came out of the shower she picked up her phone, which she had left charging, and went back to sit on the toilet seat.

'Hey, Kasper,' she said when he picked up.

'So, how's it going?' asked the cop from Bergen.

Servaz was smoking a cigarette outside his building on the place Victor-Hugo. If he looked up he could see his own balcony and the light in the living room and, from time to time, a figure walking past the picture window: Margot.

He smoked and thought about Gustav.

He thought again of what the headmistress had said: 'What is your tie to this boy?' and the terrible doubt, the dreadful apprehension that had come to him in the car and which had been secretly sapping his efforts to get at the truth: *Was Marianne already pregnant before Julian Hirtmann abducted her?* No, it was impossible. And yet he could not help but take out the photograph at every opportunity to look at the boy's face. He would rather not count how many times he had done so today, because he would have realised he was on the verge of some sort of madness. What was he looking for in the boy's features? A resemblance, or the absence of one; proof that Hirtmann really was the father?

He had the photograph in his hands at that very moment, and despite the dim light on the square, he was looking at the boy looking back at him when his telephone vibrated somewhere in his trousers. He checked the bright screen: he didn't recognise the number.

'Hello?'

'*So, how is that heart doing?*'

He gave a start and looked around him at the deserted square, the empty pavements. There was no one in sight, with or without a telephone.

'I beg your pardon?'

'That was quite a night you had, wasn't it, Martin? On that railway carriage . . .'

He knew that voice, he'd heard it somewhere before.

'Who's speaking?'

A small motorbike went by, the loud backfiring of its motor drowning out the voice on the telephone, so he couldn't be completely sure of what he heard next.

' . . . *both nearly fried* . . .'

'Jensen?'

'Because of you, I look like Freddy Krueger, for fuck's sake.'

Servaz held his breath and listened carefully.

'Jensen? Where are you? They told me you were undergoing treatment at a spa, and that—'

'Exactly. Last stage of my rehabilitation. Ever hear of Saint-Martin-de-Comminges? I saw you there today, my friend. Going in and out of the town hall.'

The figure down on the square, in a black coat, face turned up, while the passers-by streamed around him . . . And yet that man had seemed tall whereas Jensen was short.

'What do you want?'

A moment of silence.

'We have to talk.'

Servaz resisted the desire to hang up. To hell with him. He had to keep away from that guy, at any cost. He had been cleared, it was legitimate self-defence, but he was sure that the disciplinary inspectors were still sniffing around, waiting for him to slip up. He moved into the shadow of the arcade that ran around the market, as if he wanted to hide from anyone who might be looking his way.

'Talk about what?'

'You know.'

He closed his eyes and clenched his jaw. The man was bluffing.

'I'm sorry, but I have other things to do.'

'Your daughter, I know . . .'

This time, he felt a familiar heat radiating from his solar plexus: anger.

'*What did you say?*'

'How long does it take to get to Saint-Martin? I'll wait for you outside the thermal baths at midnight. See you later, amigo.'

There was a short silence.

'And say good evening to your daughter for me.'

Servaz looked at his phone, wishing he could hurl it against the concrete wall of the market. Jensen had hung up.

He drove there far too quickly. The motorway was deserted, apart from a few heavy goods vehicles whose rear lights were all too suddenly upon him.

He thought he probably ought to file a report. What would he put in it? That he'd had no choice because Jensen had mentioned his daughter? No police disciplinary body would be prepared to accept such an excuse. He simply shouldn't have gone there, they would say. He should have informed his superiors and he should not have acted alone. For goodness' sake, Martin . . . Now what was going to happen? What did Jensen want with him?

As soon as he left the motorway he was deep in dark countryside, where any link with those beyond it slackened, and the moon was often the only visible light. Then the mountain darkness engulfed him. He drove up the same broad valley as before, as if he were speeding through great ruined temples, crushed by a double presence: the night, and the mountains.

The streets of Saint-Martin were deserted when he arrived; there wasn't a soul in sight, and almost every window was dark. In this provincial sleep there was something of a foretaste of death. But he was no longer afraid of death. He had looked it in the face.

He parked at the entrance to the vast esplanade. There was no one in sight. On his left were the dark trees and bushes of the public gardens, where someone could easily hide; on his right, the colonnade of the thermal baths.

Suddenly he wished he could run away. He didn't want to be here. He didn't want to talk to Jensen without a witness; it was a very bad idea.

Say good evening to your daughter for me.

He got out.

He closed the car door as quietly as possible. Everything was silent. He expected to see Jensen emerge from behind a column; if he'd been in a film, that's what would have happened. Instead, Servaz scrutinised the bushes and shadows in the public garden opposite him. The wind had dropped and the bare branches of the trees were as inert as the limbs of a skeleton.

He walked further onto the esplanade.

'Jensen!'

The call reminded him of another identical one, on a stormy night, and fear came over him. That time, too, he had left his gun in the glove compartment. He was tempted to go back to his car but instead, he kept heading towards the buildings and the colonnade on his right. The moon was the only witness to his movements. Unless . . . He shivered, thinking that Jensen might be so nearby. He had a flashback: the rain pouring on the roof of the carriage, the lightning in the sky, and Jensen turning around, the flame bursting from the barrel of his gun and a projectile piercing his heart. He had felt almost nothing at the time . . . as if someone had simply punched him in the chest . . . Was he going to shoot him, like last time? *How is that heart doing?* Jensen had not been charged with the three rapes. Why did he want to see him now? And why didn't he show his face?

'Jensen?'

The arcade behind the colonnade was equally deserted. He went back out onto the vast esplanade, between two columns, and again scrutinised the shadows in the garden. Suddenly his gaze settled on one of them, roughly thirty metres away. It wasn't a bush; it was a figure. Black. Motionless. At the edge of the public garden. He narrowed his eyes. Between the trees the figure was becoming clearer: a human shape.

'Jensen!'

He began crossing the esplanade in the shadow's direction. That was when the figure moved. Not closer to him, but deeper into the garden. Servaz gave a start. For Christ's sake, where was he going?

'Hey!'

He began running. The figure was walking very quickly now between the hedges in the public garden, turning around from time to time to gauge the distance separating them. As Servaz was gaining ground, the figure began to run. Servaz ran faster. All of a sudden, he saw the figure branch off to the right. He climbed up the sloping gravel path, which then became a hiking trail, and went deeper into the forest. Servaz ran behind him, and felt a stitch in his side as if a nail had suddenly been hammered in there. He slowed down when he saw the wall of black fir trees ahead of him.

The wooded mountain rose above him, under a clear sky, and the moonlight illuminated the outline of the huge mass.

He paused to catch his breath, his hands on his knees, and he realised he was in very poor physical condition. He thought for a moment. If he went into the forest, he would not be able to see. He had neither weapon nor torch on him. Anything could happen in there. What did Jensen want? What was the point of his little game? Suddenly it occurred to him that Jensen did have a good reason to shoot him a second time: hatred. Because Jensen must hold him responsible for what had happened to him: his face disfigured forever. No doubt Jensen was hiding there, waiting for him. But to do what?

Servaz felt goosepimples on his forearms. Yet he kept moving. He followed the path that went deeper into the forest. It was pitch black in there. He went only a few metres into the woods and then stopped. He couldn't see a thing. He realised then that his frantic breathing was due not only to the fact he'd been running, but also to the fact that the only other living person in there did not necessarily wish him well.

'Jensen?'

He didn't like the sound of his own voice at all. He had tried to mask his fear, but was sure his voice had given him away, and that if he were hiding nearby, Jensen must be relishing the panic he was causing.

Servaz stayed almost twenty minutes in the same spot without moving, mindful of every movement of the shadows when the wind blew through the foliage. Once he was convinced that he was finally alone, that Jensen had left a long time ago, he came back out of the forest, frustrated but relieved, and returned to his car. That was when he saw it, the note on the windscreen, stuck under the wiper:

Were you afraid?

Kasper Strand was waiting until midnight. He lived in a three-room flat with a balcony high above Bergen, not far from the funicular, with a view over the city and the port. That was the main advantage of his exorbitantly priced flat. Even when it rained – which, in Bergen, meant every other day – he never tired of seeing the city with its seven hills and seven fjords light up when evening fell. And God knows that evening fell quickly in Bergen in the winter.

He knew he was betraying all the principles that had guided him thus far in his professional life, and that after this he wouldn't be able to look at himself in the mirror. But he needed the money. And the information he was preparing to convert into cash was worth its weight in gold, to the right person. What Kirsten Nigaard had just told him was simply incredible. Now he had to see how much he could get for it.

He gazed at the mess in the middle of the living room: one of those bloody DIY furniture flat packs that had made the fortune of a Swedish furniture salesman. After spending two hours on it he realised he had put the rails supporting the drawers on backwards. It wasn't his fault: the instructions had been drawn by people who obviously never bought flat-pack furniture. As he threw the screwdriver off into the mess somewhere, he mused that this was what his life had come to since his wife died: a flat-pack existence delivered with incomprehensible instructions. He was not equipped to live alone. Even less so to raise a fourteen-year-old girl who was in her existential crisis phase. There were so many things he had been screwing up since his wife died.

He checked his watch. Marit should have been home over an hour ago. As usual, she was late. She wouldn't even apologise. He had tried everything: scolding, the threat of grounding, careful explanations, attempts at conciliation. Nothing worked. His daughter was impervious to his every argument. And yet it was for her sake that he wanted to keep this flat which she loved but which was way beyond their means – his late wife had earned much more than him and had paid the mortgage – and that he was getting ready to make this phone call. And to mop up a few gambling debts.

He walked over to the glassed-in balcony, where he had put an armchair and a little table, and set down his whiskey glass. He took the telephone number he had found online from his pocket and scribbled on a piece of paper.

He focused on the money. He needed it, urgently; he couldn't allow himself to act like a squeamish schoolgirl, so he dialled the number, his stomach in knots.

19

Bang

In the refuge, she was woken by their breathing and sighs.

She had a headache, and the impression that everything was spinning crazily around her. Probably the brunette and that idiot guide. On second thoughts, the breathing was coming from one person: a man. The other person remained silent. And they were right nearby, only a few inches away from her.

She was afraid she might scream. But what would they think if she woke up the entire refuge for nothing? Besides, the breathing had suddenly stopped. She couldn't hear anything now, other than the blood pounding in her ears.

Had she been dreaming?

Later, Emmanuelle thought she heard another sound. Because of her fear she couldn't get back to sleep. It was dark, but she was sure someone was moving over there by the kitchen. Someone was walking without making a sound, furtively, like a thief . . .

She could feel her heart beating faster. There was something about the way the shadow was moving that paralysed her, glued her to her mattress. Something cunning, hidden, *hostile* . . . She thought about the sound they had heard earlier, in the evening, and how Corinne had been convinced she had seen someone outside. Emmanuelle snuggled deeper into her sleeping bag, telling herself that when she awoke her reaction would seem ridiculous, irrational, infantile – night-time fantasies. But she didn't feel reassured. She would have liked to disappear, or wake the others. But she couldn't make a sound. Because now she could see it clearly in the grey darkness – *the shadow was coming towards her* . . .

A hand covered her mouth just as something sharp jabbed her in the neck.

'Shush.'

She could smell the metallic, acrid odour of the hand gagging her. She associated it, oddly, with the smell of a copper pipe: she had repaired all the plumbing in her house herself, and she knew that smell. Then she understood it was the smell of blood, and it was in her nostrils: as was often the case when she fell prey to violent emotions, she was having a nosebleed.

The voice in her ear – even more hissing and sibilant than before – said, 'If you cry out, if you try to struggle, I'll kill you. And then I'll kill all the others.'

As if to convince her, the tip dug a little deeper into her neck and she could feel the bite of the blade in her skin. It felt like a huge slab of stone had been placed on her chest, preventing her from breathing. She could hear the zip of the sleeping bag being opened in the dark.

'Now you get out of there and stand up, and not a sound.'

She tried, she wanted to do what he told her, but her legs were trembling so violently that she stumbled and banged her knee against the wooden bench. She let out a little cry, a whimper. He immediately grabbed her and his hand crushed her thin arm through her pyjamas.

'Shut up!' he growled in a low voice. 'Or else.'

Now she could see him fairly distinctly in the half-light; he was still wearing his hood. He must not even have got undressed, just waited until the others were asleep. She could hear snoring coming from the bunks. Under her bare feet the floor of the refuge was like ice. He was holding her by the arm.

'Let's go.'

She knew they were going outside where he could rape her without fear of being disturbed. And would he kill her afterwards? Now was the time to do something. He must have felt her resistance, because the blade went deeper into the left side of her neck.

'You make a move or a sound and I'll cut your throat.'

She knew what it must feel like, to be a gazelle or a baby elephant that a predator has cut off from the rest of the herd. Never leave the circle. The cold outside went straight through her winter pyjamas. Her toes curled when her feet hit the snow and she trembled even more violently. She had never felt more alone.

'Why are you doing this?' she asked.

She could hear her plaintive, tearful tone. She needed to speak, to stop him; perhaps, if she could make him listen to reason . . .

'Why? Why?'

'Shut your gob!'

Now that they were outside and the wind was whirling with snow-flakes all around them, he no longer kept his voice down.

'Don't do this! Please! Please don't! Don't hurt me!'

'Will you shut up!'

'I'll give you money, I won't say anything. I'll . . . you . . .'

She no longer knew what she was saying, a flood of incoherent words in no order.

'Shut the fuck up!'

He gave her a punch in the stomach that took her breath away and she fell to her knees in the snow, her lungs empty. Bile rose in her throat then subsided; her belly was burning. Suddenly she felt she was being pulled by her feet and she fell backwards. Her skull hit the stone wall of the refuge and she saw stars. A moment later the man was on top of her. She could feel the snow against her buttocks as he feverishly sought to pull her pyjamas down her legs. She saw his eyes like those of a wild animal gleaming in the shadow of his hood; he had bad breath and she felt a wave of nausea. With one hand he was pressing the cold tip of the knife against her throat, almost stopping her breathing; with the other he began to undo his trousers.

When she felt the man's hands between her thighs she struggled and said, 'No, no, no!' but the tip of the blade went a bit deeper, stopping her words. She stayed with her mouth open, and the man was about to lean down to kiss her when something happened behind him. At first she couldn't tell what it was, other than that it was even more frightening than the burned man himself. She glimpsed a dark shadow emerging from the woods and rushing at them, growing larger with incredible speed. Her aggressor could not see what was coming. The shadow that came from the woods threw itself on him and practically lay on his back – as if it too wanted to rape her – and she saw a hand wearing a black glove, and extending from that hand, a gun, its barrel now pressing against the burned man's right temple.

This was the first time she had ever seen a gun, other than in a film, but she knew exactly what she was seeing. Cinema and television have made us familiar with a world the majority of us do not know in real life: a world of violence, firearms and blood.

'What the—?' was all the burned face had time to say, when he felt the weight of another body on his back.

One second afterwards a flame burst into the space between the barrel of the gun and the burned man's hood, and there was a single, deafening detonation, which caused the night to tremble. She felt the pressure of it in her eardrums, which immediately began to ring. Her aggressor's neck seemed to break, his head falling to one side like a dead chicken's, and a dark cloud of particles – blood, bone, brains – splattered in the opposite direction from the hood like a black geyser, before his entire body collapsed onto the snow, dead, freeing her from its weight. She thought she heard herself scream. The shadow was already on its feet, the smoking gun dangling in its hand.

For a split second she thought that the shadow looking down at her was going to kill her, too. Instead, it disappeared the way it had come.

This time, she was certain: she screamed.

The loud detonation and her hysterical screaming woke the entire refuge. One after the other the occupants sat up in their bunks, reached for their anoraks and rushed outside. First they called her, and when she did not reply they went around the refuge.

'Fuck!' exclaimed the guide, who was the first to find them: Emmanuelle in her pyjamas, and the corpse. He recoiled.

The snow was absorbing the blood so that the puddle forming underneath the rapist's skull was not that big: on the contrary, the hot blood and brain matter had formed a little hollow, an almost vertical funnel in the fresh snow.

Emmanuelle was trembling violently, both from the cold and the shock; her mouth wide open, she gasped and sobbed. The guide knelt down next to her and took her by the shoulders.

'It's all over,' he said. 'It's over.'

But what was over? He hadn't the slightest idea what had happened out here, for fuck's sake. He pulled Emmanuelle to him and held her closer to comfort her and warm her up.

'Did you do it?' he asked quietly. 'Did you do . . . this? *Who shot him?*'

She shook her head vigorously in denial, still gasping and sobbing on his shoulder, unable to say a word. The others had surrounded them now. They looked from the corpse to Emmanuelle, and then to the woods, their eyes like frightened animals'.

'Don't touch anything,' said Beltran suddenly. 'We have to call the police.'

He took out his mobile and looked at the screen.

'Shit, no network. We're too high up.'

'Use the emergency phone in the refuge,' said the guide, still on his knees, looking up at him, then he turned back to Emmanuelle.

'Can you stand?'

He helped Emmanuelle to her feet and supported her, because her legs were shaking and threatened to collapse beneath her. They went cautiously around the dead body, and he took her back inside, where the other two had already taken refuge.

'What happened?' asked Corinne as gently as possible.

'You . . . you were . . . right: there really was . . . someone.'

Emmanuelle's teeth were chattering noisily.

'Yes. He's out there,' said the guide with a shudder. 'And what's more, he's armed.'

20

Gold Dot

The first glow of day was tingeing the sky with pink between the clouds and the mountaintops when the forensic identification specialists from the national gendarmerie arrived at last, along with the crew from the Research Unit. Captain Saint-Germès was not sorry to see the headlights flashing through the trees: he had compiled his initial findings, and sealed the perimeter with his team, fear in his gut. The fear of messing up. It wasn't every day that the gendarmerie from Saint-Martin-de-Comminges was entrusted with a case like this one.

He watched the convoy coming his way, jolting along through the snow. Five vehicles, including a small truck with a raised roof, which he recognised as the itinerant laboratory of the Pau Research Unit. Saint-Germès had never seen a crew like this before. Like everyone around here, he had heard about the events of the winter 2008–9 – they belonged to local legend, and his senior colleagues enjoyed talking about them, particularly when winter set in – but back then he hadn't yet started in this position. It was his predecessor, Captain Maillard, who had overseen the whole affair, with the Pau Research Unit and the Toulouse crime unit. Maillard had been transferred, as had a good number of the gendarmes who had been here at the time. This was the first violent death the force had been confronted with since. And what had actually happened last night? He didn't have a clue, it was all extremely muddled. Total chaos in fact. The witness statements had merely added to the confusion. What they'd gleaned made no sense: a hiker had dragged one of the women in the group outside in the snow at three o'clock in the morning to rape her, and a shadow appeared out of nowhere to shoot him in the temple, then vanished. A complete cock-and-bull story.

The vehicles pulled up outside the refuge, and several members of the Research Unit got out. In the lead was a man with glasses and a square jaw. Like the others he was wearing a thick jumper beneath his tactical vest. His light blue eyes examined Saint-Germès through his lenses as he walked towards him, and he conscientiously squeezed the captain's hand in his own.

'What have we got?'

'Let's see now. She says the victim dragged her outside to rape her, threatening her with a knife, and that some guy burst out of the woods and shot him in the head, is that right?'

'Correct.'

'I've never heard anything so absurd,' concluded the man with the blue eyes, whose name was Morel.

'But we did find the knife,' protested Saint-Germès, who already hated the guy, with his superior attitude.

'So what? She could very well have put it there herself. We'll have to check whether this woman has any psychiatric history, whether she belongs to a shooting range, if she's already had relationship issues with men, and whether she and the victim knew each other before the hike. The whole business seems dodgy.'

Implying, *you didn't interview the witnesses properly.*

Saint-Germès shrugged: it was no longer his problem. He observed the maelstrom around them. There were electrical cables running all over the place, and lamps had been lit, making the crime scene and the refuge as bright as day. The technicians in white overalls almost blended in with the snow, as if they were wearing camouflage gear. They came and went around the policemen, shovelling the snow, lifting fingerprints and shot residue and biological samples; they took measurements, called out to each other. It gave a deceptive impression of chaos, but every man knew what he was supposed to do. Crouching by the victim's head, the pathologist looked up at them and pulled down the blue mask on his chin, a little xenon lamp in his hand.

'The bullet entered the skull and came out again, terminating all vital functions. The man didn't have time to feel a thing. As if someone flicked a switch. *Off.* Looks like he didn't have a very good year,' he added, pointing with a gloved finger to the burn marks around the man's mouth and on one cheek, where the scars had scarcely had time to form. 'Given the nearly constant temperature during the night, I would say that this happened between three and five o'clock in the morning.'

Which tallied with the witnesses' statements.

'There are footprints here that do not match either the victim's shoes, or the woman's,' a technician called out a bit further along. 'Someone came out of the woods and went over to them, then left again the way they had come.' He pointed to the footprints. 'And he ran on his way here: the tip of his shoe sunk in much deeper than the heel. Then he stood here without moving: the footprints are uniform. He turned towards him' – he pointed to the body – 'and left again the way he came. Not running, this time.'

Saint-Germès glanced at Morel, who didn't blink.

'Where's the canine unit?' asked Morel.

'They're on their way,' someone said.

'Hey, come and have a look at this!' called another voice a few yards away.

They turned towards a technician who was using a thermal camera. *Infrared thermography*, thought Saint-Germès. He saw the technician put the camera down next to him, take a pair of tweezers out of his overalls and squat down, motioning to them to come closer. Then the man stood up. In the tweezers in his blue-gloved hand he was holding a used casing. *The* casing – because only one projectile had been fired.

'What is it?' asked Morel.

The technician pulled his blue mask down onto his chin just as the pathologist had done. He was frowning, puzzled.

'A dum-dum bullet,' he replied.

Saint-Germès raised an eyebrow. The sale of expanding bullets was outlawed in France, except to hunters, sports marksmen, *and cops*.

'It's a 9 mm,' added the technician, turning it slowly before his eyes, seeming more and more concerned. 'Captain,' he said suddenly, in a changed voice.

'What's the matter?' asked Morel.

'The matter is, that this is a Speer Gold Dot. Fucking hell . . .'

'Are you sure?'

The technician nodded slowly. Saint-Germès and Morel exchanged a glance. Well well, now Morel had come down off his high horse. *He can see the shit is about to hit the fan*, thought Saint-Germès. *That's not good. Not good at all.* There was virtually only one category of individual in France who used Speer Gold Dot bullets: cops and gendarmes.

21

Belvedere

Despite the cold weather – at least it wasn't raining – Kirsten was having her breakfast at a pavement café on the place du Capitole – a French breakfast: coffee with milk, croissants, and orange juice – when she saw Servaz coming towards her across the esplanade. She immediately sensed that something had happened.

And that he hadn't got a lot of sleep.

And that he was in what is commonly referred to as a bad mood, although she had rarely seen him smile since their first meeting in the office of the head of the crime unit.

When he sat down across from her she realised it was more serious than that: he seemed disorientated. Like a child who's lost his parents in the crowd.

'What's going on?' she asked, in English.

He seemed to be in urgent need of a cup of coffee, so she ordered two more from the waiter. Martin turned to look at her. Then, in a toneless voice he related not only the night's events, but also what had happened before Kirsten had arrived in Toulouse.

'Why didn't you ask me to go with you last night?' she said, when he had finished.

'Because it has nothing to do with your reason for being in Toulouse.'

'Have you told Stehlin about it?'

'Not yet.'

'Hmm. But are you going to?'

'Yes.'

The waiter arrived with their coffees and she saw Martin's hand was trembling as he lifted the cup to his lips, so much so that drops of coffee fell on the table and on his thighs.

'So you were in a coma all that time? And that's why I found you a bit . . . *strange* in the beginning?'

'Possibly.'

'Shit, that's a hell of a story.'

He could not help but smile.

'I'll give you that.'

'Martin . . .'

'Yes?'

'You have to trust me, and above all, I would like you to see me as a partner, not just some policewoman from the cold north who doesn't speak a word of French. Do you hear me?'

This time he smiled openly when she gave him a stern look, because he knew that her sternness concealed a newfound affection.

'Martin, for fuck's sake, you went there in the middle of the night without telling anyone!'

Stehlin looked as if he were about to explode. Literally. A thick, sinuous vein appeared beneath the skin on his left temple, and his face was the colour of a watermelon.

'I had no choice,' said Servaz, to exonerate himself. 'He threatened to go after Margot.'

That wasn't exactly what Jensen had done, but never mind.

'Yes, you did have a choice!' barked the director of the crime unit, sputtering. 'You could have told us. Dammit, we would have sent someone in your place!'

'I wanted to hear what he had to tell me.'

'Oh, really? Well I'm sorry, but it seems to me that the guy took you for a ride and you're no further ahead than you were; correct me if I'm wrong.'

Servaz didn't reply.

'The problem is that if the police inspectors find out, you'll be in deep shit, and so will I,' said the director.

Here we go, thought Servaz. 'Why should they find out? Who would tell them? Jensen? He's going to explain that he enjoyed giving me the run-around at night and talked to me about my daughter on the telephone?'

Stehlin glanced cautiously at Kirsten, as if her presence prevented Martin from saying certain things.

'Martin, you have to file a report, and Florian Jensen has to be interviewed. And what will he say, in your opinion?'

'I have no idea.'

'I don't like this business one bit.'

'Neither do I.'

'Do you think he was bluffing, about your daughter?'

'I don't know. The guy has it in for me.'

'Do you want me to send someone for your daughter?'

Servaz hesitated. He thought about Hirtmann.

'Yes,' he said finally. 'Not just because of Jensen. If Hirtmann is anywhere around, I don't want Margot to end up like Marianne Bokhanowsky. It's time for me to persuade her to go back to Quebec. She'll be safe there.'

In Vienna, Bernhard Zehetmayer was gazing out of the window at the rain-swept gardens of the Belvedere Museum. Dotted with trimmed hedges, pools and sculptures, they sloped gently down to the Rennweg. As they did every day, mysterious sphinxes sat smiling on the grand terrace, indifferent to the pouring rain. This was the Vienna he loved, this eternal Vienna which had hardly changed since Canaletto. Indifferent to fashion, decadence, the degradation of manners, or the ugliness that to his mind governed the modern world.

Zehetmayer turned around.

A crowd of people in wet anoraks hurried in, dripping onto the floors of the museum. Most of them had come to admire Klimt's minor works. So much devotion for a vulgar interior decorator. What a bunch of imbeciles. Yet another Gustav. But one was a gnome compared to the other . . . He greatly preferred Schiele's *Death and the Maiden* to Klimt's *The Kiss*. At least Schiele didn't sprinkle his paintings with gilt confetti, flimflam, and artifices scarcely worthy of a cabaret poster. His style was raw, without flourishes, unrestrained. Schiele's last works had been drawings of his wife Edith, six months pregnant and mortally ill, on her deathbed, drawings he made before he himself succumbed to Spanish flu three days later. He really had guts, my God . . . The fact that Klimt had become Vienna's most emblematic artist was proof of how low the city had fallen.

He saw Wieser's short stocky figure approaching through the crowd.

'Hi,' said Wieser when he drew level. 'You have news?'

'They've picked up Gustav's trail,' he said.

Wieser gave a start.

'The boy?'

Zehetmayer shrugged irritably. *No, Gustav Klimt, idiot.*

'He was staying in the southwest of France, in a little town in the mountains. He even went to school there, until last summer.'

'How do we know it's him?'

'There isn't the slightest doubt: the headmistress recognised his photograph, and he was going by the name of that policeman, the one Hirtmann seems to be obsessed with.'

'What? I don't understand.'

I'm not surprised, thought the Emperor.

'The main thing is that we're getting closer,' he said, forcing himself to stay calm. 'In fact, we've never been closer. This is a unique opportunity. Hirtmann will probably visit the child as soon as he can. If we can pick up his trail, we will find out where, sooner or later, Hirtmann will turn up. This time we have to pull out all the stops. Finding this child is a gift from heaven.'

22

Facial Composite

'Did you see his face?'

Emmanuelle Vengud frowned.

'He was wearing a hood like . . . like *the other guy*,' she answered, after thinking for a moment. 'And it was dark. I couldn't see much. But I got a glimpse of him, yes, in the shadow of his hood. He was very close, you see, and—'

'How old would you say he was?'

Again, she hesitated.

'Forty, forty-five, I guess . . . Not young, in any case.'

'Fair, dark?'

'He was wearing a—'

'A hood, yes, I know,' he said, his tone understanding but impatient all the same. 'Do you know anything about weapons?'

'No. Nothing at all.'

He sighed and typed something on his keyboard.

'Wait,' she said.

Morel looked up.

'I thought I saw something.'

Her tone of voice immediately alerted him. He swung around on his chair and nodded discreetly, not wanting to distract her from her thoughts.

'To do with the weapon, I mean.'

'Go on.'

'I think he was wearing a holster. I saw it when he stood up and leaned over . . . the victim.'

'A holster?'

Morel felt as if he had been punched. He took a deep breath, and cracked the knuckles of his interwoven fingers.

'Yes. On his hip, there,' she added, showing him where she meant.

'Are you sure?'

He was aware that the tone of his voice had alerted her in turn.

'Why, is it important?'

'Well, yes, rather.'

'Yes, I'm sure. He had a case attached to his belt, right here.'

Good God!

'One moment, please.'

He picked up his telephone.

'Sir,' he said after waiting a moment, 'Captain Morel speaking. I have to talk to you, but not over the phone. As soon as possible.'

Then he turned back to the young woman.

'We're going to try to draw up a composite. With the hood,' he specified. 'Don't be anxious, don't put any pressure on yourself: this is just to get a few buried memories to come to the surface, all right? You never know. Maybe you saw more than you think.'

Stehlin was very pale when he hung up. He had just called the gendarmerie in Saint-Martin to tell them to take Jensen into custody. By mutual agreement, they had finally decided that Servaz would file a report: he would detail Jensen's call and his indirect threat regarding Margot, but he would deny it if Jensen claimed to have seen him in Saint-Martin. After all, there were no witnesses. The only risk was Martin's mobile, which must have activated a few transmitters along his route, but Stehlin figured that no lawyer could obtain a requisition on the basis of his client's statement alone.

It was a risk they could afford to take. And if it backfired, Stehlin could cover himself by saying he hadn't known the full story. Servaz had accepted the deal.

'What's the matter?' asked Servaz when he saw Stehlin's face.

The man was looking at him as if he were a stranger. A mystery. Servaz felt as if someone were injecting cold liquid into his spine.

'What did they say?'

Stehlin seemed to wake up. He looked first at Servaz, then Kirsten, then back at Servaz.

'Jensen is dead. Someone shot him. Last night. In the head, point blank. They think it was a cop.'

MARTIN

23

Mother Nature, That Bloodthirsty Dog

Subsequently, no one could explain how the news had got out so quickly. Did the leak come from the gendarmerie, the public prosecutor's office, or the police? Still, by the end of the day, the rumour had gone through every department, with a number of variants but one common foundation: basically, a cop had killed that little shithead Jensen just as he was about to commit another rape.

It was like something in a Marvel or a DC comic, where at the last minute masked avengers appear out of the night to come to the rescue of the good citizens of Gotham or NYC.

In some versions the rape had been committed, in others it had not. Jensen had been killed by a bullet to the head, or the heart, or even – in one of the most daring versions – the avenging gunman had first blown his balls to bits. Everyone agreed that no one on this earth – other than his ageing mother – would mourn the death of that scumbag, and that it would surely make the air more pleasant to breathe, and the highways safer for a number of women in the region; nevertheless, fear was growing among the forces of the law, because the avenger (virtually no one used the word killer) came from among their ranks, and the policemen's police would have a field day.

And then another name popped up in all the conversations.

Servaz.

Every cop in Toulouse knew what had happened on the roof of that railway carriage, and that after Jensen shot him Servaz had gone into a coma. And it took only a few hours for the boldest theories to start making the rounds. But no one in the regional crime unit was more worried and perturbed than Divisional Commissioner Stehlin. He kept going over and over the conversation he had had with Martin when he'd emerged from his coma and told Stehlin of his conviction that it was Florian Jensen who had killed the woman in Montauban. Some ridiculous story about a white cat that was missing an ear.

It had also not escaped his attention that Martin had changed since his coma. In fact everyone had noticed it – even if they avoided talking about it. Something had happened while he was unconscious. Could he have become a murderer? Stehlin found it hard to believe, but the suspicion never completely left him – and suspicion is a far more dreadful poison than any certainty, even when it's about something unpleasant.

He had read somewhere that by using a scanner and a computer, scientists had been able to decode several participants' brain signals and reconstitute the images of the film they were watching; other scientists had perfected a brain–computer interface that could, in a similar fashion, reconstitute the words the participant had just read. They were on the verge of being able to read minds . . . What an absolute nightmare that would be: a life without secrets, without the possibility of lying, of hiding. Without lies, or at least a few compromises with the truth, life would quickly become unbearable. But it would mean terrific progress for the police. Except that before long they'd be able to replace investigators with technicians and machines. Today, however, Stehlin would have liked to have such technology at his fingertips.

What part was truth, what part lies, in Servaz's story? One thing was certain: Servaz really had gone to Saint-Martin-de-Comminges the previous night. He had approached Jensen. And that same night, a few hours later, Jensen had been shot dead with a policeman's gun.

No one in the crime unit was more worried and perturbed than Divisional Commissioner Stehlin – except perhaps Vincent Espérandieu and Samira Cheung. Like everyone else, they had heard the rumours – Jensen had been killed, and Martin had seen him, alone, that same night. They shared an office and ever since the rumour had reached them they had been cautiously refraining from saying a single word. But the rumour filled their thoughts, nevertheless.

In the end, it was Samira who cleared her throat.

'Do you think he could have done it?'

Espérandieu removed the headphones from his ears, where M83 had been unfurling its delicate rhythms.

'What?'

'Do you think he could have done it?'

He shot her a dark look.

'You must be joking.'

'Do I sound like it?'

Espérandieu swivelled around on his chair.

'Fuck, Samira! It's Martin we're talking about!'

'I know that very well,' she said, annoyed. 'The question is, which Martin, exactly? The one from before the coma or the one from after?'

He gave a wave of his hand and turned back to his screen.

'Drop it. I don't want to hear it.'

'Don't tell me you haven't noticed.'

He sighed, then swivelled around again.

'Noticed what?'

'That he's changed.'

Espérandieu didn't answer.

'He doesn't even bother with us now.'

'Give him time. He's only just come back to work.'

'And that woman, what's she doing here?'

'The Norwegian? You heard the same thing I did.'

'The fact remains that he only has time for her.'

'Are you jealous?'

He saw Samira frown.

'Fuck, you can be such a cretin sometimes. Don't you think it's strange how he's more trusting around a stranger than with us?'

'I don't know.'

Samira shook her head.

'It scares me, it really does. Fuck, even if it's not him, they're going to give him a really hard time. It's a foregone conclusion.'

'Unless they do find who did it,' snapped Vincent.

'Oh yeah? And what if they find out that person is him?'

The next day, Olga Lumbroso, deputy public prosecutor at the county court in Saint-Gaudens, looked exhausted. She did not hide her weariness. A case like this was every investigating magistrate's dream – but as it happened, the magistrate who was officiating in that position at the county court in Saint-Gaudens was not even an investigating magistrate. Lumbroso had just listened to the gendarme seated across from her, she had read his report, and in her opinion the young judge who ordinarily dealt in family law was not cut out to deal with this matter. She had merely been assigned to the case in the absence of an actual investigating magistrate. When the court reopened in 2014, a major regional newspaper had published a triumphant headline about 'the return of law and order to Comminges', but since then the little court had merely been getting by.

There were eleven civil servants in all, and their workload was getting heavier by the day; the files piled up and they shared them out as best they could. And now they'd been landed with this whacking great case.

'A policeman, you said?'

'Or someone posing as one,' specified Morel.

The woman across from him went back to reading the report.

'And he came out of the forest at three o'clock in the morning, when it was several degrees below zero, to shoot this Jensen guy, then vanished into thin air?'

She had read that part of the report the way she would have read a fairy tale to her son.

'I know, I know. I thought the same as you: put like that, it seems insane. But that is what happened.'

She closed the file and placed her freckled hands on it firmly, as if it might open again against her will.

'This is a matter for the court of appeal,' she said decisively. 'We have neither the technical nor the human resources to deal with a case like this here. I'm going to call Cathy d'Humières in Toulouse. In my opinion, they will refer the case to the Inspectorate.'

The policemen's police. Morel nodded cautiously. The whole business smelled of sulphur, shit and trouble. And a load of bloody great hassle as well. The deputy prosecutor across from him was well aware of this.

'How many people know about the weapon and holster?'

'Too many,' he replied. 'There were masses of people at the crime scene. We tried to limit the damage, but it's impossible to say who heard what.'

He saw her frown.

'So, sooner or later, there'll be a leak to the press.' She reached for her telephone. 'We have to act quickly. At least show we haven't been caught unawares, and that we got onto it right away.'

She paused for a second.

'But, in any case, let's not kid ourselves: the storm is coming, and it will sweep everything in its wake. A cop playing avenger in the night: what a shambles. The press will have a field day.'

In Toulouse, Cathy d'Humières was at Les Sales Gosses dining on a perfectly cooked egg and a *souris d'agneau* when her mobile rang in her handbag.

The presiding magistrate of the Toulouse county court had risen through the ranks, having started at the bottom as public prosecutor in Saint-Martin-de-Comminges, where the case of the decapitated horse and the holiday camp had earned her a passing notoriety.

Physically, she was something of a cliché: a stern face, aquiline profile, sparkling gaze, thin mouth and wilful chin. Most of the people who did not know her found her intimidating; those who did know her either admired her or feared her, frequently both at the same time. And there was a third category: those she had humiliated – primarily people who were incompetent or scheming – and who despised her.

Cathy d'Humières took out her phone and listened to the deputy prosecutor from Saint-Gaudens without saying a word. When Olga Lumbroso had finished, she simply said, 'Fine, send the file on to me.'

A new wrinkle appeared on her brow.

'Your favourite dessert?' suggested the waiter.

This was a mixture of banoffee pie and *feuillantine* with Carambar ice cream.

'No, not today. A double espresso. No, make that a triple. Thank you. And do you by any chance have an aspirin?'

'Do you have a headache?'

She smiled at the young man's perspicacity.

'Not yet. But I feel one coming on.'

'You'll have to change your report,' said Stehlin; he had just got back from another meeting with the prosecutor.

Servaz said nothing.

'Sooner or later, they're going to take an interest in you – and your movements that night. If they find out you went to Saint-Martin, and you didn't mention it, can you imagine the consequences?'

'I know.'

'Good job I haven't sent it yet, that report . . .'

Servaz felt a surge of anger. He had immediately perceived Stehlin's wariness when he got back from the court. As if they had said things there which had changed his point of view. Shouldn't he have started by giving the benefit of the doubt to his subordinate, someone he'd been working with for years? Servaz wondered what would happen if things really got out of hand. Would Stehlin fight his corner, or would he instead try to cover his arse and think of his own career? Stehlin was fair, unlike Vilmer, his predecessor, and Servaz got along well with him. But it was when things got rough that you judged your friends, and your bosses, too.

'Martin . . .'

'Yes?'

'Two nights ago, in Saint-Martin, did you see him or not?'

'Jensen? No.' He hesitated. 'That is, I did see someone, but I'll say it again: I ran after someone who *could have been* Jensen. But he vanished into the forest behind the thermal baths. That was after midnight. I went back to my car and found a note on my windscreen.'

'A note? You didn't mention that last time.'

'Yes. It said, "Were you afraid?"'

'Good God.'

Stehlin looked as if he had seen his wife's ghost; she had died two years earlier.

'Jensen was killed by a cop's weapon,' he said. 'They're going to be looking for a motive. And the one that will immediately capture their attention is yours.'

Servaz stiffened. He thought about the first thing he had done when he'd found out that Jensen had been killed with a police weapon: he went to make sure his own gun was still where it belonged.

'What? What motive?'

'For Christ's sake, Martin! The man shot you in the heart and you almost died! You told me yourself when you came out of the coma that you were convinced he was the one who had murdered the woman in Montauban. And he's threatened your daughter!'

'He just made an allusion to—'

'And you went running back to Saint-Martin double-quick,' Stehlin said. 'In the middle of the night, goddammit. And you saw Jensen a few hours before he was shot. Bloody hell!'

So there it was: Stehlin had shown what was really on his mind.

Servaz could hear the tone of fear in his boss's voice. This wasn't the first time he had found him too cautious, too fearful, and he suspected him of wanting to avoid making waves at any cost – even if it interfered with the smooth running of his department. Suddenly Servaz was absolutely convinced that Stehlin would not hesitate to dump him in order to save his own skin. He looked at him. His boss's complexion was ashen; he'd already gone back into his shell.

'I will assume my responsibility,' he said firmly.

'I want a new report without any grey areas,' said Stehlin, looking up at him as if he were waking up. 'You have to write exactly what happened.'

'May I remind you whose idea it was not to mention my trip to Saint-Martin?' replied Servaz, standing up and pushing back his chair a bit too aggressively.

Stehlin did not react. Again, he was elsewhere. Probably busy thinking about securing his own interests. Thinking about the consequences for his career, which thus far had been pleasantly linear and on the rise.

How to cut off the rotten branch before it contaminated the whole tree.

How to build a firewall between himself and Servaz.

'Well?' asked Kirsten when they were on the terrace at the Cactus.

'Well nothing,' said Servaz, sitting down. 'There's going to be an internal investigation.'

The last internal investigation she remembered in Norway was the one that had been carried out after the massacre at Utøya, that little island where Anders Breivik had killed sixty-nine victims, most of them teenagers: to find out why the Norwegian police had arrived so late. Informed of the shooting on the island, they had taken an hour and a half to get there, leaving the adolescents at the mercy of Breivik's lethal fury. The police had had to explain why they had gone by land and boat rather than use a helicopter, and why their boat had broken down. (It was too small for the number of passengers and the amount of equipment on board, and had begun to take on water.)

'What did he say?'

'That I have to file a report. In it I will explain that I met a guy who would be killed by a cop's weapon three hours later, in the middle of the night, a guy who months earlier had landed me in hospital, and who had threatened my daughter, and whom I suspected of an unsolved murder . . . Give or take a few things.'

He said these words with a certain fatalism.

'I think I'll go back to Norway,' Kirsten said. 'I've nothing more to do here. We've reached an impasse.'

He looked at her. Instinctively his fingers felt for the picture of Gustav in his pocket.

'When will you leave?'

'Tomorrow. I have a flight at seven in the morning, with a one-hour stopover at Charles de Gaulle.'

He nodded, and said nothing. She stood up.

'I'll do some sightseeing in the meantime. Shall we meet for dinner this evening?'

He nodded again and watched as she walked away. As soon as she was out of sight he took out his mobile.

'Imagination can run from normal to pathological. This includes dreams, fantasies, hallucinations, and so on,' said Dr Xavier, sitting in his swivel chair.

'I'm not talking about hallucinations, but amnesia,' Servaz replied. 'Amnesia would be the opposite of imagination, wouldn't it?'

'What exactly are you getting at?'

'Just suppose . . . just suppose I went to Saint-Martin one night, and I thought I did one thing but in fact I did something else, far more serious, and I forgot what it was . . .'

There was a pause behind him.

'Can you be a bit more precise?'

'No.'

'Okay. There are several forms of amnesia. The ones that might correspond to what you are describing – at least based on the little information I have – are: partial amnesia, which is a disturbance of the memory in a given time lapse, generally following a head injury or mental confusion . . . Did you hurt your head on the night in question?'

'No. At least not to my knowledge.'

'Okay, sure. Then there is the second form, lacunar amnesia, which is based on one or more very precise events. The same goes for elective amnesia. This type of amnesia can be observed in patients presenting, um, neurosis or a psychiatric disturbance.'

Xavier paused.

'Finally, there is anterograde amnesia, which means an inability to create memories. This thing you think you did and have forgotten—'

'No, no. I don't think I did it. It's a purely hypothetical question.'

'Right, okay. But this "purely hypothetical question": does it have anything to do with the fact that two nights ago a man was killed not far from here with a policeman's gun?'

Five p.m. When he left Dr Xavier's surgery, evening was already falling in the streets of Saint-Martin, and the air was fragrant with the smoke from wood-burning stoves, fir trees on the nearby mountain, and car exhaust fumes. A few snow flurries whirled in the cold air. The sculpted wooden balconies, the imitation chalet pediments, and the dark little cobblestoned streets gave this part of the town a fairy-tale atmosphere that was both childlike and sinister. He had left his car by the river, and in the darkness he felt the damp chill rising from the fast-moving waters below the promenade.

When he sat behind the wheel of his car, for a moment he froze. What was that? There was a smell inside the car. Like a trace of aftershave. He turned to look behind him, but of course there was no one. He leaned towards the glove compartment: his gun was still there, in its holster.

He drove out of town and was about to turn off by the sign pointing to the valley and the motorway when he felt an itch at the back of his head. He drove past the sign. And the following exit, which led to the campsites and a small industrial estate. He took the third exit. Immediately afterwards the road began to climb. After two hairpin bends he could see the roofs of Saint-Martin below him.

The itch got worse. He hadn't come this way in years. It was completely dark outside now. Below him the little lights of Saint-Martin on their blanket of snow looked like a river of gems in a jeweller's window, nestled in their dark Alpine setting. He thought that this sort of landscape must seem quite familiar to Kirsten, and he suddenly had a pang of regret that she was not there.

He went through a hamlet consisting of four houses. Then a second one, a kilometre further along, full of white roofs and closed shutters. At the next fork in the road he turned left, and the road led down a gentle slope. The snowy meadows shone faintly blue in the evening light, and banks of mist were beginning to rise from the hollows. He drove down the hill and into a new village that was slightly bigger but just as sleepy as all the others. He left the village almost at once and continued on his way into the forest.

Before long he could see the ruined buildings of Les Isards holiday camp, although the rusty sign at the entrance to the drive had vanished. But he hadn't come for the holiday camp; he drove right past. His headlights bore a tunnel of light through the fir trees, piercing the ever-denser mist, sculpting the low-lying snow-laden branches that bordered the road as if they were paper cutouts. The only other source of light was the blue gleam from the dials on his dashboard. All notion of time and space suddenly seemed abolished.

But not memory . . .

Images surfaced as if there were a cinema screen inside his head. Before long he entered a tunnel carved through the rock.

He wondered if the sign would still be there, right after the tunnel. It was. Fastened to the parapet of the little bridge that crossed the cascade: CHARLES WARGNIER INSTITUTE FOR FORENSIC PSYCHIATRY.

As he took the steep road, it was as if he had stepped into a time machine.

The fire started by Lisa Ferney, the head nurse, had left nothing of the walls but stumps, and when he stepped out of the car into the icy night air, they reminded him of the great standing stones at Stonehenge.

There wasn't much left, but you could tell how imposing the building must have been; it was like strolling through the remains of the Forum in Rome. That towering style that had been used all over the Pyrenees region, and which dated from the first half of the twentieth century, to build hotels, power plants, thermal baths, ski resorts . . . But this place hosted neither spa-goers nor tourists. For a few years the Wargnier Institute had housed eighty-eight extremely dangerous individuals, presenting mental health issues compounded by violence and criminality: patients who were too violent even for an ordinary psychiatric hospital, inmates whose psychoses were too serious for them to be left in prison, rapists and murderers from all over Europe whom the courts had judged insane. The Wargnier Institute was a pilot project. They had been shut away in these mountains, far out of reach of society. All sorts of treatments had been tested on them, of a more or less experimental nature. Servaz recalled that the young psychologist Diane Berg had compared them to 'mountain tigers'. And in the middle of the pride, the alpha male.

The Lion King.

The individual at the top of the food chain.

Julian Hirtmann.

Suddenly he felt a film of ice close around his heart as he thought of Gustav, who was living within reach of one of those monsters. And of Jensen, killed by a policeman's gun. Ghosts of the past and shadows of the present. He felt his fear growing. The stratagem was obvious: *someone wanted him to take the rap.*

Why had he come here? What had got into him? What was the point? And what did he hope to find? It was absolutely calm but then suddenly he heard a dull, distant sound below him in the valley. Like the hum of an insect.

Down below him a car was coming nearer.

He squinted until the headlights reappeared in the forest. For several minutes he watched their flashing progression through the trees on the road below; then they vanished into the tunnel.

He expected to see the headlights emerge 100 metres from there at any moment and come straight at him. Who could be driving along this road at this hour? Had he been followed? Not once had he looked in his rearview mirror during the entire drive between Saint-Martin and the valley: why should he?

He returned quickly to the car, opened the passenger door and the glove compartment and took his gun out of its holster. As he pulled it out he realised that his palm was damp on the grip.

He left the Cordura holster on the passenger seat, and heard the sound of the motor struggling up the hill on the other side. He slotted a cartridge into the barrel, removed the safety catch and held his arm down at his side.

The car was heading straight for him now. Each jolt caused the beam of the headlights to dance in his eyes like the luminous lashing of a whip. Blinded, he held up his free hand as a visor.

He heard the accelerator as the driver stepped on the pedal.

He raised his gun.

The car was speeding towards him, but then it suddenly slowed. He blinked from the sweat dripping from his eyebrows into his eyes, and his vision blurred as if they were full of tears. He wasn't even sure he could hit the vehicle if he fired: there was no worse marksman in the entire crime unit than Servaz. He wiped the sweat away with his cuff. Bloody coma, he thought.

The sound of the motor faded abruptly as the driver shifted from third to second and the car slowed and stopped a dozen metres or so away, in a crunching of gravel and snow. He waited. Heard his own breathing, heavy and uneasy. He sensed the door opening, beyond the glare of headlights.

He could see nothing but a figure sharply defined against the paler night.

'Martin!' shouted the figure. 'Don't shoot! Put your gun down, please!'

He did as he was asked. The sudden drop of adrenaline made him feel dizzy and he had to lean on the bonnet of the car, his legs like jelly. It was Dr Xavier who walked towards him in the glare of the headlights.

'Doc,' breathed Martin. 'You scared the shit out of me.'

'I'm sorry, I'm sorry!'

Xavier seemed out of breath, no doubt from the stress of having a gun pointed at him.

'What the hell are you doing here?'

Xavier came closer. He had something in his hand, but Servaz could not tell what it was.

'I often come here.'

Xavier's voice: strange, tense, hesitant.

'What?'

'Very often . . . at the end of the day . . . I come to gaze at these ruins. The ruins of my former glory, the ruins of a shattered dream, gone . . . This place means a lot to me, you understand . . .'

Xavier was still walking towards him. Servaz looked down at his arm dangling by his side, the hand holding a cylindrical object. He couldn't see what it was. Xavier was only 3 metres away now.

'When I saw there was already someone here, I almost turned back. And then . . . I saw it was you . . .'

He lifted his hand; Servaz was on edge. He looked at the object at the same time: it was a torch.

'Why don't we take a tour?' said Xavier, switching it on and shining it at the ruins. 'Come on, I have something to tell you.'

24

The Tree

A single light was burning on the top floor of the former imperial villa on Elsslergasse, in the Hietzing district of Vienna. In his study Bernhard Zehetmayer, in a damask dressing gown, silk pyjamas and slippers, was listening to Debussy's *Trois Nocturnes* before going to bed.

The little palace was very draughty, so the orchestra conductor had transformed the top floor into a luxury flat with two bathrooms, and closed off the other parts of the building. Marble fountains, tangled ivy on the facade, bow windows, and a garden that was more of a park conferred a somewhat dated nobility upon the ensemble.

He was completely alone in his draughty palace: Maria had gone home two hours earlier, after preparing his dinner, drawing his bath, and turning down his bed. Tassilo, his chauffeur, would not be back until the following morning and Brigitta, the nurse – every time he saw her the sight of her legs stirred him and filled him with yearning – would not be coming again until the following evening. He knew that the night would be long and bring little sleep, purveying, rather, dark thoughts and sombre ruminations. At the heart of these thoughts there would – as always – be the memory of Anna. The iris of her eyes. His beloved child.

Her light.

All through her childhood and youth she had been light, and now she belonged to the darkness. Such a beautiful, gifted child. Born late of a mother who cultivated a unique ability: that of knowing how to tell men what they wanted to hear. The good fairies of beauty, intelligence and talent had all leaned over her cradle at her birth. She was meant for a future that would be the pride of her parents and the envy of their friends.

When she turned three he discovered, in a moment of near ecstasy, that she had perfect pitch. Anna then displayed her incredibly precocious aptitude for the piano – playing, composing and improvising even when she was very young. At fifteen she enrolled in the Salzburg Servazeum. Salzburg . . . a city he had not visited for decades. Cursed, venal, criminal city. It was no doubt in the streets of Salzburg that Hirtmann first saw her. How did he go about approaching her? Probably through music: Zehetmayer was stunned to learn that Hirtmann was an admirer of Mahler's music, as he was.

No one knew what had happened after that, but the orchestra conductor had imagined it thousands of times: they had found a diary where Anna wrote about a 'mysterious stranger' with whom she had 'a secret appointment, for the third time'. She wondered whether she was 'falling in love', whether it was madness, 'because of our age difference'. She also wondered why he had not yet 'touched or kissed' her. She was seventeen . . . Her whole future ahead of her. She disappeared a few days later.

They had found her naked body at the end of an interminable month, at the bottom of a ditch, not far from a hiking trail that overlooked the city. Zehetmayer had nearly gone mad when he heard of the number and nature of the violations she had suffered. He cursed God, Salzburg, humankind; he insulted policemen and journalists, punched one of them; he had been tempted to take his own life. Anna's death had also come between him and his wife and destroyed their marriage – but what did that matter next to the loss of the creature who was more dear to him than anyone on earth? When he was informed of the identity of the perpetrator at last he had someone on whom he could focus his rage.

He would never have thought it possible to hate so much. Or that hatred is an emotion purer than love: literature has not stopped filling us with the notion since Cain and Abel. Without music he would be lost, he thought, listening to the final bars of the third *Nocturne*. But even music had not managed to crush the madness that was blossoming in him like a poisoned flower. Zehetmayer was an arrogant man, stubborn and spiteful. After his wife had died of cancer, in the solitude of his ivory tower his madness had found fertile terrain. Until he met Wieser, however, he had never envisaged that it might find an outlet in action.

And now hope had just been reborn, in the features of a child. He stood up, because the final notes were fading inside the two spherical white loudspeakers on either side of the room, the only futuristic element, which clashed with the rest of the furniture. As he was walking over to his cutting-edge French stereo system, he felt a violent pain in his belly. He stopped for a moment, his face contorted.

That afternoon he had again found blood in his stools. He had not told the nurse. It was out of the question for him to spend weeks stuck in hospital like the last time. He switched off the stereo, then the lights, and headed down the long corridor to his room. Although in public he was always vigorous and full of energy, in the privacy of his palace he tended to drag his feet across the star-shaped parquet. As he slipped into bed he wondered if the same cancer that had killed his wife and had now come back for him would leave him the time to savour his revenge.

Kirsten Nigaard was window-shopping in the centre of town to kill time when yet again she caught sight of the man in the reflection in the glass. A man with glasses . . . A childish lock of hair falling over his eyes. He had his back to her and pretended to be interested in another window but she was no fool: from time to time he turned around and glanced in her direction.

Had Martin sent a cop to keep an eye on her? He would have told her. And the guy didn't look like a cop. He did, however, look like a pervert. His little eyes kept darting around behind his thick lenses, and he looked like one of those Minion characters. She smiled. Yes, that was exactly what he reminded her of.

Kirsten resumed her stroll along the cobblestoned shopping street.

Night had fallen over Toulouse, but the streets in the centre were still packed with people. She felt an unpleasant frisson all the same. She knew from experience that a crowd was only a thin protection against rape or assault. Had he merely taken a shine to her by chance, or was there something more to it?

A sexual predator? Pathologically shy? Or maybe . . . There was another hypothesis, but it couldn't be, no.

She came out onto the place Wilson and headed towards one of the pavement cafés. Sitting down at a table, she waved to a waiter. For a minute she looked all around for the man and thought he had gone. Then she spotted him, sitting on one of the benches in the middle of the square by the fountain. She could see only his head above the hedges that surrounded the square. An icy shiver went through her. She had first noticed him when she was having lunch on the place Saint-Georges. He was seated three tables over, biting into a huge cheeseburger and never taking his eyes off her.

When the waiter brought her Coke Zero, for a moment she glanced away. She looked again immediately afterwards but he was gone. Her gaze swept the square. He had vanished into thin air. A sensation as unpleasant as a whiff of ammonia made her tense every muscle. She cursed Servaz for letting her down, for calling to tell her he wouldn't be able to meet her for dinner that evening but that he'd be there the next morning to say goodbye. She would take a taxi back to her hotel and she would ask the driver to wait until he saw she was inside. She had no desire to walk on a night like this with that shadow behind her.

Roxane Varin could not believe her eyes when she stared at the letter that lay on her desk. Against all expectations, the search for academic enrolment they had sent to the local school administration had triggered a response from one of the schools: L'Hospitalet-en-Comminges primary school, where the headmaster had confirmed that Gustav was enrolled. There was a telephone number. Roxane picked up the receiver . . .

'Jean-Paul Rossignol,' said the man who answered.

'Roxane Varin, Child Protection in Toulouse. I'm calling with regards to this boy Gustav. Are you sure he's enrolled in your school?'

'Of course I'm sure. What is the issue with this child?'

'I can't discuss it over the phone, but we will explain. Has anyone else seen the search for enrolment?'

'Gustav's teacher.'

'Listen: don't mention it to anyone else. And tell his teacher as well. It's very important.'

'Can't you tell me a bit—'

'Later,' said Roxane, hanging up.

She dialled another number but got only an answering machine. *For Christ's sake, where are you, Martin?*

'I've always dreamt of going to Norway,' said the man, who had been sitting at her table for three minutes.

Kirsten gave him a faint smile. In his forties, wearing a suit and tie, and married, according to his wedding ring. Initially he had spoken to her from the neighbouring table, then asked permission to bring his beer and sit with her.

'The fjords, the Vikings, the triathlon . . . all that, you know.'

Now she refrained from asking him if they really ate frogs and mouldy cheese in this country. And whether strikes really were a national sport. And were they really all useless at living languages. But beyond that, he had an interesting body – not ordinary, but interesting. Perhaps she could kill two birds with one stone: take him back to her hotel and dissuade Mr Minion from picking on her. Yes, but still . . . Looks were not everything, even just for one night. And besides, it was another Frenchman who had been occupying her thoughts for a while now.

She was at a complete loss as to how to proceed when her telephone vibrated. She could see the Frenchie looked annoyed. Well well, apparently Mr King-of-clichés-about-Norway did not like competition or interruptions.

'Kirsten,' she said.

'Kirsten, here is Roxane,' said Roxane Varin in her broken English. 'You know where is Martin? I found Gustav!'

'*What?*'

The moon, which had been casting its light upon the gutted building, now disappeared behind the clouds, and it was snowing again. As the minutes went by, the number of snowflakes falling and whirling among the walls of the former Wargnier Institute increased steadily. Broken-off stairways, charred metallic doorframes deformed by fire, former rooms now open to the four winds and buried under the snow . . . Clearly Xavier had not forgotten the layout of the place. He made his way around the labyrinth with ease.

'I think I saw him,' he said suddenly as they were walking between two high walls.

'Pardon?'

'Hirtmann. I think I saw him one day.'

Servaz stopped walking.

'Where?'

'In Vienna, almost two years ago. At the 23rd Congress of the European Psychiatry Association, which has over a thousand member delegates. The Association claims to have over seventy thousand members.'

Vienna . . . Servaz had the photograph in his pocket, the one where Gustav appeared in one of the most famous landscapes in Austria.

'I didn't know there were so many psychiatrists in Europe,' he said, while the snow-laden wind whistled ever louder among the ruins. It was stinging his neck; he lifted the collar of his coat.

'It's because there is madness everywhere, Martin. I would even go so far as to say that madness rules the world. In short, with over a thousand delegates from all over Europe, it's not difficult to pass unnoticed.'

'Why didn't you tell me?'

'Because for a long time I believed I'd imagined it all. But the more I think about it, the more I believe it had to be him. And I think about it often.'

'Tell me more.'

Xavier turned around and they retraced their footprints, climbing over a pile of rubble and metal beams that had fallen to the ground. The snowflakes clung like dandruff to their shoulders.

'I was attending one of the lectures when a fellow asked if he could sit next to me. He introduced himself, said his name was Hasanovic. He was very friendly and we quickly exchanged a few pleasantries in English because the lecture was fairly boring and the speaker wasn't good. Then he suggested we go for a coffee at the snack bar.'

Xavier waited until they were on the other side of the pile of rubble to continue.

'He told me he was a psychiatrist in Sarajevo. Twenty years after the end of the war in Bosnia, he was still treating very severe cases of post traumatic stress disorder.'

'And you think this guy was Hirtmann? What did he look like?'

'He was the right age and size. He was unrecognisable, naturally. His eye colour, the shape of his face, his nose, his hairline – even his voice. And he was wearing glasses.'

Servaz paused. He was trying to control his feelings of anxiety.

'Had he put on weight? Or got thinner?'

'I'd say he was roughly the same build. That evening we met up again at a reception. He was with a very beautiful woman, very classy, wearing a dress that made heads turn. We went on talking about our profession and when I told him I'd been the director of the Wargnier Institute he became very interested: I have to say that with everything that happened, the Institute has become almost legendary among the psychiatric community . . . He told me he had long been fascinated by the subject and he had recognised my name, but he didn't know if I would feel like talking about it, so he'd refrained from mentioning it . . .'

Legendary . . . Not only among shrinks, thought Servaz. But he said nothing.

'He asked me lots of questions. About the treatments, the inmates, the security, what happened at the end . . . And then we started on Hirtmann, naturally . . .'

Xavier's voice had grown thinner. They had almost reached the way out.

'I realised he knew an awful lot about the subject, both what had happened here and about the Swiss killer himself. He didn't merely ask questions. He had very clear opinions, and astonishing background knowledge. Certain details in particular caught my attention. I didn't recall the press ever having talked about them.

'For example, he described the view that Hirtmann had from the window in his cell at the Institute.'

'That could have got out in the press . . .'

'You think so? Where? And the information would have reached a Bosnian psychiatrist?'

'Was that the only thing?'

'No. He began to dwell on a tall fir tree – Hirtmann could see the treetop from his window – and on the symbolism of trees in general, "connecting the three levels of the cosmos: the subterranean, into which it plunges its roots, the surface, and the sky", and about the tree of life, and the tree of the knowledge of good and evil in the Bible, and the tree where Buddha attained enlightenment, as well as the tree of death in the Kabbalah. He was very well informed on the subject of all these symbols.'

'And then?'

'That was when I realised that Hirtmann had spoken to me one day about all these things in practically the same terms.'

Servaz stopped walking yet again. He shuddered; perhaps it was the cold.

'Are you sure?'

'At the time I was absolutely sure, yes. It gave me quite a shock. And I could tell that Hasanovic was getting a kick out of seeing how unsettled I was. And then, you know how it is: I began to doubt what

I had heard, exactly; to wonder if my memory hadn't been playing tricks on me. The more time went by, the more unsure I became.'

'You should have told me.'

'Perhaps I should have, yes. But what would that have changed?'

They emerged from the ruins. It was snowing heavily now and the cars were covered in white.

'And now, what do you think?' asked Servaz as he moved towards his vehicle through the snowstorm.

'I believe it was him,' said Xavier, looking up at Servaz.

'Did you check whether there really is a Dr Hasanovic, psychiatrist, in Sarajevo?'

'Yes, I did. He exists.'

'And what does he look like?'

'I have no idea. I didn't dig any deeper. At the time, I was convinced I'd been imagining things.'

'But now you think otherwise?'

'Yes.'

Suddenly Servaz's mobile rang: he had picked up the network again. While he'd been out of range, he had received several calls. He took out the phone. There were also two voicemails.

His heart began to beat faster.

Kirsten and Roxane.

25

An Encounter

'What are you doing?'

He looked up. Margot was standing at the door to the room, shoulder against the doorframe.

'I have to go away for a few days,' he replied, folding a cardigan and putting it on top of his other clothes in the suitcase. 'For work.'

'You what?'

He looked up again. She was pink with anger and her eyes were sparkling. Margot had always been like this: she could fly into a rage in half a second.

He stopped what he was doing.

'What's the matter?' he asked with a sigh.

'You're going away?'

'Only for a few days.'

She shook her head.

'I can't believe it. Ever since I got here I've hardly seen you. You disappear, you come back in the middle of the night . . . You've barely been home an hour, Dad. And now you're packing your suitcase! Can you tell me what the hell I'm doing here? What's the point? May I remind you that not that long ago you were in a coma!'

Now he felt his own anger coming over him. He could not stand being told off. And yet, he knew she was right.

'Don't worry,' he said, trying to stay calm. 'I'm fine. You shouldn't worry about me. In fact, you should go back to your life in Quebec. You're not happy here.'

He immediately regretted these last words. He knew she would pounce on him like a dog on a bone. Margot knew how to take a sentence out of context and send it back to you like a boomerang.

'What?' Her voice had become even more strident. 'Fuck, I don't believe it!'

'Stop being a mother hen, please. I'm fine.'

'Oh, fuck off!'

He heard her stomp out of the room. He closed his suitcase and went after her.

'Margot!'

He saw her grab her pea coat from the back of a chair and her iPod from the living-room table.

'Where are you going?'

She had her back to him. He could tell she was fiddling with her device because all of a sudden an infernal noise burst from her headphones. She held the phones out from her ears.

'Don't worry. When you get back, I'll be gone.'

'Margot . . .'

She didn't hear him. She had put the headphones back on and was avoiding his gaze. He wondered just what he could say to her at that moment; she was on the verge of tears and he had never been very good at dealing with other people's emotions. Let alone his daughter's recurring bouts of unhappiness.

'Margot!' he shouted, even louder, but she was already heading towards the door.

He saw her pick up her keys on the way. She slammed the door behind her without looking at him.

'Shit!' he shouted. 'Shit, shit, shit!'

Half an hour later, she still hadn't come back. He'd finished packing, and had sent her a good half-dozen text messages. His phone rang and he hurried to swipe the green button on the screen.

'I'm downstairs,' announced Kirsten.

'I'm coming,' he said, hiding his disappointment.

I have to go. Kirsten is here. Call me back, please, he texted.

He would have liked to tell her he loved her, and that he was going to try to change, but though he was overflowing with love for his daughter and felt devastated, he switched off his telephone. As he headed towards the door, he remembered that Stehlin had promised to send protection for Margot, but had done no such thing.

First thing tomorrow he would demand that Stehlin do something.

★

'Are you sure he was following you?'

Servaz asked the question while staring at the black ribbon of motorway vanishing into their headlights. He heard Kirsten's voice beside him.

'Yes.'

'Maybe it was just some pervert who likes following women in the street.'

'Maybe. But . . .'

He glanced at her. She too was staring at the motorway through the windscreen, her profile emphasised by the faint glow from the dashboard.

'But you don't believe that, do you?' he said.

'No.'

'Because it's too much of a coincidence that a guy would follow you around Toulouse at this particular point.'

'Precisely.'

They were speeding westward along the A64 towards the village of L'Hospitalet-en-Comminges. Towards the snowstorm as well, apparently, judging by the way the wind was tormenting the trees along the embankments.

'Do you really think we'll find Gustav there?' she asked.

'It seems too easy, doesn't it?'

'Let's just say it's not Hirtmann's usual style.'

Servaz nodded, but could find nothing to say.

'And once we're there, what do we do?' she asked.

'First of all, we find a hotel. And tomorrow morning, we start again: town hall, schools . . . Maybe this time someone will know something. There are two hundred inhabitants in L'Hospitalet. If he's there, we'll find him.'

Did he believe it? No, there was something wrong: it couldn't be that simple. Not with Hirtmann.

Sitting at the window in the VH Café, Margot watched her father leave the building and go up to the Norwegian policewoman on the pavement.

She had acted on impulse, to test her father. She had wanted to force him to react, to oblige him to choose, for once, between his work and her. She had hoped he would abandon his expedition for her sake. That was stupid. She looked down at the screen of her smartphone, next to her glass of wine, where his latest message was still visible:

I have to go. Kirsten is here. Call me back, please.

She had her answer.

'We have to stop,' he said suddenly, pointing to the signboard crowded with symbols that signalled a rest stop 1 kilometre further along. 'We're low on petrol.'

'Fine. I need the toilet.'

He drove cautiously down the flooded little slip road to the service station car park, sending up sprays of water wherever the road met a slight dip, until they reached the car park. As soon as Servaz had switched off the ignition Kirsten tore off her seatbelt, opened the door, pulled up her collar and rushed towards the lights. He got out in turn. Even beneath the shelter where the pumps were the wind hurled the rain at him. In addition to the van two other cars were parked at the nearby pumps. He reached for the nozzle; mindlessly squeezing the release, Servaz thought back to what Xavier had told him in the ruins.

Of course, that would be the easiest explanation: Hirtmann had changed his appearance. But Servaz thought of the image on the video Kirsten had shown him. Hirtmann resembled the man he had known, and it post-dated the meeting between Xavier and the Bosnian psychiatrist. Perhaps Xavier was mistaken? Perhaps his friend's memory was indeed playing tricks on him? Or could the Swiss criminal have used disguises: a fake beard, coloured lenses, a few removable prostheses like the ones used in the cinema for the jaw and the nose?

He looked at the blue van parked just on the other side of the pumps: it had traces of rust on the chassis and the doors. The side door was wide open, and it was as dark as a cave in there.

The driver must be inside paying. Servaz glanced mechanically towards the till, through the streaming windows of the minimarket: there was no one there, either.

He shuddered.

He hated vans. It was in a thing like that that Marianne had been abducted. They had found the vehicle in a motorway rest area just like this one. A navy blue van . . . with rust streaks . . . like this one. He remembered there had been a rosary with olivewood beads and a silver cross hanging from the rearview mirror.

He glanced over at the front of the van.

Something was hanging from the rearview mirror. In the darkness, through the dirty window, he couldn't make out what it was.

But he would have sworn it was a rosary.

He took a breath. Letting go of the pump's nozzle, he slipped between the two petrol pumps and walked slowly around the vehicle. He glanced at the number plate and froze.

There were enough erased letters and numbers to make it perfectly indecipherable.

Kirsten, he thought.

He began running through the rain.

As she entered the women's toilets, Kirsten noticed the perfume still drifting through the ambient air, mingled with the smell of industrial cleaner. A man's scent. But there was no one there. Perhaps an employee, or a man who had come in and gone out again when he realised his mistake.

There appeared to be a leak in the roof because a bucket was standing in the middle of the room with a mop in it, in front of two doors with identical 'Out of Order' signs on them. She looked up but could see no spot on the ceiling. A little skylight at the back was open, however, and she could hear the rain. Of the three lights that were supposed to illuminate the toilets only one was working, giving off a pale glow, intermittent and sinister, that left the other corners in deep shadow.

She made a face but went to the third door, the only one available, closed it behind her, and sat down. She thought about what Servaz had said: too easy. The photograph of Gustav left behind on the oil platform, and now, the school. Too easy, was his opinion. Of course it was too easy.

She gave a start. She thought she heard a sound: one of the doors creaking. She listened. But the roar of the rain drowned out all other noise.

She stood up and pulled the flush. She hesitated for a moment before opening the door, but she could no longer hear anything. As she came out, she looked at the row of mirrors across from her. Saw the figure reflected in one of them, to her left, in addition to her own.

He was standing next to the bucket, with the mop in his hand, the tall man who'd followed her through the streets of Toulouse. Then he raised the handle of the mop and gave a sharp blow to the last light shining above him.

Darkness.

Before she knew it he was on her, pressing her against the back wall near the open skylight.

'Hello, *Kirsten.*'

She swallowed her saliva. *Kirsten* . . . She tried to breathe calmly but couldn't. The blood was pounding in her temples; she saw little sparks before her eyes. She could vaguely make out his features in the light from the car park and her heart leapt into her throat: now that they were so close she recognised him. He had done something to his mouth and eyes, changed his hairline and the colour of his hair – unless it was a wig – but without a doubt, it was *him*.

'What do you want?' she said hoarsely.

'Shhh . . .'

Suddenly, his hand was beneath her skirt. First above her right knee, she felt it caressing her thigh through the tights, then moving higher up. A large, warm hand. Kirsten bit her lip.

'I've been wanting to do this for a long time,' he murmured in her ear.

She didn't answer, but her pulse was racing and her legs began to tremble. His fingers touched her through her tights and knickers and she automatically squeezed her legs closed. She shut her eyes.

Servaz came into the shop at a run, shoving a couple who were slow to get out of his way.

'Hey!' yelled the man behind him.

But Servaz was already rushing towards the toilets. Men to the right, women to the left.

He flung the door open. Called her name.

It was dark in there and he immediately felt all his senses on the alert. Then he saw her. Sitting on the floor at the back by a skylight that let in the only light and a little bit of rain. She was sobbing almost hysterically. He went closer to her, knelt down, held out his arms and almost at once she huddled into him.

'What did he do to you?'

She was fully dressed and he could see no sign of a struggle, or any disorder in her clothes.

'He just . . . he just touched me . . .'

★

'He must have got away,' he said, after they had searched all over, inside and out, and realised that the van had been abandoned by its owner. He'd had it all planned.

'Can't we close the motorway?'

'There's an exit three kilometres from here. But he'll have left the motorway ages ago.'

A few minutes earlier one of the customers in the minimarket had complained that he couldn't find his car. Servaz thought of transmitting the car's registration to the gendarmes but by the time they set up roadblocks Hirtmann would have vanished. He hesitated to call the CSI team. He knew that if he did, Stehlin and all his superiors would immediately be informed and that they would take him off the case and entrust it to someone who was not 'convalescing'. That was out of the question, and in any case, he didn't need any confirmation: he was sure of it, they had just crossed paths with the Swiss killer.

'I can't believe it. How did he arrange to be here at the same time as us?' she asked.

Her eyes were still damp.

'He must have been driving just ahead of us for a while. Before that he'd have been following us. After that it was just a question of finding the right moment. He seized his chance. Hirtmann is a past master in the art of improvisation.'

He glanced over at the door to the toilets.

'How are you feeling?' he asked.

'I'm okay.'

'Are you sure? Do you want to go back to Toulouse? Do you want to see someone?'

'I'm fine, Martin. I promise you.'

'Okay. Then let's go,' he said. 'We have nothing more to do here.'

'Aren't you going to tell the others?'

'What for? He got away. And if I tell them, Stehlin will take me off the case,' he added. 'Let's find a hotel. We'll keep going tomorrow.'

'At least we know one thing: he's here, right nearby,' she said. 'And he's following us, wherever we go.'

Yes, he thought. *Like a cat chasing a mouse.* He checked the text message he had received a few minutes earlier. He had called Margot twice after they'd stopped at the rest area. Both times he'd got her voicemail.

The message said:
Stop calling. I'm fine.

Beyond the hotel windows it was still pouring, and as he turned towards the black night Servaz saw his reflection in the window. The expression on his face was that of a desperate man, but also an angry one. He was alone. The only customer in the entire restaurant. Kirsten had gone straight up to her room. She told him she wanted to take a shower. He ordered an entrecote and chips, which was on the greasy side. He wasn't all that hungry and left more than half the meal.

'Was it not good?' asked the *patronne*.

He reassured her as best he could, and she understood he wasn't in the mood to talk, and went away.

He thought of Gustav. Did Hirtmann know where they were headed and who they intended to see? He was suddenly afraid that Hirtmann would make the kid vanish yet again. Like a magician showing you a dove and then conjuring it away. Servaz was tempted to call the nearest gendarmerie, to ask them to find the boy and keep him safe.

But he was too exhausted to attempt anything tonight.

And besides, he couldn't figure out why Hirtmann had behaved the way he had. If he knew their plans, he would have been better off simply taking the boy away without drawing attention to himself. Unless he already had.

In which case there was nothing more they could do.

Thinking about Gustav made him uneasy. He imagined a scene that he didn't like at all. He pictured himself raising a little boy, but the thought was so disturbing that he hurried to banish it. Another thought was haunting him: Jensen's death. The ammunition used had been a cop's. And suspicions would, inevitably, be focused on him.

He felt very alone. Everything was silent and he wondered if he and Kirsten were the only customers in the hotel. He'd had a headache since the episode on the motorway and it was getting worse. He was gazing into the bottom of his coffee cup as if the solution could be found there, when his phone rang.

It was Kirsten.

'I'm scared,' she said simply. 'Can you come up, please?'

*

He emerged from the lift and walked to room 13, just across from his own, room 14. He knocked. No answer. He waited a few seconds before knocking again. Still no answer. He was beginning to feel nervous and was about to pound on the door when it opened. Kirsten Nigaard appeared, in a bathrobe, her hair wet.

She held the door, closed it behind him, backed up and leaned against the little desk where there were packets of Nescafé and a kettle. He didn't know what to do. What sort of support could he offer, and how? He didn't feel very comfortable in this hotel room. She really was a very attractive woman, and in light of what she had just been through, he wanted to avoid embarrassing her at all costs.

'I'm directly across the corridor,' he said. 'Double-lock your door and don't hesitate to call me. I'll keep my phone right by me.'

'I'd rather you slept here,' she answered.

He looked around him. Saw only an armchair that didn't look at all comfortable.

'We could ask for connecting rooms if they have any,' he suggested.

Afterwards he would try to recall who had made the first move, broken the ice. He would remember that he could see the hotel's blue neon light beyond her shoulder, while she was nestled against him, and that it was reflected in the cars parked below. And that at the entrance to the car park there were two tall fir trees. That he knew the Pyrenees must begin somewhere just beyond there, straight ahead, but they were hidden by the night.

As they were kissing he could see that her eyes were wide open, as if each of them was waiting for the other to close them first; they were so close that their gazes seemed to be one. Her gaze foraging in his, no doubt looking for some truth buried beneath the layers of civility.

Then she backed over to the bed and lay down. She opened her bathrobe completely, revealing a tattoo from her groin to her hip, a sentence, in Norwegian probably – letters and numbers. Only the little bedside lamp was lit, leaving the recesses of the room in deep shadow, where the ghosts of her life were hiding. Night enveloped them.

GUSTAV

26

Contacts

Kirsten woke up at six and looked at Servaz, still sleeping. Oddly, after the events of the night, she felt rested. She put on a pair of cotton boyshorts with the name of a Norwegian rock group printed on the buttocks, a T-shirt, and a tracksuit, and once she was outside, she set off at a run around the little park surrounding the hotel. It took her five minutes to go around it, and she started again a half-dozen times, running on the gravel and the snow, never going any further away.

The icy air burned her lungs but she felt good. She stopped by a bench and the statue of a faun to do some stretches, her gaze fixed on the Pyrenees, a few summits lit by the dawn. She missed her boxing. That was both her safety valve and her way of staying balanced. To hit a bag or a sparring partner helped her to clear away some of the frustration of her job. As soon as she got back to Oslo she would head for the gym. She had a brief vision – the dark ladies' toilet with the bucket and mop in the middle – but she banished it by focusing on what lay ahead.

At half past six Servaz woke up and saw the empty bed. The sheets still bore Kirsten's imprint and her smell. He listened out, but the room, like the bathroom, was silent. He concluded that she hadn't wanted to disturb him and had gone down for breakfast. He got up, got dressed, and went back to his room.

In the shower he thought about the night he had just spent. After their lovemaking they had talked, first out on the balcony where they shared a cigarette, then in bed, and he had eventually told her about the woman who might be Gustav's mother. She had questioned him at length about what had happened in Marsac, about Marianne, and about his past. He opened up to her in a way he had rarely done since the tragic events in Marsac, and she had listened, watching him with a calm, kindly expression. He was grateful to her for not commiserating, and he in turn avoided any self-pity. After all, she surely had her own share of problems. Who didn't? Then he remembered her question. She was smart. She had put her finger on it almost right away. The question he'd been circling around for a long time without daring to voice it: 'So, he could be your son?'

He put on clean clothes and took the lift to the ground floor. When he went into the breakfast room, he looked for her but she was nowhere to be seen. She couldn't have gone far. He felt a bittersweet pang of disappointment, chased it away, and headed to the buffet and the coffee machine.

Once he had sat down he took out his phone and called Margot. Voicemail.

She unlocked the door to her room with her electronic key and was surprised to find the bed empty.

'Martin?'

No answer. He'd gone back to his room. She felt a faint stab in her stomach. Better not to think about it. She undressed quickly and headed to the shower. She was beginning to feel seriously hungry.

When she entered the bathroom she realised he hadn't even had his shower there: the towels were folded and hanging in place; the shower cubicle was unused and dry. The hurt returned, a touch stronger. They had slept together, fine. They'd had a good time, but it would go no further. They wouldn't get to know each other any better than that: this was the message he had left for her.

She looked at her face in the big mirror above the basin.

'Okay,' she said out loud. 'That's what you planned, wasn't it?'

On entering the breakfast room she saw him sitting alone at a table and went to join him.

'Hey,' she said, reaching for her cup. 'Sleep well?'

'Yes. And you? Where were you?'

'Running,' she said, then went to the coffee-maker.

Servaz watched her walk away. Their exchange had been short and without warmth. She didn't need to say anything more, he got it straight away: what had happened last night would not be mentioned.

He felt intense frustration; he'd intended to tell her how it had done him good to talk last night, that he hadn't felt that good with someone in a very long time. The sort of thing you sometimes feel like saying, without getting too heavy. And now he felt stupid. *Right*, he thought. *Back to work. We're keeping our distance.*

Kirsten devoured bread and jam, sausages and scrambled eggs, drank a big cup of coffee and two glasses of orange juice filled to the brim – in Norway, breakfast was the biggest meal of the day – while Servaz made do with an espresso coffee, half a croissant and a glass of water.

'You're not eating much,' she pointed out.

She expected him to come out with one of those bloody clichés about Norwegians being built like lumberjacks, but he merely smiled.

'You can't think as fast on a full stomach,' he said eventually.

She didn't know that when people spoke about food, he sometimes still thought about a sublime but poisoned meal, and the fine wines that had gone with it, that a judge had served him once upon a time.

L'Hospitalet was a *village perché* high on a slope only a short distance from the Spanish border. The road was narrow and winding, bordered in places with stone parapets, and in others hanging over the void with nothing to stop a car if it suddenly veered out of control.

Once they were over the mountain and had started down the other side they could see a church steeple and the white, luminous roofs of a village below them, huddling together like a herd of sheep seeking out the warmth of their own kind.

The village, at first, seemed dreary, monastic and hostile to outsiders. Its steep, narrow streets – the houses were set out in tiers on the slope – must only have caught a few hours of sun a day. And yet they emerged onto an ordinary square with an extraordinary view: the sky was clear, the clouds had scattered, and you could see for miles, to the place where the three valleys converged; all the way to the streets and roofs of Saint-Martin-de-Comminges, in fact. The town hall was modest, simple and grey, but it had the same amazing view.

They got out. From the moment they passed the sign at the entrance to the village Servaz could think of only one thing: Gustav.

He looked all around him, as if the boy might appear at any moment. There was not a soul around.

He went up the two steps leading into the town hall, beneath a rather faded tricolour flag, tried to open the glass door but found it was locked. He knocked but no one came. The snow had been swept from the steps, haphazardly, and he took care not to slip as he went back down them.

But on the corner of the square, at the entrance to a narrow, curving street, there was a sign that read: 'Pasteur Primary School'.

Servaz looked at Kirsten, who nodded, and they started walking cautiously down the steep, slippery slope. He noticed a curtain being pulled to one side on the first floor of one of the houses, but there was no one there, as if the village were inhabited by ghosts.

When they had come round the bend they could see the playground just below them. Yet another place that evoked childhood, with its covered courtyard and playground, and the rusty clock by the gate. Servaz felt a pang of anguish.

It was break time, and the children were running, shoving and screaming joyfully around the single plane tree. The roots of the old tree had forced their way up through the tarmac, and here too the snow had been swept to one side. There was a man watching the children from the covered yard. He was wearing grey overalls and glasses. There was something strangely anachronistic about the whole tableau, as if they had gone back in time a hundred years.

Suddenly Servaz froze. He felt as if he had been punched in the face.

Kirsten had continued on her way down, but now she stopped and looked back. She saw him standing there, a cloud of vapour in front of his open mouth. She deciphered his gaze and turned around to look in the same direction towards the playground. To see what he had seen.

And she understood.

He was there.

Gustav.

The blond boy, among the other children. The boy in the photograph. Who might be his son.

27

An Apparition

'Martin.'

No reply.

'Martin!'

His voice was low, soft, forceful. Martin opened his eyes.

'Papa?'

'Get up,' said his father. 'Come with me.'

'What time is it?'

His father merely smiled as he stood by the bed. Martin got up, groggy and lethargic, his eyelids heavy. In his blue pyjamas, barefoot on the cold tiles.

'Follow me.'

He had followed him. Through the silent house: the corridor, the stairs, the front room full of light, rays of dawn flooding through the curtainless windows on the east side. He glanced at the clock. Five o'clock in the morning! He was very sleepy. And he wanted only one thing: to go back to bed. But he'd followed his papa outside because he'd never dared disobey. In those days, you didn't disobey. And because he loved him, too. More than anything on earth. Except – perhaps – his maman.

Outside, the sun was beginning to peer over the hill, 500 metres away. It was summertime. Everything was still. Even the ripe wheat. There wasn't a shiver, either, in the lacy leaves of the oak trees. He had squinted as he stared at the sun's rays flooding the countryside all around. The morning calm was bursting with bird song.

'What is it?' he asked.

'This,' replied his papa, opening his arms wide to take in the landscape.

He didn't understand.

'Papa?'

'What, son?'

'Where should I look?'

His father smiled.

'Everywhere, son.' He ruffled his hair. 'I wanted you to see this, just once in your life: the sun rising at dawn, the morning . . .'

He could hear the emotion in his father's voice.

'My life is just beginning, Papa.'

His father looked at him with a smile and put his big hand on his shoulder.

'I have a very smart little boy,' he said. 'But sometimes you have to forget your intelligence and let your senses and your heart do the talking.'

Servaz was too young at the time to understand, but now he knew. Then something happened: a deer appeared at the foot of the hill. Silently, cautiously. Like an apparition. She had emerged from the woods into the open, her neck outstretched. Little Martin had never seen anything so beautiful. It was as if all of nature was holding its breath. As if something was about to happen that would splinter this magic into a thousand pieces. Servaz remembered: his heart was pounding like a drum.

And indeed, something did happen. A sharp popping sound. He didn't immediately understand what it was. But he saw the deer freeze, then fall.

'Papa, what happened?'

'Let's go now,' said his father, his voice full of anger.

'Papa? What was that sound?'

'Nothing. Come.'

It was the first shot he had ever heard, but not the last.

'She's dead, is that it? They killed her.'

'Are you crying, son? There, there. Don't cry. Come on. It's over. It's over.'

He wanted to run to the deer, but his father was holding him. Then he saw the men come out of the woods at the foot of the hill, their rifles over their shoulders, and he was overwhelmed with rage.

'Papa!' he screamed. 'Are they allowed to do that? Do they have the right?'

'Yes. They have the right. Come on, Martin. Let's go home.'

★

He shook himself, standing there in the middle of the street. He noticed Kirsten's gaze as she walked towards him. *And Hirtmann,* he wondered, *what is he teaching his son? Or mine?*

She held her breath, and had the feeling that time was standing still. The children's cries pierced the cold air like shards of glass; the school seemed to be the only living place in this dead village. Nothing moved around them except that little playground and covered courtyard, and one car, way down in the valley, no bigger than an ant; they could hardly hear it.

Servaz was transformed into a pillar of salt. She went back up the slope to him.

'He's there,' she said.

He said nothing, but let his eyes follow Gustav's movements across the playground. He was silent and motionless, apart from his darting gaze which never left the child, and his woollen scarf dancing in the wind, and she sensed how much he must be feeling. She let a few seconds go by, and observed the boy herself. He was shorter and smaller than the others. His cheeks were as red as apples from the cold but he was bundled up in a blue down jacket and a poppy-red scarf. At that moment he seemed full of the joy of living. There was nothing of the sickly child that had been described to them, other than his small stature. He did not seem solitary, either: he joined in the playground games with enthusiasm. Kirsten stood for a moment observing him, waiting for Martin to react. But she was too impatient a person to wait for long.

'What shall we do?' she said eventually.

He looked around.

'Shall we go down?' she pressed. 'We could speak to the guy there.'

'No.'

It was a very definite no. Again he looked around him.

'What's the matter?'

'We can't stay here. Someone will notice us.'

'Who?'

'The people whose job it is to take care of Gustav, for God's sake.'

'There's no one.'

'At the moment.'

'So what do we do?'

He pointed to the road they had come down.

'This is a cul-de-sac, and the only access to the school. When they come to get Gustav they have to come this way. So either they live in the village and they come on foot, or they leave their car on the square.'

He began to go back the way they had come, up the slope on the slippery paving stones.

'We'll wait for them. But if we stay in the car' – he pointed to the window where he'd seen the twitching curtain – 'the entire village will know we are here within the hour.'

They came out onto the square. Servaz pointed to the town hall, which stood in the centre and faced east.

'This would be a good lookout point.'

'It's closed.'

He looked at his watch.

'Not any more.'

The mayor was a stocky little man with close-set eyes, a heavy jaw and a thin brown moustache like a shoelace beneath widespread, hairy nostrils. He greeted their request enthusiastically.

'Here, what do you think?' he asked, showing them the windows of a room on the second floor.

Judging by the long waxed wooden table and the number of chairs, it was here that the town council held its meetings. Against the wall opposite the windows stood a tall dresser with glass doors, behind which shone bound municipal ledgers, which looked as old as the dresser itself. Servaz thought that this village must be full of similar furnishings – heavy, old-fashioned, maintained by the calloused hands of cabinetmakers who were now long dead, well away from the flat-pack furniture of the big cities. The windows had dusty cretonne curtains, and they looked out over the square; the start of the cul-de-sac leading to the school was clearly visible.

'This is perfect. Thank you.'

'Don't mention it. In these troubled times, we must all do our duty as citizens. You do what you can, but nowadays we must all feel concerned by everyone's safety. *We are at war.*'

Servaz nodded prudently. Kirsten, who had not understood a single word, frowned as she looked at him, and Martin shrugged as the mayor turned to leave. Then he stood with his nose to the windowpane, blew a circle of vapour on the glass, and checked his watch.

'All we can do now is wait.'

At around noon parents began to appear one after the other on the square and head down the cul-de-sac towards the school. Servaz and Kirsten heard the rusty clang of the bell, full of the echoes of childhood, and they squeezed up against the windows. The parents reappeared a few minutes later, holding their chattering offspring by the hand. Apparently no one had school lunches here.

Servaz swallowed, his stomach twisted with anxiety. Gustav was bound to come out soon, holding someone by the hand.

But the flow of parents and children gradually ceased. Something was not right.

Servaz looked out of the window again, resisting the temptation to open it. He checked his watch. Five minutes past noon. The square was empty: no Gustav. Shit, did this mean he lived in one of the houses along the cul-de-sac? If so, with the mayor's cooperation, it should be easy to set up a hideout . . .

He was just pulling back from the window when a metallic grey Volvo came onto the square a bit too quickly and braked with a squeal of tyres. Kirsten and Servaz simultaneously turned just in time to see an elegant man in his late thirties, with a neatly trimmed goatee and well-cut winter coat, burst out of the car. He began running towards the cul-de-sac, checking his watch.

Servaz and Kirsten exchanged glances. Servaz felt his pulse begin to race. They waited in silence. After the racket made by the children, the silence on the square seemed deafening. Then there was the sound of footsteps and they could hear two voices – one adult, the other a child's. Again, Servaz did not dare open the window so they could hear better. A few seconds later the man with the goatee emerged from the cul-de-sac.

With Gustav.

'*Dammit!*' exclaimed Kirsten.

The man with the goatee walked under their window, leading Gustav. Servaz heard him say, 'You've been running too much. You know you're not supposed to get tired, with your illness.'

'When is Papa coming?' asked the child who, all of a sudden, seemed pale and worn out.

'Shh! Not here,' said the man, annoyed, looking all around him.

Close up, he looked older than his build and his gait had suggested: getting on for fifty or more. A senior executive in business or at a bank: he reeked of money earned without getting his hands dirty. As for the boy, his eyes were ringed with shadows and he had a yellowish, waxen complexion, despite the colour the cold air had restored to his cheeks, and Servaz recalled the headmistress's words: 'He often missed school – flu, a cold, an upset stomach . . .' He turned to Kirsten and they rushed together towards the door, barrelled down the two flights of stairs, and crossed the polished, slippery floor of the entrance. They opened the door to leave the town hall, letting in a few snow flurries, just as the grey Volvo was leaving the square.

They ran to the car, hoping there was not another way out of the village.

A bit too quickly, Servaz drove up the street that had brought them to the square, and lifted his foot off the accelerator when they saw the Volvo a bit further ahead. He felt hot, and with his free hand he loosened the scarf around his neck and tossed it behind him, then unzipped his down jacket. He slowed down. He did not know whether the man at the wheel was on his guard, but he supposed that Hirtmann would have given him instructions to that effect.

Who was he?

One thing was certain: Hirtmann it was not. Even surgery had its limits.

Servaz was overcome with a feeling of elation, but also disorientation – the disturbing impression that they were like mice in a maze. And then there was the investigation into Jensen's death. The synchronicity of the two events – the death of the rapist and the presence of the Swiss serial killer in the vicinity – constantly preyed on his mind. The fact remained that he felt not so much that they were following but that they were being followed – observed, spied on, even guided . . . Straight into a trap?

The cop from the General Inspectorate of the National Police was called Rimbaud, like the poet, but Roland Rimbaud had never read any of his namesake's verses. He did not know that the poet who shared his name had written *A Season in Hell*. Otherwise he would surely have found the title appropriate for the experience he was about to put one of his colleagues through.

Sitting in the office of Judge Desgranges, Rimbaud could smell blood. A prize case of misconduct. The disciplinary commissioner, whom some of his colleagues – as keen on poetry as he was – had nicknamed 'Rambo', was a famished wolf, tirelessly flushing out crooked cops. Or at least that was how he liked to see himself. Since Rimbaud had been running the regional branch of the policemen's police, he had brought down a few heavyweights from Public Security and Narcotics, and had dismantled an anti-crime brigade whose members had been indicted for 'organised gang theft, extortion, and unauthorised acquisition and detention of narcotics'. The fact that he resorted to methods that elsewhere would have qualified as harassment, or that he had based his investigation on the dubious reliability of a dealer's testimony and that the accusations had been debunked in the meantime, did not seem to overly bother his superiors. You can't make an omelette without, etc. For Rimbaud, the police was not one indivisible institution but a loose conglomeration of cliques, private domains, rivalries, walking egos – in short, a jungle with its big cats, its apes, its snakes and its parasites. He also knew that you don't go filing the fangs of a guard dog. You just, from time to time, remind him of the length of his lead.

'What do we know?' asked Desgranges.

If anyone resembled a poet, then it was the magistrate, with his too-long hair, his twisted black knitted tie, and his plaid jacket that looked as if it had been to the dry cleaner over a thousand times.

'We know that Jensen, in all likelihood, was shot with a cop's gun while he was trying to rape a young woman; that for a time he was suspected, then cleared, of the rapes of three joggers and the murder of one of them; that he was electrocuted by catenary during an interrogation that went wrong . . .'

He broke off. Up to this point he'd been on solid ground, merely quoting facts. Now, he was about to venture into slipperier, even downright swampy, terrain.

'During the interrogation, he shot Commandant Martin Servaz from the Toulouse crime unit, who got a bullet to the heart and spent several days in a coma; this same commandant suspected him of murdering one Monique Duquerroy, sixty-nine years of age, in her home in Montauban in June. I should add that this policeman, Servaz—'

'I know who Servaz is,' interrupted Desgranges. 'Go on.'

'Hmm . . . Jensen's lawyer wanted to sue the police: he has asserted that Servaz, er, threatened his client with a gun and forced him to climb onto the roof of the railway carriage, even though he knew full well that Jensen was at risk of being electrocuted . . .'

'And he *wasn't*?' retorted Desgranges. 'If I'm not mistaken, he was there, too, on that roof. And Jensen did shoot him, didn't he? He too was armed, so it would seem . . .'

Rimbaud saw a deep triple crease take its place among the already numerous wrinkles on the judge's brow.

'In fact, Jensen's counsel maintains that Commandant Servaz tried to kill his client by electrocuting him,' he asserted.

The magistrate coughed.

'Surely you aren't going to credit such statements, are you, Commissaire? I know you give greater credence to the words of a dealer than to those of a policeman, but still . . .'

Rimbaud was outraged. Desgranges went on looking at him without flinching. Then the policeman took out a folder and shoved it across the judge's desk.

'What's this?' the judge asked.

'The gendarmerie has drawn up a facial composite of the man who shot Jensen, from the testimony of Emmanuelle Vengud, the young woman who nearly got raped.'

Desgranges honoured him with a grunt. He reached for the drawing: a face with regular features, partly hidden by a hood. Only the mouth, nose and eyes were faintly visible. There wasn't much to get your teeth into.

'Good luck,' he said, handing the drawing back to Rimbaud.

'Don't you think it looks like him?'

'Excuse me? Like who?'

'Servaz.'

Desgranges sighed. His face turned purple.

'I see,' he said softly. 'Listen, Commissaire, I've heard about your methods. I'll have you know I don't approve of them. With regard to the anti-crime brigade that you dismantled, it would seem that my colleagues are beginning to reconsider elements of the case: the testimony on which you based your investigation for the prosecution is unreliable, to say the least. What's more, some officers in other departments have sent a letter to the regional director of Public Security to denounce what they call harassment on your part. Take my advice: take it easy this time.'

Desgranges had not raised his voice. But the threat was there, not even veiled.

'However, I won't have it said that I cover up these kinds of incidents if they occur. Carry on with your investigation, within the limits I have just set out. If you bring me something concrete, real, tangible, whether it concerns Servaz or not, justice will prevail, I promise you.'

'I would like a letter of request for ballistic analysis,' continued Rimbaud, remaining calm.

'Ballistic analysis? Do you know how many cops and gendarmes there are in this *département*? You want to analyse all their weapons?'

'Only Commandant Servaz's.'

'Commissaire, I told you—'

'He was in Saint-Martin-de-Comminges that night!' said Rimbaud. 'The night Jensen got shot, a few kilometres from there. It says so in the report he filed!'

He took a bundle of papers from his folder and handed them to the judge.

'It says here that Jensen called him in the middle of the night! He told Servaz he'd seen him earlier in Saint-Martin. He also refers to that famous evening when he was electrocuted on the railway carriage, and he blames him for fucking up his life. Then he asked to speak to him face to face, and when Servaz refused, he made an allusion to his daughter.'

Desgranges suddenly perked up, interested.

'What sort of allusion?'

Rimbaud checked his own copy of the report.

'He didn't say much. But it was enough to get Servaz hopping mad and he charged over to Saint-Martin in the middle of the night. If it's true, the transmitter will have picked up his mobile signal at the entrance to town. After that . . . this is where it gets juicy.'

The cop glanced at the judge, who was staring at him coldly. He did not seem the least bit perturbed. But Rimbaud knew that what was coming would take him down a peg or two.

'Servaz asserts that someone was hiding in the gardens of the thermal baths in Saint-Martin and that when he tried to get closer, they ran away. He went after them but they disappeared into the forest. Servaz didn't dare go any further, or so he says. He went back to his car, and found a note on his windscreen.'

'Which said?'

'"Were you afraid?" That's what he says it said.'

'Did he keep the note?'

'The report doesn't say.'

The magistrate was staring at him ever more sceptically.

'So, he claims he was in touch with Jensen the night Jensen was killed, is that it?'

'Killed by a cop's gun,' insisted Rimbaud.

'Or by a weapon stolen from a cop. Did you enquire if anyone had reported their gun missing?'

'Enquiries are being made as we speak.'

'I don't understand. Jensen was killed at three o'clock in the morning up in the mountains, and Servaz asserts he went to Saint-Martin at midnight. And what, in your opinion, happened in between?'

'Maybe he lied. The transmitters will tell us. Or there could be another possibility: he's no fool, he knew his telephone would betray him. Or that someone might have seen him in Saint-Martin. So he went back to Toulouse, dropped off his telephone, and returned to the scene . . .'

'Did you find out what Jensen was doing around midnight?'

'We're looking into that now.'

This was a lie, Rimbaud already knew. According to all the witnesses, Jensen could not have been in Saint-Martin at around midnight: at the time, he was in the refuge with the others. Unless he had gone back out when they were all asleep. But there was one other hypothesis: that Servaz had made it all up. And that one way or another he'd found out where his victim was. He'd made a return trip so that his phone would trigger the towers in both directions. Before going back to the scene without a telephone . . . A somewhat twisted alibi, but if you're a cop you would know not to have your phone with you if you were about to commit a crime.

He picked up the facial composite. True enough, you couldn't see much, but it could easily be Servaz.

Or not.

The gun.

The gun would tell. Provided Servaz didn't come out and say he'd lost it. He thought about the footprints in the snow.

'I don't know,' said Desgranges, crossing his hands under his chin and rubbing both thumbs against his lower lip. 'I get the unfortunate impression that you are following only one lead.'

'Oh, for heaven's sake, everything points to him!' protested Rimbaud, rolling his eyes towards the ceiling. 'He was there on the night of the murder! And he has a motive!'

'Don't speak to me as if I were an idiot!' scolded the judge. 'What motive? To carry out justice on his own? I know Servaz; you don't. That's not his style.'

'I've already questioned some of his colleagues: they say he's changed since his coma.'

'All right, I'll grant your request. But under no circumstances is he to be fed to the press, is that clear? It doesn't take much for a leak. Get a ballistic analysis for the entire crime unit, drown the fish.'

Rimbaud nodded briefly, a big smile on his lips.

'I want to interview him, too, along with his superiors and the members of his investigative team,' he said.

'You can call them as witnesses,' said the judge, decisively.

He stood up to indicate that the meeting was over. They shook hands, without warmth.

28

The Chalet

The road wound its way along the icy mountainside, marking a deep groove in all the immaculate whiteness. Servaz was tense. If they went on like this, the only spot of colour against this white wilderness, they would be noticed.

They seemed to be alone on the little road, apart from the Volvo. They saw it turn into a village perched on the mountainside; there was only an abandoned sawmill at the entrance to the village, thirty-odd houses, a few shops, and a hotel. When Servaz emerged from the tight bend on the way out of the village, in front of the hotel, he slowed abruptly: less than three hundred metres from there, after a broader bend, the Volvo had stopped outside a big Alpine chalet that overlooked the entire valley. The road went no further.

He parked below the deserted hotel terrace. They turned to look at the two individuals getting out of the Volvo, their plume-like breath at their lips. The chalet was luxurious, covered with rough wood, with several terraces and balconies, of the kind you saw in Megève, Gstaad, or Courchevel. It could house quite a number of people, but the garage was open and Servaz saw only one other car inside.

A couple? Was this really where Gustav lived? With this man? Who else?

Servaz saw them go inside. He opened his car door.

'Care for a coffee?' he said.

A moment later, Kirsten and Servaz were sitting on the terrace at the hotel, like two tourists on a recce; he had a double espresso, she had a Coke Zero (she'd tossed the ice out of her glass, as if they were in one of those countries where you can't drink the water). It was freezing cold, but the sun shone on the sparkling snow and warmed them up a little. Hiding behind his sunglasses, Servaz stared at the chalet, on the lookout for the slightest movement.

Suddenly he motioned to Kirsten, who turned around. A tall blonde woman had come out on one of the balconies, wearing a beige jumper and brown trousers. They were too far away to tell exactly how old she was, but Servaz would have guessed in her forties. She was slim, even slender, her hair pulled up in a ponytail.

When the manager came back out, even though there were no other customers on the terrace, Servaz motioned to him.

'That big chalet, there – do you know if it's to let?'

'No. It's not. It belongs to a professor from the university in Toulouse.'

'And they live there just the two of them?' asked Servaz, pretending to be full of admiration and envy.

The manager smiled.

'There are three of them. They have a child. Adopted. I know, some people have what it takes . . .'

Servaz hesitated to ask any more questions. He did not want to attract attention for the time being.

'And do you have rooms to let?'

'Of course.'

'What did he say?' asked Kirsten when the manager had gone.

He translated.

One hour later, the man with the goatee left the chalet with Gustav to take him back to school. Clearly, the professor was not working in Toulouse that day. They'd been sitting on that terrace for an hour. It was time to move, if they didn't want to attract attention.

'We'll get a room, go for a walk, and come back this evening,' he said, in English.

'One room or two?' she asked.

He looked at her. Clearly she had no intention of picking up where they had left off last night. She was beautiful in the light, with her close-fitting polo-neck jumper, and her big sunglasses hiding her face. He felt a sudden pang in his stomach. He didn't know exactly what had happened between them, still less what was going to happen now. It was hard to make her out. Had it merely been a reaction to the rush of adrenaline and fear? Or had Kirsten simply needed a presence in her bed at that moment? She had just alluded very clearly to the fact that she did not want to take things any further.

He decided to drop the subject for the moment.

'The guns of the entire crime unit?' repeated Stehlin incredulously.

'That's right.'

'And Judge Desgranges has authorised this?'

'Yes.'

Stehlin raised his coffee cup to his lips to give himself time to think.

'Who is going to be in charge of the ballistic analysis?' he asked.

'Is it a problem?' answered Rimbaud.

'No. But I'm wondering: are you going to put all the guns in a bulletproof truck at the same time? And head for Bordeaux? All those weapons on the motorway? Seriously?'

Rimbaud wriggled in his chair, leaning towards Stehlin's imposing desk.

'We won't disarm all your men at the same time, and the guns will not leave the premises: the analysis will take place here in your lab, under our supervision.'

'Why the crime unit? Why not the gendarmerie, or Public Security? What makes you think the culprit is here? I don't think any of my men could be mixed up in the case,' said Stehlin, not without a fleeting thought for Servaz.

'In chess, the bishops are the ones closest to kings,' said Rimbaud cryptically.

They had spent the afternoon wandering around L'Hospitalet and Saint-Martin, coming up with various theories, drinking so much coffee that Servaz felt nauseous. As soon as the light began to fade they went back to the hotel, on the pretext that they were tired, and shut themselves in the room. There were two beds, a double and a single, which seemed to both of them to be a sign. Servaz hadn't wanted to attract attention by asking for two rooms. He had been prepared to sleep in an armchair if there was one, but this settled the matter.

His problem, however, was that they had not planned to find themselves in the same hotel room after what had happened the night before, and that to be forced by events to do so made the situation even more embarrassing. He could tell that Kirsten felt just as awkward as he did.

Every movement she made in the small space seemed as controlled as that of an astronaut on board the International Space Station. And there was only one window – which meant they could not avoid bumping into each other, and that they were so close he could almost feel the heat coming off her body, or the perfume from her neck and wrists.

While they were wandering around, Servaz had obtained confirmation of the Volvo's registration and more information about the couple: Roland and Aurore Labarthe, forty-eight and forty-two years of age. Officially childless. According to Espérandieu, the husband taught intercultural psychology and psychopathology at the Université Jean Jaurès in Toulouse; the wife had no official profession. They would have to look into Gustav's adoption. Was it possible, in 2016, to be raising a child who did not belong to you? Probably. Temporarily, anyway.

Outside, night was falling rapidly over the mountain of ice. Labarthe and Gustav had not yet returned home, however. From time to time Servaz and Kirsten could see the haughty, slender figure of the lady of the house moving from one room to the next, sometimes with a phone to her ear or typing messages on the device. Servaz thought he ought to ask the judge for a wire tap. Then suddenly they saw the Volvo go by beneath their window, driving slowly and silently over the white drifts of the snow-covered road; they hadn't heard it coming. The brake lights were like two incandescent red eyes. The blonde woman came out on the front steps and stood in the glow of the headlights, all smiles. She greeted Gustav with a hug and hurried him inside, then she kissed her husband. Servaz thought there was something artificial and forced about their body language. He had taken his binoculars from the glove compartment and now he handed them to Kirsten.

Aurore Labarthe appeared more clearly in the binocular lenses. She was a domineering-looking sort of woman with a frosty socialite's looks, a nose that was on the long side, thin lips, a swan's neck, and extremely pale skin. He figured she must be at least 1 metre 75. An athletic but hard figure. She was wearing a long off-white outfit that went down to her ankles, which made her look like a Vestal Virgin. Servaz saw she was barefoot, even when she was out on the wooden doorstep, where there were still traces of snow. Something about her made him deeply uneasy. He thought that instead of Aurore she should have been called 'Umbra' or 'Night'.

'Look,' said Kirsten suddenly, next to him.

She had her laptop on her knees and had been checking the Internet.

She turned the screen towards him. Servaz saw the website of an online bookseller. All the covers were titles of books by Roland Labarthe. He read through them: *The Marquis de Sade: Freedom through Confinement*; *Do What Thou Wilt: From Rabelais' Thélème to Aleister Crowley*; *In Praise of Evil and Freedom*; *The Garden of Delights: From Sacher-Masoch to BDSM*. Suddenly on the fifth volume his gaze froze.

Julian Hirtmann or the Prometheus Complex.

He shuddered, recalling a sentence: 'Demons are malicious and powerful.' Where had he read that? There it was, the connection . . . A direct link between the two men. Hirtmann had been a topic of study for Labarthe. Had intellectual curiosity been driven to fascination? Or even complicity? Here was the proof, apparently, before his eyes. Servaz knew that Hirtmann had a number of fans on the Internet – this marvellous invention that had changed the world, enabling Islamic State to contaminate fragile brains with its lethal beliefs, and kids to harass their peers to the point of suicide, and paedophiles to pass around pictures of naked children, and millions of individuals to unleash their hatred on others . . .

He had to get hold of that book. *The Prometheus Complex* . . . Servaz vaguely remembered his philosophy classes, from that long-ago era when he wanted to become a writer and was studying literature. The Prometheus complex had been described in a book by Gaston Bachelard, *The Psychoanalysis of Fire*. It was a long time ago, but he recalled that, according to Bachelard, to conquer fire, in other words knowledge and sexuality, little Prometheus had to disobey his father's prohibition of these things; the Prometheus complex referred to the tendency of sons to want to surpass their fathers in intelligence and knowledge. Something like that anyway . . . Had Labarthe stumbled upon something in Hirtmann's past? Had Hirtmann got in touch with Labarthe after reading the book the professor had devoted to him?

He looked out of the window.

It was completely dark now. Only the bluish cast of snow emerged from the night like a sheet tossed over furniture in a darkened room. The windows at the chalet were streaming with light. Suddenly Servaz saw Gustav go up to one of them and press his nose against the pane. Through the binoculars Servaz saw that the boy was in his pyjamas. He seemed to be lost in a daydream. Servaz could not help but stare at the sad, tired little face, and he felt an abyss open in his guts. He looked away. Was he looking at his own son? The prospect terrified him beyond measure. What would happen if that were the case? He didn't want a son who hadn't been desired. He rejected the responsibility. *His son* . . . Living with an intellectual who was obsessed with transgression, and his ice cube of a wife. No, it was absurd. Still, he turned to Kirsten:

'We need his DNA.'

She nodded. She didn't ask whose DNA: she knew what he was thinking.

'At the school,' she said, 'they're bound to have things that belong to him.'

He shook his head.

'It's too risky. What if they say something to the Labarthes?'

'What will we do, then?'

'I don't know. But we have to get it.'

Kirsten's telephone rang in her pocket. The opening bars of 'Sweet Child o' Mine' by Guns N' Roses. She swiped the green button of her Samsung phone to the right.

'Kasper?'

'So what's happening?' said the cop from Bergen. 'Anything new?'

It was 18.12 at the Toulouse crime unit when Samira Cheung handed her Sig Sauer to Rimbaud. That day she was wearing a T-shirt illustrated with the logo of the Misfits, a horror punk band that had split up a long time ago. She also had two new piercings: one in her left nostril, the other on her lower lip.

'Is it just me or does it smell of dead rats in here?'

'It must be coming from the sewers,' said Espérandieu, taking his gun from the drawer.

'So you're poets, is that it?' said Rimbaud.

'Ah, with a name like that, you must really know your poetry, Commissaire.'

'Cheung, take it easy. It's just a routine check. I've got nothing against you. You're a good cop.'

'What do you know about being a cop? Hey, be careful with that, Commissaire,' she added, as he was walking away with their guns. 'They're not toys, you might get hurt.'

'Where is Servaz?' asked Rimbaud, ignoring her words.

'I don't know. You know, Vincent?'

'Haven't a clue.'

'Tell him I need his gun, too, when you see him.'

Samira burst out laughing.

'Martin couldn't hit the Death Star if it was in front of him. His scores at the shooting range are downright ridiculous. He's the sort who could literally shoot himself in the foot.'

Rimbaud later regretted saying this, but as was often the case, at the time he could not resist:

'That may well be what he's done,' he said, on his way out.

At 18.19, Servaz switched off his phone.

'I have to go to the car,' he said. 'I'll be right back.'

'What's happening?'

'Nothing. I need a smoke. I have a packet in the car.'

He felt nervous all of a sudden: Samira had just called; they were checking everyone's guns. But he had no reason to feel this way, since he'd always had it with him.

On leaving the hotel he was met with an icy wind. Gusts penetrated his too-thin jumper. He should have put on his down jacket. A powerful gust nearly drove him back towards the hotel entrance, but he went on tramping through the snow towards the steps that led down to the road. He looked up and there they were. Labarthe and Gustav. They had come out and were walking into the wind, laughing. They were heading towards the hotel – in other words, towards him. *Shit.*

He couldn't go back to the hotel now. He didn't want Labarthe to see his face too close up. That would complicate things if he needed to shadow him later. He went gingerly down the snowy steps, opened the passenger door and then the glove compartment. The packet of cigarettes was there. He looked up and craned his neck to see above the stone retaining wall. Labarthe and Gustav were climbing up to the terrace via another flight of steps. He instantly ducked into the car and pretended to be looking for something else. When he stood up straight, they had disappeared inside.

He looked up. His heart leapt when he saw Aurore Labarthe on her balcony, watching the hotel. Shit! Had she seen his little performance? He couldn't stay there much longer. He was going to have to walk past them, because the hotel reception, next to the bar, was tiny, and the lift, no bigger than a matchbox, was right next to it.

He glanced furtively at the woman on the balcony. Was she watching him? Or the hotel? He went back up the steps and crossed the terrace.

Labarthe and Gustav had their backs to him; Labarthe was talking with the manager, who was handing something to him.

'Thanks, this will really help us out,' said Labarthe. 'How much do I owe you?'

He was fishing through his wallet. Servaz began to walk across the lobby. Gustav must have heard his footsteps crunching on the snow as he approached the door, because he turned around. The boy's big blue eyes stared right at him. Servaz felt as if all his innards were being siphoned out of him and replaced with air. His head was spinning. The little boy was still looking at him.

'You are my son, aren't you?'

The little boy didn't answer.

'You're my son, I know you are.'

He shook himself. Banished the fantasy. Walked past them. Labarthe turned his head as he did.

'Good evening.'

'Good evening,' he replied.

The manager was looking at him, Labarthe was looking at him, the boy was looking at him. He pressed the button for the lift and resisted the urge to turn around.

'Excuse me,' said Labarthe behind him.

Was he talking to him or to the manager?

'Excuse me.'

This time, there could be no doubt. The voice was behind him; he turned around. Labarthe was looking at him.

'Did you love torture, Servaz, did you love pain?'

'What?'

'I'm afraid you left your headlights on,' said the professor for the second time.

'Oh!'

He thanked him and returned to the car. Aurore Labarthe had vanished from her balcony.

He went back up to the room.

'What happened?' asked Kirsten.

'Nothing. I ran into Labarthe. And Gustav. Downstairs, in the lobby.'

Zehetmayer was sitting in one of those Viennese cafés that didn't seem to have changed since the days when Stefan Zweig portrayed them in *The World of Yesterday*, not long before taking his own life. Those cafés that were among the rare vestiges of a bygone Vienna, a city that loved theatre, literature and the arts, cafés that once resonated with conversations that were so much more enlightened than those of the present day, in his opinion.

What did remain, in fact? What was left of the Jews who had made the reputation of this city? Men like Mahler, Schoenberg, Strauss, Hofmannsthal, Schnitzler, Beer-Hofmann, Reinhardt, Zweig – and even Freud, that sniffer of ladies' underwear?

Sitting in a booth at the very back of the former gallery of the Café Landtmann (for nothing on earth would he sit outside among the tourists, in the new glassed-in terrace), the orchestra conductor was eating a schnitzel and reading the *Krone,* glancing from time to time through the heavy curtains out at the Rathausplatz, which was turning white before his eyes. A short while ago he had glimpsed his reflection in a mirror, and he looked like the person he was: an old man with wrinkled, yellowed skin, his gaze full of malevolence, but his air of distinction was indisputable, with his long black overcoat and its collar of otter's fur. The opening bars of Brahms' *Hungarian Dance No. 1* drifted up from the right pocket of his coat. All his important contacts had their own ringtone, and this music corresponded to an *extremely* important contact.

'Hello?' he said simply.

'We've found the boy,' said the voice on the other end.

'Where?'

'A village in the Pyrenees.'

'And him?'

'Not yet. Sooner or later, he'll show his face.'

'If you walk on snow you cannot hide your footprints,' said Zehetmayer, quoting a Chinese proverb. 'Good work.'

The only response he got was the dialling tone at the other end: politeness was also a notion that belonged to the past. Perhaps it was time to call the other number. The one he'd obtained when he was teaching music to prisoners. He helped them to 'escape', thanks to Mahler. After all, that's what he was doing, too: through music, escaping from this modern world he loathed.

29

Ruthless

That night, in their little mountain hotel, Servaz dreamt that he was in the Métro in Paris, and that he spotted Gustav in the crowd. His heart pounding, he stood up and threaded his way, pushing and shoving, towards the boy, just as the train was pulling into a station called Saint-Martin. He could not recall ever hearing of a station with that name, except in his dream. The passengers he pushed shot him hostile, disapproving looks. With great effort, he had nearly made it when the train came to a halt: the doors opened and the crowd got out. Servaz rushed out onto the platform. Gustav was already heading towards the escalator. Servaz went on bumping into people, but the mass of bodies slowed him down and pushed him even further away from the boy.

'Gustav!' he cried.

The boy turned around and looked at him. Servaz thought his heart would burst with joy. But now the fear in the child's eyes was obvious and he in turn began to weave his way through the crowd . . . to get away from him. Servaz began climbing the escalator steps two by two. He reached the crossroads of corridors at the top and froze. There was no one there. All of a sudden, the corridors were completely empty.

He was alone.

He looked at the endless corridors around him: there was not a soul to be seen. The very silence seemed to have a particular frequency. He spun around. The escalator he had taken was just as empty – its steps moving uselessly – as the platform below. He called out to Gustav, but got only an echo in response. It suddenly seemed to him that there was no way out, and no hope. He was trapped here, in this underground warren, for all eternity. He wanted to shout but instead, he woke up. Kirsten was asleep. He could hear his own breathing.

They had not drawn the curtains and a faint phosphorescence inscribed a rectangle of light in the window, in the blue, unreal darkness of the room. He pushed back the eiderdown and the sheet and went over to the window. All the lights in the chalet were out, and the building was plunged in darkness. Its dark shape stood out against the lighter night; there was something hostile and disquieting about it. All around, the snow-covered landscape made him think of the moat of a fortress, protecting the chalet's occupants from the invader.

Then the vapour on the window blurred his vision, and he went back to bed.

'I'll stay here,' declared Kirsten that morning at breakfast. 'I'll see if I can go snowshoeing, and I'll keep an eye on the chalet at the same time. Just so I'm not stuck indoors the whole time.'

'Fine.'

He intended to go back to Toulouse, where he would hand in his gun, then hurry to the library or a bookshop to get hold of Labarthe's book. He would be back by evening. It was Saturday, but he also wanted to call Roxane Varin so that she could look into Gustav's adoption first thing on Monday morning. He reached for his phone and called Espérandieu at home. Vincent was listening to 'We're on Fire' by Airplane Man when his phone rang.

'Roland and Aurore Labarthe: can you check them for criminal records? In the usual police files but also in the sex offenders' and the gendarmerie's crime research databases.'

'You know it's Saturday?'

'Monday first thing,' he said. 'Give Charlène a hug for me.'

'Does this have something to do with that kid?'

'We found him. They're the people looking after him.'

There was a pause on the line.

'So now you tell me?'

'We only found out yesterday.'

He could tell his assistant was angry.

'Martin, ever since you hooked up with your lady from Lapland, you seem to have forgotten your friends. I'm going to start feeling jealous soon. And watch out, there's someone waiting for you here. I think he has his eye on you. And he's also waiting for your gun.'

'I know. I have an appointment with him.'

He didn't feel like saying more than that. Not now. He hung up, and slowly pulled out onto the icy road. It took him two hours to get to Toulouse and police headquarters. On Saturday morning it was three-quarters empty, but Rimbaud had nevertheless insisted on seeing him without further delay. Since he could not see him on his own territory, the commissaire was waiting for him in a little office that he'd commandeered for the purpose. Servaz thought he looked like a former boxer, with his flat nose and bulldog jaw. A boxer who had received more blows than he'd struck. But Servaz knew that it was now his turn to act as punching bag.

'Your mobile, Commandant, please,' said Rimbaud, wasting no time.

'I beg your pardon?'

'Your mobile, put it on "Do Not Disturb" mode.'

Servaz handed him the device.

'Do it yourself. I don't know how.'

Rimbaud stared at him with an expression that implied he thought Servaz was making fun of him. He reluctantly did as he was told then handed the phone back to Servaz.

'My purpose is to question you regarding the murder of Florian Jensen,' he announced. 'As you can imagine, this is a matter of the utmost importance, given the fact he was killed with a service weapon. It is a very delicate matter.'

'In what regard? Because of the suspect?'

Rimbaud did not reply. Servaz wondered what attitude he would adopt: confrontation or collaboration? They were sitting on either side of the desk, facing each other: confrontation, then.

'I would like you to tell me what happened on the roof of the railway carriage, and about the night you went to Saint-Martin.'

'It's all in my report.'

'I've read it. I was told you spent several days in a coma; how are you feeling?'

An open question, thought Servaz. According to the police manual, 'open questions encouraged the speaker to talk and give as much information as possible'. Then you moved progressively to closed questions: the tunnel technique. The problem was that offenders were almost as familiar with these interrogation techniques as the cops were. And the problem with the cops from the Inspectorate was that they were interrogating other cops, so they had to be all the wilier.

But that was Rimbaud's problem.

'How am I feeling? Do you really want to know?'

'Yes.'

'Drop it, Rimbaud. If I need a shrink I'll find one myself.'

'Hmm. Do you need a shrink, Commandant?'

'Ah, is that your thing? To repeat what the other person says?'

'And you, what's your thing?'

'For Christ's sake! How long are we going to play at this?'

'I'm not playing, Commandant.'

'Just drop it . . .'

'Okay, fine – what were you doing on the roof? Why did you go up there in the middle of the storm? You could have been burned to a crisp.'

'I was pursuing a suspect who had fled after threatening us with his gun.'

'But by this point, some time had passed since he'd threatened you, no?'

'Do you mean I should have let him get away?'

'You had your gun in your hand when you went onto the roof, didn't you? You had it pointed at Jensen?'

'What? I wasn't armed! The gun was, er, still in the glove compartment.'

'You're telling me that you were pursuing a suspect who was armed and high on drugs and who had already taken aim at you and you weren't even armed?'

'You could say that, yes,' he replied.

'You could say that?'

'Are you going to start repeating everything I say again?'

'Right. So, Jensen shoots you and at the same time gets that fucking electrical shock that turns him into a Christmas tree.'

'You like metaphors, Rimbaud. It must be because of your name.'

'Enough bullshit, Servaz. That was damned unlucky, all the same: if only he'd been fried a second earlier, you would have been spared all those days and nights in a coma.'

'Or he might have fried my brain.'

'Do you think you've changed since you came out of the coma?'

He swallowed. Maybe Rimbaud was more cunning than he seemed.

'Everyone changes, Commissaire, whether or not they've been in a coma.'

'Did you have visions? Did you see things – your dead parents, anything like that?'

Bastard, he thought.

'No.'

'Everything working just like before?'

'How about you, Rimbaud?'

Rimbaud merely nodded without reacting. He was used to sharp customers; he wouldn't let himself be rattled that easily. *Nor will I*, thought Servaz.

'When Jensen called you late the other night, do you recall the first thing he said to you?'

Servaz thought.

'"How is that heart doing?"'

'Right. And then?'

'He talked about that night on the train carriage . . . *quite a night you had*, or something like that.'

'Right. Go on.'

'He said that because of me he looked like – I can't remember who, some name I'd never heard.'

'Okay.'

'He said he had seen me that day, in Saint-Martin.'

'Oh, really? What were you doing there?'

'Working on a case. At the town hall. A missing child.'

'Missing children – is that a matter for the crime brigade?'

'It hardly matters. It has nothing to do with Jensen.'

'So it doesn't. Right. How did you react?'

'I asked him what he wanted.'

'And what did he say?'

'He wanted to talk to me.'

Rimbaud gave him a funny look.

'I asked him what about,' added Servaz without waiting for the next question, even though he knew he shouldn't make the job easier for the man sitting across from him.

'And what did he say?'

'That I knew.'

'And was that true?'

'No.'

'Right. And then what did you say to him?'

'That I had other things to do.'

'And that's when he mentioned your daughter,' asserted Rimbaud. This was what he had been driving at, right from the start.

'Yes.'

'How did he refer to her?'

'All he said was, "Your daughter, I know."'

'And was that when you decided to go there?'

'No.'

'How did you react when he mentioned your daughter?'

'I asked him to repeat what he'd said.'

'Were you angry?'

'Yes.'

'Then what did he say?'

'That he would wait for me at midnight outside the thermal baths in Saint-Martin.'

'Did he mention your daughter again?'

'Yes.'

'Okay. What did he say?'

'"And say good evening to your daughter for me."'

'Hmm. Which made you even angrier.'

'Yes.'

Rimbaud's eyes had narrowed to slits. Servaz remained impassive, but he felt insulted. He viewed Rimbaud's very existence as a personal offence.

'We checked the times your phone indicated your position on the transmitters between Toulouse and Saint-Martin. Some minor calculations enabled us to determine that you were driving well above the speed limit that night, Commandant. What did you have in mind as you went tearing down the motorway like that to Saint-Martin?'

'Nothing.'

'Nothing?'

'Nothing in particular. I just wanted to see him face to face and tell him to stay away from my daughter.'

'So, you intended to *threaten* him?'

Servaz could see very well where Rimbaud wanted to get him, the same way fish can sense where the net is dragging them – but by then it's already too late.

'I wouldn't use that word.'

'And what word would you use?'

'Warn. I wanted to warn him.'

'About what?'

'That if he went any closer to my daughter, he would be in trouble.'

Rimbaud seemed to savour the expression, giving a faint smile, transcribing something into his notebook before typing on his keyboard.

'What sort of trouble?'

'What's the point of speculating, since I didn't actually see him?'

'What sort of trouble were you thinking of, Commandant?'

'Don't wear yourself out, Rimbaud. I mean legal trouble.'

The commissaire nodded, clearly unconvinced.

'Tell me about Saint-Martin. What happened there?'

'I already told you everything.'

'What was the weather like? Was it snowing?'

'No.'

'Was the sky clear? Was there a moon?'

'Yes.'

'So, you could see as if it were broad daylight?'

'No, no, not broad daylight. But it was a fairly clear night, yes.'

'Okay. Tell me: if the night was that clear, why did you not recognise Jensen, with his bloody burned mouth that made him look like Freddy Krueger?'

'That's it, that's the name.'

'What?'

'When he said that it was my fault he looked like someone, that was the name he mentioned.'

Rimbaud shook his head, looking annoyed, and Servaz suppressed a smile.

'Fine, fine. The fact remains that you didn't recognise him.'

'He was standing under the trees, a good thirty metres away. If it was him.'

'You're not sure?'

'How could he have been there and at the refuge at the same time?'

'How indeed? So, you don't think it was him?'

'It seems obvious, no?'

'And do you have any idea who it could have been?'

'No,' he lied.

'You have to admit it's a strange business, Servaz.'

He didn't reply.

'And so the voice on the telephone, who was it?'

Servaz hesitated.

'At the time, I thought it was Jensen. But thinking back, it could easily have been someone else. After all, everything they said was in the newspapers.'

'Hmm. Who would want to do that, that's what I find so hard to grasp.'

Servaz felt the anger spreading through him. He wanted to explode, but he knew that if he did, Rimbaud would use it against him.

'Where were you that night at around three o'clock in the morning?'

'In my bed.'

'In Toulouse?'

'Yes.'

'Did your daughter hear you come back?'

Rimbaud knew more than he was willing to disclose.

'No. She was asleep.'

'So, you came back from Saint-Martin, and you went to bed?'

'Correct.'

'What size shoe do you wear, Servaz?'

'What?'

'Your shoe size . . .'

'Forty-two. Why?'

'Hmm. Fine. No more questions for the time being. As for your weapon, you can pick it up here in a few days. We'll keep you informed.'

Rimbaud stood up.

'Servaz . . .'

Rimbaud had spoken so softly he almost didn't hear him. He turned around.

'I don't believe you for one second. And I will prove that you have been lying.'

Servaz looked at the cop from the Inspectorate, almost said something, thought better of it, shrugged and went out.

30

A Strange Pair

'They're a strange pair, your Labarthe couple.'

He was sitting on the terrace at the Café des Thermes, on the boulevard Lazare-Carnot, with Lhoumeau, the cop from the anti-procurement brigade. After delivering his neat judgement, Lhoumeau raised his beer to his lips. His habit of going out after sunset to 'sniff' the pavements, or to keep an eye on the all-night bars in the Matabiau-Bayard-Embouchure sector, had resulted in an ashen complexion and huge bags under his eyes. His hollow cheeks and bony nose – where Servaz could make out a network of tiny veins that was no doubt due to his penchant for strong drink – further enhanced his appearance as a night owl. His feverish gaze was constantly on the lookout.

'We caught them more than once, propositioning whores.'

'Both of them?'

'Both of them. The woman was doing the choosing.'

Servaz knew that there were roughly 130 women working as prostitutes in Toulouse, most of them Bulgarian, Romanian, Albanian and Nigerian. Almost all of them belonged to a network. And they moved from one city to another, or even one country to another. 'The Europe of Sex', as Lhoumeau put it. He took a drag on his cigarette to get warm.

'One of the girls eventually filed a complaint: against her wishes she had ended up at an S&M party, where she was allegedly abused. But she withdrew her complaint. Since then, the pair have been lying low in the country.'

'I know,' said Servaz, his tone sinister.

'Why are you interested in them?'

'They've turned up in a case.'

The cop shrugged his skinny shoulders.

'Right. You can't tell me anything more, I understand. But you should know that the Labarthes are as twisted as they come. I've always thought that the crime unit will have to deal with them some day.'

'Why's that?'

Servaz had put Labarthe's book on the table between them. The sky hung low and grey over Toulouse. In the December light, Lhoumeau's avian face looked almost like a mask.

'The parties they organised were violent. Sometimes very violent. The Labarthes had a lot of connections in the sex trade in Toulouse, and both they and their rich guests were eager for new experiences, new sensations.'

Servaz thought about similar parties Julian Hirtmann used to organise at his villa on Lake Geneva, back in the days when he was a prosecutor there. Yet another connection.

'How do you know all this?'

Lhoumeau shrugged, but avoided Servaz's gaze.

'It's my job to know these things.'

'In what way violent?'

'The usual stuff. But sometimes it would go a bit too far. Some of the girls wanted to file a complaint, but they were dissuaded.'

'By who?'

'By money, for a start. The Labarthes' guests had a lot of it. They even paid an entry fee. And there were powerful people there: magistrates, politicians, even cops.'

Always the same rumours, thought Servaz. This city loved rumours. He narrowed his eyes, the better to study Lhoumeau.

'Could you be a little more precise?'

'No.'

Lhoumeau's attitude was beginning to exasperate him. He suspected he didn't know as much as he was implying. He looked at a young couple kissing, not five metres from them: the boy was leaning against a car, the girl was leaning against him.

Then he turned his attention back to Lhoumeau and suddenly he twigged: Lhoumeau had been a participant. He would be neither the first nor the last cop to frequent such clandestine events, or gambling circles, or orgies.

'The woman was the worst,' said Lhoumeau suddenly.

'Why?'

'She's a dominatrix, you know the type. But it wasn't just that. The moment she sensed that a girl was vulnerable, she homed in. And she would arouse the men, provoke them. Sometimes there would be more than a dozen of them around the girl. And the more terrified the girl was, the more excited this woman became. She was scary, all right.'

'Were you there?'

Lhoumeau cleared his throat. He looked as if he were about to throw up.

'Once, yes. Only once. Don't ask me what the fuck I was doing there.'

He saw Lhoumeau gulp and give him a strange look.

'That woman, take it from me – keep away from her.'

'And what about him?'

'He's an intellectual. Takes himself very seriously. Arrogant, smug, but servile around the more influential guests. He thinks he's in charge but she's the one wearing the trousers.'

What a charming pair, thought Servaz, crushing his cigarette. On the boulevard, the young couple had moved apart. Suddenly the girl slapped the boy in the face and walked away.

He thought about Margot. The girl in the young couple was a few years younger but looked a little bit like her. And obviously she had just as much of a temper. On his way here he had decided he would go and see his daughter. But now he wondered how she'd take it when he told her he wouldn't be staying. Badly, no doubt. Suddenly he realised he no longer had the courage to deal with yet another crisis.

He was back by the end of the day, although the sun had already vanished behind the peaks a while earlier. Above the mountains the sky was red, and the snow itself had a pinkish tinge, while the water of the stream he was driving alongside looked like copper leaf. Then he left the valley to start up towards the mountaintops, and snowflakes came to greet him, downy and whirling. Clearly the snowplough had not been through there, and he had to drive extremely cautiously all the way to the hotel. Once or twice he got a fright when his rear wheels skidded at the edge of a fairly steep slope and by the time he parked the car, his legs were trembling slightly.

As on every evening, everything was veiled in shadow, and the valley below them was drifting slowly into the mist. The little lights of the villages were coming on and twinkling through the fog. The manager had hung red and yellow Christmas lights beneath the eaves.

He found Kirsten at the bar, chatting with the manager. She had caught the sun, and her hair was even lighter because of it. She sat drinking a hot chocolate. She is beautiful, he thought. And they were going to have to spend another night together.

'Well?' he said.

'It's been dead calm. The woman took Gustav to school this morning and brought him back at noon. In the afternoon a woman came to do the cleaning. Gustav made a snowman and went sledging. No sign of the guy since this morning. He must be in Toulouse . . .' She hesitated. 'It's all too normal, in fact.'

'What do you mean?'

'I'm wondering if they haven't spotted us.'

'That soon?'

'They're on their guard. And your Labarthe may have spoken to the manager yesterday.'

He shrugged.

'You're imagining things. The fact they're behaving normally, that's what's normal,' he concluded, with a smile.

31

Abandon All Pride,
Oh Ye Who Enter Here

He put Labarthe's book back down, disappointed. It was fiction based on facts – phoney, meaningless stuff.

Everything in it was common knowledge, although Labarthe had added some personal ideas, putting himself in the killer's shoes. At the end of the day it was a pretentious, bombastic thing, passing itself off as literature.

He thought about what his father had said to him again and again, when he was making his first efforts at writing: 'I believe more in the scissors than I do in the pencil.' He later found out that these were not his father's words, but Truman Capote's. What he had before his eyes was verbose, complacent and posturing.

Could Hirtmann really have been seduced by such a book? Pride provokes blindness. The portrait that Labarthe had given of him was virtually hagiographic; it was easy to sense the fascination that Hirtmann's acts held for the scribe. Perhaps he had dreamt of doing the same thing but had never dared take the first step? It was certainly not morality that held Labarthe back, but rather fear of prison; everyone knew what happened inside to people like him. So why had he agreed to take Gustav in? Why run such a risk? Had Hirtmann forced their hand in one way or another?

Servaz had already found two connections: the S&M parties and the book. Were there others? Kirsten was asleep. For a moment he gazed at her profile. Like many adults, in her sleep she looked like a child, as if every night we return to our origins.

He reached for the binoculars and went to the window. Aurore Labarthe was standing at one of the first-floor windows, the only one where a light was still shining. She was wearing a very tight outfit in black leather – like a motorcyclist's – and she was looking over at the hotel. Her armour was split down the middle, with a zip that went all the way to her crotch. Servaz saw her fingers move up to the top of the zip and slowly open it. He felt his throat go dry. He stepped back so he wouldn't be seen.

A ritual, he thought. *Someone is watching.*

The manager?

Exhibitionism was clearly one of the other little pleasures Aurore Labarthe indulged in during her leisure time. Did her husband know? Probably. The two of them were on the same wavelength.

He'd seen enough, and he moved away from the window.

He looked at Kirsten still deep in the sleep of the innocent. As if she'd found refuge from her diurnal nightmares. He was oddly grateful to her for it.

He positioned himself in one corner of the Victor-Hugo market, standing behind a row of tall dustbins in a dark spot where his shadow melted into others. From where he stood he had a perfect view of the balcony, the illuminated picture windows of the living room and kitchen, and the area surrounding the building.

From time to time a car, a couple, or a solitary individual with a dog went by in the street, and he recoiled still further into the shadow. A while ago he'd noticed the bloke in the car, a dozen metres away. The bonnet was pointed towards the entrance to the building.

Apparently, in spite of Jensen's death, they had not lifted the surveillance.

His headphones were playing the first movement of the *Symphony No. 7: langsam – allegro risoluto, ma non troppo.*

He thought of Martin in that hotel and smiled. Was he fucking the Norwegian woman? Hirtmann bet he wasn't. In the meantime, Hirtmann was observing the balcony and the windows, and from time to time Margot's silhouette passed in front of them. He had not yet decided how to proceed. To do what he'd done with Marianne seemed drearily repetitive. Besides, the surveillance made everything more complicated.

But he needed Martin. He was going to have to put pressure on him, one way or another. For Gustav's sake.

Right, he thought. *Off we go.*

He left his hiding place and began walking quickly along the pavement, like someone who was late, a bottle of champagne in his hand. He walked past the car. He sensed that the cop at the wheel turned his head and looked at him as he went by.

There was a party on the top floor of the building, two floors above Servaz's flat. You could hear the music from the street. Hirtmann stopped outside the glass door. Pretended to press the button for the intercom, then speak. In fact, he had memorised the door code long ago, the day an old lady had punched it in in front of him, while he stood there wearing an impeccable suit and tie and spoke into his mobile as loudly as possible, 'Yes, it's me, tell me the door code, please – the intercom isn't working.'

He typed the code and the door buzzed. He went through. There were no cops in the entrance hall.

Julian Hirtmann walked over to the lift, pressed the call button but took the stairs that wound their way around the wire cage. There was another cop on the second floor, sitting on a chair in the corner of the landing by the door. He looked up from his paper. Hirtmann looked surprised: it's not every day you come upon a bloke reading the newspaper on the landing.

'Good evening,' he said. 'Uh, where's the party?'

The cop pointed wearily up the stairs with one finger, not speaking. How many times that evening had he made the same gesture? Nevertheless he narrowed his eyes to get a good look at Hirtmann.

'Thank you,' said Hirtmann, continuing to climb.

He did not stop outside the flat where the party was, but kept climbing up to the short little door that led into the attic. There he sat down on the last step, uncorked the champagne, put his headphones back on and raised the bottle to his lips. It was an excellent champagne. An Armand de Brignac brut blanc de blanc.

Two hours later, he had a sore arse and his knees ached when he stood back up. He dusted off his behind, then went back down to Servaz's floor, tottering, leaning on the railing.

'You still here?' he said, his voice slurred. Now the cop was drinking a cup of coffee. 'What you doing here? You live here?'

The cop shot him an irritated look. Hirtmann went closer, wobbling his head, his gait unsteady.

'Why you out on the landing? Your wife chuck you out or something?'

He gave a silly laugh, raised one finger to his nose.

'You really goin' spend the night here? Don't b'lieve it, thass crazy . . .'

'Sir,' said the cop, looking very annoyed, 'please go away.'

Hirtmann frowned, and staggered even more.

'Hey! Don' you speak t' me like that!'

The man flashed a red, white and blue card.

'Get out of here, I said.'

'Ah, okay, who th' fuck lives here, anyway?'

'Get out!'

Hirtmann pretended to stumble, and his hand knocked the coffee cup from the cop's fingers; a brown spot appeared on his light blue shirt and grey jacket.

'Shit!' shouted the cop, shoving him violently. 'I told you to get out of here, you pillock!'

Hirtmann fell backwards on his arse. Just then the door to the flat opened and Margot Servaz appeared in her pyjamas and dressing gown, barefoot, her hair dishevelled. Hirtmann thought she resembled her father, with that little bump on her nose.

'What's going on?' she asked, one hand on the door handle, looking first at Hirtmann and then at the cop.

He could see the cop's nervousness increasing exponentially, his eyes darting from Hirtmann to Servaz's daughter and back.

'Get back inside! Get back inside! And lock the door!'

Now the cop was pointing his gun at him and speaking into his Bluetooth at the same time:

'Get up here, I've got a problem!'

The second cop appeared a few seconds later. The one from the car. There were only two of them.

'Take this drunk and get him out of here, for fuck's sake!'

On Sunday morning, Servaz and Kirsten could see heightened activity and preparations under way at the chalet: skis and snowboard on the roof of the Volvo, clothing in the boot, picnic basket on the back seat. The Labarthes and Gustav climbed into the car and drove past the hotel.

They would be gone for the day.

Kirsten and Servaz exchanged a glance. 'A very bad idea, going out there today,' she said.

At around noon a thick fog settled, and the chalet was nothing but a blurry outline in the pea soup. Servaz and Kirsten were snow-shoeing above the hamlet, near the col du Couret; the manager had assured them that the snowpack was stable.

Servaz stopped at the edge of the forest, out of breath, and looked down at the scarcely visible roofs below them, then at Kirsten.

'With weather like this, they're bound to come back,' she added, to dissuade him, after interpreting his gaze.

'Take the car,' he said. 'Go down to the valley. And let me know if you see them go by.'

He switched on his mobile and showed her the screen.

'It's okay. I have a signal.'

Then he vanished into the mist, taking great strides down the slope.

The dark mass of the chalet emerged slowly from the fog, even more imposing up close. He went around it, along the side away from the hotel. Seeing it at close quarters, Servaz realised it must originally have been a mountain farm which had been rebuilt: he could make out the stone foundations which would have accommodated the occupants and the livestock, and the wooden structure above, where straw and grain had been stored.

Everything had been transformed, redesigned, with vast glass surfaces to let the light in, like something out of an interior design magazine, and with a great deal of money spent to achieve the desired effect. This was, in its way, the architectural equivalent of cosmetic surgery: all these rehabilitated facades ended up looking the same.

In some resorts in the Alps a house like this would have been worth millions of euros. But here, the darkened wood of the facing needed refreshing and the door and window frames, licked by the fog, seemed in a sorry condition. Even with a university professor's salary, the purchase and upkeep of such a building must be astro-nomical. Did the Labarthes have delusions of grandeur? Or hidden resources? Were they hard-pressed, financially? Servaz made a note to call his mates at economic and financial affairs the very next day.

There was no sign of any alarm system or sensor.

Servaz looked all around: no one. As he had done outside Jensen's house, he reached into his pocket for some bump keys. If things went on like this, he'd have to start thinking about a new career. He studied the lock. Unlike the door, it had been changed recently. So much the better. Rusty locks were trickier to deal with.

Seven minutes and thirty-five seconds later he was inside, in a little boiler room with a washer-dryer, where it was pleasantly warm and there was a nice smell of laundry. He walked past some metal shelving, down a corridor, and came out into a large cathedral-ceilinged living room. A pyramid chimney took centre stage, suspended above an open hearth. When the weather was clear the picture windows must command a breathtaking view. Eggshell leather sofas, stone, light wood, black-and-white photographs, spotlights: when it came to interior design, the Labarthes seemed to conform to mainstream taste.

Outside, whorls of fog rolled across the terrace as if it were the deck of a ghost ship.

Servaz took a few cautious steps forward. There was something unreal about the silence. He looked around for the little red eye of a movement sensor. Saw nothing. He began to search, avoiding the windows on the east side, which were visible from the hotel, even in this weather.

Sixteen minutes later he had to face facts: there was nothing to report in this main room, or in the kitchen.

Labarthe's study was hardly any less disappointing. A room with windows on two of the four sides, wedged in a corner between the two wings of the chalet. Labarthe's reading material was unsurprising, given his interests: Bataille, Sade, Guyotat – and also Deleuze, Foucault, Althusser . . . Labarthe's own books had pride of place. On the desk were a Mac, an anglepoise lamp and a letter-opener with a leather handle. Also a pile of bills and indecipherable notes for classes or some future book, who knew.

Beyond the study was a little corridor. Servaz came upon a bathroom at the very end, as well as a sauna and a room that had been made into a gym, with an indoor rowing machine, weightlifting bench, punching bag, and rack of weights.

He went up the wide staircase. On the first floor there were three bedrooms, a bathroom and a separate toilet.

The first two bedrooms were obviously spare; the last one was Gustav's – it said as much on the door in big blue letters. As Servaz pushed it open he felt a mixture of apprehension and excitement – there, in the nerve centre of the silent house.

It was decorated the way a little boy's room is meant to be decorated. There were posters on the walls, picture books on a shelf, a duvet decorated with a multitude of Spider-Men swinging in all sorts of acrobatic positions, and soft toys, including a huge one a metre long that looked like an elk or a caribou. Servaz went closer and looked at the label: *Made in Norway*.

Don't stay here.

He checked his watch. The time was speeding by. He went over to the bed, looked at it; did the same with the boy's clothes in the dresser. He eventually found what he was looking for: a blond hair. His pulse began to race. He took a transparent Ziploc from his jacket and slipped the hair into it. He would have liked to search the room from top to bottom but he doubted he had much time, so he left and went up the stairs that led towards the roof. His legs were trembling. There was a small landing and beyond it an open door, the parents' suite. He went in, walked across a thick carpet. Outside, through the French windows, he could see a misty white landscape and a tall fir tree, its branches stippled with snow. He thought of the view Hirtmann used to have from his cell.

Nearly the entire room was white: the panels of the sloping ceiling, the bed, the carpet. He recalled the off-white tunic Aurore Labarthe had been wearing the first time he saw her.

The bed was not made. It was piled with clothes, as was an adjacent chair. He went closer, sniffed the sheets on both sides: she slept on the right. Her perfume was the heady, overwhelming sort; it impregnated the sheets. He opened the drawers on the bedside tables. Magazines, earplugs, an eye mask, a tube of paracetamol and some reading glasses.

Nothing else.

The two adjacent walk-in wardrobes were the size of a student's garret. Jeans, dresses and several outfits in white or black leather for the lady; jackets, shirts, jumpers and suits for the gentleman.

When he was sure he wouldn't find anything there, either, he went back down to the kitchen. There was a door next to the huge freezer. He opened it. A spiral staircase, made of rough concrete. He switched on the light and started down it.

Perhaps he was on to something at last . . .

The stairs arrived at a metal door. He turned the handle. His pulse went up another gear.

The door resisted slightly, then gave way with a creaking sound. Yet another disappointment: the door opened into the big garage they could see from the hotel. The second vehicle was a small four-wheel drive. He walked quickly around the garage, then back up to the ground floor, his frustration and impatience increasing rapidly.

He looked outside: the day was fading. He thought quickly. Suddenly he had an idea.

Of course, why hadn't he realised earlier?

He went back to the top floor, to the little landing before the parents' suite. He looked up: there it was, the trap door to the loft.

He brought a chair from the next room, climbed onto it, reached up and grabbed the handle. The trap door creaked open – a dark, gaping mouth – and he pulled down the metal ladder and replaced the chair.

He climbed up the rungs, and pressed a switch next to the opening. A neon light flickered above him; he put his head through the hole.

Bingo.

The Labarthes' secret lair, their 'garden of delights'. No doubt about it. On the wall opposite him, in Gothic letters, was a framed notice:

> ABANDON ALL PRIDE
> OH YE WHO ENTER HERE
> ENTER INTO THE TYRANNICAL CRYPT
> DO NOT PITY US
> SEEK KNOWLEDGE AND PLEASURE
> MAKE EACH HOUR EXQUISITE
> SUFFER AND CRY
> TAKE YOUR PLEASURE

The sight of it filled him with gloom.

The immensity of the loops, twists and deviations of the human mind were enough to make him dizzy. In any other circumstances this jargon would have been laughable, but here, it was somehow sinister.

He pulled himself through the hole and stood on the floor, which was covered with a plastic coating. The place reminded him of a private dance club: there were benches, a dance floor, a bar, a sound system, and soundproofing of the kind found in recording studios.

The heat was suffocating and there was a cloying smell of hot dust.

Then his attention was caught by the wall bars at the far end, the kind they had in gyms. He got the suspicion that they were not used for working on one's abdominal muscles. He also saw a pulley and two hooks beneath the sloping ceiling, two other hooks on the wall, a camera on a tripod and video recording equipment at the back. A large old-fashioned oak armoire with bevelled mirrors stood out a bit further along, just before an opening without a door that gave on to another room.

He went in: translucent windowpanes, lockers and a shower. He returned to the first room. Opened the armoire. And felt as if he himself was a voyeur, when he saw the sinister shine of whips, crops, ball gags, leather shackles, chains and snap hooks – all politely lined up like tools on a handyman's rack. The Labarthes had enough to outfit a battalion in there. He thought back to Lhomeau's reflections about Aurore Labarthe and felt a shiver run down his spine. How far did these little games in the attic go?

He checked his watch.

He had been there for nearly an hour and still had not found the slightest trace of Hirtmann.

You've got to get out of here, he thought.

He was walking over to the trap door when he heard the sound of an engine.

He stiffened. It was heading towards the chalet. No. It was already here. The engine had just been switched off. *Shit!* He heard doors slamming, and voices outside, muffled by the snow. He looked at his phone. Why hadn't Kirsten warned him? *No signal!* The attic must be equipped with a frequency jammer.

He stopped at the edge of the trap door. Below him, the front door had just opened and he heard three voices, including Gustav's clear, cheerful tones.

He was for it now.

With damp hands, he pulled the metal ladder and the trap door towards him, as quietly as possible. Just before closing it, he slid his hand outside and switched off the light.

In the dark, he tried very hard to breathe regularly. Not altogether successfully.

32

The Fair-Eyed Captive

Night had fallen a while ago. From the hotel, Kirsten had her eye on the illuminated chalet. From time to time she saw a figure walk by a window.

Martin, where the hell are you?

She had tried to call at least a dozen times since she'd seen the Volvo, at the foot of the winding road, and sent just as many messages. Every time, she got his voicemail.

Now she had been back in their room for at least an hour and he still hadn't returned.

Something had happened. Was he simply hiding somewhere, or had they found him? The more time went by, the more the answer to this question seemed to be vitally important. Should she call for backup? Martin had broken every rule by going in there. With the suspicions that had been weighing upon him since Jensen's death, this would be the end of his career. Did that even matter? She could not possibly leave Martin at the mercy of those two individuals.

She felt a stiffness in her neck and the onset of a headache, both probably due to stress. She massaged her neck and took a paracetamol, before going back to the window.

As long as Gustav was awake, they wouldn't act. They would wait until he was asleep. Unless they had already . . . she banished the thought. Had Hirtmann told them about Martin? She had to act, to do something. But what? Once again she tapped on her mobile.

Where are you? Answer!

She gazed desperately at the empty screen. *Shit!* Why did he have to go and sneak inside the chalet? Over there, at the window, Labarthe was swinging Gustav in his arms, then the boy ran off, laughing. A touching family scene.

He was lying on his side in the darkness, his ear glued to the linoleum.

In the dark, a thin strip of light ran around the trap door like a rectangle burned with a blowtorch.

While he occasionally heard Gustav's high-pitched voice from the ground floor, the adults' voices were less distinct. Very soon they would put Gustav to bed. How long before they were all sound asleep? And even then, the trap door was right next to their bedroom. He recalled the creaking of the metal ladder when he extended it: it would be impossible to use it. There would be only one option: to jump straight down to the floor below and get the hell out of there.

He couldn't wait all night. What if someone came up to the attic?

He could feel the damp in his armpits. It was very hot. He was thirsty, too, a nagging thirst that thickened his dry, swollen tongue like boiled cardboard. And both his elbow and shoulder were stiff from staying in the same position.

He looked at his telephone. Not a single one of the messages he had sent had been transmitted.

He wiped the sweat from his brow with the back of his sleeve and listened out. The television had just been switched on. A cartoon. He could identify the sounds coming from the big living room from the slight echo they made. Suddenly he heard heavy steps resounding on the floor below. Someone had come upstairs. Then the shower in the bathroom in the parents' suite came on.

Five minutes later, whoever it was came back out. And stopped just below the trap door.

Servaz's Adam's apple bobbed up and down. He was willing to bet it was Aurore Labarthe. Did she come up every evening to gaze at her secret garden, her infernal little paradise? Or had she heard some noise he'd made?

He rolled over, moving quickly to one side: someone had just grabbed the handle on the other side and was opening the trap door.

Kirsten looked at her watch. Two hours had gone by since she'd returned to the hotel. Shit, she couldn't stand this waiting. The fog had lifted, with the exception of a few clouds of mist in the hollows, but it was snowing again, fairly heavily. The landscape looked like one of those virtual animated Christmas cards people send by email. Everything was drowned in a yellowish darkness.

Over there, a light was flickering in the living room: the television. Kirsten was beginning to get pins and needles in her legs. She was constructing all sorts of scenarios in her mind – and some of them were fairly sinister. An American study had shown that uncertainty wrought more havoc on people's minds and health than negative certainties.

That she could confirm. The question was, had Hirtmann mentioned Martin to the Labarthes, and did they know how important the cop was to him. It seemed unlikely. Most probably Hirtmann had not told them any more than they needed to know.

Light poured from the opening like glowing lava from a volcano. Servaz held his breath. The trap door was wide open. But whoever was standing underneath had not yet pulled down the ladder. He was frightened that his breathing, or the mad beating of his heart, would be audible. It was Aurore Labarthe, without a doubt: her heady, venomous perfume drifted up to him.

Down below there was no movement, no sound. Was her face raised towards the attic? Could she sense his presence? Did she suspect that someone was hiding there in the dark?

Then he heard the doorbell.

Whatever she had planned to do, she thought better of it, because the trap door closed. His cheek against the plastic flooring, he began to breathe again.

She rang the bell a second time. The door opened at last and Aurore Labarthe appeared. She was even taller than Kirsten had imagined: almost 1 metre 80. She was wearing an old dressing gown that looked warm and comfortable, and her hair, wet from the shower, was the colour of damp hay and fell around her severe face like a curtain. She planted herself in front of Kirsten. She had a long slender figure, her body all bone and muscle. Her pale blue eyes were totally devoid of warmth.

'Hi,' said Kirsten in English, with a big smile.

He listened out. A new voice. *Familiar*. He couldn't hear what she was saying, and it took him a few moments to realise why. *English. Kirsten!* Good Lord! What was she up to? He became aware that for a while now he'd had a terrible urge to urinate. He stood up and walked tentatively through the dark to the shower, where he relieved himself without really caring whether he was pissing in the right spot. Then he returned to his post.

Everyone was downstairs. He had to risk it. He opened the trap door a few centimetres and the voices reached him more distinctly.

'Do you speak English?' Kirsten asked, at the front door.

The Labarthe woman answered with a simple nod, neither unclenching her jaw nor taking her eyes off her.

'I – I'm staying at the hotel. I'm an architect in Oslo, in Norway, and I've been looking at your chalet since this morning.'

The blonde was listening without batting an eyelid, completely indifferent to what she was saying.

'I'm completely fascinated. I took a few pictures of the facade. I would like your written permission to publish them in a Norwegian journal, as an example of French mountain architecture. Would you allow me to have a look inside?'

That was all she had come up with. Improbable enough to be credible. She had the advantage of not looking like a French police officer – none of the ones she had met spoke English as impeccably as she did – and she did look like a foreigner. However, the woman at the door had not yet said a word and her expression was indecipherable. Kirsten felt the hair on the back of her neck stand on end: there was something utterly chilling about this woman. For a split second she wondered if she should reveal her true identity.

'I realise it's late and I'm disturbing you. I apologise. I'll come back tomorrow.'

All of a sudden Aurore Labarthe's face lit up.

'Not at all. Come in,' she said, with a broad smile.

Servaz heard the voices below, but could not make out what they were saying. The conversation sounded light. Nothing aggressive or threatening. This did not reassure him. God only knew what the Labarthes would be capable of in the presence of a lone woman as attractive as Kirsten. She had entered their lair, she had thrown herself into the lion's jaws. Now that he had seen all the paraphernalia in the attic, he wondered if anyone had ever been brought up here against their will.

The tension was exhausting and the situation was getting out of hand. He had to do something.

They were still chatting downstairs, the television blasting out its cartoon. This meant Gustav was not in bed yet. As long as that was the case, they would not go after Kirsten. He pushed the trap door wider, slid out, hanging from his arms, swung and let go. The moment his fingers were free he felt his shirt tear somewhere on his back.

He landed on the floor a bit too loudly, but at least the sound was muffled by the thick carpet. He wondered if anyone had heard him, but in addition to the racket of the cartoon, there was a shutter banging somewhere. He listened for a moment and could hear Aurore Labarthe's sinister laugh. He took out his telephone and switched it to silent. Hunted for Kirsten in his contacts. Typed in English:

Get out of here!

'How interesting,' said Aurore Labarthe, pouring Kirsten another glass of the sweet white wine which was, she said, a speciality of the southwest. 'Architecture is one of my passions,' she added, with a faint smile and a wink. 'Santiago Calatrava, Frank Gehry, Renzo Piano, Jean Nouvel . . . Do you know what Churchill said? "We shape our buildings; thereafter they shape us."'

Her English was perfect. Kirsten had a moment of panic. Truthfully, architecture was far from being one of her specialist subjects. She looked up from her glass, flashed Aurore Labarthe an indulgent smile, which she hoped would appear to be that of a professional who has already heard this a thousand times from enlightened, enthusiastic amateurs. Only one name came to mind.

'Ah, we have several remarkable architects in Norway,' she said with a smile. 'Kjetil Thorsen Traedal to start with.'

The co-architect of the Oslo Opera, known to all the inhabitants of the city. Aurore nodded cautiously, narrowing her eyes. Kirsten didn't like that look. She noted that they were sitting face to face in the living-room area, while Roland Labarthe was standing slightly to one side. From where he stood he could observe Kirsten at his leisure. Kirsten put down her glass. She had drunk enough. Her telephone vibrated in her pocket. A message.

'Shall we get Gustave to bed?' said Aurore Labarthe to her husband.

Kirsten saw the look they gave each other, and she was immediately on her guard. Where was Martin? His absence was increasingly worrying. She wondered again whether she ought to reveal her true identity. She tried desperately to pick up a sound, a sign. She hoped that Martin had heard her and that he would take advantage of the fact she was distracting the Labarthes' attention to find a way to get out. But what if he were tied up somewhere? She felt close to panic.

Labarthe switched off the television.

'Are you coming, Gustav?' he said.

Gustav . . . She swallowed her saliva. The little blond boy stood up.

'Your little boy is very sweet,' she said. 'And very well behaved.'

'Yes,' said Aurore Labarthe. 'Gustav is a good little boy. Aren't you, my treasure?'

She caressed his blond hair. The boy could have been hers. The couple headed towards the stairs, with Gustav between them.

'We won't be long,' said Aurore Labarthe.

Kirsten became aware of the sudden silence in the house. She took out her mobile. She had a signal. Four bars. She saw the message. Martin! His text in English was as explicit as could be:

Get out of here!

He scarcely had time to slip into one of the first-floor bedrooms before they were there. Through the narrow opening of the door, he saw them walk down the corridor towards the boy's room, with Gustav in his pyjamas. Aurore was much taller than her husband.

'I want her,' said the blonde woman.

'Aurore, not in front of the kid.'

'I fancy her,' she insisted, paying no attention to what he had said. 'I *really* fancy her.'

'What do you have in mind?' asked Labarthe, his voice warm and refined. Servaz was hearing it for the first time, as they walked by. 'It's a bit too good to be true, don't you think?'

'I want you to take her up there for me,' the woman declared. 'She'll be perfect.'

'Isn't it a bit dangerous? She's staying at the hotel next door.'

They were moving away, towards Gustav's room.

'With what I put in her wine, she won't remember a thing tomorrow,' answered the woman.

'You drugged her?' he said, incredulously.

Servaz suddenly felt cold fear grip his insides. He leaned closer to the opening in the door to be able to hear, but the tension was making his ears buzz.

'What are you talking about?' asked Gustav.

'Nothing, treasure. Get into bed now.'

'I have a tummy-ache.'

'I'll get you something.'

'A sedative for Gustav, then?' said the man, calmly.

'Yes – I'll get a glass of water.'

Servaz heard the woman coming and quickly stepped back. She went into the bathroom on the other side of the corridor and turned on the tap. Then she passed him again, a glass in her hand. He saw her hard profile, her gaze without warmth, and it was as if his centre of gravity suddenly plummeted. The Labarthes' intentions were as clear as could be.

'May I use your toilet?'

Kirsten's voice, now, from the ground floor.

'I'll go,' said the man. 'Make sure Gustav is asleep.'

Servaz resisted the urge to jump on Labarthe as he went past. He would have the advantage of surprise for a brief moment, but there was the woman – and he suspected that they were resourceful. He remembered the rowing machine, the weightlifting bench, the weights and the punching bag. He would never get the better of them. Not one against two, with his gun at police headquarters and Kirsten drugged. He was going to have to outsmart them.

'May I use your toilet?' she called, looking upstairs.

She heard heavy steps coming down, and Labarthe appeared. First his legs then his narrow face, with his ambiguous little smile.

'It's this way,' he said, showing her. 'Please.'

Once she was inside, Kirsten turned on the tap and ran her face under the cold water. What was happening to her? She felt woozy; as if she was going to be sick. Her forehead was damp with sweat. She pulled down her trousers and pants, and sat on the toilet seat. As she was relieving herself she felt as if her heart kept changing pace, beating faster, then slower.

What the hell was going on? She stood up painfully, took a deep breath and went back out.

The Labarthes were both sitting in the living-room area now. Their gazes swung towards her in unison, as if they were being moved by the same puppeteer, and she almost burst out laughing.

Don't laugh. You ought to be wary of these two, my dear, said a little voice inside. *If I were you I'd get out of here as fast as possible.*

She was sure that in the state she was in – if she ran to the door

– they would catch up with her in no time. And besides, they had just said they would have a drink and show her pictures of the chalet when it was being built – or renovated, rather, since it was an old farmhouse.

She was thinking about all this as she walked towards them across the big living room. She suddenly wondered how long it had taken her to do that. For fuck's sake, she was losing all sense of time and space, and the floor seemed to be moving in waves. Aurore Labarthe patted the space next to her on the sofa, and she flopped down.

The blonde smiled, and never took her eyes off Kirsten; nor did her husband.

If you think I've lost control, you're kidding yourself!

'Some more wine?' said the blonde.

'No, thank you.'

'I'll have another one,' said the man.

'Here,' said Aurore Labarthe, putting the iPad on her lap, 'here are the photographs of the chalet as it was being renovated.'

'Oh!'

Kirsten looked down at the screen, tried to focus on the photographs, but she found it difficult – and the colours seemed strangely saturated, like those of a poorly adjusted television: glaring reds, greens and yellows, all running into each other.

'The colours are strange, don't you think?' she said, and her voice seemed thick.

She could hear Roland Labarthe's short, ironic laugh, oddly distorted by a sort of echo in her ears. What was he laughing about? She wanted to let herself go, to lie down on the sofa. She felt weak, drained of strength.

Suddenly she remembered Martin's message:

Get out of here!

Shit, get a hold of yourself.

'I don't feel very well,' she said.

There was an echo in her voice. Aurore Labarthe stroked her cheek with her index finger. She leaned towards her, pressing her breast against her arm.

'Look,' she said, showing her the pictures.

Her fingernails were black and very long.

'It's . . .' she began.

What did she say? She had mixed up Norwegian and English! Her hosts were looking at her, amused. There was something besides mere amusement in their identical expressions, though: something sly, false, covetous . . . A shiver went through her. They said something to each other and laughed, but her brain must have disconnected for a moment, because she couldn't remember what had made them laugh.

She realised she was on her feet, and that they were leading her towards the staircase, holding her by both arms. *When did I stand up?* She couldn't remember.

'Where are we going?' she asked.

'You have to get some rest,' said Aurore Labarthe gently. 'We're taking you somewhere quieter.'

'Y-yes,' she stammered. 'I want to be left alone, I want some peace and quiet.'

Suddenly Aurore Labarthe turned to her, grabbed her chin and kissed her. The woman's tongue forced its way into her mouth. Kirsten let it. Something in her brain – a barrier, a lock – was preventing her from reacting.

'You fancy her,' said the man, behind them.

'Oh, yes. Very much. Let's go.'

Servaz looked at Gustav. The boy was sound asleep in the soft blue glow of his nightlight. It made the twirling Spider-Men on the duvet turn purple. Once again he wondered who this boy was – and above all, who his father was.

He had the blond hair in his pocket, deep inside the Ziploc bag.

He had heard Kirsten's voice downstairs as it changed and became thick and shrill. He had heard the Labarthes laughing, their honeyed voices, and he felt a rage in his belly.

But he knew that if he confronted them, both he and Kirsten were in danger of ending up in chains upstairs in that den. He had to outwit them.

Suddenly he heard a sound on the staircase and he hid behind the open door. There was a heavy thud. *Kirsten.*

'Help me,' said the man. 'She can't stand up.'

He took a peep, and saw them go by, heading towards the next floor, with Kirsten between them. She was half unconscious, allowing herself, more or less, to be dragged.

Servaz heard the noise of the trap door opening and the ladder being pulled down.

'You're beautiful, you know that,' said Aurore.

'Really?' asked Kirsten, as if she appreciated the compliment.

'You'll have to help us now,' said Labarthe, more coldly.

'Of course,' said Kirsten, 'but I can't feel my legs.'

'It doesn't matter,' said Aurore Labarthe, her tone soothing.

'Go and make sure Gustav is asleep,' ordered the man.

Servaz panicked. Aurore Labarthe's steps were already hurrying down the stairs and echoing along the corridor. He hid behind the door again – which was then flung wide open. He pressed his back against the wall.

But the door went back to its initial position and the steps retreated. Gustav moaned softly in his sleep and changed position. He put his thumb in his mouth.

Servaz felt as if his brain were about to explode. He had been roasting ever since his stay up in the overheated attic. He needed more than anything to get out of there, to breathe some fresh air.

He walked resolutely towards the stairs. On the floor above, they were climbing up the ladder, and it creaked and groaned under their weight. He went back down to the ground floor, treading lightly, and headed towards the front door in the same way.

The frigid night air was like a slap in the face. It woke him up.

He took deep, thirsty breaths, his hands on his knees, as if he'd been running a hundred-metre sprint. And then he went down the steps, took a handful of snow and rubbed it all over his face.

Finally, he took out his mobile, to call for backup.

He stopped. How long would it take them to get there? What would happen up there in the meantime? And what if the gendarmes refused to get involved? It wouldn't be the first time. And then their cover would be blown. Any chance that Hirtmann would ever show himself would be gone.

He thought for a moment, went back up the stairs, took another deep breath and rang the bell.

33

Poker Trick

The door only opened after the fifth time he had buzzed and held his finger down.

'Good God!' exclaimed Labarthe. 'What on . . . ?'

Servaz had taken out his red, white and blue badge and flashed it under the university professor's nose. He instantly put it away, before the man in front of him began to wonder why it was a cop at his door and not a gendarme.

'There has been a complaint from the hotel,' he said. 'Are you having a party here? People have complained about the noise. Have you seen the time?'

Labarthe stared at him, completely bewildered. Visibly he was trying to understand what was going on. Behind him, the house was perfectly silent and dark.

'What? Noise? What noise?' Incredulous, the professor gestured towards the interior. 'You can see perfectly well they can't mean here!'

He seemed to be in a hurry to curtail the discussion.

'We were about to go to bed,' he added, then narrowed his eyes. 'I've seen you somewhere before, haven't I? You're the guy from the hotel, yesterday . . . You left your headlights on.'

'You don't mind if I just take a quick look?' insisted Servaz, not answering.

He did mind. Quite obviously. And yet the professor smiled.

'I don't believe you have the right to do that,' he said. 'Good night.'

But before he could step back and close the door, Servaz had pushed past him and walked in.

'Hey! Where the fuck do you think you're going? You have no right! Come back here! We have a child sleeping upstairs!'

A child that you've drugged, you son of a bitch, thought Servaz, walking into the big cathedral-ceilinged living room. They had switched off all the lamps on the ground floor and the only light came from the snow beyond the windows; the dark shapes of the furniture were barely visible. Clearly, the Labarthes were ready for their very private little party. He resisted the temptation to turn around and kick the professor in his private parts, just so he wouldn't feel like partying any more.

'You cannot barge in here on the basis of a simple neighbourhood complaint; you can see there is nothing happening! Get the hell out of here!'

Labarthe seemed more worried than furious. Servaz heard a noise upstairs; perhaps it was the ladder being pulled up.

'What's that noise?' he said.

He saw Labarthe stiffen.

'What noise?'

'I heard a noise.'

He made as if to start up the stairs. The professor stood between him and the staircase.

'Stop! You have no right!'

'What's making you so nervous? What are you hiding up there?'

'What? What are you talking about, for fuck's sake? I told you, my son is asleep up there.'

'Your son?'

'Yes! My son!'

'What do you have up there?'

'What? Nothing! What do you think you're doing? You have no right to—'

'What are you hiding?'

'You're absolutely mad! Who are you, for God's sake? You're not a gendarme, and you were at the hotel yesterday. What do you want from us?'

Just then, Servaz's phone began to ping in his pocket. He knew what it was: all the messages Kirsten had sent him while he was in the attic; all the times she'd rung him in vain. They had decided that now was the moment to remind him of their presence.

'What's . . . ? Your phone's ringing,' said the man, his tone increasingly suspicious.

He mustn't let the professor regain the upper hand.

'Okay. I'll take a look,' said Servaz, walking around him and heading towards the stairs.

'Wait! Wait!'

'What?'

'You need a warrant, you have no right to do this!'

'A warrant? You've been watching too many films, mate.'

'No, no. A letter of request . . . something like that . . . Whatever it's called, I don't give a damn. You know very well what I mean. You can't just go marching into people's houses like this. I don't know who you are, but I'm going to call the gendarmes,' he said, taking out his phone.

'Okay,' said Servaz, unflinching. 'Be my guest.'

Labarthe switched it on, waited for a second, then put it away.

'All right, fine – what do you want?'

'Why aren't you calling the gendarmes?'

'Because . . .'

'What is your problem? There's something going on up there. Something not quite right. And I'm going to find out what it is. Get to the bottom of it. I'm going to go down to Saint-Martin, get a judge out of bed and come back here with a letter of request.'

He headed for the front door, and as he walked away towards the car Kirsten had left outside the hotel he felt Labarthe's gaze at his back, in the cold night.

Labarthe was already in a sweat when he put his head through the trap door. He saw that the Norwegian woman was attached to the pulley by her wrists, her arms raised. Aurore was wiping her face, hair and neck with a damp flannel to wake her up. All her gestures were filled with great tenderness, until she gave her a slap that rang out like the cracking of a whip and left a mark on her left cheek.

'We've got a really dodgy situation downstairs!' exclaimed her husband as he burst into the attic. 'She mustn't stay here! We have to take her back to the hotel!'

The blonde turned around.

'Who was it?'

Labarthe glanced cautiously at Kirsten, with her wobbling head and blinking eyes: she was completely out of it.

'A cop!'

He saw his wife stiffen.

'What? What did he want?'

'He claims that someone at the hotel made a noise complaint. It's total bullshit!'

Labarthe was waving his arms. 'I saw him at the hotel yesterday. What was he doing there? He told me he's coming back. We're in trouble!'

'What are you on about?' said Aurore Labarthe, unruffled.

But her husband seemed far more worried.

'We've got to hurry and get her out of here! We have to take her back to the hotel! Right away! We'll say she's had too much to drink.'

Now it was her turn to glance over at Kirsten. She handed the Norwegian woman's mobile to her husband. A message appeared on the screen:

Get out of here!

'That's what I keep telling you! We have to—'

'Shut up,' she interrupted. 'Take a breath. Calm down. And tell me everything from the start.'

From his room, he watched the chalet. If nothing happened in the next three minutes he would go back. He had pretended to drive away with the car, had left it by the side of the road after the first bend, and then returned to the hotel on foot.

He checked his watch. Two more minutes. He wished he had his gun with him.

He froze.

A figure had just appeared at the top of the steps. Labarthe. He was looking towards the hotel, then Servaz saw him gesture to someone inside the chalet. Aurore Labarthe appeared, supporting Kirsten. They helped her down the steps, then began walking, one on either side, holding her up as if she were drunk. And that was indeed the impression she gave.

Servaz took a deep breath. Fourteen minutes had gone by since he'd left the chalet. They wouldn't have had time to do her much harm.

34

Food

He wiped a cool, damp cloth across Kirsten's sweat-soaked face. Then he sat up straight and went to the bathroom for another glass of water. He tried to make her drink, but on the second swallow, she gagged and pushed the glass to one side.

It was the manager who had brought her up to him.

The Labarthes had informed him that the Norwegian woman who was staying in his hotel was interested in architecture, and that they'd invited her to stay for a glass of wine, and now she was completely drunk. It was probably customary in her country, they said, to drink more than was reasonable.

Servaz did not know what the manager had replied, but as they headed back to the chalet, they'd turned around several times to look back at the hotel windows. Every time, he'd moved to one side.

His and Kirsten's cover was blown. From now on, the Labarthes would be on the alert, more than ever.

They must already have informed Hirtmann of the incident.

How did they go about contacting him? He probably had a fake email account that was accessible only through the dark web, or through a chat on Telegram or ChatSecure. Encrypted messages that were rerouted: Vincent had demonstrated to him the numerous possibilities available on the Internet to those who liked to keep things confidential.

'Fuck, I feel like absolute shit,' Kirsten declared suddenly.

He turned around. She was lying on her bed, her neck and shoulders propped against three pillows, pale, her hair clinging with sweat to her brow and temples.

'I must look awful.'

'Atrocious,' he confirmed.

'That was a major cock-up,' she said. Servaz had some trouble translating her words. 'That sadistic little Labarthe bitch, she really screwed us over. She's brought out all my murderous tendencies.'

You're not the only one, he thought.

'I think I'm going to be sick,' she added.

Then she stood up and ran to the bathroom. He heard her vomit three times, taking deep breaths in between, then flush the toilet.

Zehetmayer was having breakfast at the Prague Sheraton, surrounded by Chinese tourists. He hated that. He had slept in room 429, after spending the evening walking around Malá Strana and the Old Town. Of course he had stopped off at the Jewish Cemetery, and as it did every time, there in the middle of the chaos of gravestones, in the gloom of silence and twilight, among the old facades preserving the memory of centuries, time had dissolved and he had been moved to tears.

He was momentarily ashamed to feel the tears on his cheeks, but he did nothing, leaving them to dampen his shirt collar as he tasted the salt on his lips. There was no reason for him to be ashamed: all his life he had seen brave men weep, and cowards with dry eyes. He had felt penetrated and purified by the light and silence, and the thought of all those souls and their past lives. He thought of Kafka, and the Golem – and of his daughter, violated and killed by a monster. Because there was purity in hatred, as there is purity in love.

The man he was waiting for that morning was called Jiri. He was Czech.

Zehetmayer saw him walking towards him, past the tables. Jiri had the face of a bearded wildcat, a face you could not easily forget, which could be something of a handicap in his profession: cheeks furrowed with deep wrinkles as if by the blade of a cutter, a powerful chest, and an incandescent gaze. He looked less like a killer than a poet, or a man of the theatre. He could have been an actor in a play by Chekhov, or an opera singer. For all that Zehetmayer knew, Jiri might be an artist, in his way.

Fine. Zehetmayer did not believe all that romantic bullshit about thieves and murderers. All that mythology for the bourgeois who dreamt of mixing with the riff-raff.

Jiri sat down across from him and motioned to the waiter.

'Coffee,' he said. 'Black.'

He got up, walked over to the buffet, then came back with a plate full of sausages, scrambled eggs, bacon, pastries and fruit.

'I love hotel breakfasts,' said Jiri.

He began wolfing it down.

'I have been told that you are a true professional,' declared Zehetmayer by way of introduction.

'Who told you that?'

'Our mutual friend.'

'He's not a friend,' corrected Jiri. 'He's a client. Do you like your work, Mr Zehetmayer?'

'It's more than work, it's—'

'Do you like your work?'

Zehetmayer frowned.

'Yes, passionately.'

'It's important to love what one does. *To love* . . . There's nothing more important in life.'

Zehetmayer frowned again. On an early morning in Prague he was sitting opposite a killer who was talking to him about love.

At a few minutes past nine on that Monday morning Roland Labarthe logged in to the Telegram app on his iPhone. The messaging service had recently become famous in the media as the preferred messaging service of terrorists. While the free publicity had attracted the ephemeral glare of the media spotlight, Telegram was anything but a confidential service. However, one of its features was the transmission of fully encrypted messages and their self-destruction after a time lapse set by the user.

It was the 'secret chat' feature that Labarthe activated that Monday morning. The recipient at the other end went by the name 'Mary Shelley', but Labarthe knew that it was not a woman. The only thing Julian Hirtmann and the author of Frankenstein had in common was Cologny, the village in the canton of Geneva where they had both lived. Hirtmann's first message arrived almost immediately.

[I got an alert. What's going on?]

[Something weird happened last night]

[Concerning Gustav?]

[No]

[Where?]

[At the chalet]

[Tell me. In detail. Be precise.
Concise. The facts.]

Adding as few details as possible, Labarthe related the previous evening's episode: the visit of the Norwegian woman, a so-called architect, then the cop whom he had already seen at the hotel the night before, and the way the guy had wanted to snoop everywhere.

He did, however, leave out the fact they had tried to take the woman up to the attic. And above all, the fact they had drugged Gustav. The first time they did it, it had been Aurore's idea. Labarthe didn't approve. He dared not think of the consequences were Hirtmann to find out; just the thought of it made his blood run cold. But, as usual, Aurore got her way.

[Don't panic. Nothing's amiss]

[Nothing's amiss? What if they begin to show an interest in Gustav?]

[That's what they're doing]

[In what way?]

[They're there because of Gustav.
And because of me.]

[How do you know?]

[I just do.]

Labarthe let out a silent oath. There were times when his Master got on his nerves.

[What should we do?]

[Stay on your guard.
Keep an eye on them, too.
Act normally]

[Until when?]

[They won't do anything as long as I
don't show myself.]

[And do you intend to?]

[You'll see]

[You know you can trust us
completely]

It took a while for the answer to come.

[Because you think I would have
entrusted you with Gustav if it had
been otherwise? Carry on. Change
nothing]

[Fine]

Roland Labarthe wanted to add something, but he saw that his
interlocutor had gone offline. He did likewise. In a few seconds their
conversation would self-destruct and there would be no trace of it
anywhere.

Hirtmann switched off his phone and looked up. A few metres away
from him Margot Servaz was walking down the aisles of the large
Victor-Hugo covered market, with its abundance of sounds and smells.
She lingered by the displays of fruit, fish and cheese, all incredibly
tempting. She examined, weighed, evaluated and bought, then went
on her way. Three metres behind her, lost in the crowd, a plain-clothes
policeman did not take his eyes off her.

Mistake, thought Julian Hirtmann as he sipped his coffee at the
little counter. He would have done better to show an interest in what
was going on *around her*. Hirtmann put down his cup, paid and
walked on. Margot had stopped by the Garcia charcuterie stand.
Hirtmann went behind her, then around the counter that extended
on three sides and over to where the master of the premises was
slicing his exorbitant Iberian *pata negra* ham.

Exorbitant, but sublime.

Hirtmann ordered 200 grams of the most expensive cut, keeping
an eye on Margot, who was filling up her bag. She was truly beautiful,

the way he liked them. As fresh in her winter coat as the fish lying on ice, as tender as Garcia's ham, and her cheeks, red and shiny from the heat and the cold, were like the lovely apples on the greengrocer's stand.

Martin, he thought, *I really fancy your daughter. But I suspect you would take a dim view of a son-in-law like me, wouldn't you? Will you allow me just to take her to the ball?*

While Servaz watched the chalet through the window, Kirsten was throwing up in the bathroom. He wondered what the Labarthes had given her. He had questioned her, but her memory of the evening remained very confused.

His phone rang. He checked the screen and swore to himself. Margot! Recent events had completely erased her from his mind. He swiped the green button, dreading that she would tell him off again.

'Dad,' said his daughter, her voice contrite. 'Can I speak to you?'

Behind him he heard Kirsten spewing her guts out, then say something he didn't understand.

'Of course you can. I'll call you back in five minutes, all right?'

Five minutes.

He hung up. Kirsten was talking to him, but all his thoughts were circling around Margot.

'Martin?' she called, finally, from the bathroom.

'Margot just rang,' he replied, without turning around, and he heard the door open.

'Is everything all right?'

'I don't know. I'll go downstairs to call her back. I could use a bit of fresh air.'

'Martin . . .'

He headed towards the door, but was stopped by his colleague's questioning look from where she stood on the threshold to the bathroom.

'What?' he said.

'The medicine – would you mind getting it for me?'

'What medicine?' he asked, feeling a bit stupid.

'I told you, there's a pharmacy at the entrance to the village, three hundred metres from here. Could you go and get me something to make this nausea stop,' she replied patiently.

'Yes, of course.'

'Thank you.'

He realised Kirsten must have asked him the same thing more than once. But his brain had completely blanked it out. Suddenly he had a terrible thought: could a coma induce this sort of thing? Or was he merely distracted? He tried desperately to remember if this was the first time this had happened to him since he'd regained consciousness.

Troubled, he walked out to the lift, and looked at his phone as he got into it. There were several messages, all from Margot. She had called a number of times during the night, and the last message had been sent a few minutes before she rang. He opened it:

Dad, I wasn't being serious. And I know you weren't, either. But please tell me you're fine. I worry about you.

When he emerged into the lobby he saw the manager walking towards him.

'How's your colleague doing?' he asked. 'She was pretty far gone last night.'

Servaz stopped.

'My what?'

'You're with the police, aren't you?'

He didn't reply.

'Have you got the chalet under surveillance?'

Servaz remained silent, merely staring at the man.

'I didn't say anything,' said the man reassuringly. 'When they brought your . . . colleague back last night, I didn't mention you. I kept my bloody mouth shut and pretended to believe their crap. I don't know what they've done wrong, but I may as well tell you, I've always thought they were a bit off, those two. Good call, if you want my opinion.'

This mania people had nowadays for giving you their opinion, even when you didn't ask for it, thought Servaz. He watched him walk away.

35

Bile

We spend our lives comparing. We compare houses, televisions, cars; we compare hotels, sunsets, cities, countries. We compare a film and its remake, or two performances of the same role. We compare our life the way it was before to the way it is now, friends the way they were to what they've become. As for the police, they compare finger-prints, DNA, witness statements, successive depositions from detainees, and, when it's called for, weapons and ammunition.

This is called test firing. In Toulouse, it was the ballistics department of the Police Forensics Laboratory, at police headquarters on the third floor, that was in charge. The shooting range and the ballistic baffles on the other hand, were in the basement. The first step was examining the weapon. For example, traces of dust could indicate how much time had gone by since the gun had last been used, particularly if there was more dust near the barrel than near the breech, which would imply that the weapon had not been used for some time. This was not the case with the Sig the engineer had there before him. And yet its owner, Commandant Servaz, maintained that he had not used his gun in months. He said that the last time had been at the shooting range, with the aforementioned pitiful results. This was odd, thought Torossian, grimacing. He liked Servaz. But this weapon seemed to have been used much more recently than that.

He made a note of it, then put the gun away next to the other weapons. When he had finished, he would get started with the test firing.

Calling Margot.

It rang as he went down the steps of the terrace then along the snowy street in the direction of the shops.

'Dad,' she said at last. 'Tell me you're all right. I've been worried.'

Her voice was tight with emotion . . . She seemed on the verge of tears, and he felt a knot in his stomach.

'I'm fine,' he said, tramping clumsily through the snowdrifts on the side of the road. 'We had a rather . . . eventful night. I didn't see your messages. I just got them, I'm sorry.'

'It doesn't matter, I was very angry. I didn't really mean all those things.'

'It's not important,' he said.

But in fact, it was. Because he had just read the messages. They were full of melancholy and complaint. For the first time in her life, his daughter had told him outright that she felt as if she was his lowest priority. Who knew, he thought – there might be more than a grain of truth in that. Perhaps, without realising, he had become a crap father . . .

'What do you mean, it's not important?' she said at once.

Shit. I don't believe it, here we go again. He would have liked to tell her right away that he loved her, that he was going to find the time, that she had to give him a chance. Instead, for the remaining 300 metres, he listened to Margot lecturing him and twice nearly went flying on a mound of snow, replying monosyllabically, unable to stem the flow of filial reproach. With her words still pouring inexorably into his ear, he stood outside the pharmacy for at least five minutes before he made up his mind to go in. He hid the telephone with one hand and asked for some Primperan.

'Was there a party in the village last night?' asked the pharmacist with a smile.

Servaz raised his eyebrows, failing to understand.

'You're the second person in five minutes who's come in asking for some.'

He went back out, saw a pavement café and sat outside despite the cold. On his phone, Margot was still easing her conscience with everything she had on her mind.

'Good morning,' said the waiter.

'A coffee, please.'

'Who are you talking to?' asked his daughter suddenly, interrupting her monologue.

'The waiter,' he replied, with a hint of annoyance.

'Fine. I'll let you go. Please, don't ever tell me again that I behave like a mother hen. The truth is, it's you who behaves like a little boy. And you don't make things easy, Dad.'

'I'm sorry,' he said, in spite of himself.

'Don't be. Change. Kisses.'

He looked at his mobile, incredulous. She had hung up! After at least fifteen minutes of lecturing him and not letting him get a word in edgeways, she had hung up.

Kirsten's stomach continued to contract, but not as harshly: the nausea was receding. What the hell was Martin doing? He'd left at least twenty minutes earlier for the pharmacy. Now she had a headache, and her mouth felt as if it were filled with sand. She had a sharp pain between her shoulder blades, probably the result of emptying her guts so violently all night long. She went into the bathroom. She must stink.

She brushed her teeth, tossed the towel on the floor, got undressed and stepped into the shower.

Four minutes later she came back out with a towel wrapped around herself. She thought the room must smell stuffy, so she went to the window and opened it wide.

The cold air was like a balm, the sun like a caress, the wind stirring the snow into little clouds. A dog barked. A bell rang in the distance. One voice called to another. *It feels good to be alive*, she thought.

She glimpsed a car to her left, heading in her direction, and immediately turned her attention to the chalet. *The Volvo had vanished. Shit.* Kirsten went to fetch the binoculars from Martin's unmade bed.

It was indeed the Volvo. But from this angle she could not tell who was inside. She turned the binoculars towards the chalet. One of the windows was wide open, the wind lifting the curtains and causing them to flutter outside.

For several seconds Kirsten gazed hypnotised at the silent dance, the white, luminous flight.

Until suddenly Aurore Labarthe appeared and broke the spell. Kirsten saw her lean out to pull the curtains back, then close the window.

It had lasted no more than ten seconds, but she'd obtained some of the information she wanted. There were only two possible options regarding the car's occupants:

1. That bastard Labarthe.
2. That bastard + Gustav.

Aurore Labarthe shut the window after glancing out at the Volvo on its way back from the pharmacy. What the fuck had he been doing? The pharmacy was not even one kilometre from the chalet. Drive more slowly while you're at it! That spineless husband of hers . . . He exasperated her but for once she had to admit he was right: they had screwed up. And what made her even angrier was that it was her fault. She had underestimated the side effects of the sedative on Gustav. And yet she was perfectly well acquainted with the child's illness, the extreme fragility of his liver. Hirtmann had cautioned them about it at length.

'Biliary atresia', it was called. An illness whose cause was unknown, affecting roughly one child out of ten or twenty thousand, characterised by an obstruction which prevented bile from evacuating the liver. Left untreated, it could cause death through liver failure.

If Hirtmann found out that they had drugged the boy on two occasions, so he wouldn't bother them during their little parties, Aurore had no doubt that they would be dead meat. He would be ruthless. Hirtmann cared more about that kid than his own life. Who was this child, anyway? She had often wondered. Was he really Hirtmann's son? And if so, where was the mother?

She went down the corridor and into Gustav's room. Pinched her nostrils at the smell of vomit. She took the duvet and the soiled sheets and yanked them from the bed, dropping them on the floor.

She heard a gurgling sound from the adjacent bathroom.

She walked around the bed and into the bathroom. Gustav was kneeling by the toilet in his blue pyjamas, throwing up.

The poor boy was gasping, wheezing, his blond hair clumping in tufts from the sweat, revealing his pink scalp. On hearing her he straightened and shot her a sad, pained look. Dear Lord, this boy never complained, except to ask for his father, she thought. A wave of shame almost stifled her.

She went closer and put her hand on his little brow. It was burning.

She heard the front door.

Then Roland's step on the stairs.

She helped Gustav get undressed, checked the temperature of the shower with the back of her hand, and pushed him gently inside the cubicle.

'It will do you good, treasure.'

Gustav nodded silently, then slipped under the showerhead. He jumped.

'It's hot!' he said.

'It will do you good,' she said again, adjusting the temperature.

Labarthe came into the room.

'That cop,' he said right away, 'he was at the pharmacy!'

She turned around and shot him a look as sharp as a razor. Still soaping Gustav's back, with her free hand she pointed to the bag Labarthe was holding.

'Give me that.'

'Did you hear what I said?' he said, handing her the Primperan.

'Gustav, look at me,' she said gently, ignoring her husband.

She unscrewed the plastic bottle and raised it towards the boy's lips. He made a face.

'It tastes bad.'

'I know, my love. But it will make you better.'

'Steady!' exclaimed Labarthe, watching her. 'You're giving him too much!'

Aurore took the bottle from Gustav's lips, looking daggers at her husband.

'I got the bed dirty,' said the boy guiltily.

She kissed his forehead and caressed his damp blond hair.

'It doesn't matter, we'll change the sheets right away.'

She turned to her husband. 'Can you help me, please? And tidy the room?'

Her tone was hostile. He nodded, clenching his jaw, and went back out. Aurore dried Gustav off, rubbed him down, then handed him some clean pyjamas.

'There, is that better?'

'A little bit, yes.'

'Where does it hurt, exactly?'

He put one hand on his tummy, and she felt it: it was hard, and swollen.

'You're a very brave little boy, you know that?'

She saw him give a weak smile. It was true, she thought, that the boy was brave. No doubt he got it from his father. He confronted his illness like a valiant little soldier. But had he ever known anything else in his short life? Crouched down next to him, she looked at him for a moment, smiling. Then she stood up.

'Off we go,' she said. 'We'll get you back into bed, all right? No school today.'

When they came back out of the bathroom the bed was made but the window was wide open.

'Hop into bed,' said Aurore, hurrying to close it. 'I'll be right back. Is it true that you feel a bit better?'

Gustav nodded, very seriously, from his bed.

'Good. When you're hungry, let me know.'

She went out and headed towards the stairs.

'The guy last night—' Labarthe began, the moment she came into the kitchen.

'Yes. I heard you. It's very windy. Why did you leave the boy's window open?'

'Because it stank.'

'Perhaps you'd like it if in addition to vomiting he caught his death?'

'When I came out I waited to see where he was going,' he continued, as if he had not heard her. 'The cop. He didn't see me. He had his phone to his ear and seemed very annoyed. I wanted to see if he was going back to the hotel.'

'And was he?'

She placed a black capsule in the coffee machine and switched it on.

'He sat outdoors to drink a coffee. I left him there and came home, as . . . as the situation here was more urgent.'

His tone was almost apologetic, something he instantly regretted: if you acted weak around Aurore, it made her want to sink her fangs into you.

'Yes, I even began to wonder if they were making the bloody medication themselves,' she said. 'The kid is going to cause us a ton of problems. He hasn't stopped vomiting.'

She pressed a button and the coffee machine began groaning and belching, spitting out its brown liquid. Labarthe had heard the reproach in her voice. He wondered why she was blaming him. True, he was the one who had first suggested to the Master that they look

260

after the boy, when the headmistress of the previous school had begun asking the 'grandfather' too many questions, but Aurore had been enthusiastic. They had never been able to have children. And he saw how Aurore looked after Gustav, spending time with him, enjoying his company. The fact remained that it had been her idea to sedate him. Although he had tried to dissuade her.

But he knew it was pointless to try and reason with Aurore.

'Perhaps we should let *Him* know,' was all he said.

The silence that followed seemed like a bad sign. Her answer came like the crack of a whip.

'Let him know? Are you stupid, or have you gone mad?'

Kirsten saw him coming back to the hotel. She crushed her cigarette, closed the window, and took off the coat she had thrown over her shoulders. She hurried to the bathroom and checked herself in the mirror.

It was impossible not to see the yellow-brown shadows under her eyes. Or her corpse-like complexion. She checked her breath.

When Martin came into the room he was puffing from the exertion. He handed her the little bag from the pharmacy. She took out the Primperan and drank it from the bottle as if it were water, then caught his gaze.

'I saw someone leave the chalet then go back in,' she said.

'Who?'

'Labarthe. He had a bag in his hand. Like this one.'

'A bag from the pharmacy – are you sure?'

'Sure? No. He was too far away. But it did look like this. In any case, he seemed to be in a hurry.'

Servaz went to the window and looked at the chalet. He realised he was worried – worried about Gustav.

On the desk, the telephone rang. Not the everyday telephone. *The other telephone.* Labarthe shuddered. Shit, could Hirtmann, somehow or other, already have got wind of what was happening? He was becoming paranoid. He looked at his screen.

[Are you there?]

Labarthe typed his response with his middle finger.

[Yes]

[Good. There has been a change]

[What sort?]

[I want to see Gustav. Tonight. At
the usual place]

Good Lord. Labarthe let out a breath. He suddenly felt as if
something enormous was lodged in his throat, preventing him from
breathing.

[What's up?]

[Nothing. I want to see Gustav.
That's all. Tonight]

Labarthe's heart skipped a beat. He wanted to call Aurore to the
rescue. But the seconds were ticking by. He had to answer. Otherwise
Hirtmann would suspect something. And in fact, the next message
proved this was already the case:

[Is there a problem?]

Bloody hell! Answer! Something!

[Just that Gustav is sick right now,
he's coming down with the flu]

[Has he got a fever?]

[Yes. A little]

[Since when?]

[Last night]

[Has he seen the doctor?]

[Yes.]

Labarthe's heart was racing. He stared at the luminous screen,
waiting for the next message.

[The usual one?]

Labarthe hesitated. Did Hirtmann suspect something? Was he trying to trap him?

[No. Another one. It was Sunday]

[What are you giving him?]

[Aurore took care of it. Do you want me to go and fetch her?]

[No, there's no point. I'll come by this evening]

[What? But there are some policemen at the hotel, watching the chalet!]

[That's my problem]

[Master, I don't think it's a good idea]

[I'll be the judge of that. Tonight. 20.00]

Hirtmann had logged off.

Fuck! Labarthe swallowed. He felt as if a thousand ants were crawling around his neck. He needed air . . . He went to the window and opened it. Breathed in, looking at the sparkling white landscape.

Julian Hirtmann would be there that evening.

Why had he said it was the flu, for God's sake? Instead of gastro-enteritis? Fuck, what had come over him?

And what if Gustav told his father that he hadn't seen a doctor?

The entire time he was writing his book, he had imagined himself in Hirtmann's skin; he liked thinking he was him. When he walked down the street in Toulouse and looked at the women, he looked at them with Hirtmann's eyes; he felt strong, powerful, cruel and ruthless. What a joke! They were nothing but words. Was he frightened? Of course he was frightened! Julian Hirtmann was no fiction, he was fucking reality – and he had entered their lives.

He remembered their first encounter: he was signing books in a bookshop in Toulouse. Or at least he was supposed to be signing, but in the half-hour he had been there he had seen no one. And then finally one reader came up to have his book signed. When Labarthe asked him his first name, the man replied, 'Julian.' Labarthe had laughed. But the man standing before him on the other side of the table remained impassive – and the way his eyes examined Labarthe from behind his glasses sent a little shiver down Labarthe's spine.

Labarthe was heading for his car in the Jean-Jaurès car park when the man suddenly emerged from a dark corner, causing him to jump out of his skin.

'Christ, you frightened me!'

'You made a mistake on page 153,' said Hirtmann. 'That's not the way it happened.'

Without knowing why – perhaps because of the intruder's tone, or his aloof calm – Labarthe instantly knew he was not dealing with an impostor. That he had the real Julian Hirtmann there before him.

'Is it you?' he stammered.

'Don't be afraid. It's a good book. If it were not, you would be well advised to be afraid.'

Labarthe tried to laugh it off, but his laughter caught in his throat.

'I . . . I . . . I don't know what to say. It's a great . . . honour.'

He had looked up, at the face in the shadow of the ceiling: Labarthe was no taller than 1 metre 70. Hirtmann took a mobile from his pocket and handed it to him.

'Here. We will meet again soon. Don't mention this to anyone.'

But Labarthe had mentioned it. To Aurore. He had no secrets from her.

'I want to meet him,' she said at once.

Now he left his study then looked in vain for her on the ground floor. He could hear voices upstairs. He went up the stairs and down the corridor at a run. Aurore and Gustav were together in the boy's bathroom.

'It's getting worse,' she cried, wiping a damp sponge over the boy's forehead. 'His temperature has risen.'

It can't have!

'I just spoke to Hirtmann.'

'Did you call him?'

Her tone was incredulous.

'No! He messaged me. I don't know what's got into him. He wants to see the boy!'

'What?'

'He's coming tonight.'

'What did you tell him?'

'That Gustav is ill, that he has . . . the flu.'

'The flu? Why the hell did you say the flu?'

'I don't know! It was all I could think of, on the spot like that. He also wanted to know whether Gustav had seen the doctor.'

She looked cautiously at the boy, then stared straight at her husband.

'And what did you tell him?'

'That he had.'

He saw Aurore turn pale. She turned to look at Gustav, who returned her gaze with a sad, exhausted, almost tearful look, but one that was also full of affection and trust, and for the first time, this hard-hearted woman felt a truly human emotion and was wracked with guilt. She stroked his cheek then hugged him, on impulse, feeling his damp hair against her face. She almost felt like crying.

'Don't worry, treasure. It will be all right. It will be all right.'

She turned to Labarthe.

'We have to take him to A&E,' she said.

'Not a moment too soon, dammit.'

'They're going out,' said Kirsten.

Servaz joined her at the window.

'Look how they've bundled Gustav up. He doesn't look well, even at this distance.'

She handed him the binoculars.

'He didn't go to school today,' he observed.

The anxiety was there again. He checked his watch. Nearly three o'clock. Over three hours had passed since Labarthe had got back from the pharmacy, if that was where he had been. Clearly Gustav's condition had got worse. Servaz would have given anything to know what the boy was suffering from.

He saw them place Gustav on the back seat; Labarthe's wife put a blanket over his lap and stroked his hair. Her husband sat behind the wheel, not without first glancing over at the hotel.

'What shall we do?' asked Kirsten.

'We leave things as they are. There are already on their guard. On these roads, they'd spot us in no time. And you're in no fit condition anyway. We'll wait until they get back.'

'Are you sure?'

'Yes.'

But he knew he wouldn't be able to put up with this uncertainty for long. Where were they taking him? He didn't give a damn about the Labarthes, or even Julian Hirtmann. At that very moment, he could think of only one thing: Gustav. *Why am I so worried?* he wondered. If the kid is not mine, why should I feel so concerned?

Aurore sat in the back, holding Gustav. She'd dressed in the first trousers and jumper she could find. The chill in the car was damp and penetrating; she had wrapped the boy in the blanket, but he wouldn't stop shivering.

'Are you trying to freeze us or what?' she shouted towards the front.

Labarthe put the heating on as high as it would go and said nothing, keeping his eyes on the tricky road.

At the end of the hairpin bends they came out onto a wider road cleared of snow. He took a left, in the direction of Saint-Martin.

He accelerated.

'I'm going to throw up,' said the little boy.

Dr Franck Vassard was on his break in the lounge when the nurse came for him.

'They've just brought in a kid who can't stop vomiting.'

The young intern sat up on the worn sofa, looked at her and stretched, his arms spread. He rubbed his hipster beard and looked at the nurse.

'How old?'

'Five. And he has a few symptoms of jaundice. It could be liver failure.'

'Is he with his parents?'

'Yes.'

'Any fever?'

'38.5.'

'I'm coming.'

He stood up and went over to the coffee machine. Drat, he'd hoped his siesta would last a little longer. Saint-Martin was a little hospital, and the emergency services rarely had to deal with the chaos that characterised A&E in major cities.

Two minutes later Vassard left the little room and went down the corridor full of carts, nurses and commotion. The child was sitting on a gurney. The couple watched him walk towards them. Without knowing why, he thought there was something strange and mismatched about the pair and he felt uneasy.

'Are you the boy's parents?'

'No, we're friends,' replied the man with the goatee. 'His father should be here shortly.'

'Right then, what's the matter?' he asked, moving closer to the blond kid with the feverish gaze.

'We'll give him some activated charcoal and an anti-emetic,' he said. 'I'm not a fan of stomach pumping. And besides, we only use it when a highly toxic substance has been ingested, which is not the case with the sedative you gave him.' Here, he could not help but tinge his words with a frankly disapproving tone. 'Then we'll keep him under observation until tomorrow morning. What worries me most are his symptoms: the jaundice, his swollen liver, his abdominal pain. Biliary atresia is no laughing matter. Is he being treated for it?'

His gaze met the blonde woman's, which was shifty, and hyper-vigilant.

'He has had the Kasai procedure,' she replied. 'He is being treated by Dr Barrot.'

The young intern nodded. He knew Barrot. A competent physician. The Kasai procedure was a surgical intervention that sought to restore the flow of bile from the liver to the intestine by replacing the duct damaged by the disease with a new system grafted from the small intestine. The surgery was successful in one case out of three. But even when it did succeed, it did not prevent the cirrhosis from slowly progressing. *Biliary atresia is a cruel, nasty disease,* thought the intern, looking at the boy.

'It would seem the surgery has failed,' he said, frowning as he looked at Gustav. 'We might want to consider a transplant. Do you know if one is planned? What does Dr Barrot think?'

They were staring at him as if he were speaking Chinese. What a strange couple, he thought.

'Next time, don't use a sedative,' he insisted, as they didn't reply. 'Even if he is very agitated.'

He looked at them one after the other, wishing he could shake them. The woman nodded.

*

He observed the hospital entrance and the vast esplanade from a doorway 100 metres away. Night had fallen. The streetlamps outside the big building cast yellow circles on its brick facade. A few isolated snowflakes drifted through their halo. He puffed nervously on his cigarette, his little eyes on the lookout behind his glasses.

Everything was so calm, so dark. Nothing moved. Where did the inhabitants of Saint-Martin-de-Comminges go once it got dark? He tossed his cigarette into the snow on the pavement.

He looked all around then calmly crossed the deserted esplanade, despite his overwhelming impatience. He went over to reception.

'A five-year-old boy was admitted to the emergency department this afternoon,' he said when the nurse behind the counter condescended to pay him a little attention. 'Gustave Servaz. I'm his father.'

She checked her computer screen.

'Oh yes,' she said, pointing to a glass door to the left of the counter. 'Go through this door, all the way to the end of the corridor, and then right. You'll see, it's signposted. Ask there. And visiting time ends in fifteen minutes.'

He stared at her a fraction too long.

For a split second he imagined himself leaning over the counter, grabbing her by her hair, taking the cutter out of his pocket and slitting her throat.

'Thank you,' said Julian Hirtmann.

He walked away and followed her directions. At the end of the second corridor was another office. He asked again.

'Please follow me,' said the nurse with limp hair and a weary face.

He saw the Labarthes at the end of the corridor. Roland rushed forward to greet him, Aurore stayed behind, looking at him cautiously. He embraced the cretinous university professor the way the pope gives his blessing, keeping his gaze riveted all the while on the woman. For a moment he relived that time in the attic, when he'd taken her, bound and hanging by her wrists from the rings on the ceiling, completely naked and at his mercy, while Labarthe waited patiently down in the living room for them to finish.

'Where is he?'

Labarthe pointed to the door.

'He's sleeping. They've given him a tranquilliser and an anti-emetic.'

He refrained from mentioning the activated charcoal, but he knew that sooner or later the Master would find out what had happened.

'What happened?' asked Hirtmann, as if he could read his thoughts. 'You said something about the flu?'

Labarthe had messaged him to tell him they'd had to take the boy to hospital.

'He took a sudden turn for the worse,' said Aurore, walking towards them. 'He was very restless, and so I gave him a light sedative.'

'You what?'

Hirtmann's voice turned vicious.

'The doctor said it had nothing to do with it,' she lied. 'And Gustave is fine.'

He suddenly felt like grabbing her by the neck, shoving her up against the wall, and squeezing until her face turned purple. His voice was dangerously calm:

'We'll talk about it another time,' he said. 'Go home. I'll stay here.'

'We can stay too, if you like,' said Labarthe.

He stared at the little man with the goatee, and the tall blonde woman. He pictured them dead, cold and stiff.

'Go home. And drop this envelope off at the hotel.'

Labarthe glanced at it quickly. It was addressed to Martin Servaz. Of course he knew the name. He'd even wondered, last night, when the man came to his house. He'd looked vaguely familiar. For Christ's sake, what was going on?

Hirtmann watched them walk away. Then he went into the room. Gustav was sleeping, his features relaxed. He stood for a long moment at the foot of the bed, watching the little boy, then he sat on the only available chair.

Servaz stood looking out of the window.

He listened and watched. Desperately. He stared at the deserted, darkened chalet, the empty night. With butterflies in his stomach.

They had left several hours earlier. He couldn't stand this waiting and was beginning to regret not following them. Kirsten, too, had been champing at the bit.

Now, exhausted by nerves and the nausea from the previous night, she had collapsed on her bed, snoring faintly.

Suddenly he heard an engine approaching. He put his nose to the glass and saw it: the Labarthes' Volvo had come back! He saw it slow down and stop outside the hotel.

Labarthe got out, stepped onto the terrace of the hotel and went inside. He came back out a few moments later and the car continued on its way to the chalet.

Servaz felt his heart sink when the doors opened. Labarthe and his wife got out alone. *Gustav was not in the car.* Where was the boy? What had they done with him?

Just then the telephone rang. Not his mobile, but the big black antediluvian hotel telephone on the little table that served as a desk, and he reached for it before the ringing had time to wake Kirsten.

'We have an envelope for you,' said the manager.

Labarthe. What was going on? Once again he felt as if invisible wires were being pulled by a puppeteer. Once again, he was one move behind.

'I'll be right down.'

He burst into the lobby less than a minute later. A brown envelope was waiting for him, his name written by hand:

MARTIN SERVAZ

'That moron dropped it off,' said the manager.

Servaz's hand was trembling when he ripped it open and took out the piece of paper.

He felt the hotel lobby begin to spin, the entire universe rotating – planets, stars, space, void. All creation overturned in a fraction of a second, the world off kilter, all familiar landmarks gone. The note said:

Gustav is in hospital in Saint-Martin. I'm waiting for you. Come alone. If we join forces, there will be no Kindertotenlieder. *J.*

36

H

He left Kirsten at the hotel, asleep. The blood was pounding in his temples, as if he were being drip-fed adrenaline. He drove fast. Tore around the bends and gave himself a fright when the car skidded onto the snow-covered verge, dangerously close to the slope, before it stabilised on the icy road.

One sentence haunted him: '*If we join forces there will be no* Kindertotenlieder.'

'Songs on the Death of Children'. Gustav Mahler. 'J.' Only one person could have written that note. And it told him that Gustav was in mortal danger. That his salvation depended on them. It occurred to him that it could be a trap, but he brushed the thought aside. Hirtmann had been taking his photograph for months, and he'd had ample opportunity to set all the traps he liked. Besides, there were better places for a trap than a hospital.

On entering Saint-Martin, he took his foot off the accelerator. Saw the sign indicating 'H' and went straight on from the roundabout. Six minutes later he parked in a spot reserved for staff and hurried into the hospital reception area.

'Visiting time is over,' said the person seated behind the counter, not even looking up from her mobile telephone.

He leaned over the counter and flashed his red, white and blue card between her nose and her screen. The woman looked up, her gaze furious.

'No need to be unpleasant,' she said. 'What do you want?'

'A kid was brought into emergency this afternoon.'

She narrowed her eyes, looking at him defiantly, then checked her file.

'Gustave Servaz,' she confirmed.

For the second time he felt an abyss open in his guts on hearing that first name associated with his last name. Was it possible? Now that his hopes and fears were taking shape, he wondered which he wanted most: for Gustav to be his son, or not. But another vaguer, more dangerous hope was aroused at the same time. A hope he'd abandoned years before, but which had been secretly waiting to be reborn: Marianne. Would he find out at last what had happened to her? His mind tried in vain to brush the question aside, to relegate it to a dark corner, far from the light.

The woman pointed to the glass door to the left of the counter.

'Take this corridor,' she said, 'then the next corridor to the right.'

'Thanks.'

She was already staring at her screen again. Servaz went through the swinging door.

His steps rang out on the varnished floor; otherwise, there was complete silence. Another door. Another corridor. At the end of it was a luminous sign: 'Emergencies'.

There was only one person in the cluttered office, its walls covered with planning charts with columns full of coloured stickers.

Once again he took out his badge.

'Gustav,' he said; he didn't have the courage to use the last name. 'The boy who came in this afternoon.'

She looked at him, not understanding. She looked so tired. Then she stood up, stepped out of her tiny office, and pointed to a door.

'Third on the right.'

A beep rang out somewhere and she turned and went in the other direction.

He stepped forward, his legs as wobbly as jelly. He had a persistent sensation of unreality. The door she'd shown him was only 4 metres away. He stifled the voice inside that was whispering to him to turn and run.

His heart was pounding in his ears, a wind of panic in his skull.

Three metres.

Two.

One.

The sound of ventilation; the door wide open. A figure in the room sitting on a chair, his back to him. A man's voice saying: 'Come in, Martin. I've been waiting for you. Welcome. It's been so long. It took you a while – our paths crossed hundreds of times, and a hundred times you didn't see me. But now you're here, at last. Come in, don't be shy! Come closer. Come and see your son.'

MARTIN AND JULIAN

37

A Child Makes You Vulnerable

'Come in, Martin.'

That same voice: an actor's, an orator's. Deep, warm. Those same worldly tones. He had almost forgotten.

'Come in.'

Servaz moved closer. In the bed on the left, Gustav was asleep (Servaz felt a heavy thud in his chest), looking peaceful and carefree, but his cheeks were flushed from the heat in the room. Through the window at the back the light from the streetlamps painted horizontal streaks between the blinds.

There was no other light.

He could hardly make out the seated figure with its back to him.

'You won't arrest me, will you? Not until we've had time to talk.'

He said nothing, but took another step, keeping Hirtmann on his left. Servaz gazed at his profile. He was wearing glasses, his hair fell over his forehead, and his nose had changed shape. If he'd passed him on the street he wouldn't have recognised him.

But when Hirtmann turned his head and raised his chin to look at him, Servaz recognised his smile and his slightly feminine mouth.

'Hello, Martin. I'm glad to see you.'

He still didn't say anything, and wondered whether Hirtmann could hear the pounding in his chest.

'I sent the Labarthes home. They're good little soldiers, but they're as thick as they come. He's a real idiot. His book is worthless. Did you read it? She's far more dangerous. You know they had the nerve to drug Gustav.' His voice suddenly sounded like a flow of icy water. 'They think they'll just get a ticking-off. But you know it won't be like that.'

Servaz said nothing.

'I'm still not sure how I'll deal with it. We'll see. I prefer spontaneity.'

Servaz listened carefully. Tried to detect other sounds behind the voice. There were none. Everything was calm.

'Do you recall our first conversation?' said Hirtmann suddenly.

Of course he remembered. As a matter of fact, there had not been a single day in eight years that he had not thought about that moment in one way or another. Sometimes only for a few seconds, sometimes more.

'Do you remember the first word you said?'

Servaz remembered. But he let Hirtmann say it.

'Mahler.'

Hirtmann smiled, and his face lit up as he looked at him.

'You said "Mahler". And that's when I immediately understood that something was happening. Do you remember the music?'

Oh yes, he remembered.

'The Fourth, first movement,' Servaz replied, his voice gravelly, as if he had not spoken for days.

Hirtmann nodded with satisfaction.

'*Bedächtig . . . Nicht eilen . . . Recht gemächlich . . .*'

He lifted his hands and they fluttered, as if he could hear the music.

'"Moderately, not rushed, rather leisurely",' translated Servaz.

'I have to admit you made quite an impression on me that day. Yes. And I'm not someone who is easily impressed.'

'Are we here to talk about the good old days?'

Hirtmann gave a good-natured little laugh. Almost a cough. Then he turned to the bed.

'Don't speak so loudly. You'll wake him up.'

Servaz felt his stomach lurch.

'Who is this child?' he asked.

For a moment neither one of them spoke.

'Can't you guess?'

He gulped.

'Did I ever tell you that once, in my previous profession, I found a child's dead body?' continued Hirtmann. 'I was young, I had started work at the court in Geneva three weeks earlier. The police called me in the middle of the night. The guy on the phone seemed very upset. I went to the address they'd given me. It was a depressing place; a miserable little house where some junkies were squatting. When I went inside I immediately noticed the odour: a stench of vomit, cat piss, food, shit, tobacco, filth, but also burned aluminium foil. There were cockroaches in the corridor and in the kitchen; it was infested. I went into the living room. They were all completely high, sprawled on the sofas; the mother was lying across two guys' laps, her head wobbling, and one of the guys was insulting the police; there were still tourniquets and syringes on the coffee table. The kid was in her room at the end of the corridor, lying on her bed. At the time I thought she was around four or five years old. In fact she was seven. But years of abuse and malnutrition had made her look much smaller and frailer than her age.'

He glanced over at the bed.

'The pathologist was a guy close to retirement, someone who had seen worse, but he went very pale. He was examining her very gently, as if to make up for the rage with which she had been beaten. The emergency services were still outside the house. One of them had gone to throw up in the grass. They had done everything they could to resuscitate the little girl – cardiac massage, defibrillator . . . One of the guys wanted to go in and beat the living daylights out of the parents. The cops had to hold him back. The little girl's room was full of rubbish, like all the rest of the house: bottles, cans, food mouldering in boxes; stains everywhere, even on the bed.'

Hirtmann fell silent, lost in thought.

'We eventually arrested the person who'd killed her – not one of the wasters on the sofa, but the father, every bit as high, who had shown up and found the mother asleep with the other two. So he took his revenge on the kid. I killed the mother two months later. After torturing her. I didn't rape her. She was too disgusting.'

'Why are you telling me all this?'

Hirtmann didn't seem to have heard.

'You have a daughter, Martin. You've known for a long time.'

Servaz felt himself stiffen.

Don't you talk about my daughter, you bastard.

'I've known what?' he asked, his voice icy.

'That when you have a child, you stop reasoning the way you used to. When you have a child, the world becomes dangerous again, doesn't it? Having children means learning all over again that we are fragile. A child makes you vulnerable. But you know all this, of course.

Look at him, Martin. What will happen if I disappear? If I die? If I go to prison? What will become of him? Who will look after him?'

'Is he your son?' asked Servaz, with a lump in his throat.

Hirtmann looked away from Gustav to stare at Servaz through his glasses, eyes narrowed.

'Yes, he is my son. I raised him, I watched him grow. You cannot imagine what a wonderful kid he is.'

He paused.

'Gustav is my son, and he is also yours. I raised him as my own son – because that's what he is – but it's your DNA he has in his cells. Not mine.'

Martin was no longer listening. His ears were buzzing. His throat seemed to be lined with sandpaper.

'Can you prove it?' he asked suddenly.

Hirtmann took out a transparent plastic bag. Inside was a lock of hair. Blond. Identical to the one he had in his own pocket.

'I thought you might ask me that. Here, go ahead, do the test. But I've already done it for you: I wanted to find out whether he was yours or mine . . .'

Hirtmann paused.

'Gustav. *Your son.* He needs you.'

'Does he? Oh, so that's why . . .'

'That's why what?'

'We found him so easily. You arranged it all so that we would find him, in fact.'

'You're clever, Martin. Very clever.'

'But not as clever as you, is that it?'

'I am fairly clever, that's true. You know me well enough to be aware that I don't often make mistakes, as a rule. It should have started you thinking.'

'It did. But even if I did think that you were pulling the strings, that you were behind it all, I figured you must have your reasons – and that the puppeteer would eventually come out of hiding. I was right, was I not?'

'Very good. So, here we are.'

'The problem is that all the exits to this hospital are being watched by the police. There's no escape.'

'I don't think so. Are you going to arrest me? Here? In the room of *your ailing son*? To be honest, I think that's in very poor taste.'

Servaz looked at Gustav, his blond hair still glued to his brow with sweat, his lips parted, his narrow ribcage rising gently beneath the flannel pyjamas. His blond lashes lay against his closed eyelids like the whiskers of a brush.

Hirtmann stood up to his full 1 metre 88. Servaz noticed he had put on a few pounds. He was wearing an old-fashioned Fair Isle jumper and shapeless corduroy trousers. But he still emanated something magnetic and formidable.

'You're tired, Martin. I suggest we—'

'What's wrong with him?' interrupted Servaz, his voice altered.

'Biliary atresia.'

Servaz had never heard of this disease.

'Is it serious?'

'Mortal if nothing is done.'

'Explain it to me,' he said firmly.

'It will take a while.'

'I don't care. I have all the time in the world.'

'It's a nasty disease that starts even before the child is born, in its mother's womb. Basically, the ducts which allow the liver to evacuate bile shrink and become blocked, and the bile retained in the liver causes irreparable damage which, if left untreated, will prove mortal. You've heard of cirrhosis of the liver, which alcoholics get. Well, that's what happens here: the presence of bile in the liver causes fibrosis, then a secondary biliary cirrhosis. That is what the child dies of: good old cirrhosis of the liver.'

Hirtmann paused and glanced at Gustav before continuing.

'The cause is unknown. Children who have it suffer from constant health problems. They are smaller than average, and often catch infections. They have abdominal pain and swelling, jaundice, sleep issues, and gastrointestinal bleeding. In short, as I said, a nasty disease.'

There was no particular emotion in his voice, merely the brutal enunciation of facts.

'The initial treatment consists in restoring the flow of bile. This operation is known as the Kasai procedure, from the name of the surgeon who developed it. Gustav has had this operation. One out of three operations are successful. In his case, it seems to have failed.'

He paused.

'From this point on, liver failure develops and the child is in danger of dying.'

Servaz got the impression the silence reigning in the hospital was producing a sort of vibration – or was it his ears?

'Is there any other treatment?'

Hirtmann looked deep into his eyes.

'Yes. A liver transplant.'

Servaz waited for what came next, his heart in his throat.

'Biliary atresia is the primary reason for liver transplants among children,' explained Hirtmann. 'The main obstacle to the transplant – as you can imagine, Martin – is the lack of donors in this age group.

'And, in Gustav's case,' continued Hirtmann, 'it would involve a lot of formalities; bringing him out of hiding, which would no doubt mean he would end up in a foster family – strangers, for fuck's sake. People I would have no control over, people I haven't chosen.'

Servaz refrained from pointing out that his choice of the Labarthes hardly seemed optimal.

'But there is another option – for Gustav, in fact, the only one: a transplant from a compatible living donor. Roughly 60 to 70 per cent of a healthy donor's liver is removed, and this is not a problem, because the liver grows back. And it is transplanted to the child. But not just any donor will do. It has to be a close relative: a brother, a mother, a father . . .'

So that was it. Servaz resisted the urge to grab Hirtmann by the collar. Marianne, he thought suddenly. He had said, 'a mother, a father'. Why not Marianne?

'Why not his mother, Marianne? Why not her?' he asked, his voice hoarse. 'Why can't she donate her liver?'

Hirtmann stared at him gravely; he seemed to be groping for the right words.

'Let's just say that her liver is not available.'

Servaz took a deep breath.

'She's dead, is that it?'

Hirtmann's gaze was full of feigned compassion, and again Servaz wanted to grab him by the throat.

'And if I refuse?' he said. 'What then?'

'Well, in that case, your son will die, Martin.'

'Why?' he said suddenly.

'Pardon?'

'Why didn't you kill him? Why did you raise him as your son?'

They both gazed at the sleeping boy; his lips were moving in silent speech.

'I don't kill children,' answered Hirtmann coldly. 'And fate placed this kid in my hands. Did I tell you that when I found out Marianne was pregnant, I was livid? For weeks I starved her, hoping she would lose it. I didn't want to kill the child, I wanted it to die a natural death. But the little devil clung on for dear life. Except that with all the drugs I was making her take, Marianne was in a pitiful state. I had to wean her off them, feed her, and inject her intravenously with vitamins.'

'In Poland?' asked Servaz.

Hirtmann looked at him.

'Marianne never set foot in Poland. That was just so I could see you squirm. I added her DNA to the others', that's all.'

'How did she die?'

'When the boy was born, I took a paternity test and found out he wasn't mine,' continued Hirtmann, ignoring Martin's question. 'I realised he must be yours. So I came to Toulouse and, without you realising, I got hold of a bit of your DNA. It wasn't hard. No harder than borrowing your gun. In both cases, all I had to do was break into your car.'

Servaz held his breath; he was trying to think.

'Because it was indeed your gun that killed Jensen,' Hirtmann confirmed. 'And I'm the one who pressed the trigger. I borrowed it the night you pursued me in the gardens at the thermal baths. I replaced it with another, identical one, then put it back a few days later.'

Servaz thought of the perfume he had smelled in the car, the day he came out of the therapist's office, then of his weapon in Rimbaud's hands, and the test firing they would soon be carrying out. He looked at the child in the bed.

'At the same time, I checked to see whether your blood groups were compatible,' added Hirtmann.

Servaz listened to his words, unable to shake off an impression of unreality. He felt as if he were dreaming, that he would eventually wake up.

'Just supposing . . . just supposing I do it, how can I be sure you won't finish me off after the operation?'

The pale light above the bed was reflected in Hirtmann's glasses, like a reflection on the surface of a pond at night.

'You can't,' he replied. 'But after that, Gustav will owe you his life. A life for a life. Let's just say that will be my way of paying my debts. Of course you're not obliged to believe me. I might change my mind and finish you both off. It would make my life a lot simpler.'

'I have one condition,' said Servaz after a moment.

'I don't think you're in a position to negotiate, Martin.'

'How could you entrust him to those idiots, the Labarthes, for God's sake!' he said, in a sudden burst of anger.

Hirtmann started but didn't say anything.

'So who do you suggest?' he asked, looking surprised.

'He's my son, after all.'

'So?'

'It's my duty to bring him up.'

Hirtmann stared at him, flabbergasted.

'I beg your pardon?'

'You heard me. Where will the operation take place?'

He sensed that Hirtmann was thinking.

'Abroad. It's too risky here, both for him and for me.'

Now it was Servaz's turn to be surprised.

'Where abroad?'

'You'll see.'

'And how do you plan to get him out of the country?'

'So, will you do it?' asked Hirtmann without replying.

Servaz did not take his eyes off Gustav. He was sick with fear. A fear that reminded him of when Margot was Gustav's age.

'I don't really have any choice, do I?'

38

A Wolf Surrounded by Lambs

'This child: do you believe that *Someone* sent him to us? Do you believe in God, Martin? I think I've already asked you that, at some point. He would have to be a bloody twisted sort of God, if he exists, don't you think?'

They had gone outside to breathe the night air, and were watching the snowflakes fall. Hirtmann took a drag on his cigarette.

'Have you heard of Marcion of Sinope, Martin? Marcion was a Christian who lived in Rome eighteen hundred years ago. As he looked around him, as he looked at this world full of suffering, slaughter, disease, war and violence, Marcion the heretic concluded that the God who had created all this could not be good, and that evil was a component of his creation. The screenwriters of Christianity had come up with a fairly murky twist to respond to the question of evil: they invented Lucifer. But Marcion's version was much better: God is responsible for evil along with everything else; he is responsible for Gustav's disease as well. Not only is evil an intrinsic part of his creation, it also acts as a lever to that creation. It is thanks to violence and conflict that creation evolves towards ever higher forms. Look at Rome. According to Plutarch, Julius Caesar conquered over eight hundred cities, subjugated three hundred nations, took one million prisoners, and killed another million of his enemies. Rome was a vicious society, with a definite taste for cruelty. However, its rise enabled the world to evolve, with an empire that unified nations, allowed ideas to circulate, and invented new forms of society.'

'I'm tired of your rambling,' said Servaz, taking out his own packet of cigarettes.

'We dream of peace, but it's an illusion,' continued Hirtmann, ignoring the interruption. 'At every level you find rivalry, competition and warfare. William James, the father of American psychology, has suggested that civilised life makes it possible for many people to go from cradle to grave without ever experiencing the slightest moment of true fear. Therefore, many of these people do not understand the nature of violence, hatred and evil; and yet they're surrounded by it all. Is it not marvellous to be a wolf surrounded by lambs?'

'What did you do with Marianne? How did she die?'

Hirtmann glanced at him, irritated this time, as if he found it rude to be interrupted on two occasions.

'Did I tell you that when I was Gustav's age I hit my uncle with a hammer? He was sitting in the living room with my mother. He had stopped by for some reason while my father was absent, and they were chatting. To this day I cannot explain why I did what I did. In fact, I had forgotten all about it until my mother brought it up years later, on her deathbed. I don't know . . . it was probably simply because the hammer was there. I grabbed it, I went up behind him, and bang! I bashed him hard on the skull. According to my mother, there was blood everywhere.'

Servaz held the flame from his lighter up to his fag.

'One of the last things my mother said, a few seconds before her cancer finally got the better of her, was, "You've always been bad." I was sixteen. I answered her with a smile: "Bad like cancer, mother."'

Suddenly, Hirtmann tore the cigarette from Servaz's lips and tossed it into the fine layer of snow on the pavement.

'What did you do th—?'

'Have you never heard that a donor mustn't smoke? It's a bit late, but from now on, no more cigarettes,' decreed Hirtmann, turning around and going back in the door. 'Are you taking medication for your heart?'

Servaz almost replied, but he thought of Gustav. Was this real? Was he really talking about his medication with Julian Hirtmann?

'Not really for my heart,' he replied. 'It's not as if I had a bypass or a transplant. And I stopped the painkillers and anti-inflammatories. I don't think they had too much time to damage my liver, if that's what you're worried about. Where is she? What did you do with Marianne?' he growled at Hirtmann's back, following in his footsteps.

The doors closed behind them. It was the service entrance. Servaz looked all around. There was no one.

'Where is she?' he said, grabbing him by the collar and pushing him up against the wall.

Hirtmann put up no resistance.

'Marianne,' said Servaz again, his features twisted with rage.

'Do you want to save your son or not? Let me go. You'll find out when the time comes, don't worry.'

Servaz tightened his grip. He wanted to strike, to hit, to hurt.

'Your son will die if we do nothing. We can't wait any longer. One last thing, in case you've got it into your head that Gustav can be operated on here: think of Margot. Two nights ago, I saw her, she was scantily dressed . . . I'd spilled some coffee on her bodyguard's suit and she opened the door. She's quite a beauty.'

This time, he lashed out – he smashed his nose. Hirtmann roared like a beast when Servaz let go of him. He leaned forward, took out a handkerchief and held it against his nose to staunch the flow of blood.

'I could kill you for this,' Hirtmann growled. 'You know as well as I do,' he continued, 'that it's impossible to protect your daughter from someone like me. Speaking of Margot, don't you think she looks tired these days? Have you seen the shadows under her eyes?'

'You fucking bastard!'

He was prepared to hit him again. His heart was pounding wildly. And then he saw the sign on the wall, next to the sliding door:

Any physical and/or verbal aggression displayed towards hospital staff is punishable by law.
Art. 222-7 and 433-3 of the Criminal Code

Well, he thought, it wasn't as if Hirtmann was a member of hospital staff. Suddenly, he reached for his handcuffs.

'What are you doing?' asked Hirtmann, his eyes darting with rage.

Not answering, he closed one of the cuffs around Hirtmann's wrist and swung him around briskly.

'Stop it. This is nonsense.'

He did the same with the other handcuff, grabbed him by the arm, and led him towards the way out.

'What are you doing, for God's sake?' shouted Hirtmann. 'Think of Gustav! The time we're wasting.'

His voice was smooth and cold, and Servaz felt as if he were walking on thin ice that was about to crack.

The nurse in the little office saw them go by and rushed out of the room. Without turning around, Servaz waved his badge and walked on with his prisoner.

'You seem upset, Martin,' said Hirtmann, his voice both mocking and nasty now. 'You're like a cat with its tail caught in the door. Take these off. I didn't touch your daughter. And I will not touch her. If you do what you have to do . . . Ultimately, everything – absolutely everything – depends on you.'

'Shut up.'

He pushed the swinging door into the entrance hall and again held out his badge to the woman at reception – who stared round-eyed at Hirtmann's bloodied face – then he turned and led Hirtmann out of the door.

There was a rush of cold air, but Servaz didn't notice. They went down the steps and headed towards his car.

'Think,' said Hirtmann, walking next to him. 'You're going to be convicted of murder. I'm the only person who can clear you.'

'Precisely. I'd rather know you're in prison by then and not at large,' he said, opening the passenger door.

'And Gustav?'

'That's my problem.'

'Oh, really? Once you're in jail, how are you going to donate your liver?'

Hirtmann was leaning against the car, his bound wrists crossed over his abdomen; he looked him up and down. Servaz hesitated.

'All right, I'll do it, but on my terms,' he said.

'Which are?'

'You'll go to prison, I will be free. I'll follow your instructions. I'll go to your clinic and donate my liver. We'll save Gustav. But you'll be in jail all that time.'

Hirtmann made a sound between a laugh and a roar.

'You think you can dictate your terms? You have no choice, Martin, if you want to save your son. And your daughter . . . Even if I'm in prison, think of what the Labarthes could do to her. Or if it's not them, other people like them – acquaintances of mine. You look very pale, Martin . . .'

His eyes had narrowed to two slits, but Servaz could make out a metallic gleam between his eyelids. He did not doubt for one second that the man would make good on his threat.

He struck him in his liver, as hard as he could, and Hirtmann screamed in pain and rage, bending his knees.

'You'll pay for this,' he said. 'Sooner or later, you'll pay. But not now.'

Servaz removed the handcuffs.

It was four o'clock in the morning when he went back up to the hotel. He saw a light shining in the window of the room. Kirsten was awake.

When he went in, she was sitting with her back to him, on the chair by the little desk, at her computer.

'Where were you?' she asked, not turning round.

He didn't answer right away. Kirsten spun around and looked at him.

'What happened? You look as if you've aged ten years in one day.'

39

Margot

'And you didn't see fit to tell me?'

She was furious. She did not seem to have got much sleep, and the shadows beneath her eyes made her look frailer than usual.

'You spent five hours in the damn hospital with that kid and you couldn't find a single moment to call me?'

'You were sleeping . . .'

'Fuck off!'

He took this as a warning and fell silent.

'And where is he now?'

'I don't know.'

'What?'

'I don't know.'

'You . . . you *let him get away*? Just like that?'

'Didn't you hear what I said? Gustav may be my son. And he is mortally ill.'

'And so . . . ?'

'Hirtmann has everything planned. The clinic abroad, the surgeon who is going to operate on him . . .'

'Shit, Martin! They can just as easily operate on the kid here, if you're the donor. You don't need to—'

'No,' he interrupted.

She looked at him.

'Why?'

'I have my reasons.'

'Bloody hell!' she swore.

'He threatened to go after Margot.'

'You could ask to have her detail reinforced.'

'You know as well as I do that it's impossible to protect someone

one hundred per cent of the time,' he said, thinking of what Hirtmann had said about Margot. 'I won't take that risk. Besides, who knows how long it will take to sort Gustav's situation here. He's *ill*. There's no time to lose. They have to operate *now*.'

His tone was firm, and categorical. Kirsten nodded, with solemn intensity.

'So you're going to let him play this out, is that it? You're going to obey him?'

'For the time being. I have no choice.'

'You always have a choice.'

She seemed very annoyed.

'When are you due to see him again?'

'He's going to contact me.'

Again she nodded, not without shooting him a sharp look.

'I have to go,' he said, gathering his things.

'Where are you going?' she asked, exasperated and dumbfounded.

'To see my daughter.'

It was still dark when Servaz reached Toulouse, parked his car in the Victor-Hugo car park, went down to street level, crossed the road and entered his building, with a wave of his hand to the cop sitting in his car. He greeted the other cop outside his door, wondering how long he'd been there. It was 6.12 in the morning.

'Coffee?' he said.

The cop accepted and stood up. He unlocked the door carefully, so as not to wake Margot. He heard someone moving in the kitchen.

'Margot?'

His daughter's face appeared in the doorway.

'Dad? What are you doing here?'

'Good morning, mademoiselle,' said the cop behind him.

'Good morning,' she replied. 'Would you like a coffee?'

'You're already up?' asked her father, studying her tired face, the bluish shadows beneath her eyes.

She looked at him without answering and turned around to go back into the kitchen. Even her shoulders seemed to droop more than usual in her worn dressing gown. He remembered what Hirtmann had said: 'Don't you think she looks tired these days?'

He walked into the kitchen and took the cup Margot held out to him.

'I'm going back to bed,' said Margot, stifling a yawn.

She kissed him and walked away, through the living room. He watched her go. She really didn't seem herself. He also noticed the effects of her recent inactivity: she had put on a few kilos since she'd arrived, and her face was rounder. Did Hirtmann know more than he was letting on? From Hirtmann, his thoughts turned to Gustav. The hospital was keeping him under observation until the end of the day. After that he would go home – to the Labarthes', in other words. The very thought of it made his stomach churn.

He was hungry. He looked for a pizza in the freezer, but there were none left. The microwave meals had vanished, too. Yet again he felt a wave of irritation. The fridge had also been emptied of hamburgers, replaced by industrial quantities of fruit and veg. Organic, obviously.

He headed towards his daughter's room. The door was ajar, and he opened it quietly. She was already asleep. Even in her sleep she looked exhausted.

'Your *son?*' said Vincent Espérandieu, incredulous.

Servaz was looking at the bottom of his coffee cup, as if a message were written there.

'Martin, this is unbelievable. *Your son.*'

'Maybe,' amended Servaz, sliding two Ziploc bags over to him, one containing a lock of blond hair, the other a single hair. 'Or maybe he's just bluffing. I need the results as quickly as possible. For both of them.'

Espérandieu studied the bags, then picked them up.

'Why two? I don't understand.'

'I'll explain.'

It was too cold to sit on the terrace so they had taken refuge indoors, by the window. There were not many passers-by on the place du Capitole.

'Don't you think you could have told me about this before?'

Servaz said nothing. He glanced at his assistant. He was approaching forty, but with his hair falling over his face, his chubby cheeks and his adolescent expression, time had no purchase on him. Servaz thought he hadn't changed a bit since the day he had first come through the door to his office, ten years earlier.

Vincent was a true geek and a mild-mannered young man. In the beginning he had been the target of jibes and homophobic insults, until Servaz put a stop to it. Subsequently they had become the best of friends – to be honest, Vincent was the only true friend he had in the police, or anywhere else, for that matter. Servaz was even godfather to Vincent's son.

'I'm sorry,' he said.

'No, but really! How long have we known each other, Martin?'

'What?'

'For God's sake, you never tell me anything any more. Not me *or* Samira.'

'I'm not sure I understand what you're getting at.'

'You've changed, Martin, since your coma.'

He stiffened.

'Not at all,' he replied, firmly. 'The proof is that I've told you before anyone else.'

'And I'm glad you have. Bloody hell, I don't know what to say. You saw Hirtmann, you were in the same room as him. And you let him get away. Bloody hell, Martin! It's complete madness!'

'What else was I supposed to do? You think I've given up on the idea of arresting him? The boy could die. And he may be my son.'

'Is there no way to have him treated here?'

'Are you going to help me or not?'

'What do you want me to do?'

'The guy from the Inspectorate: what stage is he at?'

'Rimbaud? He's convinced you killed Jensen.'

'That's ridiculous.'

Espérandieu looked at him intently.

'Of course it's ridiculous. But the jerk has no other leads, so he's clinging to it. In any case, once they've done the test firing he won't have anything on you.'

Servaz avoided his assistant's gaze.

'So the question remains,' continued Vincent, 'who would have wanted to bump off that scumbag?'

'Besides me, you mean.'

'Fuck, Martin, I didn't mean that.'

Servaz nodded. But Vincent Espérandieu was determined not to leave it at that.

'Since when have you been taking everything your friends say the wrong way? Shit, you want me to tell you? Ever since you came out of your coma, I've been wondering who I'm speaking to: you, or someone else.'

That's something I've been wondering, too.

'Can you keep an eye on Rimbaud?' he asked.

'It's going to be tricky. He doesn't trust Samira and me.'

'Who's doing the test firing?'

'Torossian.'

'Well, we know him. Could you sound him out?'

'All right,' said Vincent. 'I'll see what I can do.'

He shook the two Ziploc bags.

'What will you do if he is your son?'

'I have no idea.'

'How's Margot?'

Servaz was instantly on the alert.

'Why do you ask?'

'Because I saw her two days ago in town and she really didn't look well.'

He hesitated.

'So you've noticed, too?'

He looked down, and then up again.

'I feel guilty,' he said. 'She dropped everything to be near me, and I'm constantly leaving her on her own. And then, I wonder if . . . I don't know . . . I get the impression there's something . . . But she won't tell me anything. Things are awkward between us at the moment. I don't know what to do.'

'It's simple.'

Servaz looked at his assistant, astonished.

'Ask her. Straight out.'

Servaz nodded. Vincent was right.

'And what about the Norwegian woman, is there anything between you?'

'Is that any of your business?'

Espérandieu sighed, a gleam of irritation in his eyes.

'No, of course not. Except that in the old days you would never have spoken to me like that. Seriously, you're spooking me.'

Espérandieu stood up. 'I've got to go. I've got work. I'll keep you posted about the DNA.'

Kirsten saw the Labarthes come back with the boy at around three in the afternoon. She watched them for a moment through the binoculars, then suddenly she was fed up. What was the point? She tossed the binoculars onto the bed and was about to lie down when her phone vibrated. She looked at the screen.

Kasper. Calling for news.

She didn't reply. She didn't feel like talking to him. His interest in the investigation was all to his credit, but she was beginning to find his repeated phone calls a touch suspicious: after all, he hadn't seemed that interested when she was in Bergen. She had been careful not to tell him that Hirtmann had been found. He would have told his superiors in no time. Servaz had not informed his own superiors, either. Why? Because he didn't want to be taken off the case – or was there another reason? She herself had not told Oslo much of anything. If there was one thing she wanted to avoid, it was having the Kripos prying into what was happening here.

She stared at the ceiling and thought about the Labarthes. About what they had put her through. And above all, what they hadn't had time to put her through . . . The very thought of it filled her with a murderous rage. It shouldn't have happened. It wasn't her style to just let things drop. She remembered her early days as a uniformed policewoman on the streets of Oslo. She had been called to Rosenkrantzgate regarding a fight in a bar and had stopped a drunken man and his mate. As she expected, the man in question went for her from the start, spitting in her face words that certain men automatically use the moment a woman stands in their way. Despite this, the man was released the next morning, and as he was leaving the station he jeered at the policemen on duty.

No doubt he didn't understand why, the following evening, as he was staggering home, drunk yet again, a shadowy figure had appeared out of nowhere and assaulted him. The drunk ended up with several broken ribs, a crushed jaw, a dislocated shoulder, and three fingers of his right hand bent back. To this day he must wonder what had happened to him.

She'd had enough of going round in circles. So she put on her boots, her anorak and her hat and went out for a walk in the snow. As her ankles sank into 20 centimetres of powder, she thought about Martin and the night they had spent together. It had been more than just a one-night stand. At the time, she'd felt as if something else was beginning. Had he felt it too?

*

'What shall we do?' asked Aurore Labarthe.

'What do you mean, what shall we do?'

She shot her husband a look of exasperation. It was nine o'clock in the evening and she had just put Gustav to bed. Night had fallen long ago, and the chalet was silent.

'Didn't you see his face at the hospital?' she said. 'He's going to come back. And this time he's going to punish us.'

She saw Roland go very pale, and his features lost their composure.

'What do you mean, *punish us*?'

'Are you going to go on parroting me?' she snapped.

She did not see the murderous look he gave her, because she had turned to the window.

'We have to get out of here,' she declared.

'What?'

'Before he comes to deal with us.'

'Why . . . why would he do that?'

His voice was practically trembling. He was such a wuss.

'That's his thing, punishment. You ought to know, you're his biographer,' she snorted. 'We screwed up.'

'You screwed up,' he corrected her. 'It was your idea to drug the kid. And your second mistake was to tell him.'

'Because you think that little twit of an intern wouldn't have told him? Shut up. And stop shitting yourself.'

'Aurore, don't speak to me like that.'

'Shut up. There's only one thing for us to do: take as many things as we can carry and get out of here.'

'And the kid?'

'As soon as we're gone, you call Hirtmann and tell him to come and get him, that the keys to the chalet are in the exhaust of my car and that Gustav is sound asleep in his bed.'

'And where will we go, for fuck's sake?'

'Far away. For a change of air. And we'll change our names if we have to. There are plenty of people who do that, who disappear overnight. We have enough money put aside.'

'And my work at the university?'

'Do you think I give a fuck?' she replied.

'May I remind you that it's thanks to my position that we've been able to buy this place and that we—'

There was the sound of an engine. They fell silent. For the first time, he saw Aurore's face contorted with fear when she turned again to the window. He looked in turn, and froze. A car was driving very slowly through the snow; it had passed the hotel and was headed now towards the chalet, its headlights like two bright suns.

'It's him,' she said.

'What are we going to do?'

'The same thing we did to that Norwegian,' she declared. 'Then we'll kill him. After we've had a little bit of fun.'

She turned to face him and he felt an icy chill: Aurore Labarthe's eyes were sparkling with cruelty.

Kirsten saw him get out of the car and go up the snowy steps to the door.

Julian.

She moved the binoculars and saw Aurore Labarthe at one of the windows on the first floor. She focused on the blonde woman. She looked preoccupied, but there was something else in her expression, too: wiliness, treachery, scheming . . . Kirsten suddenly felt all her senses on the alert. Something was brewing.

Clearly, Aurore Labarthe was fully aware of the danger she and her husband were in. As for Hirtmann, was he aware of the danger that was stalking him? Kirsten felt as if a cloud of black ink were obscuring her thoughts. What should she do? She had come without her gun. Where was Martin? Probably on the road. She dialled his number – and got his voicemail.

Shit.

He was standing on the steps, his shadow wrapped in a dark winter coat sprinkled with snow, his hair dancing in the wind above his glasses. Aurore Labarthe had put on the black silk dressing gown with red braid he liked so much, but when she opened the door, he did not pay her the slightest attention. Any more than he noticed her body which, ordinarily, he always stopped to appreciate. At no point did his eyes ever leave hers.

'Good evening, Aurore,' he said.

His tone was as chilly as the night outside. She felt a shiver in every one of her vertebrae, beneath the silk, like the caress of an icy finger. She saw his battered, swollen nose, and the cotton protruding from his nostrils. What had happened?

'Good evening, Julian. Come in.'

She wondered, as she stood to one side, when he was going to throw himself on her, but he did nothing of the kind, and headed towards the living room. She thought of Roland, in the kitchen mixing the cocktails. His hands must be trembling, her coward of a husband. He had better not make any mistakes with the dosage.

All the same, when Julian walked past her, she felt the heady mixture of excitement and fear she always experienced in his presence. He strode into the living room like an animal. Certain of his strength, but wary. Ready for action and reaction. Aurore tightened the sash of her dressing gown around her waist before walking over to him. Roland came out of the kitchen carrying a tray with three big cocktail glasses, and she saw right away that he had been drinking to give himself courage.

'Master,' he said respectfully. 'Please have a seat.'

'Stop talking rubbish, Roland, will you please?' said Hirtmann, removing his damp coat and tossing it onto the sofa.

Labarthe nodded his head, not daring to look at him. He set the creamy white cocktail down in front of him.

'A White Russian, as usual?'

Hirtmann nodded, never taking his eyes off Labarthe. Labarthe put Aurore's champagne cocktail and his own Old-Fashioned down on the coffee table. Cocktails were another of Roland's passions. Which had come in useful more than once when they had to 'help' their guests relax and take part in their games.

'Have I ever told you that I have Russian roots?' said Hirtmann, raising his glass. Roland was staring at the cocktail. Aurore wanted to shout at him to be more discreet. But then she turned her attention back to Hirtmann, who had paused with his glass a few inches from his lips. 'Aristocratic Russian, in fact. My maternal grandfather was a minister in the Kerensky government, before the October Revolution. The family lived in Saint Petersburg, on Bolshaya Morskaya street, a stone's throw away from the Nabokovs.'

At last he took a sip of the mixture, which looked like whipped cream, then another one.

'Delicious, Roland. It's perfect.'

He set his glass back down. Roland glanced furtively at Aurore. He had added almost 3 grams of GHB to the cocktail. A huge dose. In a few minutes, the substance would make its way to Hirtmann's brain, changing his mood, making him euphoric, dissolving his fears and paranoia, and altering his motor functions. He would then cease to be the formidable Julian Hirtmann, and become easier prey.

Aurore went and sat opposite Hirtmann. Ostensibly spreading her legs. This time, Hirtmann's gaze lingered at the woman's thighs, and for a moment it shone with pure lust, but also rage.

'What you did was unforgivable,' he said suddenly, his voice as sharp as a knife, as he set his glass back down.

Aurore tensed. Labarthe felt his stomach drop to his shoes. It was Hirtmann's tone, more than what he said, which was so chilling. She thought about the loaded gun she had hidden behind him, in an open drawer in the sideboard. She wondered if she would have time to reach for it.

'You shouldn't have done it. Really. It's very . . . disappointing.'

His suave, honeyed voice, as soft as a caress. Or a doctor's cotton swab before the injection.

'Julian,' Aurore began.

'Shut up, you bitch.'

She recoiled. He had never spoken to her like that. No one had ever spoken to her like that. But she remained silent.

'To be honest, it's something that I cannot . . . forgive. And so, as you will easily understand, it must be punished.'

Aurore wanted to say something, but she realised it was pointless. Only the drug could save them now. *If it worked in time* . . . Hirtmann's eyes were darting from her to Roland and back, and for the moment, they did not show the slightest sign of any altered consciousness.

'You are going to—'

He broke off. Raised one hand to his face. Rubbed his eyelids. When he opened them, his gaze had changed. His dilated pupils were two black holes. His gaze was hazy, and he had difficulty focusing.

'This cocktail,' he said, 'this cocktail is absolutely . . . delicious.'

He flung himself back against the sofa, his neck on the cushions, his eyes staring at the ceiling, and he smiled.

'Among humans as among the rats, control stimulates the mind, you know that? The absence of control, it is said, can paralyse mental function. But sometimes it's good to lose control, isn't it?'

He laughed, sat up again, raised the glass to his lips, then took a long swallow. Suddenly he burst out laughing.

'Shit, I don't know what is in this, but I have never felt so fucking good!'

There was no trace of threat in his voice.

'"*Now I know when the last morning will come: when the Light will no longer bring fear . . . neither Night nor Love . . . when slumber has become eternal, a single . . . a single . . . inexhaustible dream . . . and . . . I feel a celestial fatigue . . .*"'

He put his glass back down and lay on his side on the sofa, his knees tucked up.

'Shit . . . I think I'm going to sleep . . .'

Aurore peered at him. He closed his eyes. Then opened them. Then closed them again. She was silent for a moment. Then she looked at her husband and motioned towards the kitchen with her chin. Labarthe was about to get up when Hirtmann opened his eyes and stared at him. The professor felt his blood go cold. But then Hirtmann's eyes closed again and his head fell back against the cushion. Unsteadily, Labarthe followed Aurore into the kitchen.

'What the fuck did you do?' she hissed as soon as he came in. 'Have you seen the state he's in? How are we going to get him up there?'

Roland opened his eyes wide.

'So? He's at our mercy! All we have to do is finish him off. Now. Right away.'

She shook her head.

'I told you I wanted to have some fun with him.'

Labarthe couldn't believe his ears. Had his wife gone mad? He could see the irritation and frustration in her eyes.

'Shit, the man is dangerous, even drugged! We have to finish him off, Aurore! Now! Just in case you hadn't noticed, this time it's murder.'

She gave him a penetrating look, her eyes flashing.

'You're nothing but a coward, you know that? All your so-called fantasies – it's all hot air. Why do you have to screw everything up? Do everything all wrong?'

'What did you do all wrong?' came a voice from the door, behind Labarthe's back.

Julian Hirtmann's tall figure was framed in the threshold to the kitchen, and he had a broad smile across his face. Labarthe felt his heart beating fit to burst. Had Hirtmann heard the beginning of their conversation?

'I thought maybe we could have some fun before I take Gustav away,' said Hirtmann, his voice unsteady. 'What do you think? A sort of farewell party . . . shall we?'

His head was wobbling. He was blinking, as if he were having trouble keeping his eyes open; they were rolling in their sockets, unable to stay in place. Aurore looked at him warily, then her smile spread. The cretin was going to hurry into the trap all by himself, the great Julian Hirtmann would be at her mercy. A shiver of excitement went all through her like an electric shock.

'Of course.'

Labarthe looked at her in turn, and his look said, *Aha, you see?* Hirtmann went back out of the kitchen and staggered towards the staircase.

'Are you sure he's not faking?' Labarthe murmured behind his back. Aurore pointed to the cocktail glass. It was empty.

'How much did you put in?'

'Almost three grams.'

'That's impossible. Even for him,' she said.

As if to prove Labarthe was right, Hirtmann stumbled on the first step, laughed, went up another step, and stumbled again.

'Fuck, I'm drunk as a skunk!'

The spouses looked at each other. Roland went over to Hirtmann and put his arm around his waist. Hirtmann put his free arm around the professor's shoulder and squeezed him affectionately. Labarthe looked tiny next to Hirtmann; the huge man could snap his neck just like that, and the professor felt every hair on his body stand on end.

'My friend,' said Hirtmann, 'my faithful, loyal friend.'

'Always,' answered Labarthe, subject in spite of himself to a strange and powerful emotion which wasn't only fear.

'Always,' echoed Hirtmann, with the solemn conviction of a drunk.

With Aurore following behind, they climbed up the steps. On the final landing, Hirtmann held out his arm. He was tall enough to reach the trap door handle on the ceiling; he opened it then pulled down the metal ladder, which descended with a creak. Hirtmann grabbed hold of the ladder and climbed up the first rungs like a child eager to play.

He suddenly stopped halfway up and leaned towards them, looking concerned.

'Are you sure Gustav is asleep?'

She gave her husband a questioning look.

'I'll go and check,' he said. 'Go ahead and start without me.'

She wanted to tell him to do no such thing. She didn't like the idea of going up there alone with Julian Hirtmann. But Hirtmann was watching them and she reluctantly agreed.

Labarthe went back down to the floor below. She heard his steps heading along the corridor towards the boy's room. Hirtmann flipped the light switch and disappeared into the attic. She put her foot on the ladder.

Why did she feel as if she were climbing up to the gallows?

With each rung she told herself this wasn't such a good idea, after all. Perhaps Roland was right: they should have finished the job downstairs. When she put her head through the hole, she shuddered: he was standing right next to the trap door, towering over her, observing her with his shining little eyes.

She saw her own reflection in the lenses of his glasses. For a split second she was tempted to go back down and run away.

She pulled herself out onto the floor and stood up. Hirtmann gazed at her, lustfully. The wind was howling against the roof. Outside, the temperature must be arctic, but the heat up here made her dizzy.

'Take it off,' he said.

She did as she was told, and the bathrobe dropped to her feet with an almost imperceptible rustle of silk. He gazed at her for a long time, his look this time one of pure desire, not missing a single part of her body.

'I'm in charge here, don't forget,' she said.

He nodded, his head still shaky, his eyelids visibly heavy. She put one hand flat on his chest, near his heart, and pushed him gently but firmly, and he stepped back, docile. She reached for a leather bracelet attached to a cable, tugged on the pulley, and fastened it around his left wrist. He complied with a smile.

'Bring your face closer,' he said. 'Kiss me.'

She hesitated but lifted her face to him; their chests were almost touching. He leaned slightly forward, put his free hand behind her neck and kissed her on the mouth. She responded to his kiss. He tasted like coffee liqueur and vodka. Suddenly Hirtmann's large hand left the back of her neck and closed around her throat.

'What did you put in my cocktail?'

Her neck in a vice, she opened her mouth, struggling for the air blocked by his grip. She saw black spots before her eyes, like a swarm of midges.

'Let me go!'

'Answer me.'

'Nothing . . . I . . . swear.'

She punched him in the chest, with surprising force despite the lack of room, but he held on regardless. She wanted to shout, but all she managed to produce was a sound halfway between a whistle and a croak. Hirtmann's hand was crushing her carotid artery, and the blood flow to her brain was getting weaker. She would pass out before long. The pain in her larynx was unbearable. She tried to breathe but her throat was blocked. Her heart was pounding like a drum.

Suddenly Hirtmann let her go.

She wanted to step back but, before she had time to grasp what was happening, he punched her so hard she could feel her nose breaking, staining the linoleum with a cloud of black blood, and she collapsed, all awareness snuffed out like a taper.

He picked up one of the candles. Went closer. Held it before her eyes, a few centimetres away, passing the light over her cornea from one eye to the other like an ophthalmologist's lamp.

She struggled feebly, naked and exposed, shivering despite the heat in the attic, but her wrists were bound in a V above her head, she had a gag over her mouth, and her eyes were wide and full of tears. Her broken nose was excruciating, and she could taste blood.

Roland's steps resounded on the vibrating steel ladder and Hirtmann went over to the trap door.

'Come on up,' he said encouragingly.

He could hear Aurore moaning behind him. Roland froze. His eyes grew wide with terror. He was about to go back down and run away when Hirtmann grabbed him by the collar and lifted him effortlessly up through the opening. He shoved him with a thump and the professor rolled across the floor.

'I beg you, please, Master, don't hurt me!'

Labarthe pointed at Aurore.

'It was her! That bitch! I . . . I didn't want to!'

His eyes filled with tears. Hirtmann turned to Aurore. He could see rage and deadly hatred in her eyes. He almost admired her.

'Get up,' he said to Labarthe.

The professor obeyed. His legs were trembling violently, as was his lower lip. Soon he would start weeping. Gusts of wind were banging a shutter somewhere. For a moment, Hirtmann was afraid the noise might wake Gustav. He listened out, but no sound came through the open trap door.

His hand on Labarthe's shoulder, he steered him into the middle of the room. Resigned, trembling, the professor yielded like a lamb being led to slaughter. Hirtmann tied him up. A lamb who had thought he was a wolf. Now he was sobbing openly, his arms in a V like his wife's.

Hirtmann removed the gag from Aurore's mouth. She spat in his face, an impressive gob, which he wiped off nonchalantly. He looked at the streak of blood on the back of his hand with a smile. She turned to her husband:

'You're just a shit, Roland!' she spat. 'A useless weakling.'

Her eyes blazed with anger.

'Hey, hey,' said Hirtmann, his voice no longer hesitant or slurred. 'You can settle your differences some other time. Well . . . perhaps not . . .'

'Go fuck yourself,' she replied.

'It's you, darling, who will be fucked, and after that you will die,' he said calmly.

'Fuck off, Hirtmann!'

With the speed of a rattlesnake, a sharp little knife appeared in his fist and he drew two deep vertical slashes in Aurore's cheeks. The blood soaked her chin and neck before dripping onto her breasts.

She screamed.

The sweat was pouring off her profusely now, every pore of her naked body exuding it, like a tree trunk oozing sap. She was gasping, her chin and chest smeared with blood, her blonde hair clumping with sweat.

'You see, you shouldn't resist me,' he said calmly. 'Your bloody drug is beginning to work; I feel dizzy. It's time for me to leave. It's a good job I ate a kilo of lard and took a few amphetamines before I came, isn't it, darling? Lard is very effective: it slows down the absorption of the drug through the stomach. And the amphetamine counteracts the effect of the GHB. Or the Rohypnol. It's some sort of crap like that you gave me, isn't it? Like you gave that Norwegian woman the other night. You seem to have a rare old time of it in your chalet.'

He glanced over at Labarthe.

'I'll be back in a minute.'

It was three minutes, in fact, which Aurore spent exclusively insulting her husband. When Hirtmann reappeared he had a can of petrol in his hand. He set it down in front of Aurore, lit another candle, walked over to a curtain of garnet-coloured velvet, and held a flame up to the cloth.

The flames devoured the cloth as they crackled and rose to the ceiling in no time at all. Hirtmann went back to the couple, his form outlined against the rising intensity of the flames. He unscrewed the container and poured it onto Aurore, who writhed and screamed.

'Fuck, no! Not like this! *Not like this!*'

Hirtmann left the open container at her feet as if he hadn't heard and turned to Roland.

'You might have a chance to make it out alive, who knows?'

The professor shot him a dubious look: a mixture of hope, doubt and absolute terror. He was about to beg for mercy when the little blade in Hirtmann's hand inscribed the almost horizontal arc of a circle and came to lodge in his carotid. Hirtmann withdrew it and plunged it in again, this time level with his subclavian artery. It was as if two holes had been drilled into a barrel: two little ruby fountains spouted from the professor's neck and torso. Hirtmann read the stupor and weakness in Labarthe's gaze, the disbelief that takes hold of certain men at the threshold of death – before life quickly left him.

'But I don't think so,' added Hirtmann.

He tossed the bloody blade to the floor and walked over to the trap door.

40

Two Down

Tall flames rose to the sky, illuminating the night and devouring what was left of the chalet. Rising cinders met falling snowflakes, like two columns of luminous ants. The glow from the fire was reflected on the edge of the woods slightly higher up. Kirsten was leaning against a police car, wrapped in a survival blanket. Her cup of coffee was steaming in the cold air. A dozen metres away, firemen's hoses made huge columns of hissing steam where the water met the flames. When the fire was extinguished on one side, it started up on the other.

Kirsten gazed at the spectacle, glinting fire reflected in her eyes. She knew she was going to have to explain it to Martin. She'd heard Aurore's inhuman screams as the flames devoured her, as her eyes popped out of her head and her flesh melted like wax in the inferno. Kirsten had held her breath, felt the pressure of her screams against her ears, until suddenly they stopped. Not long afterwards, a large portion of the chalet had collapsed on itself and the sirens had drowned out all other sound.

'What happened?' asked a voice next to her.

She turned her head and saw him.

'He let them burn, inside,' she said. 'He must have tied them up somewhere. Where did you get to?'

'And what happened to you?' asked Martin, when he saw her face was black with soot.

'I tried to get in; the fire had already started.'

'To . . . save them?'

She gave him a look of surprise.

'So? It's not because—'

'And did you see Hirtmann?'

She made a face.

'Yes. He left with Gustav. The fire had already started by then.'

Servaz looked at her intently.

'Without a gun, there was nothing I could do. To arrest him, I mean. He walked right past me without saying a word, holding the boy's hand. He put him in the back of the car and they drove away.'

She shook her head, tears in her eyes.

'He killed them, Martin. And I just let him get away!'

He said nothing.

'Don't stay here,' someone said. 'Move away. It's going to collapse.'

They went back to the hotel. The terrace was full of curious onlookers from the village. It was like Bastille Day, except for the cold that went right to the bone.

He put his arm around her shoulders and she let herself lean against him as they walked.

'Don't worry,' he said. 'It will soon be over.'

His phone vibrated in his pocket. He took it out and looked at the text message that had just arrived. A place, a time, nothing more. And two words: *Come alone*.

He looked up at Kirsten.

'That was him,' he said. 'He wants me to come alone.'

'Where?'

'I'll tell you later.'

Her expression went blank. But for a moment he saw a flash of black anger in her eyes, and her features were transformed, so much so he hardly recognised her. Then her face regained one of its usual expressions and she nodded, reluctantly.

41

Trust

'Do you trust me, son?'

Gustav stared at his father. He nodded with conviction. Hirtmann looked out and measured the 100 metres of void below the great arch dam, the tops of the frozen fir trees, the snow-covered rocks, the riverbed all the way at the bottom, buried in the moonlight beneath a sepulchral whiteness.

'Are you ready?'

'I'm afraid,' said the boy suddenly, his voice trembling.

He was dressed in a down anorak, the hood pulled up over his head. With the scarf wrapped around his neck he looked like a Russian doll.

'I'm afraid!' he said again. 'I don't want to – please, Papa!'

'The secret of life is overcoming our fears, Gustav. People who obey their fears don't get very far. Are you ready?'

'No!'

He lifted Gustav over the railing of the ice-covered dam and held him out over the dizzying void. The wind was whistling in their ears.

The boy screamed.

His shrill cry was channelled by the white mountains around them, the sound wave travelling all along the valley below. However, there was no one to hear for miles around.

Then Hirtmann saw a pair of headlights slowly moving up the winding road. He smiled. Unlike his own car, Martin's was visibly not made for a road that had not been cleared of snow. Other than maintenance vehicles, no one was supposed to come up here in the middle of winter: normally, the barrier down below was lowered. Hirtmann had broken the padlock and raised it for the occasion.

He lifted Gustav back over the railing and set him down on the dam. The boy hugged him, his arms clinging to Hirtmann's legs.

'Don't ever do that again, Papa, please.'

'All right, son.'

'I want to go home!'

'We won't be here much longer.'

The headlights were getting closer along the last portion of the icy road. They came out onto the little car park where in summer there was a temporary outdoor restaurant.

He saw Martin getting out of his car, dressed far too lightly for the Siberian cold that prevailed at this altitude. Servaz saw them. He left his door open. He got back into the car and for a moment Hirtmann thought he was going to take his gun. Instead, he manoeuvred the car so that it faced them, and the headlights caught them in their beam, blinding them, setting the entire dam ablaze in a flood of white light.

Dazzled, Gustav shielded his eyes. Hirtmann merely blinked. Now Martin was coming down the steps to the dam, walking towards them. All they could see was his outline against the glare of the headlights and his dark shadow stretching ahead of him, whereas he must be able to see them perfectly.

'Why here?' he shouted, as he got closer. 'The road is dangerous in winter. And going back down will be even worse. I thought you cared about my liver!'

'I trust you, Martin. And I have chains in the boot. You can put them on for the way down. Come closer.'

Servaz complied. He was looking not at Hirtmann, but at the boy. In return, clinging to Hirtmann, Gustav never took his eyes off Servaz, and the shadow of his hand acting as a screen formed the silhouette of a wolf on his face. Servaz felt the icy wind go right through him.

'Good evening, Gustav,' he said.

'Good evening,' replied Gustav.

'Do you know who this is?' asked Julian Hirtmann.

The boy shook his head.

'I'll tell you soon. He is someone who is very important to you.'

Servaz felt a grinding in his guts. At this altitude, the shrieking wind drowned Hirtmann's words. Hirtmann put one hand in the pocket of his coat and took out a printed paper and a passport.

'A hire car will be waiting for you tomorrow morning at Toulouse-Blagnac airport. You will drive to Hallstatt, in Austria. It takes roughly fifteen hours. Once you arrive, someone will come to meet you on the Marktplatz, by the fountain. The day after tomorrow, at noon. Don't worry, you'll recognise him.'

'Hallstatt? The place on the postcard.'

He saw Hirtmann smile.

'Poe's "Purloined Letter" once again,' said Servaz. 'No one will go looking for him there.'

'Well, not any more, now that the police have turned the village and the surrounding area upside down,' said Hirtmann.

'Is that where the clinic is?' asked Servaz.

'Just follow the instructions. Of course, should you get the bright idea of asking that little Norwegian policewoman to follow you . . . Oh, in fact, they must have nearly finished identifying your gun as the crime weapon, so you'd do well not to hang around anywhere near your regional crime unit.'

It suddenly occurred to Servaz that the double DNA test was pointless: Hirtmann would never have chosen him as donor were he not 100 per cent sure that Servaz was the father. Gustav was indeed his son. The thought made him dizzy. He looked at the boy, his expression somewhat lost.

'Papa, is he the man who's going to give me his liver?' asked Gustav, as if he were reading his thoughts.

'Yes, that's him, son.'

'So it's thanks to him that I'm going to get better?'

'Yes. You see, I told you: he's very important. You have to trust him the way you trust me. That is important too.'

Kirsten saw Martin's car drive up and park just below the terrace. A moment later he came into the room, his eyes shining, and she knew something had happened.

'He really is my son,' he said.

He looked at her, distraught. Kirsten said nothing.

'I'm leaving tomorrow,' he added.

'Tomorrow? Where are you going?'

'I'm not allowed to say.'

He saw her withdraw, read the sadness in her eyes. He took her by the shoulders.

'Kirsten, it's not a matter of trust.'

'It certainly seems like one.'

Her look was stubborn, her manner several degrees colder.

'Kirsten, I don't want to take the slightest risk, that's all. Who knows if there's not someone watching both of us.'

'Who's taken over from the Labarthes, you mean? What, you think he has an army at his disposal? You overestimate him, Martin. And anyway, he needs you. Well . . . he needs your liver.'

True enough. As long as the transplant had not been carried out, Hirtmann would not try anything against him. *And after that . . . ?* he wondered. What would happen then? Who knew if he wouldn't want to eliminate 'the other father', who would now be in the way.

'Hallstatt,' he said.

'The village on the postcard?' she said with surprise.

He nodded.

'Shit. That's clever. Where is your appointment?'

'On the marketplace, day after tomorrow at noon.'

'I could leave tonight, and get a room there,' she said. 'How are you supposed to get there?'.

'Hire car. At the airport.'

'Let's go back to Toulouse. We have nothing left to do here. You drop me off at my hotel, then I'll find a way to leave without anyone noticing. With a few hours' head start.'

He nodded. She was looking at him with a mixture of gentleness and complicity, and he felt that she must want, or need, to be closer; he too wanted contact. For a moment they didn't say anything, their arms hanging by their sides, then their hands touched. First briefly, then insistently, their fingers seeking, mingling, stroking.

She moved closer to him and their lips met. She touched his neck, while he was already undressing her, pulling her towards the bed. It was different from the previous time; less violent, more tender. She did bite him again, and scratch him – as if to leave her mark, yet again, on his flesh. She adapted to his rhythm and let him come.

'There is something I haven't told you,' she began, once they'd finished, as she lay curled next to him under the duvet, and she stroked his day-old beard, her legs mingled with his.

He turned to look at her.

'I have a sister,' she said, 'younger than me. An artist.'

He was silent, sensing that she was getting ready to tell him something she'd been keeping to herself for a long time.

'She looks like Kirsten Dunst – how she was in the *Spider-Man* trilogy, not *Fargo*; although psychologically, she's more like the character in *Melancholia*.' He refrained from telling her he hadn't seen any of those films. 'My sister has always been drawn to shadows and darkness, I don't know why. She has regular bouts of depression, and yet she's so gifted, and men all fall at her feet. But it's never enough. She always needs more: more love, more sex, more drugs, more attention, more danger. She's a painter and photographer, she's had exhibitions in Oslo, in New York, in Berlin . . . But she doesn't care. Art for her is just a way to make a living. When our father died, she didn't come to the hospital or to the funeral. She said she was afraid she'd be too *depressed*. Instead, she did a series of paintings, something like Bacon reinterpreted by David Lynch. In those paintings our father looks like a monster, arrogant and bloated, grotesque. She said that was how she saw him. Our mother never got over it.'

She shrugged her shoulders under the duvet.

'Don't get me wrong, I love my sister. Even though I spent my youth fixing all her messes, hiding them from our parents, cleaning up after her and providing her with alibis for her secret encounters with increasingly unhinged men. And then one day last year I got the impression she had changed.'

She propped herself on her elbow and her gaze, which had been focused on the window, came back to him.

'I questioned her and eventually she confessed that she had met someone. An older man – brilliant, charming, funny . . . But she didn't want to introduce him to me and I sensed something must be up. I figured he must be unhinged like all the others, just another one of those nutcases who she found so attractive. And then one day in March, she disappeared. Poof – she was gone . . . We never found her.'

He gave her a searching look.

'Hirtmann?'

She nodded.

'Who else could it be? Several women disappeared in the Oslo region just after my sister did, and the description she gave me of her friend matches up.'

'So this is why you're putting so much into this investigation – not just because he wrote your name on a scrap of paper. It's a personal matter. I should have guessed. But why did Hirtmann choose you? Why did he make you come all this way? Why did he put your name in the victim's pocket? What does any of this have to do with Gustav?'

She didn't say anything, but she looked – a sad, desperate look – deep into his eyes. He checked his watch, then gently pushed her back and sat on the edge of the bed.

'Martin,' she said. 'Wait, wait. Do you know what Barack Obama said to one of his girlfriends when she told him she loved him?'

He turned around to look at her.

'What?'

'"Thank you." That's what he said. Please don't say thank you.'

Once he had finished rehearsing Smetana's symphonic poems, Zehetmayer went back to his dressing room. As always, he had called for chocolate, Japanese whiskey, and roses. These requirements were aimed above all at maintaining his legend. He was sufficiently vain to think that his legend would outlive him, but that in no way lessened the coming horror, the prospect of his imminent annihilation and eternal night; and lately he could not think of it without trembling. Twice already the crab had loosened its claws, but this time it would not let go.

He did not believe in God, he was far too proud. His old man's mind was full of frightening lucidity, a lucidity so pure it bordered on madness. Around the Musikverein, the Viennese night had fallen yet again – a winter night of snow and wind, which for several years now had made him fear he would not see the next spring – when a knock came at his door. He thought of the statue of the Commendatore knocking at Don Giovanni's door, and the flames of hell, and he wondered if the man on the other side, in the dark corridor – that man who had so often delivered death – ever thought of his own. *Who doesn't think of it?* he wondered.

Despite his height, Jiri slipped into Zehetmayer's dressing room with the lightness of a shadow. Bernhard recalled his early conversations with Jiri, at the prison. They had been insignificant. He would scarcely have imagined that he would get in touch with him again one day for a far more sinister reason. But from the very start he had sensed that Jiri would never change, that once he came out he would resume his 'activities'. It was just who he was. Like a musician who will never give up music.

'Good evening, Jiri,' he said. 'Thank you for coming.'

The killer didn't bother to answer. He walked over to an open box of chocolates by the mirror.

'May I?'

Zehetmayer nodded. 'There has been a development,' he said, his tone impatient. 'They'll be here soon. They're coming to Austria.'

Jiri chewed on his chocolate and listened distractedly to the conductor, as if the topic did not interest him. No sooner had he finished the first chocolate than he took a second one.

'Where?' he said.

'Hallstatt. Apparently the child, Gustav, is ill. He has to have an operation there.'

'Why?' asked Jiri.

'I suppose Hirtmann knows someone there, someone from his past. He often came to Austria before he was arrested.'

'And what do you want me to do?'

'We will go there.'

'And then?'

'And then we'll see.'

The old man fell silent for a moment. Then he looked Jiri deep in the eyes.

'I'll leave it up to you: either you kill him, or you kill his son. Either way, it's all the same to me.'

'What?'

There was another moment of silence. The old man's lower lip trembled slightly.

'If you don't manage to kill him, kill the child. That gives you two options.'

Jiri seem to mull it over for a moment.

'You're crazy,' he said.

'There must be a way,' insisted the old man.

Jiri nodded his head.

'There is always a way. I want more.'

A broad smile lit up the conductor's face.

'I figured as much. One million euros.'

'Where will you get it?'

'I've been putting money aside my whole life. And I have no children. This seems to me a useful way of spending it.'

'How old is the kid, did you say?'

'Five.'

'Are you sure you want to do this?'

'One million, and one hundred thousand euros in advance,' said the old man. 'The balance when it's done.'

Suddenly both men turned their attention to the door, which had just opened. A woman's weary face emerged from the darkness, like a theatre mask, her eyes shining like pebbles. They saw a cleaning cart behind her.

'Oh, sorry. I thought the dressing room was empty.'

She closed the door. They waited for a few moments, not speaking.

'Why?' asked Jiri. 'Why do you want to go after the child as well? I'd like to understand.'

Zehetmayer's voice betrayed his emotion.

'He took my daughter, I'll take his son. It's simple arithmetic. He cares more about that child than his own life.'

'So you hate him that much?'

'More than anything.'

Jiri shrugged. The orchestra conductor was crazy, no doubt about it. Well, as long as he paid . . .

'I wouldn't know,' he replied. 'I never let my emotions get the better of me. One million euros, fair enough. And two hundred and fifty thousand in advance.'

42

Alps

The following morning, engineer Bernard Torossian reluctantly left his house in Balma, in the eastern suburbs of Toulouse, and his little family – a spirited five-year-old girl, a slightly less lively boy of twelve, and an anorexic greyhound called Winston – to head for police headquarters. He left his car in the car park and took the A line of the Métro to Jean-Jaurès station. There he changed to the B line, in the direction of Borderouge.

As he came out of the station at Canal-du-Midi that morning, he dragged his feet the last few metres to the police station as if his soles were made of lead. He had never gone to work with such a heavy heart.

Torossian showed his badge at the turnstile, then went into the lift and pressed the button for the third floor, where the ballistics section of the forensics police laboratory was located. Once he was in his office he sat down at his computer, and proceeded to think. The last few hours had been tough on his nerves, and he had only managed to fall asleep at around four o'clock in the morning. His wife asked him what was wrong, but he refused to say.

He had finished the test firing the night before. The results were devastating for someone he liked very much. Not only was it someone who'd enjoyed a near-mythic stature in the regional crime unit ever since the Saint-Martin and Marsac cases, but he was also someone Torossian respected as a man.

But ballistics and physics don't give a damn about human emotions. They are cold, factual, truthful and irrefutable. That is what he'd always liked about his profession until now: unlike his colleagues, he hadn't had to struggle through the jungle of human emotions, intuitions, theories, lies and half-truths. Until today. Today, he hated facts.

314

Because the facts had spoken: it was Servaz's weapon which had killed Jensen. Beyond a shadow of a doubt. Science does not lie.

Looking out at the rain drearily splattering the windows, he shook his head – Servaz taking his gun to kill a man in cold blood: no, it was absurd – then picked up his phone and dialled the number for the Inspectorate.

He left his car in the police car park not long after dropping Kirsten off at her hotel. It would soon be daylight. He wanted to ask Espérandieu to keep an eye on Margot – she liked and trusted him – and on the surveillance teams during his absence.

He recalled Hirtmann's words as he headed towards the building. Was he really about to walk into the lion's mouth? If the ballistics analysis had come up with anything, he figured Vincent would surely have called to warn him.

He charged through the lobby and as he came out of the lift on the second floor, he ran into Mangin, a guy from the CSI team for whom he felt no particular affinity. Ordinarily, they greeted each other as briefly as propriety would allow. This time, Mangin gave him a sharp look and kept walking without a word.

No, not a sharp look: an astonished one.

He instantly felt nervous. A few more timid good mornings in answer to his greetings and he was beginning to feel pins and needles in his legs. He resisted the urge to turn right round and get the hell out of there. *Run for it*, said a little voice inside his head. *Now. Run for it.* He took out his phone. No messages from Rimbaud. Or Vincent. Or Samira. He hastened his steps and found them in their office.

'What is going on here?' he asked from the door.

Vincent was leaning over Samira's shoulder, where she was sitting at her screen. His two assistants were speaking excitedly, then suddenly broke off. They turned to him. Their eyes grew wider.

He met their gazes.

And understood.

He felt a lump in his throat.

'I was going to call you . . .' Vincent began, hesitating somewhat. 'I was going to call you . . . your gun . . .'

Servaz was still standing in the corridor by the door to the room. His ears seemed to be ringing, and Vincent was looking at him as if he'd seen a ghost.

Something moved, over to his left.

He turned his head, looked down the corridor, and froze. Rimbaud was taking great strides in his direction.

His expression was hostile.

'It's your gun,' said Espérandieu again, as if dazed, from inside the office. 'Martin, fuck, you . . .'

He didn't hear the rest.

He swung around towards the lift. Started walking.

Slowly at first, and then more quickly.

'Hey! Servaz!' shouted the inspector behind him.

The doors were open. He stepped in. Swiped his badge.

'Servaz! Where are you going? Come back!'

Rimbaud was running now, shouting something he didn't hear. He could see faces appearing in the hallway, one after the other.

The lift didn't move.

Come on, come on . . . Rimbaud was only a few metres away. Suddenly the doors closed. But in the instant before, he had time to read not only the frustration on the man's boxer-like features but also his satisfaction at being right.

In the lift, Servaz let out a breath. He tried to think calmly and clearly. But any serenity was escaping like air from a punctured tyre. He was stuck, while up there Rimbaud would be making phone calls, sounding the alarm, rounding up the troops. His heart began beating faster.

They would nab him downstairs: just one call and they would block him at the front door.

Ever since the attacks on 13 November 2015, not only were there guards at the entrance, but junior officers at reception controlled access to the doors with a button.

His goose was cooked.

Then he thought of something else. There was one thing in his favour: it was a big building, and communication between departments was rarely optimal.

The lift opened on the ground floor, just opposite the turnstile, but he stayed at the back. He swiped his badge again and pressed another button. The lift began moving again with a slight vibration.

The basement.

The jail. The detention cells.

They must have already called reception. How long before they figured out where he had gone?

The doors opened. He entered a cold, clinical space without windows, lit solely by artificial light.

He turned right.

The cells were glass-walled; some lit, others not. Men lay on the floor inside them like puppies in a pet shop, their gazes indifferent, weary, enraged, or simply curious.

A bit further along, he passed the big glassed-in office with guards in light-coloured uniforms; he greeted them, expecting them to burst out at any moment to intercept him, but they merely returned his greeting.

Someone was being remanded in custody a bit further along – the man was going through the security checkpoint, about to be searched. Three cops from the crime brigade were with him.

His heartbeat accelerated. This might be his chance. He went through the checkpoint, and continued on his way . . .

Turned right.

Headed for the door leading to the car park *Open!*

A Ford Mondeo was waiting in the gloom near the exit for the patrol to return. There was no one inside. He swallowed, walked around and peered in the driver's side.

Christ! The keys were in the ignition!

He had a split second to decide. He was not yet a fugitive criminal, but if he took this car, there would be no going back. He glanced behind him: the men from the crime brigade had their eyes on the detainee, and were paying no attention to either Servaz or the vehicle. He heard a phone ring somewhere.

Decide, quick!

Servaz opened the door, sat at the wheel, and turned the key in the ignition. He put the car into reverse. He saw someone look over, from the building, then the policeman's stunned expression when he put the car into gear.

He backed up, causing the tyres to squeal on the floor of the car park, then drove forward through the rows of cars, charging towards the exit ramp.

Thirty seconds.

That was the time he figured he would need to reach the barrier, which would open automatically to any vehicles coming from inside and which, as a rule, were in a hurry.

He was driving fast, too fast. He almost lost control when he reached the ramp, and he hit a motorcycle with the right front wing, skidded first to the left and then to the right, but quickly regained control. The motorcycle he had just hit collapsed against the one next to it, and all the motorcycles in the car park fell one after the other in a clamour of crumpling metal and twisted handlebars, echoing all through the underground space.

He hardly heard it: he was already charging towards the exit and the barrier that gave out onto the boulevard.

He was fleeing from his workplace like a bandit! The entire police building could hear the screech of tyres.

His fingers were damp and tense on the steering wheel, and he forced himself not to think about it; he was sure the barrier would not go up, or that someone would appear, something would go wrong, and he would spend the rest of his days in . . .

Concentrate, dammit!

The barrier.

It was going up! He couldn't believe his eyes. Hope returned and the adrenaline was like a kick in the arse. He came out onto the boulevard, jumped the red light in front of a Mini coming from his right, which stopped short with a squeal of tyres and blew its horn in a rage. He turned left, scraping the pavement that went along the canal, and sped towards the Minimes bridge.

Twenty seconds.

That was roughly how long it took him to cover the 300 metres to the bridge.

He was across the canal fifteen seconds later.

Avenue Honoré-Serres now.

Fifty more interminable seconds because of a traffic jam – not a single siren, yet – his heart pounding wildly. For a moment he was even tempted to turn round and go back to the police station. 'All right, I did something stupid, I'm sorry.' But he knew there was no going back.

Nearly there: 200 metres more and he turned left onto the rue Godolin – he thought he could hear sirens in the distance – then after 150 metres, down the rue de la Balance; a few seconds more and he was lost in the labyrinth of the Les Chalets district. He abandoned the vehicle and continued on foot.

He was dying for a cigarette, and to see his daughter, but that was impossible now, too. A door – an invisible one – had just closed in that direction as well. He thought about Hirtmann, who had forbidden him from smoking. The urge was overwhelming. He took out his packet, still striding down the pavement, feeling completely, utterly alone.

At the car hire agency, a glassed-in office right in the middle of the car park opposite the arrivals hall at Toulouse-Blagnac airport, he handed over his passport in the name of Émile Cazzaniga, filled out the form, and took possession of the vehicle. In the boot he placed the little suitcase and handful of belongings he had bought at the Galeries Lafayette in the centre of town, and turned the key in the ignition.

Fifteen minutes later he was driving towards the Mediterranean. The little Peugeot 308 GTI was brand new, the tank was full, and the sun was shining. For a few minutes he was filled with the headiness of freedom – checking, nonetheless, that he was driving well below the speed limit. Then he suddenly recalled what the doctors had told him: avoid long car trips. This one would take fifteen hours. What if he had a heart attack driving at 130kph down the motorway? He preferred not to think about it. He did, however, think of Gustav and Hirtmann on the dam, and his daughter who looked so tired, and Rimbaud saying, 'I will prove that you have been lying,' and of Kirsten's sister, the artist who liked shadows and who had gone to be with them. And then he saw Kirsten again, saying, 'Please, don't say thank you.'

What exactly did he feel? He had to admit that this Norwegian woman had filled his thoughts a good part of the time recently. What would happen now? He was on the run, and she would have to go back to Norway. Would they go their separate ways for good?

A few hours later, after he had passed Nîmes and Orange, he was heading up the Rhone Valley, where a violent mistral was blowing. He stopped to have a tuna and mayonnaise sandwich and a double espresso at a motorway rest stop not far from Bourgoin-Jallieu, then continued towards the Alps, Annecy and Geneva, which he reached as night was falling.

He drove along the northeast shore of Lake Geneva, leaving it after Morges to set a northward course towards Lake Neuchâtel, then turned towards the immaculate whiteness of the Bernese Alps. The mountains stood out against a cloudless night like meringues against a black curtain, and after Zurich he left Switzerland and crossed the

Austrian border at Lustenau at around nine o'clock, then the German border near Lindau, driving around the southern edge of Lake Constance before heading due east to Munich, where he arrived at ten o'clock.

It was after eleven o'clock when he crossed the Austrian border once again, near Salzburg, and drove in among the imposing summits of the Salzkammergut. And it was after midnight when he finally reached Hallstatt, that 3D postcard of Austria nestled on the edge of a lake, obscured for now by fog and darkness. Little cobblestone streets, chalets with Tyrolean facades, fountains and panoramas: it was all straight out of a film – *Heidi*, or *The Sound of Music*.

He found the hotel Hirtmann had told him to go to – the Pension Göschlberger – and twenty minutes later he was out like a light, in a high bed piled with eiderdowns like something out of a fairy tale.

'He used his Visa card at a car hire agency in Blagnac yesterday morning,' said a cop called Quintard. 'And a few hours later at a service station near Bourgoin-Jallieu, and for the last time at the tollbooth at Annemasse-Saint-Julien just before the Swiss border.'

'Bloody hell,' exclaimed Rimbaud.

'The car, a Peugeot 308, was hired in the name of Émile Cazzaniga.'

'Great,' said the inspector. 'He could be anywhere in Europe.'

'Or he may even have come back to France,' suggested another officer from the Inspectorate. 'He would be clever enough to do that.'

Stehlin was following the conversation gravely, without getting involved. It was a nightmare.

'Does anyone have any idea where he might have gone?' asked Rimbaud, walking around the table, his attitude scathing.

Neither Samira nor Espérandieu said a thing, but when the inspector focused his attention elsewhere, they exchanged a glance.

'You need a special sticker to use the Swiss motorways,' said Rimbaud. 'Who knows, he might have been stopped by the Swiss police if he didn't have one. Can someone get in touch with them?'

An end-of-an-era atmosphere had settled over the table: the death of a department, to whom henceforth no magistrate would ever entrust any important investigations. Espérandieu mused that he could ask for a transfer. But Martin, what would become of him? Did he really kill Jensen? He still found the idea hard to believe. He looked over at Samira for support, and the young Franco-Sino-Moroccan woman laid her hand discreetly on his knee for a second. He felt infinitely sad. What had gone wrong since the gunshot? He had seen broken cops before. But Martin was his best friend – or at least he had been, before the coma.

'And what about that Norwegian policewoman, does anyone know where she is?' asked Rimbaud, looking at the director of the crime unit.

Stehlin shook his head, as slowly as a condemned man who has just been asked whether he has any last wishes.

'Great,' said the inspector. 'We'll contact Interpol to send out a Red Notice regarding Commandant Servaz.'

Is that all? thought Espérandieu. The media mistakenly referred to Red Notices as 'international arrest warrants'. In fact, they were not arrest warrants, as a policeman from one country could not arrest an individual solely upon the decision of a national judicial system; they were alerts to locate a person and request his arrest by local authorities.

'I want a detailed description – a photograph, fingerprints, the whole shebang.'

He turned to Vincent and Samira.

'Can you take care of that?' he asked them, his tone poisonous.

There was a moment of silence. Then Samira's right middle finger – bearing a skull ring – was raised elegantly above the table. She shoved back her chair and walked out.

'Same here,' said Espérandieu, getting up in turn.

Martin spent the morning wandering through the narrow streets of the picture-postcard village and along the lake, wearing sunglasses, a thick woollen scarf and a cheap cap he had bought in a local souvenir shop with his last euros. He lingered at pavement cafés, drinking so much coffee that he eventually shoved the last cup away, disgusted.

He ran no risk of attracting attention: there were many more tourists than residents. Around him he heard every language imaginable and very little German.

In spite of everything, he could not help but be impressed with the panorama: all these white roofs piled one on top of the other, the neat, almost cheerful facades, the wooden piers and, just opposite, the hostile, crushing presence of the ice-covered rock face. It loomed, white with horizontal streaks, like a drawing made by a trembling hand, dropping like a tombstone into the icy and slightly misty waters of the Hallstättersee.

At five minutes before noon he began walking towards the Marktplatz. There, too, a mass of tourists with cameras and smart-phones was snapping away at virtually anything.

He waited several minutes almost without moving, pretending to be observing the fountain and the surrounding area. He wondered where Kirsten was. She had not shown herself and he was beginning to feel worried. Then he said to himself that it was only logical: someone else might be watching him and Kirsten didn't want to take any risks.

'Mahler came here, did you know that?' one of the tourists next to him said suddenly, still snapping away.

Servaz looked at him. The man was wearing a strange yellow cap with a pompom. He was blond, suntanned, and looked healthy and sporty.

'Have you packed your bag?' said the man, putting the lens cap back on his camera.

Servaz nodded.

'Good, let's go and get it.'

They left the town a few minutes later in an ageless Range Rover, spewing black exhaust fumes over a little road that followed the western shore of the lake.

Samira Cheung looked at Vincent. That day she had put so much black pencil around her eyes that she looked like a ghost from a haunted house.

'Are you thinking what I'm thinking?'

'What are you talking about?'

'What Quintard said at the meeting: Martin's route, across the border into Switzerland. Switzerland isn't far from—'

'Austria, I know,' he said. 'Hallstatt . . .'

'Do you really think he could be there?'

'It seems absurd, don't you think?'

'But that is the way he went,' she pointed out.

'Yes,' he agreed, 'that is the way. It's also the way to Geneva, where Hirtmann is from. And what about the Norwegian woman: do you think she's with him?'

Samira didn't answer. She was already typing on her keyboard. 'Look.'

He went over and saw an ordinary homepage, and then he read: 'Polizei Hallstatt, Seelände 30'. There was an email address that ended with 'polizei.gv.at', and even a website. Samira clicked on it and despite the gravity of the situation they smiled: two Barbie and Ken lookalike models in police uniforms standing next to a squad car, about as credible as Steven Seagal playing the President of the United States.

'Do you speak German?' she asked.

He shook his head.

'Neither do I.'

'But I speak English,' he said, picking up his telephone. 'Austrians must speak the Queen's English, don't you think?'

She let go of the curtain. From her window in the Hotel Grüner Baum, Kirsten had seen Martin speaking with a man in a yellow cap. Now they had set off together. She rushed out of her room on the first floor, down the steps, and out onto the square, just in time to see them leaving the square and heading down a side street. Instead of following them, she went in the opposite direction.

Espérandieu put the phone down. The Austrian cop – a man named Reger – had turned out to be surprisingly cooperative. He seemed to be delighted to collaborate with the French police, even if their request had drawn a blank at the other end of the line. Espérandieu figured that it must be a change of routine for him. How many murders did they have in Hallstatt? A Chinese tourist killed with a pickaxe by a Sinophobic mountain climber? A jealous husband tying a flowerpot to his wife's ankles before sending her to the bottom of the lake? Reger had a strong Austrian accent, but his English was impeccable.

Espérandieu motioned to Samira, who keyed in the email address they'd found on the Austrian website and added a photograph of Martin to the text in English.

Martin and his guide with the yellow cap came back to Hallstatt at around two in the afternoon. They went through a tunnel in the mountain and parked in the P1 car park, then walked back to the

323

centre of town along the lake. It was cold. There were snow flurries above the lake and the light seemed as leaden as if it were late afternoon.

'Why did we take that detour?' asked Servaz, once again dragging his suitcase behind him.

'I wanted to make sure no one is following us.'

'And now what will we do?'

'You will go back to your hotel, and don't go out: wait there for someone to come for you. Don't call anyone, do you understand? No alcohol, no cigarettes. And no coffee either. Drink plenty of water, get some rest, and sleep.'

Neither Servaz nor the man with the yellow cap saw the green Lada Niva pull into the same car park a few minutes later. Zehetmayer got out first. He was wearing his usual coat with the otter's fur collar and, on his bald head, a battered felt hat. Jiri was wearing a simple anorak, jeans and fur-lined boots, and looked like any ordinary tourist. They left the car and hurried straight to the centre of the village.

An odd couple, fox and wolf, they sat down in a café and watched the tourists go by.

After three hours shut in his room, Servaz was beginning to get restless. He could not stop thinking about Margot. How tired and drained she looked. He had left without saying goodbye and she must be worried sick. He had to speak to her.

Would they already have permission from the judge to tap his phone? It was possible, given the circumstances. But not certain. The French police and justice system did not operate like they did on TV.

He had to take the risk. He took out the little prepaid mobile he had bought in the centre of Toulouse before rushing to the airport, and dialled the number.

'Hello?'

'It's me,' he said.

'Dad? Where are you?'

Her voice was full of concern.

'I can't tell you,' he replied.

There was a pause.

'You what?'

Anger, again, in his daughter's voice. Through the window, he could see a white boat coming closer across the grey water, through the fog; it was bringing tourists from the railway station on the other side of the lake.

'Listen. They're going to question you about me. The police. They're going to talk to you about me as if I were a . . . criminal . . .'

'The police? But you're the police. I don't understand.'

'It's complicated. I had to leave.'

'Leave? Leave where? Can't you be a bit more—'

'Let me finish. I've been framed. I've been accused of something I didn't do. I had to run away. But I'll . . . I'll come back.'

More silence.

'You're frightening me, Dad,' she said suddenly.

'I know. I'm sorry, sweetheart.'

'Are you all right?'

'Yes, don't worry.'

'Of course I worry,' she replied. 'How do you expect me—'

'There's something else I want to tell you.'

She was silent. He hesitated.

'You have a little brother. His name is Gustav. He's five years old.'

Another silence.

'A . . . *little brother*? Called Gustav?'

He could picture the disbelief on her features.

'Who is his mother?' she immediately asked.

'It's a long story.'

He swallowed a glass of mineral water from the minibar.

'I have time,' she replied, her voice cold again.

'It's a woman I knew a long time ago, and who was kidnapped.'

'Kidnapped? Marianne? Is it Marianne?'

'Yes.'

'Good Lord. He's back, isn't he?'

'Who?'

'You know who.'

'Yes.'

'Oh, fuck, Dad, I don't believe it. Tell me it isn't true. Tell me this bloody nightmare isn't going to start all over again!'

'Margot, I—'

'This child, where is he?'

He remembered what Espérandieu said: 'Ask her straight out.'

'Never mind where he is,' he said. 'What's done is done. It's my

325

turn, now, to ask you a question: what exactly is the matter with you, Margot? Answer me, this time. I want the truth.'

This time, there was a longer silence on the line.

'Well, it would seem that you don't just have a second child, you're also about to become a grandfather.'

'What?'

'I'm nearly three months now,' she added.

He thought about all the little physical and psychological changes, how she'd felt sick in the morning, her sensitivity, her mood swings, the fridge full of healthy things, the weight she had put on.

He must have been blind.

Even Hirtmann, just watching Margot from the car park across the street, had understood.

'The father . . .' he said. 'Do I know him?'

'Yes,' she replied. 'It's Élias.'

At first, he didn't know who she was talking about. Then it came to him. He saw again the tall, silent young man, his long hair covering half his face, his resemblance to a beanpole that's sprouted too quickly. Élias had been with Margot when she'd come to find him in that Spanish village where he had taken refuge after Marianne disappeared and was spending his days and nights drinking. Servaz recalled that Élias was not exactly talkative, but when he did speak he always had something to say.

'I didn't know you were still seeing him,' he said.

'I wasn't. He showed up in Montreal last year, supposedly just for a visit. We hadn't seen each other for three years, but we'd stayed in touch. He went back to Paris after four weeks, and we went on writing to each other. And then he came back again. For good, this time.'

Margot had always had a gift for summing up complicated situations in a few sentences.

'And are you going to . . . ?'

'No, Dad, no: that's not on the agenda, at all.'

'But are you . . . living together?'

'Does it matter? Dad, whatever's happened, you have to come back. You can't run away like a criminal.'

'I can't come back,' he said. 'Not right away. Listen, I—'

There was a sound on the line, perhaps a door closing, and then a voice: 'Margot? Sweetie, it's me!' Alexandra, his ex-wife.

'Don't say anything to your mother,' he said.

He hung up.

A vision came to him suddenly, of a happy moment a very long time ago: that same young woman who was now pregnant babbling and chirping in a language only she understood, climbing onto her parents' bed. She nearly always came onto the bed when her mother was asleep. Her own personal Kilimanjaro. Climbing, conquering, making her niche, then nestling her little body between theirs. Her baby smell. Her fine hair. He could not remember anything more delightful than burying his nose in his little girl's sweet-smelling round tummy. Her infant's smell mingled with the acidity of the milk in the bottle, and eau de Cologne. That was the perfume of early morning. His daughter . . . who would soon have a round tummy again.

He hoped she would be a good mother, that she would cope well with motherhood. And that her relationship would not go to pieces the way her parents' had. That she would be happier as a mother than she had been as a daughter. That the child would grow up in a close family. He was trying to think but it was all spinning . . . He felt as if another Margot had taken his daughter's place.

He went over to the window and saw his ghostly face juxtaposed on the image of the white boat and the grey water.

My daughter, he thought, a lump in his throat. *I know you will be a good, an excellent mother. And that your child will be happy. I don't know how long I'll be gone, but I . . . I hope you will think about me from time to time, and that you will understand.*

Kirsten's telephone rang as she was resuming her surveillance, along with a pastry and a coffee.

'Hey, Kasper,' she said.

There was a moment's silence on the line. She thought that even there she could hear the inexhaustible rain of Bergen.

'Where are you?' he asked.

'Having a pastry and coffee.'

'Still at the hotel?'

'Why do you want to know?' she asked suddenly.

'Pardon?'

'Why do you want to know where I am?'

'I don't understand your question.'

'Why are you so interested in where someone is and what they're doing?'

Silence.

'What's all this bullshit?' he said. 'I want to know how things are going, that's all.'

'Kasper, I called Oslo yesterday. Apparently, they don't know anything. No one had told them that we've picked up the little boy's trail. And yet I told you. Why didn't you mention it to your superiors?'

Nothing but the sound of rain on the line.

'I don't know,' he said finally. 'I wanted to give you time to do it yourself, I suppose. You didn't mention it to anyone either, apparently.'

Score one for you, she thought.

'You're not the only one with a professional conscience,' he said. 'I'm just as eager to find that bastard as you are. Except that no one has paid me to travel to France.'

Score two.

'Okay. I'm sorry. I'm a little bit on edge at the moment.'

'Why?' A pause. 'Don't tell me . . . don't tell me he has shown up again?'

'I have to go,' she said.

'What are you going to do?'

'I don't know.'

'Take care of yourself.'

'Okay.'

He hung up and looked over to the harbour. He hadn't gone to work today. He'd taken the day off to finish assembling his furniture. This rain . . .

Then he thought about the money in his bank account. The money that had already been deposited in exchange for his information. And which had enabled him to pay off some of his debts. Not as much as he would have liked, but it was something at least. He checked the time and dialled the other number. The one that had nothing to do with the police.

43

Getting Ready

'Do you feel all right, Gustav?'

Hirtmann looked at the boy lying in the hospital bed. Then he went over to the window. He could see the white roofs of Hallstatt. The clinic was on a hill above the village.

'Yes, Papa,' said Gustav behind him.

'That's good,' he said, turning around. 'It will be this evening, you know.'

This time the blond child said nothing.

'You mustn't be afraid, Gustav. Everything will be fine.'

'Let's go,' said the man with the yellow cap. 'Take your suitcase.'

'Where are we going?' he asked.

He was fed up with all the secrecy. He had spent the entire afternoon and evening yesterday pacing his room like a wild animal, before eventually drifting into a sleep filled with nightmares.

'To the clinic,' replied the blond man.

'What do you do for a living?' asked Servaz.

'I beg your pardon? I'm a nurse,' said the man, seeming surprised. 'At the clinic. What a question! They asked me to welcome you.'

'And our little drive yesterday, to see whether I was being followed: was that also to welcome me?'

The man gave him a disconcerting smile as he locked the door. They headed towards the tiny lift.

'I follow the instructions I've been given, that's all,' he said.

'And you never ask any questions?' asked Servaz, as the door closed on the lift, which was far too small for two adults.

'Dr Dreissinger simply told me you were well known in France and you didn't want any . . . publicity, paparazzi – that sort of thing.'

To Servaz's great relief the doors opened almost immediately, and they went over to the little reception area to return his key. He thought about what the blond man had just said. Something occurred to him.

'Why would I need to avoid publicity?' he asked. 'What do you normally do at your clinic?'

Yellow-Cap looked at him, astonished.

'Well, facelifts, nose and eyelid jobs, breast enhancement, implants – even phalloplasties and labiaplasties . . . that sort of thing.'

It was Servaz's turn to look stunned.

'You mean we're going to a plastic surgery clinic?'

They drove only a few hundred metres along the cobblestoned streets, up to the top of the village, then pulled into the clinic's little car park. Yellow-Cap got out first and opened the boot, then handed the suitcase to Servaz, who now had butterflies in his stomach. He had read online that a liver transplant was a complicated, delicate operation, both for the living donor and the recipient. *Scared to death? Yes, you could say that.* For reassurance, he reminded himself that Hirtmann was far too fond of his son to hand him over to anyone inexperienced.

His son. He still couldn't get used to the idea. He was here to give part of his liver to his own son. Phrased like this, it sounded like science fiction.

'What is phalloplasty?' he asked suddenly as they were walking across the car park and climbing up the steps to the entrance.

'Surgery to the penis.'

'And labiaplasty?'

'The inner labia. They are reduced in size, when they're too big.'

'Charming.'

Lothar Dreissinger was a living advertisement for cosmetic surgery, of the before and after variety. He embodied 'before': he was one of the ugliest men Servaz had ever seen. His nose and ears were too big and too fleshy, his eyes were too small, his jaw too narrow, he had the lips of a toad, his skull was bald and pointed like an Easter egg – and in addition to all this, he had yellow, bloodshot eyes, and pitted skin as if he'd had smallpox in his youth.

Servaz wondered how this was supposed to inspire his clients to hurry to the operating theatre.

He was wearing a doctor's coat over a white shirt and his manicured hands, by contrast, were beautiful. Servaz noticed them when he crossed them under his chin.

'Did you have a pleasant trip?' he asked in English.

'Does it matter?'

The director of the clinic stared unpleasantly at him with his yellow eyes.

'Not really,' he said. 'All that matters is that you are in good health.'

'You have a very fine clinic here,' remarked Servaz. 'Cosmetic surgery, is that correct?'

'Indeed.'

'Now, answer me, are you qualified to perform this type of operation?'

'Before I converted to this more . . . lucrative . . . activity, it was my specialisation, you understand. My reputation had spread well beyond the borders of Austria.'

'Do you know who I am?' asked Servaz.

'The child's father.'

'And besides that?'

'No, and I don't care.'

'What did he tell you?'

'About what?'

'About this operation.'

'That Gustav needed a transplant. As quickly as possible.'

'And what else?'

'That you were shot in the heart a few months ago. And were in a coma for a few days.'

'And this doesn't worry you?'

'Why should it worry me? It was in the heart, not the liver.'

'Isn't it a bit . . . risky?'

'Of course it's risky. Every operation has a degree of risk.'

Dreissinger waved his fine pianist's hands.

Servaz felt a twinge in his stomach.

'But the fact I had a heart operation two months ago: doesn't that considerably increase the risk?'

'Not for the child: the donor could be deceased, and that is actually the most common procedure.'

'And for me?'

'For you without a doubt.'

His tone was almost jocular, and Servaz felt his throat go dry. *He doesn't give a toss whether I die or not.*

'You are sheltering a murderer,' Servaz said suddenly. 'And not just any murderer.'

The surgeon's face went blank.

'Did you know?'

Dreissinger nodded.

'So, why?' asked Servaz.

The little man seemed to hesitate.

'Let's just say I'm indebted to him . . .'

Servaz raised an eyebrow.

'What sort of debt could warrant taking such a risk?'

'It's difficult to explain.'

'Well, try anyway.'

'Why should I? Are you a cop?'

'I am indeed.'

Dreissinger stared at him, stunned.

'Don't worry,' Servaz said, 'I'm not here in my capacity as a cop, but to give you my liver – as you know. Well?'

'He killed my daughter.'

The answer came without the slightest hesitation. Servaz looked at the little man, not understanding. Fleetingly, a veil of sadness came over his ugly face. A moment of weakness that quickly vanished: now Dreissinger stared fixedly at him again.

'I don't understand.'

'He murdered her. At my request. Eighteen years ago.'

Servaz looked at him with growing disbelief.

'You asked Hirtmann to kill your daughter? *Why?*'

'You see, Monsieur Servaz, you only have to look at my face to understand that nature is not as perfect as some people maintain. My daughter was as ugly as her father, and it made her very . . . *depressed*. But, as if that were not enough, she was also afflicted with a rare, incurable disease that caused her unbearable suffering. To this day there is no treatment. I spoke of it with Julian one day. And he offered to do it for me. I'd envisaged it myself on several occasions. But in this country only passive euthanasia is tolerated, and I was afraid of going to prison. As I told you: I'm indebted to him, and can never repay what I owe him.'

'But you could go to prison for this, too.'

The surgeon's eyes narrowed to two slits.

'Why? Do you intend to expose me?'

Servaz did not reply but he felt as if he had swallowed a refrigerant: on the operating table this man would have his life in his hands, and as he had said, the donor could just as easily be dead.

'Would you like to know more about the procedure?' asked Lothar Dreissinger, in honeyed tones.

Servaz nodded cautiously. He was not too sure he did.

'We will start by removing your liver. Then we will perform the hepatectomy—'

'The what?'

'The exeresis or ablation of Gustav's diseased liver. This involves sectioning the ligaments and blood vessels – the hepatic artery and the portal vein – as well as the biliary ducts. However, because of his hepatic insufficiency, we have to be particularly vigilant, because there could be problems with coagulation. And the last stage is to transplant the organ. Priority will be given to re-attaching the blood vessels, in order to irrigate the organ again. Then the ones that conduct bile. Finally, before we close up, we will insert drains to evacuate any blood, lymph or bile that might have accumulated. Obviously this is all under general anaesthesia. An operation like this can last up to fifteen hours.'

He was not sure he had grasped all of Dreissinger's medical English, but he didn't like the sound of any of it. And where was Hirtmann? And Gustav? He had not seen either one of them since he'd arrived. Yellow-Cap had brought him straight here.

'We will spend the morning conducting a series of tests,' added the little man. 'And then you will rest until it is time for the operation, and you won't have anything more to eat for the rest of the day. No cigarettes either, obviously.'

'And when will the operation take place?'

'This evening.'

Servaz raised an eyebrow.

'Why this evening? Why not tomorrow? When it's daylight?'

'Because that is when my biological cycle is at its peak,' answered Dreissinger with a smile. 'Some people are morning people, others are night people. I'm at my best at night.'

Servaz didn't say anything. Frankly, he felt a little bit out of it. And this guy sent a chill down his spine.

'Someone will take you to your room. I'll see you again in theatre. Give me your phone, please.'

'What?'

'Your phone, give it to me.'

Lothar Dreissinger waited until the steps had faded down the corridor before he left his office and went through the next door. It led to a tiny room stacked with shelves with dozens of binders and labelled boxes. There was a little window at the back. A tall figure stood out against the backdrop of mountains, looking out of the window.

'Are you sure he's in a fit state to undergo the operation?' asked the surgeon, closing the door behind him.

'It is his liver you want, I think,' answered Hirtmann, without turning around. 'And it would be even easier with a dead donor, wouldn't it?'

He did not see Dreissinger slowly nodding his head. The reply was not altogether to his liking.

'And supposing the guy survives – what will happen if, once he gets home, he denounces me: have you thought of that? You didn't tell me he was a cop!'

His great friend shrugged.

'That's your problem. You will have his life in your hands in theatre.'

Dreissinger gratified him with an ill-tempered grunt.

'If he dies, I will have to report his death, and they will ask me for an explanation. There will be an investigation. Sooner or later, the truth will come out. I cannot allow that.'

'Well then, let him live.'

'And besides, I've never killed anyone,' added the Austrian, tonelessly. 'Shit, I'm a doctor. I am not . . . like you.'

'You killed your daughter.'

'No!'

'Yes. I was merely your tool; you're the one who made the decision. You're the one who killed her.'

The surgeon fell silent. Hirtmann turned around. As always, the director of the clinic felt a cold draught down his spine when that electrifying gaze focused on him. A taser shock would hardly have produced a greater effect. He handed Hirtmann the cop's phone.

'On the other hand, my dear Lothar, you must be aware that if anything should happen to Gustav, I don't think you'll be long for this world.'

Lothar Dreissinger felt a sudden, writhing panic in his stomach. But he suppressed it.

'The operation is tricky enough as it is, Julian. I don't think this sort of threat is very helpful.'

Hirtmann cackled.

'Are you afraid, my friend?'

'Of course I'm afraid. I will be eternally grateful to you for what you did for Jasmine. But the day you die, I will sleep better at night.'

A roar of laughter filled the small space.

That morning, Officer Reger came out of the Pension Göschlberger with a smile on his lips. His French colleague would be pleased. This was the fifth hotel, and he'd already hit the bull's-eye. He did not think, however, that it was so urgent that he could not stop off at Maislinger's for a cappuccino and a pastry.

Once he'd finished his little treat he began walking towards the Dreissinger clinic. The hotel manager had recognised not only the man in the photograph, but also the one he had left with that morning: Strauch. A local guy. He worked as a nurse at the clinic. Reger had known him since childhood. He walked up the steep little street with a smile on his face: this morning was certainly a bit more exciting than his typical day.

Servaz looked at the bed next to his – his was by the door, the other one by the window – as he entered the room. *A child's bed.* Clearly it had been occupied, but at the moment it was empty.

He glanced quickly out at the rows of cars in the small car park and the branches moving gently beyond the window, scratching at the grey sky, then as soon as the person who had brought him there had left, he bent double and removed a little prepaid mobile from his sock. He had figured they would take his phone away; Hirtmann trusted him only so far, and temporarily. He gazed around the room, saw another door and opened it: a tiny bathroom with a toilet. He lifted the lid of the cistern, then lowered it again and went back into the room.

The strip light above the bed.

He reached up and ran his hand over the strip, then behind the plastic casing. There was a hollow space against the wall. He made sure the sound on his device was still switched off and that there was a signal, slipped it in, took a step back, made sure it was invisible, then began to get undressed as he had been told to do, to put on the hospital gown that was waiting on the bed.

*

Reger greeted the woman at reception with a smile. Her name was Marieke. He knew her well: they belonged to the same bridge club. Marieke was divorced and bringing up her two children on her own.

'How are the boys, Marieke?' he asked. 'Does Matthias still want to be a policeman?'

'He has the flu,' she replied. 'He's in bed.'

'Ah.'

Marieke was a pretty, slightly plump blonde and Reger had had a brief affair with her after her divorce. He put the photograph the French police had sent him on the counter.

'Tell me, do you have a patient who looks like this?'

Marieke suddenly looked slightly flustered.

'Yes, why?'

'When did he get here?'

'This morning.'

This confirmed what the hotel manager had told him. Reger was feeling more and more excited.

'And do you have his room number?'

She checked her computer and gave it to him.

'What name is he registered under?'

'Dupont.'

He felt even more excited. A French name.

'Call Dr Dreissinger for me, please,' he said, taking out his mobile phone, which rang before he even had time to do anything. 'Hello?' he said, annoyed.

He listened for a few seconds.

'An accident? Where? On the Hallstättersee Landesstrasse? Where exactly? Is it serious? I'll be right there.'

He switched off his phone and looked at Marieke, distraught.

'Tell the doctor I will stop by later – I have to go.'

'Is it serious?' she asked.

'Seems like it: two cars and a lorry involved. One dead.'

'Local people?'

'I don't know, Marieke.'

Through the binoculars the windows of the clinic were perfectly visible. They were wide, tall windows that ran the entire length of the room, so that when the blinds were not lowered, the interior of the room was also visible, neon-lit even though it was daylight. He supposed that when the rooms were unlit, it must mean they were vacant.

Jiri counted half a dozen occupied rooms, on this side anyway. The Lada was parked 50 metres from the clinic, next to a stone wall with a slight overhang. Sitting at the wheel, he moved his binoculars from one window to the next. Suddenly he paused. The French cop. He had almost missed him because the first bed was empty and the cop was in the background, in another bed.

He focused on the first bed. *A child's bed.* Jiri felt his interest increase exponentially.

He wondered where Kirsten was. He had tried three times to reach her with his prepaid phone but there had been no answer. And Gustav? And Hirtmann? They had all suddenly disappeared. He couldn't sit still. He was dying to see Gustav, and he could no longer ignore his anxiety: he was afraid of seeing him for the first time on the operating table. It terrified him far more than his own presence in the same place, or his own anaesthesia: he had suffered far worse.

But he wanted to be sure of waking up. To hear that the operation had been a success. That his son was alive.

His son.

Once again, he pushed the thought away. It was too strange. This boy who had slipped into his life without anyone asking him his opinion. Unfairly, there were times he thought about him as if he were a sort of cancer, slowly growing inside him until the day came when he could no longer ignore his presence. What would happen next, if the operation was a success? Would Hirtmann let them leave together? Surely not. He would have to take the boy from him by force if he wanted him. But did he want him? In any case, Servaz would be far too weak after the operation to attempt anything.

There was a knock at the door. It opened and the blond nurse came in. He had removed his yellow cap.

'Let's go,' he said.

This seemed to be his favourite expression.

'We'll start with an electrocardiogram and a thoracic echocardiogram,' he explained, once they were out in the corridor, 'to check for any possible heart disease. Also, I was told that you are a smoker. So we will take an X-ray of your thorax, and then an abdominal ultrasound to study your vesicle and measure the size of your liver. Finally,

337

you will meet the anaesthetist. It'll take a few hours – will you be all right?' he asked, glancing at Servaz.

'How many patients are there here at the moment?' asked Servaz, following him. He was naked under the hospital gown, which was open at the back, and wearing a paper cap and plastic slippers: he felt utterly ridiculous.

'A dozen or so.'

'And that's enough to keep a place like this going?' he said, surprised.

The blond nurse smiled.

'With what they pay? Yes, believe me.'

She found the package when she came back to the hotel. The hotel manager took it out from under the counter and handed it to her: 'Someone dropped this off for you.' She went up to her room, the package under her arm, then removed the brown paper, opened the box, and unfolded the cloth that was inside. The weapon was wrapped in a greased plastic film: a semi-automatic Springfield XD pistol. A Croatian weapon, light and reliable. Along with three magazines containing fifteen 9-millimetre cartridges.

They took him back to his room at around four o'clock in the afternoon. He immediately went to his suitcase. It had been searched. The intruders had not even bothered to hide the fact. They must have done the same with his clothes. He walked over to the plastic strip light above his bed and slipped his hand inside it. The phone was still there.

He went to the window and looked outside. Clouds were massing above the mountains. They already cast a dark, colourless veil over the entire landscape. Wisps of smoke rose from the lake as if a gigantic fire were simmering beneath the surface.

It was going to snow. You could feel it in the air.

He turned around when the door opened.

Servaz looked at the gurney they brought alongside the child's bed. Then he saw the nurse ask Gustav to move from one to the other. The nurse smiled at the boy once he was in his bed and, they gave each other a high five. He went back out and was immediately replaced by another person.

'Hello, Martin,' said Hirtmann.

He felt his hair stand on end. The tall Swiss man had a four-day beard, red eyelids, and he seemed absent, preoccupied. *Haunted*, was the word that came to Servaz's mind. He suddenly felt a hot flush. He had seen in Hirtmann the same anxiety he himself felt. Or was there something else? Some other reason to be anxious? Hirtmann walked past him and looked out of the window. Outside, where the light was fading. Then he pulled down the blinds.

'What's going on?' asked Servaz.

Hirtmann did not reply. He went over to Gustav and caressed his blond hair. For a moment Servaz felt a pang of jealousy as he saw the boy smile so trustingly at Hirtmann. Then Hirtmann looked up at Servaz and he felt a chill down his spine: *Julian Hirtmann was afraid of something. Or someone.* This was the first time Servaz had ever seen fear in those eyes, and the sight of it was chilling. Because, in that moment, he understood it was not only because of the operation. Hirtmann stepped quickly to the window once more and looked out before again lowering the blinds.

Something was happening – *outside*.

Kirsten was standing next to the Catholic church, staring at the Lada through her binoculars. The tables had been turned. She was watching the car from behind but could still clearly make out the man at the wheel, who had his own binoculars trained on the clinic.

Now she focused on the neck of the car's other occupant. She had her Springfield XD wedged between her belt and her back. Then she looked at the clinic; at Martin's window. She froze. Julian Hirtmann was at the window, looking out. She saw Martin standing behind him and Gustav in his bed. Her pulse began to race.

Then Hirtmann lowered the blinds.

She put down her binoculars. The man in the car had done the same. It was obvious he had been watching that same window.

Kirsten thought about what to do next.

It was half past four. Before long it would be hard to see anything at all.

Reger watched as the last rescue vehicles drove away down the Hallstättersee Landesstrasse in a blazing maelstrom of flashing lights. What chaos! A nightmare of twisted metal and mutilated bodies, broken lives, blazing lights, messages sputtering like firecrackers over radios, and the strident buzzing of the saws slicing through the wreckage. Now that silence had finally fallen once more, he felt a violent headache coming on.

Fortunately, neither the driver of the Ford – killed on the spot – nor the three other passengers, severely injured, were people he knew. He was going to have to file a report. His legs were still trembling. It was a miracle there had only been one fatality.

Suddenly he remembered what he'd been doing that morning before the accident. Good Lord, what a day. It was always like this. You had entire days where nothing exciting came your way, and then suddenly there was a hailstorm of major incidents.

As his thoughts returned to the clinic, something terrible occurred to him. What if the man had used the opportunity to get away? How would he look then, in the eyes of his French colleagues? It was, in a way, the reputation of the entire Austrian police force that was at stake, he thought. He hurried off, and didn't even stop at the police station. He took out his telephone and called Andreas, formerly with the Bundespolizei in Lower Austria, a man with decades of experience, and explained the situation.

'Who is this guy?' asked Andreas, puzzled. 'What has he done wrong?'

Reger had to admit that the French policeman had not been very forthcoming on the matter. He had made it perfectly clear, however, that the patient must not be left unattended.

'Meet me at the clinic,' he said. 'We'll set up surveillance outside his door and make sure he doesn't leave his room – or if he does, you follow right behind. He must not leave the clinic under any circumstances,' he added. 'Is that clear? I'll have Nena take over from you in a few hours.'

'He's there,' said Espérandieu, hanging up.

It was five o'clock in the afternoon. Samira swivelled around in her chair to face him.

'He spent one night at a hotel,' he explained. 'Then packed his suitcase and left with another man.'

She waited for him to continue.

'But the hotel manager recognised the man. A local fellow. His name is Strauch, and he's a nurse in a clinic.'

'A clinic,' she echoed, thoughtfully.

Vincent nodded.

'This Reger guy just questioned someone at the clinic. Martin got there this morning.'

'What do we do?'

'*We* don't do anything,' he answered. 'But I'm going to take a day off and go to Austria to see Martin. And I asked them to place him under surveillance until I get there.'

She frowned.

'What do you intend to do?'

'Talk to him. And convince him to come back here and turn himself in.'

'After what happened yesterday,' said Samira, 'do you think he's guilty?'

'Of course not.'

'And what if he refuses to listen to you?'

She saw him hesitate.

'I'll have the Austrian police arrest him,' answered Vincent reluctantly.

'They'll want an official warrant.'

'I'll tell them that it's on its way.'

'And what will happen once they realise that they still haven't got anything?'

'We'll see. I'll be there by then. And besides, they must have got a Red Notice from Interpol. Though it would surprise me if they checked them regularly.'

He was already typing something on his keyboard.

'Shit,' he said.

'What's the matter?'

'There are no flights.'

'You could go through Paris.'

'By the time I get to Paris, catch my connection then make the trip from Vienna to Hallstatt in a hire car, I may as well drive.'

'You won't get there until tomorrow,' she pointed out.

'Precisely. Another reason to leave right away.'

He stood up and reached for his jacket.

'Keep me posted,' she called out.

Marieke looked first at Reger then at his colleague, a tall red-faced beanpole. They had just asked her where the Frenchman was.

'In theatre,' she said. 'They're operating on him.'

'Can't we interrupt the operation?'

'You must be joking! He is under general anaesthesia. He won't wake up for several hours.'

Reger frowned. What a can of worms. What should he do? Then he figured that basically, it didn't change the situation. The French cop wouldn't get here for several hours, and at least the man was hardly likely to make a run for it.

'You stay by the door to the operating theatre,' Reger told Andreas. 'Then you follow this Mr . . . um . . . Servaz to recovery, and then when he goes back to his room, you go with him.'

Reger went back to the police station.

As soon as he was inside, he called the French policeman.

'I'm on my way,' said the cop. 'Have you got him under surveillance?'

'He's in the operating theatre, under anaesthesia,' answered Reger. 'But I've got a man posted there who won't let him out of his sight. What has this guy done, exactly?'

'He is suspected of having shot a man,' answered Espérandieu. 'A repeat rapist.'

'Oh, is there an international arrest warrant out for him?' asked Reger.

'There's no such thing as an international arrest warrant,' said Espérandieu. There was a moment of silence. 'But Interpol has issued a Red Notice, yes.'

'In that case, I'll ask for help from the Salzburg Bundespolizei to have him arrested,' decided Reger.

'No, don't do anything like that, not until I get there. The man isn't dangerous. Let me deal with him.'

Reger frowned, looking at his telephone. He understood less and less.

'As you wish,' he said finally.

But he was determined to contact his superiors as soon as he put down the phone.

Marieke was mistaken: Servaz was not under anaesthesia. Not yet. But he was lying on the operating table, breathing through an oxygen mask, with an IV drip in his arm, ready to receive the injection. The medical team were busy around him.

If he turned his head he could see Gustav already asleep on the other operating table. He could see all the trappings of modern sorcery around the child: monitors like the one he was hooked up to, transfusion pouches, transparent tubes, catheters kept in place with sticking plasters, syringe pumps, and protective cushions. Gustav's blood was struggling to escape into one of the tubes.

Servaz swallowed.

The drugs were beginning to take effect and the intense stress he had felt during the first few minutes was giving way to an abnormal sensation of well-being – abnormal in the light of the rigorously hostile environment in which he found himself.

Servaz again looked over at the boy's hand where he could see the blood trying to escape into the tube. It is always thus: blood struggling to escape. Red on white skin, red in the transparent tube. Red. Red. Red like the blood from a horse's severed head, red like the bath water of an astronaut who has slashed her wrists, red like his own heart, pierced by a bullet, yet still beating.

Red.

Red.

Suddenly he felt fine. Okay. This is the end, like Espérandieu says. No, he doesn't say it, he sings it. *This is the end, my friend.* All right. Let's go. This is the end. Gustav, Kirsten's son. No, that's not right. Gustav is whose . . . whose son, already?

He was losing it.

His mind was acting up.

Red.

Like the curtain falling.

'Where are they?' asked Rimbaud.

In Toulouse, Stehlin was looking at the commissaire from the Inspectorate, and he was pale, very pale. No doubt the head of the regional crime unit was re-watching the film of his career, which until now had been following an impeccable upward trajectory. But the stain that was spreading across his CV would erase all these years of good and faithful service, and soon the stain would be all anyone would see. Years of effort, ambition, compromises, all swept away in a single day. Like a cyclone ravaging a coastal paradise in the space of a few hours.

'I don't know,' he confessed.

'You don't know where Servaz is? You haven't the faintest idea where he might have gone?'

Silence.

'No.'

'And that Norwegian policewoman, Kirsten . . . ?'

'. . . Nigaard. I don't know where she is, either.'

'One of your men is a murderer on the run, and this Norwegian policewoman who is supposed to be working with him has also disappeared: that doesn't bother you?'

His tone was scathing.

Stehlin's face was the colour of curdled milk. 'I'm sorry. We are doing everything in our power to find them.'

Rimbaud sniffed.

'Everything in your power,' he said ironically. 'You are sheltering a murderer in your ranks. This service is a calamity, a disgrace, the very example of everything that is wrong with the police – and, since you are the one in charge, this is all your responsibility,' he continued coldly. 'You will provide us with an explanation, believe me.'

He was already on his feet.

'In the meantime, pull out all the stops to find them. Try at least to do that much properly.'

As soon as the inspector had left, Stehlin picked up his phone and rang Espérandieu. If there was anyone who knew Martin, it was his assistant. Samira's voice answered.

'Yes, boss?'

'Samira? Where is Vincent?'

There was a pregnant pause.

'He took the day off.'

'What?'

'He took a day off to—'

'A whole day? *Now?* Find him! Tell him I want to speak to him. *Right away!*'

Jiri switched off the classical radio station, which had been playing symphony upon concerto upon cantata upon opera for hours.

'Put that back on,' said Zehetmayer next to him.

'No,' retorted Jiri. 'I'm sick of classical music.'

The orchestra conductor was beginning to get on his nerves. Jiri had his binoculars on his lap. There was nothing to see: the evening darkness had settled over the clinic, the blinds had been raised but the room was empty. By the looks of it, they had taken the cop and the kid to the operating theatre. He would wait until they came back to strike. When they were still woozy, unable to react.

Where was Hirtmann? he wondered. In the operating theatre, almost certainly. With the others. According to their source, that little boy was the apple of the Swiss killer's eye.

But sitting in the gloom of the Lada, Jiri felt anything but confident. He didn't like the fact that Hirtmann was nowhere to be seen. It left him with the unpleasant impression that he did not have everything under control. What was even more worrying, was that he'd had the feeling all day long that Hirtmann knew they were there, that it was a game for him, appearing and disappearing. That they were not the cat, but the mice.

Glancing around the car, he tried to reassure himself. They held all the cards. And above all, they had a major trump card. For a moment he closed his eyes, imagined his knife doing a nice clean job slitting Hirtmann's throat, the blood gushing from his carotids. He would show him who, of the two of them, was better.

Next to him the conductor coughed. This was always a sign he was about to say something. Jiri listened distractedly.

'I can transfer the rest of the money to "K",' said Zehetmayer, taking out his mobile. 'He has fulfilled his part of the contract.'

In Bergen, after walking down the hill – the same hill where the funicular was – along Øvre and Nedre Korskirkeallmenningen, Kasper Strand passed the illuminated facades of the bar and restaurant complex in the middle of the port known as Zachariasbryggen. He turned off 100 metres before the fish market and crossed the broad esplanade with its gleaming cobblestones to head towards the little pub on the other side of Torget. It was the last pub open; in Bergen, restaurants and bars closed early.

It was drizzling; an almost microscopic mist, but it hadn't left the town or the hills for days. Nor had the feeling of guilt that had been nagging at him ever since he had made the decision to sell the information Kirsten Nigaard was handing to him.

No matter how often he told himself he'd had no choice, it did not free him from the increasingly tenacious impression that he was a shit. That he had sold his soul. And for a few tens of thousands of crowns, no more. He walked into the little pub, which was exclusively frequented by authentic Bergen locals. It was a pallid, jumpy clientele; almost all the women looked tired and were wearing too much make-up; there was roughly one of them for every three men.

His contact was waiting at a table in a corner between the front of the pub and the room at the back. A discreet spot, away from the other tables.

'Hey,' said Kasper.

'Hey,' said the journalist.

He was a young man, hardly over thirty, with ginger hair, resembling a weasel or a fox. He had slightly protruding, very light blue eyes that never left his interlocutor, like the smile that never left his face.

'Are you sure that Hirtmann has resurfaced?' the journalist asked, straight out.

'Yes,' he lied, but he remembered Kirsten's voice on the telephone and her silences, and he was convinced it must be true.

'Fuck, this will make incredible copy,' said the hack. 'And you say he's been bringing up this kid, Gustav, as his own son?'

'Correct.'

'And where are they now?'

'Well . . . in France,' he said. 'In the southwest.'

'The kid, Hirtmann – and your colleague, who's on their trail. Is that it?'

The guy was taking notes.

'Yes, that's it.'

'Crikey, a serial killer saving a kid from death. And being hunted by one of our very own female cops. We can't put it off any longer. This will come out tomorrow.'

'Tomorrow?'

'Tomorrow. An entire feature.'

Kasper swallowed his saliva.

'And my money?'

The young man looked around, took an envelope from his coat and handed it to him.

'It's all there. Twenty-five thousand crowns.'

Kasper looked at the snotty-nosed guy who didn't even bother to hide his disdain for him. For a split second Kasper was tempted to shove the envelope away, to redeem his behaviour. *It's a lie*, he thought. He tried to kid himself. But he had forfeited any dignity long ago.

He looked at the envelope. The price of betrayal. Of having leaked his information to the Norwegian media. Of having systematically conveyed everything Kirsten Nigaard had told him over the telephone to a journalist. He shoved the money into the pocket of his damp jacket, and went back out into the rain.

In Toulouse, Stehlin couldn't sleep.

Now, at five o'clock in the morning, going down to the kitchen in his house in Balma for a glass of water, he thought back to the phone call he had received shortly before seven that evening.

'Norwegian police on the line,' announced his assistant, with that voice that reminded him of his mother. 'Have a good evening. That's my day over.'

A voice that said: *It's late, I'm still here, I'm sacrificing my family life to make myself available; I hope you are aware of that.*

He had thanked her and wished her a 'Nice evening to you, too,' and he took the call. In fact it wasn't the Kripos, but a department that – if he'd understood correctly – was the equivalent of the French National Police Inspectorate. In short, the man on the line, with his rasping voice, was a sort of Norwegian Rimbaud.

'Kirsten Nigaard,' he said. 'Does that name ring a bell?'

'Of course.'

'We've been trying to reach her since yesterday. Do you know where she is?'

Stehlin sighed.

'No.'

'That's unfortunate. We need her back in Norway as soon as possible.'

'May I ask why?'

There was a moment's hesitation on the line.

'She has been accused of having . . . of attacking a passenger on a train.'

'What?'

'A woman called Helga Gunnerud, on the Oslo–Bergen night train.'

'Attacking? What do you mean?' asked Stehlin, increasingly puzzled.

'She beat her black and blue, apparently. The victim had to be taken to hospital. It took her a while to agree to file a complaint because her aggressor had told her she was with the police, and she was afraid of the consequences. The victim told us she boarded the train at Finse, and that she and Kirsten Nigaard initially had a friendly rapport, but then Nigaard suddenly turned nasty. So the victim lost her temper – she admits she is quick to fly off the handle – and they started calling each other names. After that, Kirsten Nigaard threw herself on the woman and hit her, over and over.'

Stehlin could not believe his ears. That lovely Norwegian woman, so cool and distant, who had been sitting in his office: that she would hit another woman so hard as to leave her unconscious . . . It was absurd.

'Are you sure the woman isn't making it up?' he asked.

He could sense the Norwegian man's annoyance on the line.

'Well, we did conduct an investigation. There are too many incriminating elements against Nigaard, I'm afraid. Believe me, this saddens me greatly. It's a right old mess, and it will soon be in all the papers – the victim is far too talkative to hold her tongue. So you really have no idea where she could be at the moment?' he asked again. 'We've been trying to reach her since yesterday, but she's not picking up.'

With a heavy heart, Stehlin had to confess that he knew nothing, that she had vanished into thin air, and that they had also had their share of problems, there in Toulouse.

'It's as if the world has gone mad,' concluded his Norwegian counterpart, when they had finished.

Yes, he thought, drinking his glass of water, his back pressed against the kitchen worktop. Martin on the run, suspected of murder, and the Norwegian policewoman turning out to be some sort of apparent psychopath . . . Yes, it was enough to make you think the world had gone mad.

Espérandieu crossed the Austrian border two hours ahead of schedule. He had driven fast, with no thought for the speed cameras or police checks. He'd sped across Switzerland and Germany and now he was heading through the Salzkammergut at full tilt towards Hallstatt. He was feeling more and more nervous. He didn't know what to expect in Hallstatt. He was going to have to persuade Martin to turn himself in. It was the only reasonable option. They had reached the end of the line. But would Martin listen? He also had the nagging suspicion that he would get there too late. But too late for what?

44

The Bait

It was a cock-up right from the start. Thick snow was falling, fluffy and wet, when Jiri set off. He left the Lada and inched his way into the unquiet dawn. A regiment of snow-laden clouds floated above the clinic.

It was ten past eight in the morning. The nurses had brought the cop and the boy back from surgery. Jiri knew this because before they lowered the blinds he had seen the cop being wheeled on a gurney to his bed.

He walked past the low wall, and went carefully down the short icy slope between the road and the car park, then threaded his way between the cars towards the entrance. An icy wind was making the tree branches sway like semaphores.

He went briskly up the steps and into the clinic. He already knew the layout of the premises having gone in twice already, the first time with a bouquet of flowers, the second time empty-handed: as in most hospitals, to staff 'civilians' were invisible, as long as they did not enter any unauthorised areas.

He walked around reception, went through the double doors with the air of someone who knows where they're going, and turned right. He put his hand on the gun in his pocket. Small calibre, small bulk. But sufficient. He turned left: this was the corridor.

He came to a halt.

There was someone there, at the end of the corridor. Sitting on a chair outside the door. A woman. *Wearing a police uniform.*

Shit.

This was not part of the plan. Jiri spun around before the woman could see him. He leaned against the wall, out of sight, and thought. He was a good chess player. When he had been studying the windows

349

of the clinic through his binoculars, he had gone over a certain number of eventualities, the moves he could make and the possible responses of his adversary.

He went off again in the opposite direction, opened the door leading to the service stairs, went up two flights and came out on the first floor. At this time of day the nurses were busy; there were carts everywhere you looked. He would have to be quick.

He went down the corridor at a brisk pace, past several doors – some of them open, others closed – counting as he went.

This one.

The door was closed; he listened carefully but could hear nothing inside. He opened the door and went in. He recognised the woman wrapped in bandages whom he had spotted through his binoculars.

There was no one else in the room; the floor nurses had not yet got this far.

Her only visible features through the bandages were her eyes, nostrils and mouth. She looked at him in surprise. Jiri walked resolutely towards her, saw the astonishment in her eyes, reached for a pillow from beneath her head and slammed it down on her face. And pressed. Cries escaped through the pillow; her legs shook beneath the blanket like the needle of a seismograph.

He waited. The cries and shaking lessened and eventually stopped. He let go.

There was no time to lose.

He wedged the back of a chair under the doorknob, returned to the bed, pulled back the blanket and sheet, and took the woman's body in his arms. She was as light as a feather. Jiri set her down below the window and then opened it. The wind blew into the room, bringing the snow with it, and the cold from outside and the heat in the room mingled like sea and river in an estuary.

He grabbed the cords of the blinds and wrapped them around the woman's neck – once, twice, three times.

Then he tore the sheet from the bed, went back to the window, made one knot around the handle and a second one around the woman's neck. When he had finished, he lifted the body and swung it out of the open window into the grey, snowy dawn.

After that he removed his coat.

Underneath he was wearing the uniform of an Austrian policeman, bought on the dark web. He took the chair from the door and dragged it to the middle of the room where the fire alarm was mounted on the ceiling, and he climbed onto the chair.

Then he took out his lighter.

Hirtmann came to a halt at the end of the corridor. Outside Martin's door a woman had replaced the tall guy. Hallstatt police, like the previous officer, judging by the uniform. He had to find a way to get rid of her. Otherwise his trap would not work. These bloody cops were going to scare the quarry away. Following the operation he had put Gustav in a safe place. Locked behind a steel door, and Hirtmann was the only one who had the key. Zehetmayer and his acolyte must be thinking he was in the other room, the one where he had opened and closed the blinds several times. Martin's room. Where he was waiting for them. But if they found a cop outside the door, they would turn around. Unless . . . Surely some simple local policeman would not be enough to stop them.

He had got that far in his musing when the fire alarm went off. Shit, what the hell was that? *Gustav*, he thought. And hurried away.

Jiri headed for the room where the boy and the French cop were. The door was open. The woman guarding the door watched him coming towards her. She glanced quickly at his uniform.

'Who are you?' she asked.

'Someone set off the alarm,' he said. 'A woman has hanged herself out of her window. I was told she was here.'

He saw the policewoman frown. Suddenly a cry came from the room through the open door. A nurse rushed out.

'There is someone hanging from the window!' she cried, and set off down the corridor at a run.

The policewoman watched her, then turned to give Jiri a suspicious look.

'Who are you?' she said again. 'I don't know you. And what sort of uniform is that?'

He brought the butt of his weapon down on her skull.

Sounds, penetrating the mist of his consciousness. Shrill sounds. Shredding the fog in his skull. His eyelids are trembling but won't open. Through them he can sense the light – and when he breathes in, the antiseptic smell of the room.

351

He blinks several times. Each time aware of the pain to his optic nerves from the brightness of the snow. And that shrill, exasperating, constantly recurring sound. He had thought he was at home and his alarm clock was ringing, but it's not that, no. It's much louder, harsher.

He opens his eyes.

He looks at the white ceiling, the white walls. There is something swinging on the wall – a shadow – swinging like the pendulum of a clock, superimposed upon the white and grey stripes made by the blinds.

Suddenly he knows where he is. And why.

His right hand slowly lifts the blanket, then his hospital gown, cautiously. The bandages around his abdomen . . . He can feel a certain tautness. They have opened his belly, removed half his liver, closed it again and stitched it all up.

He is *alive*.

Still that strident noise. He can hear people running in the corridor. Doors slamming. Voices.

He turns his head.

There's something over there . . . behind the blinds, beyond the window – a shape barring the grey, nascent dawn, slowly swinging: like a clock pendulum. A body. There is a body hanging at the window.

In a sudden panic, he checks the other bed – Gustav's. The boy is there. He can make out his motionless form beneath the sheet and blanket. He would like to wake him up, ask him how he feels, but he knows that the boy stayed longer under the surgeon's knife than he did. He has to give him time.

And that big shadow over there . . . that body . . . whose is it?

It's swinging more and more slowly.

Maybe it's just tree branches moving with the weight of the snow? Or the medication still in his bloodstream, playing tricks on him?

No, no: it really is a body.

Through the bandage he feels his wound, and presses gently. And then he pulls the sheet and blanket aside and begins to move. He shouldn't; he knows it's a very bad idea. He swings his feet to the edge of the bed, raises his torso very slowly, and sits up. He sets his feet on the cold floor. For a second he lowers his chin onto his chest and closes his eyes. He only just came round, for Christ's sake. He's afraid of moving too quickly, of damaging something inside, but he needs to get to the bottom of this, to find out what it is, that shadow at the window.

352

He breathes in. Opens his eyes, raises his head and begins to stand.

He removes the clip from the end of his index finger. Another alarm sounds.

Leaning cautiously against the night table, he stands up slowly.

His legs seem do not seem very trustworthy, but they support him. He knows that if he falls, he will cause irreparable damage. But he starts walking all the same. Towards the window. He gets the impression that the big shadow, which is now almost motionless, is filling the entire room, finding its way inside him, occupying all the available space in his still fuddled brain.

He recalls a shadow not unlike this one, a sort of big, evil, black butterfly, hanging from the top of a cable car.

A twinge in his abdomen: he begins to feel slightly dizzy. A wave of nausea. But he keeps on walking. He wants to raise those bloody blinds, to see the body behind them.

When at last he reaches the window, he hears the door open behind him and a woman's voice cries, 'What are you doing? Come here! You mustn't move! We are going to evacuate you! We have to evacuate everyone!'

He pulls the cord and slowly the slats of the blinds rise.

The form appears.

He wonders if he is dreaming, still unconscious on the operating table. Because what he sees is a body floating miraculously in the air. A woman. Levitating. Her head a mummy's head, wrapped in bandages, and around her neck he sees the sheet, which is hanging from the floor above.

Behind him, the nurse is screaming.

He turns around. A man has come in and is closing the door behind him.

He is wearing an Austrian policeman's uniform, but his face is that of a bearded wild animal, with a piercing gaze. Servaz doesn't like the way he looks. The man is very obviously looking for someone.

He stares at Gustav's bed and Martin grows even more wary. He walks towards the intruder. Too quickly. His head is spinning; his legs start to give away. He avoids falling in the nick of time, catching himself on the wall. He's too hot, then cold, then hot again. He opens his mouth and gasps for air. He sees the man heading towards Gustav's bed. He reaches out his arm to stop him, but the man shoves him and this time he falls backwards. A flash of pain rips through his belly.

He looks up at the man; he has taken his gun out of his holster, and he glances at the door again before he pulls back the blanket and the sheet.

Servaz is about to scream but the moment he sees the look in the man's eyes he understands.

He does not need to see Gustav's bed, which the bearded wild animal is staring at with disbelief. Then he turns to Servaz. He sees the man place his gun on the bed, and he seizes him by the collar of his hospital gown and lifts him up. An excruciating pain wrenches his guts. The man brings his face up to his and shakes him. A tiger is digging its claws into his belly.

'Where are they?' screams the man. 'Where is the kid? Where is Hirtmann? Where are they?'

Now the door is opening.

45

Dead or Alive

He saw the door open behind the man's back. Kirsten! He saw her reach behind her, pull out her weapon, and aim it in their direction.

'Let him go!' she screamed.

The man obeyed and Servaz fell again, his belly burning. He would die of internal bleeding, there on the floor in this clinic. Sweat was pouring from his brows into his eyes like water. Chernobyl was exploding in his guts.

'I'm with the police,' said the man. 'A woman has hanged herself outside the window.'

'Turn around,' ordered Kirsten. 'Put your hands behind your head.'

'I said that—'

'Shut up. Raise your hands.'

The bearded man did as he was told, calmly, and Kirsten moved towards him. The gun was on the bed only a few inches from the man, but he had his hands on the back of his neck.

'Martin, are you all right?'

He nodded, but he would have liked to scream, 'No I'm not all right! It hurts! I'm going to die!' He clenched his teeth so hard his gums hurt. Footsteps sounded in the corridor. Then there was a familiar voice from the door:

'Gustav . . .' Hirtmann began to say.

That was when it started: the situation suddenly getting out of hand, the unpredictable chain of events, time accelerating and running away. He saw Hirtmann motionless in the doorway, his momentum stopped short. Out of the corner of his eye, he realised Kirsten's mistake, that split second of distraction, the fateful instant when the gun barrel shifted slightly from its target. For a man like the bearded wild animal, a split second was more than enough.

He didn't use it to rush for the gun on the bed, the way a less experienced individual might have done; no, he was not that stupid. He knew instinctively he wouldn't have time and that he had to get hold of *the other weapon* – the one that was threatening him.

In the confusion that followed Hirtmann's appearance, he threw himself on Kirsten, twisted her wrist violently and managed to get hold of the Springfield XD. He pointed the barrel towards the door, using Kirsten as a shield, but his finger did not press the trigger: there was no one there.

Hirtmann had vanished.

Nevertheless, he swung Kirsten around, twisting her arm, and with the barrel against her temple, near her blonde hair with its brown roots, he murmured in her ear:

'And now, we're getting out of here.'

Servaz watched them leave the room. He tried to get up, but his legs could only carry him as far as the bed, where he collapsed. His heart was pounding fit to burst. He pulled up his hospital gown and saw the bandage around his middle. A red flower was spreading across it.

'Where are we going?' she asked.

'There's an emergency exit just there,' said Jiri, pointing to the metal door at the end of the corridor.

'And then?'

He didn't answer, merely pushing her forward, frequently glancing behind him to where several nurses and doctors had gathered, keeping a cautious distance. The cop who had been standing guard at the door was among them. She had a huge bruise on her temple where Jiri had struck her.

But still no Hirtmann.

'*I'm on your side,*' said his hostage suddenly, her voice so faint he hardly heard her.

'What?'

'I'm the one who passed all the information to your boss,' she said more loudly. 'Fuck, it's thanks to me that you found him. Let me go.'

He continued to steer her towards the door, while looking behind him.

Where had Hirtmann got to, dammit?

'You're the source?' he asked, surprised.

'Fuck, that's what I keep telling you: I'm on your side. Just ask Zehetmayer. Let me go!'

'Where is he now?' he said, opening the metal door and shoving her through it.

The wind immediately whistled round them, surrounding them with snow.

'Where is who?'

'Hirtmann, where is he?'

'How should I know!'

He pushed her down the steps and she slipped on some black ice, almost falling and taking him with her.

'Watch out!' he said, helping her regain her balance.

But he tightened his grip on her wrist and she grimaced. Their shoes sank into the snow.

'Ouch! You're hurting me, shit!'

'Move it!'

He pushed her along the wall behind the clinic, towards the road where the Lada was parked. All around them was the white forest, fir trees standing guard. Snowflakes whirled in the fog like hornets pursued by smoke.

'Move!'

'Where are we going?'

'Shut up!'

He couldn't hear any sirens yet but it wouldn't be long. The cop in the clinic must have sounded the alert. His mind was desperately seeking a way out, a final winning shot, which would reverse the situation in his favour. To hell with Zehetmayer, to hell with the money, to hell with Hirtmann and the kid: he didn't want to go back to prison. In the grip of his inner confusion, he didn't see the figure emerging from behind a fir tree until it was too late, until he was facing them, taking aim, and firing. Kirsten let out a little cry when the flame burst from the barrel, but the bullet had already gone through her right shoulder by her deltoid muscle, coming out again without encountering any resistance and penetrating Jiri's shoulder. The impact and the pain caused him to let go of his gun and his hostage at the same time. The gun fell into the snow; Kirsten moved away from Jiri with a scream. Straight ahead of them Hirtmann was calmly taking aim at Jiri. He raised his hands in surrender.

'Fuck, Julian!' roared Kirsten Nigaard, holding her shoulder. 'You shot me!'

'I promise you it was your shoulder I was aiming at, my sweet,' answered Hirtmann, walking forward and picking up the gun. 'But consider yourself lucky: I wasn't sure I would hit my target.'

46

Dead Man

'Let's go,' said Hirtmann, handing his gun to Kirsten. She winced as she climbed slowly to her feet.

With the tip of his gun he motioned to Jiri to start walking into the forest. Jiri looked at him, then did as he was told. He was now free to study his enemy at leisure. His initial thought was that he was an interesting enemy – and a formidable one.

He did not yet know how he was going to turn the tables, when at this moment everything seemed so unfavourable, irrevocable, but he knew from experience that there would be a moment – and only one – when the opportunity would arise.

The silence could not be more total. Jiri was only slightly surprised that there was no sound of sirens. How often had he encountered this in his career: the slow reaction time of the police. A universal law. It was a pity: for once he would have liked to see the bloody cops show up sooner. His hands in the air, he climbed up the slight slope, sinking into the snow up to his ankles, followed by Hirtmann and his stooge.

'Turn right,' said Hirtmann, in front of a tall tree.

Someone had already come this way. There were two trails of footprints: one that went and came back, and the other that . . .

Jiri understood before he saw him: he was bound to a tree trunk, shivering, almost as white as the snow, and completely naked, his clothing in a pile at his feet. Not even fifty metres from the clinic.

Zehetmayer.

The orchestra conductor was shivering, his every limb trembling, his teeth chattering so violently that Jiri could hear the sound. All gone was the 'Emperor's' glory. He was sagging, only the rope around his middle keeping him in an upright position; his bare chest was heaving and his eyes were blue as ice. When he looked in their direction, it was fear, above all else, that they saw. *The oldest human emotion*, thought Jiri.

'Kirsten,' said Zehetmayer, surprised at seeing her. 'Kirsten . . . what are . . . what are you . . . ?'

He was finding it very difficult to speak.

'What am I doing here?' she said, to help him.

She didn't answer. She merely looked at Hirtmann.

'Don't you get it?' she said eventually.

She saw the dumb, incredulous look on the conductor's face.

'I brought you here, you and your mercenary. It was a trap. All your fantasies of revenge, your website, your money . . . I contacted you with only one purpose: to get you to come here.'

Hirtmann winked at the naked old man. Jiri looked at Hirtmann and understood. From the beginning he'd been pulling the strings. He felt renewed respect for his enemy. He had found his match.

'Take your clothes off,' ordered Hirtmann.

'What?'

'Don't try to play for time, you heard me.'

Jiri looked from Hirtmann to Kirsten. These two knew what they were doing. Perhaps there would be no opportunity, in the end. As he removed his down jacket, he glanced at the Norwegian woman. She had recovered her weapon and was holding it in her left hand. A dark spot was soaking her clothes on her right shoulder. She wouldn't last long, but he would still die before she did. Such a pity. One against one he might have been able to attempt something. Or maybe not. Not against such an adversary.

'Now your shoes,' said Hirtmann. 'Hurry up.'

He did as he was told. He felt the damp chill envelop his feet through his socks as they sank into the layer of fresh snow. He removed his jumper, shirt and T-shirt and stood motionless, his face and torso plumed with a cloud of vapour.

'And the rest. Trousers, pants, socks. Everything.'

'Fuck off, Hirtmann.'

The detonation blasted through the silence of the forest, made louder by the echo, and Jiri's body was projected 2 metres backwards.

'I beg you,' stammered Zehetmayer. 'I beg you. Don't . . . don't kill me . . . please.'

Hirtmann looked at Zehetmayer's wrinkled face, already showing

360

the effects of the cold, his purple lips, his bloodshot eyes, the tears streaming down his gaunt cheeks and freezing before they fell, his bent knees, his shrivelled penis, and he saw how the ropes were crushing his chest.

'I killed your daughter, you should hate me,' he said.

'No . . . no . . . I don't hate you . . . I . . . I . . .'

'Do you want to know what I did to her before I killed her?'

'*I beg you . . . don't kill me.*'

The old man was repeating himself. Kirsten saw a steaming yellow spot form a hole in the snow at his bare feet. She saw a few strands of white hair fluttering above his purplish ears like the wings of a wounded bird that cannot take flight. She aimed her gun at the conductor and fired. A tremor, then his body collapsed on itself, only held to the tree trunk by the rope, his chin on his chest.

'What the hell are you doing?' said Hirtmann, turning to face her.

He saw the smoking black barrel. Aimed at him.

'I'm getting rid of witnesses.'

He had his gun in his hand, but his arm was lowered.

'What are you playing at?' he said calmly, as if he were talking about the weather.

She paused to listen: a siren, at last, in the distance.

'I thought you liked our little games . . .' he said.

'Let's just say I've had enough. The police will be here soon, Julian, and I have no intention of spending the rest of my days in prison. Not for you, not for anyone. Thanks to him,' she added, nodding towards the dead orchestra conductor, 'I'm rich. And I will soon be handed a medal for having rendered you harmless.'

'Aren't you going to miss me?' he said ironically.

'We had some good times together, you and I, but I have no intention of letting you live.'

She had her eye on his gun, still hanging by his side. She had him in her sights but she knew that as long as she didn't shoot him, he was dangerous.

'But it's your weapon which killed the old man,' he said, motioning with his chin at the body.

'I'll find an explanation. And besides, Martin will testify that I assisted him, and that Thingummy, over there, took me hostage. There are plenty of witnesses.'

'*Martin?* Sounds like you've become quite chummy.'

'Sorry, Julian, time is running out. No more time for idle conversation.'

'Do you remember your sister?' he said suddenly.

She froze and saw a new spark in his eyes.

'You hated your sister; you despised her. I've rarely seen that sort of hatred between two siblings. It's true that your sister had everything – talent, success, men – and that she was your parents' favourite. Your sister treated you like a household pet; you were the average daughter, always in her shadow. I killed her for you, Kirsten. She was my gift to you. I restored your pride. I showed you who you could be. Thanks to me you went much further than you ever would have dared, on your own. I taught you everything I know.'

'That's true, you have been a good teacher. But you're forgetting one thing: it wasn't my sister you planned to rape and kill in that abandoned factory, it was me.'

He looked her straight in the eyes.

'Yes. And you convinced me not to do anything,' he said. 'You weren't even afraid. Anyone else would have been terrified. But not you. It was so frustrating, to see you waiting for death as a deliverance. Good God: even when I told you you would suffer, you didn't react. It made me furious. Shit, I wasn't there to facilitate a suicide. You kept encouraging me, defying me. The harder I hit you, the more you drove me into a corner. I had never seen anything like it, I have to admit. And then you offered me a bargain: your life in exchange for your sister's. It was so unexpected, so . . . twisted. Do you want to know how I killed her? You never asked. Do you want to know if she screamed a lot?'

'I hope she did,' Kirsten replied coldly. 'I hope the bitch was in agony.'

'Oh, don't worry about that. So, is this it? Have we reached the end of the road, you and I? I suppose there's no other way for us to part. Crime brought us together, crime will part us.'

'What a romantic you've suddenly become, Julian.'

'You were less ironic when you were begging me to let you come with me, my darling. You were like a little girl who's been promised the most extraordinary present. If you could have seen how your eyes were shining. But it's true it was easier to abduct those women using you as bait. A woman cop. They felt safe. They would have gone anywhere with you.'

'And they had cause to regret it,' she said, listening to the sirens in the distance: not one, but several.

'It's so ironic, don't you think? The woman appointed to investigate the disappearances was the very person who was behind them?'

'Tell me: you're not playing for time, by any chance? You don't intend to start begging like that other clown over there, do you?'

His laughter rang out in the silence of the forest. The sirens were closer now.

'If I thought it would serve any purpose, maybe I would. To think I'm the one who dropped that gun off at your hotel. That's pretty ironic, too, don't you think?'

He clung to the side of the bed and tried to move towards the door, his face and body streaming with sweat, when suddenly he saw the familiar face there before him. Servaz stopped short. He wondered again if his mind was playing tricks on him. Then he gave a faint smile.

Followed by a wince.

'Hey, Vincent.'

'Bloody hell,' exclaimed Espérandieu when he saw him. 'Where do you think you're going?'

He stood next to his boss, and put an arm around his torso to support him and steer him back to the bed.

'You shouldn't be on your—'

'We're going that way,' interrupted Servaz, pointing to the emergency exit not 5 metres from there.

Espérandieu froze.

'What?'

'Do as I said, please. Help me.'

Vincent looked around the room, then at the door. He shook his head.

'I don't know if—'

'Shut up,' interrupted Servaz. 'But thank you for coming.'

'Don't mention it. It's always nice to have such a warm welcome. It looks like I arrived just in time. I came straight here, but I think the cavalry is not far behind.'

'Let's go,' said Servaz, his legs trembling.

'Martin, you're in no fit shape, for fuck's sake. They just removed half your liver, you've got drains all over you! This is madness.'

Servaz stepped towards the door and stumbled. Espérandieu caught him in time.

'Help me!' shouted his boss.

They moved towards the metal door, arm in arm, step by step, like two walking wounded. Espérandieu put his free hand on the safety bar.

'May I ask where we're going?'

Servaz nodded, grimaced, clenched his teeth. The pain was constant now.

'Kirsten is out there . . . with another guy . . . he's armed. You left your gun in Toulouse . . .'

Espérandieu gave a funny smile. He put one hand under his anorak.

'Not really. Do you think I'll need it?'

'I hope not. But be prepared – that . . . that man is dangerous.'

Vincent walked around Martin so he could support him with his left arm and hold the gun in his right hand.

'Which other guy?' he asked. 'Hirtmann?'

'No. Someone else.'

'Maybe we should wait for backup.'

'There's no time.'

For the time being, his assistant gave up trying to understand. Martin would explain the situation when the time came. Or at least, he hoped he would. His son's godfather looked absolutely dreadful. And the thought of being out there confronted with a dangerous armed man he knew nothing about did not exactly fill him with enthusiasm. They went cautiously down the icy steps, and began walking through the snow, following the fresh footprints.

Servaz had put on his shoes and tossed a blanket over his shoulders, but the icy wind blew underneath it and around his bare legs, freezing him. Suddenly he stopped, bent forward and threw up in the snow.

'Bloody hell, Martin!' exclaimed Vincent.

He stood up straight, his forehead pearling with sweat. He wondered if he'd manage to go through with this. Vincent was right: it was madness. *But people are capable of the most unbelievable feats, are they not?* he thought. Every day the television was full of them. *So why not me?*

'I look like Jesus, don't you think, with this blanket and gown?' he grimaced, trying to smile.

'You need a bit more beard,' replied his assistant.

He wanted to laugh but he coughed, and felt another wave of nausea.

Suddenly two shots rang out in the forest, not far from there, and they froze. The sound waves caused a few clumps of snow to fall from the fir trees. The air vibrated for another second then everything was silent again. The shots had come from somewhere nearby.

'Give me your gun.'

'What?'

Martin almost tore it from Vincent's hands and he rushed forward, limping, along the trail of footprints.

'I'm the better marksman of the two of us, don't forget!' shouted Vincent, following close behind.

A laugh rang out a bit further away, beyond the fir trees, and Servaz recognised Hirtmann. He went even faster, his head spinning, his stomach burning.

After they'd passed the tall fir tree they saw the four of them: the two dead men, one tied naked to a tree, and the other, the one who had attacked him in his hospital room, lying in the snow, while Kirsten had her gun pointed at Hirtmann.

'Shit,' muttered Espérandieu behind him.

From further down the slope, on the far side of the clinic, came the wailing of sirens, very near.

'Martin,' said Kirsten when she saw him, and for a moment it seemed to him that she was not at all pleased. 'You should be in bed.'

'Martin,' said Hirtmann in turn. 'Tell her not to shoot me.'

He saw the gun hanging at Hirtmann's side.

'He killed my sister,' said Kirsten, her voice vibrant with hatred. 'He deserves to die.'

'Kirsten,' Servaz began.

'He tortured her, he raped and killed her.' Her lower lip was trembling, as was the barrel of her gun. 'I don't want him to spend the rest of his days in a psychiatric hospital, do you understand? All pampered and talking to journalists and shrinks. That's not what I want.'

'Kirsten, put down your gun,' he said, taking aim at her with his own gun.

'She's going to shoot,' said Hirtmann. 'Stop her, Martin. Fire first.'

Martin looked from Kirsten to Hirtmann, then back at Kirsten.

'Her name is Kirsten Margareta Nigaard,' said Hirtmann quickly. 'She is my mistress and my accomplice. She has a tattoo that goes from her groin to her hip. Did you sleep with her, Martin? Then you know that—'

Suddenly, he saw the barrel of her gun edge away from Hirtmann and swing in his direction. Trigger, flex index finger, press . . . Her hand was trembling – from the cold, exhaustion, stupefaction, pain, rage – trembling far too much to take proper aim. Trembling far too much to win the duel.

The details appeared to him in shattering snapshots: the boughs of the fir trees heavy with snow, suddenly swaying in a gust of wind; the naked body tied to the tree; the other body with its arms spread, looking up at the sky; the cold wind biting his bare calves, and Kirsten's gun, turning, turning . . .

He fired.

He felt the recoil in his shoulder, the pain in his belly, he heard the 'flop' of a clump of snow loosened by the sound wave, or perhaps the wind. He saw Kirsten's incredulous gaze upon him. Her arm falling, her hand letting go of the gun. Her lips forming an 'O'. Then her knees gave way, a tremor went through her as if she were shivering, and she fell, her beautiful features face down in the snow.

'Well done, Martin,' said Hirtmann.

He heard shouts behind him, or rather cries. Guttural, in German.

He supposed this meant he ought to drop his gun. It would be stupid to get shot now, wouldn't it? He looked at the three bodies in the snow, his gaze lingering on Kirsten's. Once again he felt the sting of betrayal.

He felt stupid, naïve, credulous, devastated, exasperated, sick.

Once again, life had reclaimed what it had given him. Once again blood had been shed, and there was anger and remorse. Rage and sorrow. Once again darkness had triumphed, and the shadows had returned, more powerful than ever, and daylight had fled, frightened, far from there, to a place where normal people led normal lives. Then everything disappeared. He no longer felt a thing. Only immense fatigue.

'But you needn't have fired,' added Hirtmann.

'What?'

Behind him, the cries in German had become more urgent, more imperious. They were right nearby. These were orders, no doubt about it. *Drop your gun.* They were going to fire if he didn't.

'She only had one bullet in the gun. And she'd already fired it. The magazine was empty, Martin. You killed her for nothing,' said Hirtmann, showing him the magazine he had just removed from his pocket.

He wanted to lie down in the snow and watch the snowflakes drift down from the sky, right onto him, and fall asleep.

He obeyed; he let go of his gun.

And passed out.

Epilogue

The snow fell all day long, and on the days that followed, over Hallstatt and the surrounding area. Hirtmann was interrogated at the tiny police station that looked like something straight out of *The Sound of Music*. Reger and his men began the interrogation in German, until Espérandieu asked them if they couldn't do it in English. Then a guy showed up from Vienna or Salzburg, and took control of the situation.

It would take a few more days for them to decide what to do with Hirtmann (he had killed a man on Austrian territory, so it was a matter for Austrian law), and they decided to empty out the cells of the little police station.

Servaz did not attend the interrogations. He had been transferred to the hospital in Bad Ischl, as had all the patients from the clinic. It was temporarily or permanently closed, and the director was nowhere to be found. At the hospital, Servaz was initially placed in intensive care, then kept under observation. His untimely departure from the clinic had caused damage – less, however, than anyone had expected, or than he had feared, but they had to open him up a second time all the same, to make sure. The Austrian police came to interrogate him at length about what had happened in the forest: what Espérandieu, Servaz and Reger – and even Hirtmann – had said seemed to tally almost perfectly, but the investigators were finding it very difficult to comprehend the chain of events that had led four people to shoot each other and a renowned conductor to end up naked, bound to a tree and killed.

In his hospital bed Servaz received a number of telephone calls: from Margot, three times a day, and then Samira, Judge Desgranges, Cathy d'Humières and even Charlène Espérandieu – plus Alexandra, his ex-wife. As for Vincent, he left after two days, but he had stopped off morning, afternoon, and evening to see him.

'They won't let me go,' said Servaz, smiling vaguely from his bed, as Vincent had just told him he was going back to France. 'How far have they got with Hirtmann?'

'They're still interrogating him. He did kill a man on Austrian territory, after all – they're not going to hand him over to us all that soon.'

'Hmm.'

'Take care of yourself, Martin. And come back quickly.'

He mused that this final point did not depend solely on him, but he didn't say anything. Somewhere outside bells were ringing. The landscape was completely white. All that was missing were Christmas carols, but he had no doubt that at some point there would be a 'Stille Nacht' at the hospital. He hoped he would be done with the place before then.

His phone rang shortly after Vincent left.

'How are you feeling?' asked a voice that was all too familiar.

'What do you want, Rimbaud?'

'I have good news and bad news. Where should I begin?'

'Don't you have anything less clichéd?'

'The good news is that we received a flash drive. It would seem that it was sent on the very day you had your operation. From Austria. Do you want to know what's on it?'

Servaz smiled. Rimbaud could not help torturing people one way or another.

'Out with it,' he said.

'A film,' replied the inspector. 'A film shot with a GoPro fastened to the cameraman's chest. The night Jensen was killed. It shows everything: the attempted rape, the filmmaker rushing at Jensen, shooting him point blank in the temple, then vanishing into the woods. After that, he turns the GoPro around and waves at us, stupid bastard.'

'Hirtmann?'

'Yessir.'

Servaz let his head fall back against the pillow and took a deep breath, staring at the ceiling.

'This clears you of Jensen's murder, Servaz,' said Rimbaud. 'Although I really do wonder why Hirtmann sent it to us.'

'But . . . ?'

'But it does not exonerate you for behaviour unworthy of a member of the French National Police: fleeing from police headquarters, entering Austria under a false identity, murdering Kirsten Nigaard, an officer of the Norwegian police, with a gun that was not your service weapon . . .'

'Self-defence,' he said.

'Maybe.'

'Well well, it seems you're not so quick to jump to conclusions now.'

'I'm going to ask for your dismissal,' said Rimbaud. 'The French police can no longer allow itself to have people like yourself in its ranks. And your friend Espérandieu will also be disciplined.'

After that, he hung up.

The next day, Servaz lay in his bed and watched the snowflakes falling. He could not possibly get up or walk around. The doctors kept telling him that his survival was a miracle: after the operation on his heart he should never have had an operation on his liver so soon. As for the fact that he went out to shoot and kill someone less than an hour after he'd regained consciousness, it was an exploit that would go down in the annals of Austrian medical history. He now had two huge scars that made him look like a regular Frankenstein's monster: one on his chest, the other that started below his sternum, went straight down for 6 centimetres, then suddenly veered off to the side. He asked regularly for news of Gustav, who was in an adjacent ward: Gustav was fine, but he kept asking to see his papa – Hirtmann, in other words.

On the morning of the fifth day Servaz was finally able to get up. His first visit was, of course, to see his son. The boy did not look well, and the shadows under his eyes were deeper than ever, but the physician on duty was reassuring: the initial signs were encouraging, and Gustav seemed to be tolerating the immunosuppressant treatment they'd administered to reduce the risk of transplant rejection. Servaz's mind was not fully at ease: there were still so many things that could go wrong.

Gustav was asleep when Servaz entered the room. He had his thumb in his mouth and his long blond eyelashes were quivering slightly. Servaz thought that his sleep must be full of dreams, and he wondered if they were pleasant. He looked for a long while at the calm little face, the sheet and blanket tucked under his chin, his narrow ribcage rising and falling – at that moment, Gustav seemed to be resting peacefully – then he left the room as silently as he had come.

Servaz and Gustav spent Christmas Day in hospital, among the cheerful chatter of the nurses, the blinking lights, and the little synthetic Christmas trees. Then came a freezing January, both in Austria and in France. At last in February Servaz was able to go home. He was immediately called before the disciplinary council, and got off with a temporary three-month unpaid suspension, and demotion to the rank of captain. He devoted months to doing all he could to obtain custody of Gustav, who had been placed with a foster family. France had a new president by the time his wish was granted and he found himself trying to win over the new member of his family. They were difficult days: the boy wept, called for his real father, threw tantrums. Servaz was distraught; he felt completely out of his depth, and totally incompetent. Fortunately Charlène, Vincent and their two children came to the rescue: Charlène dropped by almost every day, while Servaz gradually went back to work, and bit by bit Gustav seemed to adapt to the new situation; even to enjoy it. This made Servaz happier than he had been in a long time.

In Austria, Julian Hirtmann was transferred to the prison in Leoben, an ultra-modern glass prison commonly referred to as 'the five-star prison'. France was calling for his extradition, but Hirtmann had to be tried in Austria first. Another Christmas was approaching when, one night, he complained of nausea and stomach cramps. The doctor was sent for. He could find nothing to explain such stomach pain other than a slight swelling and, so he thought, stress. He gave Hirtmann two tablets and made out a prescription. Not long after he left, Hirtmann asked the young guard on duty for another glass of water.

'How are your children, Jürgen?' he asked, reaching for the glass of water and making sure no one else could hear. 'How are Daniel and Saskia?'

He saw the young officer turn pale.

'And your wife, Sandra, is she still teaching little ones?'

Beyond the dark windows it was snowing. The faraway drone of the wind accompanied Hirtmann's all-too-distinct voice. Somewhere a laugh rang out, then silence returned.

'How do you know the names of my children?' asked Jürgen, giving a start.

'I know everything about every one of you here,' answered Hirtmann, 'and I know a great number of people outside. I'm sorry, I was just trying to be polite.'

'I don't think so, no,' said the young guard in a voice that tried, but failed, to sound assertive.

'Indeed, you are right. I have a little favour to ask of you.'

'Forget it, Hirtmann. I'm not doing you any favours.'

'I have a lot of friends outside,' hissed Hirtmann, 'and I wouldn't want anything bad to happen to Daniel or Saskia.'

'What did you say?'

'It's really only a tiny favour. If you could just get me a Christmas card, and then send it to the address I will give you. Nothing at all bad, you see.'

'What did you say before that?' growled the young man, furious. 'Go on – repeat it.'

He was staring angrily at Hirtmann, but his anger quickly turned to fear, then a wave of pure terror, when he saw how Hirtmann's features changed before his eyes, a literal metamorphosis, the dark shadow entering his eyes and the evil spark in his gaze. And how this horrible change lent his gaze, in the cold, surgical beam of the neon light, an unbearable intensity, and gave him the face of someone who is no longer human, a face that only madness could engender. The voice that emerged then in a powerful murmur from those almost feminine lips uttered words Jürgen would never forget:

'Let me tell you that if you don't want to find your pretty little Saskia dead in the snow, her skirt pulled up by some monster like me, you'd better listen to me.'

Resilience is a mysterious quality. It refers to the faculty of the body, the mind, an organism, or a system to return to a state of balance after a serious change, to continue to function, to live, and to move on, while overcoming a traumatic shock.

Martin Servaz needed some time to return to a state of balance, but he recovered. And one event helped in particular. On Christmas Day 2017, the doorbell rang at the Espérandieus' house. Many people were gathered that morning by the Christmas tree in the living room, along with an even greater number of presents, but most spoiled of all, beyond a doubt, was Gustav.

His biological father watched him opening his presents one after the other, his little face lit with joy; there to encourage him were Margot – holding her baby in her arms – Vincent, Charlène, and their two children. With his little fingers he tore off the colourful wrapping paper, opened the boxes with quick, impatient gestures, and pulled out the toys with somewhat exaggerated exclamations of surprise. And every smile on his face was a smile in Servaz's heart. But a moment afterwards Servaz's thoughts turned darker, and all of a sudden he felt the crushing burden of responsibility on his shoulders, a responsibility that was far too great, in all honesty, for a man like him.

That Christmas morning he also thought about Kirsten. He had been thinking about her every day for a year, in fact. Yet again he had been deluded. He was angry with himself for having lowered his guard, for having let falsehood come into his life wearing a disguise; he was angry with himself for having nurtured absurd hopes, hopes that could only be disappointed. At the same time, he wondered if Kirsten Nigaard had ever been sincere. The truth was that she had come to him to guide him towards her lover and master. She had lured him into a trap, the way she had lured the orchestra conductor and his hitman. He tried not to think of those moments of shared intimacy, tried to erase them from his memory. But did he have to deny his own feelings, simply because the other person had not felt the same thing?

'Martin, Martin!' said Charlène joyfully.

He looked up. Gustav was standing before him, handing him his Transformers truck. Servaz smiled, reached out for the toy. The doorbell had just rung. Vincent left the room.

He heard someone talking in the hall, and Espérandieu saying, 'Just a moment.'

He was fiddling with the toy, holding it every which way before Gustav's attentive and, so it seemed, slightly sceptical gaze, when Vincent called to him from the door:

'Martin, can you come?'

'I'll be right back,' he said to his son.

He stood up and walked over to the front door.

He looked at the man standing there: an employee wearing a brown

373

UPS uniform. Apparently the delivery company had decided to make their personnel work on 25 December.

Then he saw his assistant's face and he felt his pulse quicken.

'It's from Austria,' said Espérandieu. 'It's addressed to you. Someone knows you're here.'

Servaz looked at the envelope. Took it. Opened it.

It was a Christmas card: holly, garlands, shining baubles. A cheap one. He opened it.

Merry Christmas, Martin
Julian

Inside there was a photograph. He recognised her at once. She was wearing the same khaki tunic dress with a woven belt as she had on one of the last times he had seen her; she had the same curly blonde hair, the same strands falling over the left-hand side of her face, the same subtle lipstick. She did not seem to have changed in all those years, in spite of the newspaper she was reading which clearly indicated that the picture had been taken scarcely three months earlier. She was smiling.

'That fucking scumbag,' roared Espérandieu next to him. 'Bastard. On Christmas Day! Throw that thing out. It's been Photoshopped.'

Servaz stared at his assistant, not seeing him. He was certain that Vincent was wrong: that it hadn't been Photoshopped, and that analysis would prove as much. It was indeed Marianne there before his eyes.

Reading a newspaper from 26 September 2017.

Suddenly he understood Hirtmann's words: 'Let's just say that her liver is not available.' Of course not: the drugs, the alcohol – how could it have been?

Marianne – alive . . .

His heart plummeting, in his chest – an endless fall.

Acknowledgements

First of all, I would like to thank everyone who saved this vessel from shipwreck and brought it to a safe harbour. In order of appearance: Caroline Ripoll, Amandine Le Goff and Virginie Plantard from XO, and Christelle Guillaumot. All through the writing of this book, Caroline steered it clear of the reefs it was headed for: she was my compass.

And then, as always, I must express my gratitude towards two people who have been with me from the very first day: my editors Édith Leblond and Bernard Fixot. And with them the entire team from Éditions XO: Valérie Taillefer, Jean-Paul Campos, Bruno Barbette, Catherine de Larouzière, Isabelle de Charon, Stéphanie Le Foll, Renaud Leblond – it is impossible to name them all. Working with you is a privilege, the coffee is good, and the view from up there is far-reaching. There is nothing like it, for gaining height.

I must also thank Marie-Christine Conchon, François Laurent and Carine Fannius for their indefatigable enthusiasm, as well as everybody at Pocket/Univers Poche.

As usual, this book could not have been written without the precious help of my contacts at the regional crime unit in Toulouse – they know who they are. If there are mistakes, they are in no way responsible. Take it out on the author; blame him, that gentle dreamer, that teller of stories, who has to juggle a thousand and one balls.

Many thanks to the staff at Air France who provided me with an abundance of information during a flight from Paris to Mexico City. They will be surprised not to have found it here. But circumstances, and the writing, decreed otherwise. It will be for another time, though – definitely, my friends.

Finally, Laura Muñoz – she took this book and its author far away from the shadows.

Ah yes, I nearly forgot: there is one last person I would like to thank. His name is Martin Servaz.